'Did anyone ... **you're suprem** ...

'Often. I'm not averse to hearing compliments, Olympia. And nor do I imagine are you. You really are stunning, *querida*.'

Up close she was even more exquisite. Nic couldn't take his eyes off her.

'Save it, Romeo. You may be infamous for your limitless wants and desires, but I'm afraid you've reached your limit with me.'

He might have believed her if he hadn't trailed the back of his index finger down her bare arm excruciatingly slowly and relished the shimmy rustling over her body. Impossible as it was, her infinitesimal gasp and the ghostly pinch of her brow gave him the notion that she hadn't known a simple touch could affect her in such a tremendous way.

'You're scared. Maybe even petrified. Afraid I will prove you wrong? Or fearful you'll enjoy every minute of it?' He was baiting her, but there was one advantage to toying with an intelligent woman: he knew exactly what buttons to push.

'I fear no one. Least of all you.'

THE 21st CENTURY GENTLEMAN'S CLUB

Where the rich, powerful and passionate come to play!

For years there have been rumours of a secret society where only the richest, the most powerful and the most decadent can embrace their every desire.

Nothing is forbidden in this private world of pleasure.

And when exclusivity is beyond notoriety only those who are invited to join ever know its name…

Q Virtus

Now the truth behind the rumours
is about to be revealed!

Find out in:

THE ULTIMATE PLAYBOY
by Maya Blake
July 2014

THE ULTIMATE SEDUCTION
by Dani Collins
August 2014

THE ULTIMATE REVENGE
by Victoria Parker
September 2014

THE ULTIMATE REVENGE

BY
VICTORIA PARKER

Published in Great Britain 2014
by Mills & Boon, an imprint of Harlequin (UK) Limited,
Eton House, 18-24 Paradise Road, Richmond, Surrey, TW9 1SR

© 2014 Victoria Parker

ISBN: 978-0-263-24996-5

Harlequin (UK) Limited's policy is to use papers that are natural,
renewable and recyclable products and made from wood grown in
sustainable forests. The logging and manufacturing processes conform
to the legal environmental regulations of the country of origin.

Printed and bound in Spain
by Blackprint CPI, Barcelona

Victoria Parker's first love was a dashing heroic fox named Robin Hood. Then came the powerful, suave Mr Darcy, Lady Chatterley's rugged Lover—the list goes on. Thinking she must be an unfaithful sort of girl, but ever the optimist, she relentlessly pursued her Mr Literary Right, eventually found him lying between the cool crisp sheets of a Mills & Boon® and her obsession was born.

If only real life was just as easy…

Alas, against the advice of her beloved English teacher to cultivate her writer's muse, she chased the corporate dream and acquired various uninspiring job-titles *and* a flesh-and-blood hero before she surrendered to that persistent voice and penned her first Mills & Boon® romance. Turns out creating havoc for feisty heroines and devilish heroes truly *is* the best job in the world.

Victoria now lives out her own happy-ever-after in the north-east of England, with her alpha exec and their two children—a masterly charmer in the making and, apparently, the next Disney Princess. Believing sleep is highly overrated, she often writes until three a.m., ignores the housework (much to her husband's dismay) and still loves nothing more than getting cosy with a romance novel. In her spare time she enjoys dabbling with interior design, discovering far-flung destinations and getting into mischief with her rather wonderful extended family.

Recent titles by the same author:

THE WOMAN SENT TO TAME HIM
A REPUTATION TO UPHOLD
PRINCESS IN THE IRON MASK

To my *Q Virtus* compatriots,
Maya Blake and Dani Collins.
Thank you for the laughs and chats as we concocted
and conceived our brave new world.
It's been an honour and an absolute pleasure.

And for the fabulous Jennifer Hayward,
my CP and best bud. Like Olympia Merisi, you rock!
So this one is for you...

CHAPTER ONE

THEY SAY YOU can't plan a hurricane.

Nicandro Carvalho could. He could wreak havoc with a smile. And after ten years of planning and months of whipping up a storm he was finally ready to unleash chaos.

Zeus. I am coming for you and I will annihilate your world. As you destroyed mine.

The Barattza in Zanzibar, this weekend's ostentatious venue for the quarterly meeting of Q Virtus, was warm, and so muggy his flimsy white shirt clung to his body like a second skin and moisture thrived beneath his mask. Still, he strode ruthlessly through the crush of elite billionaires, intent on his pretty 'Petit Q'—his backstage pass into Zeus's lair, in the form of a five-foot-three brunette in a haute couture red gown designed to attract and blend in equal measure.

Look but don't touch was the cardinal rule.

As if Nicandro had *ever* followed the rules. *'Rules are for boring fools,'* as his mother would say, although her voice was now a distant echo from the past.

Numerous greetings vied for his attention and he offered a succinct nod or a quick 'good evening' and volunteered nothing more. Conversations were like fires—they tended to sputter out if he deprived them of enough air.

His purposeful stride didn't break—hadn't since he'd been Nicandro Santos, a terrified seventeen-year-old boy who'd boarded a cargo ship in Rio to hide in a filthy container bound for New York. It hadn't faltered when he'd concocted a new identity to ensure anonymity from his past life, emerging as one Nicandro Carvalho, who'd sold his pride on the streets of Brooklyn and then wrenched it back by working his fingers raw on construction sites to put some semblance of a roof over his head.

Nor had it swayed when he'd bought his first property, then another, over endless harrowing years, to earn enough money to bring his grandfather from Brazil to be by his side.

An unrelenting purpose and a cut-throat determination that had rewarded him with obscene power and wealth—until he'd been graciously accepted into the covert ranks of Q Virtus, where his sole purpose was to infiltrate and take it down from the inside.

So here he was. And this was only the beginning.

A plan over ten years in the making. Rewriting history to make the Santos Empire—his legacy of a life that had been stolen from him, along with his parents—whole once more.

Nic shut down his thoughts as mercilessly as he did everything else. Otherwise the burning ball of rage that festered and ate away at his insides like a living, breathing entity would surely explode and incinerate everything and everyone in its path.

'Hey, Nic, what's the hurry?'

Narciso's voice shattered his ferocious intent and this time he did turn, to see his friend looking dapper in a tailored tuxedo, *sans* jacket, leaning against the main bar, Scotch glass in hand, the top half of his face shrouded in a gold leaf mask that reminded him of a laurel wreath.

Nic felt the constricting steel band around his chest slacken as a smile played at his mouth. 'All hail, Emperor Narciso. *Dios*, where do they come up with these things?'

'I have no idea, but I'm certainly feeling on top of the world.'

He resisted the urge to roll his eyes. 'Of course you are. How is the ball and chain?'

Narciso grinned at the blatant cynicism, his smile reaching the scalloped edge of gold.

Hideous masks. Requisite to afford them some anonymity, but they only served to aggravate Nic to the extreme—just as everything about Q Virtus did.

A gentlemen's club for the elite. Prestigious. Illustrious. The most sought-after membership in the world. Run by a deceitful, murdering crook.

Ironic, he thought, that grown men, multi-billionaires, would sell their soul to be a member of Q Virtus, virtually handing their business confidences, their reputation, their respect and trust to a common criminal.

Not for much longer. Not after Nic had finished exposing the cold, hard truth and crushed Zeus beneath his almighty foot.

'She's as beautiful as ever. Come, take a spin of the wheel with me. I'd like a quiet word.'

Impatience clawed at him with steel-tipped talons, slashing his insides, but Nic resisted the compulsion to decline outright. It had been too long since he'd seen his friend and he wanted a quiet word of his own.

'Let's grab a private table,' Nic said, not wasting a moment, simply ushering Narciso towards the lavish roulette room and a private table at the back.

Within ten minutes they had drinks in hand and the full attention of a male croupier dressed in red footman's livery. 'Gentlemen, please take your bets.'

Nic tossed a five-thousand-dollar chip haphazardly at the marked numbers adorning the roulette layout and waited for Narciso to make his choice.

'Twenty thousand dollars on black seventeen,' the croupier confirmed impassively.

Nic whistled a huff of air. 'Feeling reckless without your lady present?'

'Feeling lucky. That ball and chain does that to me.'

Yep, his partner in crime was still drugged on a potent cocktail of regular sex and emotion. He just hoped the hangover was a long way off. Nic didn't relish seeing the lights go out in his eyes. Sad, but inevitable.

The wheel spun in a kaleidoscopic blur and he eased back in his seat to afford them a modicum of privacy. With time at a premium and his patience dwindling he jumped right in. If he waited for Narciso to start the conversation he might be there all night.

'Tell me something. Don't you think it's odd that we've never seen a glimpse of QV's Mr Mysterious? Not once.'

Narciso didn't waste time pretending not to know exactly who they were discussing. He simply arched one dark brow and spoke in that rich, affluent tone that had used to fell women faster than a forest fire. 'So the man likes his privacy? Don't we all?'

'There's got to be more to it than that.'

'So suspicious, Carvalho.'

The white ball plopped into black seventeen and a satisfied grunt filled the air. Typical. Served Nic right for not even caring where his chip landed, but right now he had more important thoughts swirling around the vast whirlpool of his mind in ever-narrowing circles. Always leading back to the same thing. *Zeus*.

'Maybe he's not fit for polite society,' Narciso suggested. 'Ever thought of that? Rumour has it the man is associated with the Greek mafia. Maybe he's scarred with a dozen bullet holes. Maybe he's mute. Maybe he's shy. Over the last few months—since the last meeting, in fact—the rumour mill has churned up all kinds of ludicrous tales.'

Oh, he'd heard the rumours. Of course he had. He'd started most of them.

'Doesn't it bother you that Q Virtus could be dirty?' he asked, his voice all innocence with the required edge of concern. 'It obviously bothers some. There are a few members missing this weekend.'

Amazing what a few 'have you heard?' whispers in the right ears could achieve. Doubt was a powerful thing—destructive, flammable—and Nic had lit the torch with a flourish, sat back and watched it spread like wildfire.

Narciso shrugged, as if the thought of being a member of a club that was morally corrupt was water sluicing off a duck's back.

'The club might've had shady beginnings, but even my father and his cronies say the place is clean as a whistle now. You and I personally know several members, and all of them have made billions from mutually beneficial business deals, so I doubt any of it is true. Rumours are generally fairy stories born from petty jealousy or spoken from the mouths of people who have an ulterior motive.'

Very true, that. But the fact that Nic had numerous ulterior motives was something he kept to himself.

'Still, I want to meet him.' What he wanted, he realised, was back-up if something went wrong tonight. If he conveniently disappeared he wanted Narciso to know where he was headed.

'Why? What could you possibly want with Zeus?'

To bring his world crumbling down around his ears. To make him suffer as his parents had—as he had and as his grandfather had.

That old man, whom he loved so dearly, was the only family he had left. The man who'd harangued and railed at him to stand tall, who had propped him up as he'd learned how to walk again when Nic would rather have died in the same bloodbath as his parents.

'Is there something you want to tell me, Nic?'

Yes. The shock of it made him recoil, push back in his seat until he could feel the knotted gold silk poke through his shirt and agitate his skin. Problem being he didn't want

Narciso dragged into the epicentre of a storm of which he was the creator.

'Not particularly.'

Mouth pursed, his friend nodded grudgingly. 'And how do you intend to meet the mysterious, *reclusive,* notorious Zeus?'

Nic tossed back another mouthful of vodka as his gaze flickered to the Petit Q he'd been wooing since he'd arrived the night before. There she was, standing near the doors, unobtrusive as always, yet only a hand-motion away. All it had taken was one look into her heavy-lashed slumberous gaze and he'd thought, *Piece of cake.*

One romantic midnight stroll along the beach and he'd had a thumbprint lifted from her champagne flute. One lingering caress of his hand round her waist and he'd slipped the high-security access card from the folds of her red sheath. What remained was one promise of seduction in her suite that he'd fail to keep and would ensure she was gone from his side.

Narciso followed his line of sight and huffed out a breath. 'Should've known a woman would be involved. I like your style, Carvalho, even if I *do* think that vodka you drink has pickled your brain.'

Nic laughed, riding high on the narcotic mix of anticipation and exhilaration lacing his veins. That was until he looked into his friend's eyes and the mirth died in his throat.

What would Narciso and their buddy Ryzard think of him when Nic whipped the Q Virtus rug from beneath their feet? When he lost them the chance of schmoozing with the world's most powerful men, creating contacts and thriving on the deals that cultivated their already vast wealth. They would understand, wouldn't they? Narciso was the closest thing to a best friend he'd ever had and Ryzard was a good man. Surely he was doing them a favour of sorts—he knew what Zeus was capable of; they hadn't a clue.

'Speaking of rumours,' Narciso murmured, in a tone that made Nic's guts twist into an apprehensive knot. 'I hear Goldsmith made you an offer.'

He practically choked on his vodka. 'How do you know that?'

Narciso looked at him as if he'd sprouted a second head. 'Do you honestly think Goldsmith could keep the possibility of the mighty Nicandro Carvalho, an unequalled dominant force in real estate, becoming his son-in-law a secret for one second? He told my father. Who told me. And I told *him* that Goldsmith is delusional.'

Nic checked an impatient sigh. This was the last thing he wanted to discuss. Except his silence pulled the air taut, pinching Narciso's brow and turning his smart mouth into a scowl.

'Do *not* tell me you are seriously considering marrying Eloisa Goldsmith.'

No. Maybe. 'I am considering it, yes.'

'You've got to be joking, Nic!'

'Keep your voice down! Just because you've been blinded by good sex and emotion—ah, sorry—I mean to say just because you've found *everlasting bliss*,' he muttered, with no small amount of sarcasm, 'it doesn't mean I want to sign my own death warrant. A business marriage is perfect for me.'

'You're as jaded as I was. Heaven help you if you meet a woman strong enough to smash your kneecaps and drop you at her feet.'

'If that ever happens, my friend, I'll buy you a gold pig.'

Narciso shook his head. 'Eloisa Goldsmith. You're insane.'

'What I am is late for a rendezvous.' He downed the last of his drink as he bolted upright, the lock of his knees thrusting his chair backwards with an emphatic scrape.

'Why would you even consider it? She's a country mouse—you'll be bored within a week.'

Exactly. He could never fall in love with her and he'd have a sweet, gentle, caring woman to be the mother of his children. As to the why—there was only one reason Nic would walk down the aisle at twenty-nine years old. The final goal in his grand slam.

Santos Diamonds.

The business phenomenon that had taken generations to build: his great-grandfather's love affair, his *avô*'s pride and joy, the legacy Goldsmith would only gift to Nic along with his daughter's hand.

He wasn't enamoured of the idea, but he'd promised himself he'd consider it while he whisked up a vengeful hurricane for Zeus to flounder within. So consider it he would. If only for Avô to see Santos Diamonds back where it belonged. It was the least he could do for the old man.

'I will be content. Now, if you'll excuse me, I have an appointment with pleasure.'

The pleasure of the ultimate revenge.

PRIVATE. NO ENTRY.

Blood humming with a lethal combination of exhilaration and eagerness, Nic swiped his nifty keypad over the high-access security panel. While he'd loathed those early days in New York when he'd been lured to the streets of Brooklyn, he'd met some interesting if a smidgeon *degenerate* characters walking on the more dangerous side of life, who had always been willing to teach him a trick or two.

Still, his heart slammed about in his chest like a pinball machine until the fingerprint recognition flashed green and he was standing in Zeus's inner sanctum.

Moroccan-style ironwork lanterns cast eerie shadows down the long corridor and painted the white stucco walls with a brassy wash. The floor was a continuation of the small intricate mosaic that ran through the hotel but here, in Zeus's lair, the colours were richer—deep amber, bronze and heavy gold, as if gilded by Midas's touch. And that touch had embellished every scrolled door handle, finger-plate and urn.

Arched double doors, elaborately carved, encompassed the entire wall at one end of the floor, and as he drew closer faint murmurs slithered beneath the gap like wisps of smoke unfurling to reach his ears. Someone having unpleasant dreams, if he guessed right. Definitely female.

Mistress? Wife? The man was reclusive and malevolent enough to hoard a harem as far as he knew.

Gingerly Nic curled his hand around the gold handle and smirked when the lever gave way under the pressure of his palm. This was just too easy.

Door closed behind him, he stifled a whistle at the vast expanse of opulence.

Ochre walls were punctuated with arched lattice screens, allowing the shimmering light of the ornate candelabra to spin from one room to another and dance over every gilt-edged surface almost provocatively. But it was the heady scent of incense that gave the atmosphere a distinctly sultry feel, heating his blood another few degrees and coaxing his eyes towards the bed.

Mosaic steps led up to a raised dais, at least eight feet square. The entire structure was shrouded by a tented canopy made with the finest gold silk—the weighty drapes closed on all four sides, with only a small gap at the bottom edge. Clearly an invitation to take a peek as far as he was concerned.

Nic slipped off his shoes by the door and stepped closer on sock-clad feet, his pulse thrumming with the devilry of being somewhere he shouldn't and half hoping, half anxious that he'd be caught.

The sudden bolt of lightning that flashed through the room, followed by a sonorous crack of thunder didn't help. His heart leapt to his throat.

Sumptuous cushions and layers upon layers of superfine silk in white and gold embraced the still mound of a woman veiled by the caliginous shadows.

He watched, waiting to ensure she slept on, frowning at the odd sizzle of electricity that ran beneath his skin. If he were the suspicious sort who believed in Brazilian clap-trap he'd think his ancestors were trying to tell him to get the hell out of here. *As if.*

Nic shook himself from the bizarre trance and skulked round the rest of the palatial suite, prowling between over-stuffed sofas in a rich shade of cocoa, towering fern trees that plumed from barrel-wide bronze urns and the ritzy copper-toned spa tub raised on another dais in the bath-ing room.

The entire effect was stunning, but it had a homely feel—as if the guest was in fact the owner and he'd decided to give the sheikhs of the Middle East a run for their money.

Finally, in the farthest room, was the answer to his prayers. A wide leather-topped desk strewn with business files and paperwork.

Hope unfurled and he sniffed at the air tentatively, while anxiety curled its wicked tail around his ribcage. Not fear of being caught—more fear of never finding the truth. Never finding what he was looking for. Never coming eye to eye with Zeus himself. Or should he say *Antonio Merisi*.

Ah, yes, Antonio Merisi—aka Zeus. A name that had evaded him for years—as if trying to connect the god-like sacrosanct prominence of Zeus with a flesh and blood human capable of being destroyed was impossible. But Nic had friends in places both high and low, and anything was procurable for a price.

It had been a torturous exercise in patience to discover any other Merisi business interests apart from Q Virtus. Not an easy feat, considering they'd been buried in aliases, but he'd struck gold within weeks and found one or two to set the wheels in motion. Make dents in the man's bank balance. Contaminate his reputation. See how he liked his empire destroyed. As long as Nic got to watch it crumble. To see the very man responsible for his parents' death languish in hell.

Standing behind the desk, he hauled himself up from his pit of rage and resentment and fingered the portfolio at the top of towering pile.

Merpia Inc.

Merpia? The largest commodities trading house in the world.

Eros International.

That one he'd guessed, from the abundance of Greek mythological connotations surrounding the club and a brief mention of the Merisi name in the company portfolio. Consequently he'd plagued the stockmarket with rumours two weeks earlier.

Score one Carvalho.

Ophion—Greek shipping.

Rockman Oil.

Dios…

Multi-billion-pound ventures. Every single one of them. This man wasn't wealthy— he was likely one of the richest men in the world, with millions scattered across a vast financial plain.

The dents Nic had made would be a drop in the ocean.

He battled with an insurgence of disheartenment until another file snagged his eye.

Carvalho?

His hand shot out…then froze when a sharp voice splintered his rage.

'I wouldn't do that, if I were you. Hands up, back away from the table, then do not move a muscle or I'll blow your brains out.'

Busted. Just when things were getting interesting. Still, his lips twisted ruefully at the sound of a husky, sultry feminine voice.

Nic flicked his hands in the air with a high school level

of flippancy to lighten the mood and twisted his torso to spin around.

'Now, now, *querida*, let's not fight—'

The practised snick of the safety catch on a revolver made him rethink. *Fast.* It was a sound that resonated through his brain and threw him back thirteen years. Even his back stiffened, as if he were waiting for the echo of a bullet to penetrate his spine. Rob him of the dreams of his youth. End life as he knew it.

'Stay right where you are. I did *not* give you permission to move.'

A shiver glanced over his flesh at the cool, dominant tone, as if he'd been physically frisked not just verbally spanked.

'As you wish,' he said, taking his voice down an octave or three and coating it in sin. 'Though I'd much rather conduct this meeting face to face. More so if you are as beautiful as your voice.'

Maybe it was her barely audible huff or maybe it was the impatient tap of a stiletto heel on wood but Nic would swear she'd just rolled her eyes.

'Who are you and how did you get into my suite?'

Suddenly the ridiculousness of the situation hit him. Was he actually being controlled by a *woman*?

Shifting on his feet, he made to swivel. 'I'm turning around so we can have this conversation like two adul—'

A sharp sound like a whip cracking rent the air and Nic's jaw dropped as he married the sound of a silenced bullet with the precise hole in the oil painting of a wolf about three feet from his head.

How ironic. *Lobisomem.* Portuguese for werewolf. His Q Virtus moniker.

Omen? He damned well hoped not.

The smell of the gunpowder residue curled through his sinuses and the past seemed to collide with the present, making his stomach clench on a nauseating pang. Sweat trickled down his spine and he had to surreptitiously clear the thickness from his throat just to speak.

'Crack shot, *querida*.' Question was, why wouldn't she let him turn, look at her?

'The best, I assure you. Now, tell me I have your undivided attention and that you will behave.'

Nic had the distinct feeling he wasn't going to win this argument. And that voice... *Dios*, she could read him passages from the most profoundly boring literature in the world and he'd still get sweaty and hard at the sound of her licking those consonants and vowels past her lips.

'I will be on my best behaviour. Scout's honour.'

Not that he'd ever been one. At the suggestion his mother had arched one perfectly plucked, disgusted brow, told him the idea was simply not to be endured and that she'd rather take him to the country club to play poker.

How he'd loved that woman.

Ignoring the misery dragging at his heart, he strived for joviality. 'Though if it's co-operation you're looking for, I'll be far more amenable without a gun trained on my head by an expert marksman.'

'Trouble must follow you if you're familiar with the sounds of a loaded gun. Why does that not surprise me?'

'Guess I'm just that kind of guy.'

'A thief? A criminal? Insane?'

Dios! Why was everyone calling him insane today?

'*Misjudged* was more the word I was thinking of. Or maybe I'm simply enigmatic, like your lover. Or is he your boss?'

'My...*boss*?' she replied, with a haughty edge that said no man would ever lord it over *her*.

He almost rolled *his* eyes then. 'Okay, then, your lover.'

That earned him a disgruntled snicker.

'Think again. And while you're at it who are you talking about? Who is my boss supposed to be? Who are you looking for?'

'Zeus, of course—who else?'

The room hushed into a cacophony of silence; the lack of sound so loud his ears rang. No doubt a pin dropping would have detonated in an explosion of sound.

Nic pounced on the lull—he'd always liked creating a big bang. 'I have a meeting with him here. Tonight. So if you'd like to run along and get him I'd be greatly appreciative.'

A stunned pause gave way to a burst of incredulous laughter. The kind that was infectious. It was rusty—as if she didn't get much practice—but it was out there, all smoky and sultry, and it filled him with a scorching hot kind of pleasure.

Who the devil *was* she?

'A meeting, you say? I think not. And I believe you are toying with the wrong woman, stranger. So forgive me if I just *run along* and leave you with some friends of mine.'

From nowhere three hulks had three guns trained on various parts of his anatomy and he fought the violent urge to cup his crotch. Because 1) despite evidence to the contrary he was of high intellect, and 2) despite their tailored Savile Row attire their eyes were dull from a hard life and the inevitable slide into madness.

Splendid.

For pity's sake, why guns? Why not knives? He hated guns!

'Ah, come now, *querida*, this is hardly fair. Three against one?'

'I wish you the best of luck. If you survive we will meet again.'

He'd always been a lover, not a fighter. Still, living on the streets had taught him more than how to break a lock—which was just as well because he was nowhere near done with this night or this woman.

CHAPTER TWO

SHE SHOULDN'T HAVE LEFT. Walked out. Left them to rid her of the criminal in their midst. Here she'd been expecting news of his disposal to the authorities, or his being shoved onto a plane to Timbuktu, and instead she was standing in the security room faced with three decidedly sheepish guards and a fifty-two-inch plasma screen filled with the image of a prominent, high-profile billionaire tied up in her cellar!

'I don't believe this,' Pia breathed.

Exquisitely tall.

Beautifully dark.

Devastatingly handsome.

And infamous for satisfying his limitless wants and desires. *Not*—as far as she was aware, and she generally knew more than most—renowned for being a felon.

'Nicandro Carvalho. I almost shot Nicandro Carvalho!'

Pia's insides shook like a shaken soda can ready to spray. He'd been in her bedroom. Maybe watched her sleep. She'd been half naked when he'd swaggered into her rooms and for a split second she'd thought her past was catching up with her.

But what really ratcheted up her 'creeped-out' meter was the fact she'd shot her favourite painting. Of a werewolf. *Lobisomem*. How freaky was that? Considering she'd code-named him herself.

'It would have been his own fault! What was he doing, snooping around in there?'

All three testosterone-dripping men in the room flinched at Jovan's holler but Pia was used to his bark—especially where she was concerned. Protectiveness didn't come close to the way he went on. Ridiculous. You would think she was eight, not twenty-eight.

'More to the point, how did he even *get* in here?' she said, glaring at her supposed security staff, who flushed beneath her scrutiny. 'Find the breach and deal with it. Someone betrayed me today and I want them found.'

Skin visibly paled at her tone. 'Yes, *madame*.'

Purposefully avoiding the image on screen—because every time she looked at Carvalho the lamb she'd eaten for dinner threatened to reappear—she speared Jovan with her displeasure. 'Did you realise who he was before you roughed him up? Tell me you went easy on him.'

'*Easy?*' Jovan said, with a hefty amount of incredulity, and she only had to glance across the room to see why.

One of his men sported a black eye and a broken nose, the other winced with every turn and the third had a pronounced limp.

'The guy should be a cage fighter! I recognised that pretty-boy face within minutes and I *still* wanted to pulverise him, regardless. He could have hurt you, Pia! So what if the man has money? Only last year they discovered that billionaire who had buried thirty-two bodies in his back yard!'

Heaven help her.

'All right—calm down.' If he worked himself up any more he'd either have a seizure or charge back in there to finish Carvalho off. Which would now be a manageable feat, considering he'd tied the stunner to a chair so tightly the ropes were likely cutting off his circulation. 'Like every member, he's been checked out thoroughly.'

Born in Brazil to a lower class family, he'd sailed to New York to make his fortune. The fact he'd come from nothing, was a self-made man, had gained her deepest respect from the start. Pia had first-hand experience of being hungry, feeling worthless, powerless, and she never wanted to revisit *that* hellhole ever again. The amount of determination it would have taken Carvalho to rise from the ashes with no help had fascinated and charmed her in equal measure.

'If there was something amiss about him I would know.' Yet suddenly she wasn't so sure. Her instincts screamed that this man was far more than he'd initially appeared.

'People don't tend to put "serial killer" and "rapist" on their résumé, Pia.'

Valid point.

She tapped at the pounding spot between her brows, feeling as if she'd been given a complex puzzle with half the pieces left out.

'I'm missing something vital. I must be. First he breaks in, then he has a snoop at the files on my desk. Eros longer than most—I'd know that red file anywhere—and then…' She ran her tongue over her top front teeth. 'Now, isn't *that* a coincidence? That Eros International should catch his eye.'

The company had taken a suspiciously abrupt beating on the stockmarket of late. Though in all honesty Eros's share decline had been the least of her concerns. Ugly rumours were abounding, hitting her where it hurt. Her reputation.

Could he be the thorn in her side? The man who'd been making discreet enquiries about Zeus, about the club, about her businesses—the very man who'd been spreading filth and lies?

Maybe. After all, in her world anything was possible. But why?

Stuff it. She had no intention of waiting around while some property magnate ruined her life. *If* he was to blame.

'Turn off the screens. I'm going in there.'

She wanted answers and there was only one way to get them. She just hoped she was wrong and there was some perfectly good explanation for his breaking and entering.

Yeah, right. Call her foolish, but she didn't want Nicandro Carvalho to be at the centre of her current storm.

'*What?*'

'You heard me.'

While Jovan dismissed his men with a quiet word her gaze sought out Nicandro Carvalho once again. Obscenely grateful that her dinner stayed put and she remained apathetic and unflappable. As if the sight of a six-foot-plus Brazilian hunk with a bloodied lip was an everyday occurrence. She was good at that. Projecting absolute calm composure while her stomach revolted at the sight of her *Lobisomem* in a snare.

She rubbed her own upper arms, sore with the faint echoes of pain. She wanted to scream and rail at Jovan for trussing him so tightly. Perhaps she'd tie *him* up until control was lost, handed to another. See how *he* liked it.

'Did you *have* to cut off his blood supply?' she asked, cringeing inwardly at her snippy tone. Not for Jovan's sake. He was more like the bothersome older brother she'd never had, so she didn't bother to pull her punches with him. But the last thing she needed was to come over unhinged to her staff. *'Women are emotional liabilities,'* her father would say. Not her. Not since he'd made her into a living, breathing machine.

'Who cares if I did?' Jovan asked.

Pia cared—for some bizarre reason. But she wasn't about to tell him that. Just as she wasn't about to admit that at times she'd secretly watched Nicandro Carvalho over the past year. There was something darkly arresting about him. One look at his brooding beauty, at that dark skin that looked as if exotic blood ran through his veins, and she felt giddy with it all.

Pia was tall for a woman, and yet his towering height, wide shoulders and the thick biceps bulging from where his arms strained made her feel like a porcelain doll. Though he was snared, anyone could see his bearing was straight, confident, almost regal—like titan warriors and powerful gods. Not an image she would expect from a boy born in the Rio slums. The fact that he took pride in that fact, felt no shame for his poor origins and preferred to acknowledge the truth and stand tall with dignity, had lent him a kind of reverence in her eyes. *She'd* never been able to shake the stigma of it all.

Hung loosely about his face, his hair was the deepest shade of brown. She suspected it would curl when wet, drying into untamed flicks that twisted to his shoulders and fell wantonly about his face. Sharp brooding eyes almost black in their depths were framed lavishly with thick dark lashes: luscious, evocative and dominating.

And there was that word again—*regal*—rolling through her mind as she frantically tried to piece together the *how* and *why* he had broken into her suite and was now trussed to a chair. None of it made sense.

Jovan's hard voice ripped her attention from the seriously ripped Carvalho and she spun to see him leaning his six-foot-five frame against a bank of security screens.

'He did this to himself, Pia. Let me deal with him— please?' His chiselled features twisted, playing out a complex series of emotional shifts.

'No. He wants something.' Right then she flashed back to their brief conversation. 'And I suspect it is something only Zeus can give—otherwise why lie about having a meeting prearranged? So before he destroys my club with his ugly rumours, or costs me another twenty-five million on the stockmarket, I want to know why.'

Jovan grumbled in the way Pia had learned to ignore. 'So what do you intend to do with him?'

Stress and worry lined his brow, reminding her of the day they'd met. When he'd swept her into his arms as she'd lain knocking on death's door outside her father's palatial entryway. Sixteen years old and before then she hadn't even known her father existed. Without Jovan, Pia doubted she would have survived in her father's frigid Siberian world.

'I can't believe I'm saying this, but I have no idea.'

Commodities? A cinch. Juggling multi-million-dollar investments every day? A breeze. Dealing with people? Excruciating torture.

'I'll just have to play it by ear. Question him. Find out what he wants and why.'

Jovan snorted. 'Good luck with that one. He is arrogant. Overly cocky and dangerously determined.'

'Then we are equally matched. I don't believe in coincidences, Jovan. My gut tells me he's responsible for the rumours and the mayhem at Eros, and if so he wants something and won't disappear until he gets it. It would be foolish of me to take my eyes off him for one second.'

'So we put him on watch. Twenty-four-seven.'

'Or I go in there. Deal with him. Quickly. Quietly.'

'Pia, please. It is too risky.'

'Since when have I been afraid of a little risk?' *Never.* Fear would never touch her heart again. 'He's sure to tell me far more than he would ever tell you, and I'll hazard a guess he'll remain obstinate until he meets the man behind Q Virtus anyway.'

'He'll be waiting a long time.'

'Quite. So I'll put him off. Persuade him to deal with me and figure out what he's looking for. Why he'd chance his membership, his reputation, his business and fortune, by toying with the club. With me personally. He must know Zeus could bring him down.'

'But you'll place yourself in jeopardy. Under the spotlight. What if he realises you and Zeus are one and the same person? That your father is dead?'

Without thought Pia let her fingers creep up to her throat, where her pulse beat against her palm in a wild tattoo. Such an outcome wasn't even worth contemplating.

'He won't. He's a man. He's predictable and he won't

look beyond my breasts. Women are designed for whoring or childbearing in his world—the truth wouldn't occur to him in a million years. Granted, very few people know Antonio Merisi had a daughter, but my existence is no secret. If he looked in the right places he'd know I exist. When I tell him he'll think I am merely ornamental—a pampered child—so I doubt he'll crow to his friends that he was wrestled to the ground by a mere female.'

The man had a superb business mind and a vast IQ, but he was arrogant and conceited and as dominant as they came. Any battle between them would likely stay behind doors.

'This is my life we're talking about and the future of a club I swore would stand the test of time.' Damn the old rules. '*Damn* the dinosaurs that litter the ranks of my club.'

They'd never accept leadership from someone with a sullied past such as hers. Not only that, but the gentlemen's club was bound by rules—archaic, chauvinistic rules created by troglodytes—that declared only a Merisi man could lead. Only a man could own and control the largest business interests in the world.

Yet here she was. Groomed. Her path decided the moment her father had seen her, semi-conscious in Jovan's arms. She'd become the son Antonio Merisi had never had. His heir. His corporate assassin. The girl he'd called worthless, tainted, illiterate trash at first glance, making her feel dirtier than the clothes on her back. The same girl who'd then taken his fortune and quadrupled it within the first two years of living under his excessively opulent roof.

She was master of the most exclusive club in the world. Perpetually in hiding. Habitually alone. And that was the way it must stay.

'If my instincts are right he's declared war and I'm fighting blind—ignorant of the cause. If I'm to have any chance of surviving I need the right weapon to wield. Turn off the screens, Jovan.' Her tone brooked no argument. 'I'm going in.'

The monitors flickered to black and a moment later a faint tap on the door preceded Clarissa Knight, one of the Petit Qs, shifting on her feet as she was nudged through the space, a telling flush driving high on her cheekbones.

The pennies dropped more quickly than a Las Vegas slot machine flashing 'Winner' in neon lights.

Oh, wonderful. A lovesick puppy.

Pia checked a disgusted growl. 'Oh, Clarissa, tell me he promised you the world—or at least a permanent position in his bed?'

Simultaneously Clarissa's eyes fell to the floor and Jovan raised a small, flat high-tech sensor pad in the air, his expression warning her not to underestimate their intrepid foe.

Fingerprint recognition.

Her anger dissipated as fast as it came. She wasn't going to ask Clarissa how it felt to be used. She remembered humiliation and worthlessness all too well.

Somewhere in that dark abyss between unconsciousness and lucidity a razor-sharp rapping registered and Nic tried for a gentle head-shake. His temples loathed that idea, twisting his stomach into a tight knot, pleading with him not to even attempt it a second time.

Prising his bruised eye open wasn't much of a picnic either, but his heuristic brain—not to mention his sense of self-preservation—was keen to know exactly how much trouble he was in.

And he *was* in trouble. The ropes cutting into the skin of his wrists was a dead giveaway.

Well, he'd been in worse situations. *Look on the bright side, Nic. You're in. Zeus is here. Somewhere. They haven't thrown you out. Yet.*

Neck aching from being slumped forward, he cautiously raised his head to take in his surroundings.

His mind registered the darkness, the shadows prancing around the bare room, before he focused on a single stream of moonlight shining through the only small window, illuminating one stiletto-heeled foot tap-tap-tapping on the floor.

Ah. He suspected that was the culprit responsible for the lethargic woodpecker hammering at his head. Yet, oddly enough, all was forgotten as his appreciative eyes glissaded upwards.

Vintage towering black patent heels with an inch-thick sole. Sculpted ankles and toned calves. Sheer stockings draping long, long luscious legs and disappearing beneath a short, black figure-hugging pencil skirt.

His mind took another detour, wondering when he'd last had sex. Full-on, hedonistic, mind-blowing, erotic carnality usually kept his body taut, but now he thought about it he hadn't felt the need in months. Little wonder he was famished.

'Good evening, Mr Carvalho.'

A rush of heat shimmered over his skin like a phantom fire. 'Well, well, well—if it isn't my little gunslinger.'

'We meet again. How are you feeling?'

Mouth as dry and hot as the desert sands, he licked his lips. His voice *still* came out gravelly with repressed need. 'Much better for seeing you, *querida*. Or at least the half that I can see. I do wish you'd come a little closer. You can trust me.'

'Said the wolf to the lamb,' she quipped. 'Was it that charming reprobate tongue you used to gain access to my private suite, Mr Carvalho?'

'Call me Nicandro, please. I'd like to think my submissive aspect puts us on first-name terms at least. Right now you could do anything you desired to me.'

Straddling his lap would his first choice. Pressing her

breasts into his chest and licking into his mouth and down the column of his throat would be the second. The agony of feeling her all over his body but being unable to touch... Exquisite torture.

'Very well...*Nicandro*.'

His name rolled deliciously from her mouth with a hint of European inflection. Italian, or maybe Greek. He didn't miss the fact that she still hadn't given him her name, but he was too busy imagining thick, dark curling locks and hazel eyes to match that smoky, sultry voice.

'Let us discuss the misdemeanour of breaking and entering. It stands to reason—our being on first-name terms, after all—that you should tell me exactly what you were doing in my private rooms this evening.'

'Tell me your name and I will.'

That she didn't want to was clear. But two could play this game, and he hadn't needed to hear the safety click of her revolver or the commands she'd issued to the staff to tell him this woman held power. Exactly how much he had yet to figure out.

'My name is Olympia Merisi.'

Now, *that* was unexpected. He barely managed to swallow the sharp hitch in his breath.

'Ah. The little wife, then?' A healthy dose of disappointment made him frown. What did he care *who* she was chained to?

'Little? Now, *there* is something I've never been called. As for me being a wife—angels will dance in hell before I submit to any man.'

Nic could soon change that. In fact he was tempted to make it his mission. Which was incongruous, considering he hadn't even seen her face yet.

'A more accurate description for me would be...*daughter*.'

Everything stopped, as if someone had pressed 'pause' on the drama that was his life.

Zeus had a daughter. Well, now, every cloud had a silver lining and it seemed the fates were looking down on him tonight.

How utterly opportune. How devilishly delicious.

This new information gave him extra verve to break loose and he regained his attempts at loosening the knots binding his wrists as he found his tongue.

'In that case I do hope I didn't cause too much damage to your father's security staff. I was hoping to meet the man himself to apologise.' If he were Pinocchio his nose would have poked her eye out by now.

'That is very decent of you,' she said, skating the lines of sarcasm.

'I thought so too. I'm a very decent man.'

'That remains to be seen. You see, I have the very old-fashioned view that seducing a member of my staff and breaking into private quarters does not decent make.'

He flashed her a mock-aggrieved look. 'Now you are just nitpicking, *querida*. I was curious, that is all.'

A small flat black box spun through the air and landed at his feet with a clatter.

Ah. Busted.

'I would expect to find such high-tech equipment in the hands of a CIA operative, not a man who is merely curious to meet another. I very much doubt you'd find such a thing in the electronics section at the local store.'

Nic shrugged. Forgot he was slightly incapacitated and wrenched his shoulder. *Dios*, it hurt like hell. He was going to get her back for this and he'd enjoy every single second.

What had she said? The local store? He wished. It would have been a damn sight cheaper. 'Let us say I have friends in high places.'

'MI5? The White House?'

'The Bronx.'

She huffed out a genuine laugh and, just as it had earlier, a hot kind of thrilling pleasure infused his blood with a sullen pulse of want. *Come on, Olympia, show me your face. You're beautiful—I know it.*

'Any normal person would've asked for an appointment. Ever heard of a phone?'

'Believe it or not, I much prefer the personal touch—'

'Oh, I believe you,' she interrupted snarkily.

'Maybe curious was too bland a word,' he went on regardless. 'Tenacious?'

'Foolhardy? Reckless?'

He settled on, 'Intrepid.' It sounded better to him.

'Why? What exactly is it you want?'

'An audience with the all-powerful mystery man himself. One hour with your father.'

'Impossible,' she declared, without missing a beat.

There was something no-nonsense about her. She was overtly frank. And, call him a fool, but he believed her. Thinking about it, she didn't seem the type to waste time messing around. As if her time was at a premium.

He pondered that while he doubled-checked. 'He isn't here?'

'No, I'm afraid not. On this occasion the journey was too far for him to travel.'

She had an odd tone to her voice he couldn't fathom, but he still trusted her word. Dangerous? Probably. Considering who her father was. Her father who *wasn't* here.

'Pity.' Or was it? Eventually this woman would lead him directly to Zeus himself, and in the meantime…? The game was afoot and his to master.

A few days or weeks in the company of this woman would be no hardship. He could burrow into her life, find potential weak spots, and seduce her into his bed. Imagine Zeus's horror when he discovered Nic had tasted his precious daughter. It was too delicious an idea to reject outright. It needed serious consideration.

'Is it a private matter, or business?' she enquired.

'Both.'

'Then I'm happy to talk to him on your behalf, or deliver any message you wish. You have my word it will be delivered with the utmost secrecy.'

She began to lean towards him and Nic watched, mesmerised, breath held, pulse thumping frenetically, as she came into view inch by delectable inch. It occurred to him then that she was trying to gain his trust by coming out of the shadows, making eye contact, and figured it was entirely too possible that he was underestimating her.

Nic's eyes strained to focus as she leaned further still, bending that tiny waist, bringing the low, severe slash of her black V-neck shirt into the light, showcasing a deep cleavage of pearly white skin that made his blood hum.

Every blink of his eyes felt lethargic, every punch of his pulse profound, as she came closer...closer—

Dios...

Legs crossed, she sat with her elbow on her bent knee, chin resting on her lightly curled fist; she was the picture of seductive power.

His jaw dropped so fast it almost dented the floor. He felt his IQ dip fifty points. 'You are...' *Stupefyingly beautiful.* 'Blonde.'

Eyes sparkling with amusement, she tipped her head to one side, as if he'd given her a complex mathematical equation and no calculator.

'Ten out of ten, Mr Carvalho. What exactly did you expect?'

'Greek.' It was the only word he could muster. Pathetic, really, considering his reputation. But holy hell and smoke and fire, the woman looked as if she'd just stepped off a film noir set, playing the leading role of *femme fatale.* Visually dominant and unrepentant.

Thick flaxen hair the colour of champagne had been swept back from her face and perfectly pinned in a chic 1950s Grace Kelly look. Then again, the image of Grace Kelly aroused words like *innocent, serene.* Whereas Olympia Merisi exuded danger and sin. A woman who would refuse to be defined by any man or to submit to her sexuality. All mysterious and seductive. The type whose charm ensnared a man in the bonds of irresistible desire.

There was no other word for it—her beauty was otherworldly, almost supernatural. Pale flawless skin that shimmered like a pearl, high slashing cheekbones that any supermodel would weep for, huge, ever so slightly slanted violet-blue eyes thickly rimmed with black kohl, and full pouty lips painted in the deepest shade of unvirtuous red.

She should have been called Aphrodite, as undeniably goddess-like as she was. An enchantress able to weave her magical powers, leaving her morally ambiguous. She was danger personified—and didn't *that* just ratchet up his 'want meter' into the stratosphere?

This wasn't a woman you married—hell, no: the very idea was ludicrous. This was a woman you bedded. Found ecstasy in her body over and over, until neither of you could walk, talk or summon the energy to breathe.

Hauling in damp air, he silently prayed for his arousal to subside, wishing he'd felt one zillionth of this visceral attraction for the Petit Q he'd earlier declined.

'Your mother...? Norwegian? Swedish?' With that natural colouring she had to be.

If Nic had blinked he would have missed it. That pained pinch of her mouth, that subtle flinch of her flesh. It didn't take a genius to work out that her mother was a touchy subject.

'French,' she said, in a tone so cold it was a welcome blast of air-con sizzling over his hot, damp skin and leaving goosebumps in its wake.

Nic shrugged. What was a couple of thousand miles? 'European. Close enough.'

Her displeased pout told him to drop it, and even he knew some battles weren't worth fighting. So he did. Well, sort of...

'Please allow me to apologise for waking you earlier, *querida*. Or maybe you should thank me. Your dreams seemed too dark to be pleasant.'

Right there. Ah, yes. She might ooze power and control, but beneath all those chilly layers she was still a woman, swayed by emotions, capable of vulnerability. This was going to be child's play.

'What haunts your sleep, Olympia?' And since when had he ever been interested enough in a woman to care?

'A mere headache.'

Poised and graceful as a ballerina, she stood and pirouetted on her heels, turning her back on him. No doubt to soothe the raw nerve he'd struck. But what really bothered him was the weird, not to mention scary idea that he wanted to take it back, soothe her pain himself.

Instead his eyes followed her like a heat-seeking missile, and he detonated at the sight of the tight curves forming her lush heart-shaped bottom and the perfectly straight black seams splicing down her sheer stockings.

Every thought in his head exploded with the extra blast of heat to his groin.

Holy smoke. She was the sexiest thing he'd ever laid eyes on. He couldn't wait to taste her. To get up close and personal with that stunning hourglass figure. To mould his hands to her flesh, sip at her skin for days. And he would. There was no woman in the world he couldn't beguile and lure into his bed.

After she'd taken a turn around the chair she came to stand in front of him. Up close and personal.

Nic ground his back teeth, scrambling for a reprieve from the sexual tension that choked the air around them and took his hard-on from uncomfortable to agonising.

Turned out the fates had had their eye on the ball the entire time—because if there was one sure-fire way to rid him of lust they'd found it.

Olympia bent slightly at the waist—to look into his eyes

or to endeavour to intimidate him, he wasn't sure and didn't particularly care—and he reckoned he was so far gone he would have begged for her mouth right there and then. *If* a large black diamond teardrop, spectacular and rare, edged with twenty-four brilliant-cut white diamonds totalling fifty-two carats, with a net worth of approximately forty-six point two million dollars, hadn't chosen that precise moment to tumble from the sumptuous lace confection encasing her breasts.

Nic jerked as if that bruiser bodyguard was back with a fist in his guts. One punch and a tsunami of anger and hate and pain threatened to pull him under, drag him into the depths of hell. His chest felt crushed and toxic adrenaline rushed through his body, hardening his wide shoulders, searing down his arms, until he was able to contort his wrists and almost pull free of the ropes. *Just a few seconds more.*

He wanted to rip that platinum chain from around her neck, tear those jewels from the warm cavern of her skin. Just as Zeus's henchman had ripped it from his mother's lifeless body.

O Coracao da Tempestade. The heart of the storm. The Santos diamonds.

He couldn't tear his eyes away. So many memories. So much heartache. So much pain.

Nic had always surmised that Goldsmith owned the jewels, along with the rest of the company. The thought that they'd been separated thoughtlessly, like meaningless pieces of chattel, had broken his heart. He could only presume that when Zeus had sold off Santos he must have kept the diamonds to gift to his pampered daughter like some kind of obscene trophy.

Did she know how her father had come to own them?

A shudder racked his entire body and he broke out in a cold sweat.

Dios, did she know they were smothered in blood?

If she did he would make her life a living hell.

The fist gripping his heart threatened to squeeze the life out of him. It took everything he had to remain calm, not to jump to conclusions or lose the hold on his temper.

Gracefully she straightened before him, and the vigilance narrowing those striking violet eyes told him she was well aware that the *Lobisomem* now sat before her, struggling to stay leashed.

Not any more.

The rope finally fell away from his wrists and it took all his remaining strength to keep hold of the bonds, control his face into an impassive blank slate so she would be none the wiser. Timing was everything, and he hadn't bided his for years only to trip over his anger and fall at the first hurdle.

Nic discreetly cleared his throat and turned his voice to a rich, evocative volume that would diffuse her doubt.

'Apologies, *querida*, my mind wandered. While I appreciate your offer to relay my business to your father, I stand firm. Let us say the topic is of a delicate nature.'

Olympia took another step back and he dug his nails into his palms to stop himself reaching out, gripping her waist, hauling her into his lap, punishing that seductive temptation of a mouth, taking his revenge on her glorious body.

Instead he carried on—as if his heart *wasn't* tearing apart. 'I don't know you well enough to discuss it with you. I'm sure you understand.'

Stalemate. He knew it. She knew it.

Agitation leached from her. 'No' was clearly not a word she was used to hearing.

'Then I can't help you any further, Mr Carvalho. As for this evening—I'm sure *you* understand there has been a breach of trust, and as you're unwilling to explain yourself your membership will be placed under review. I can—'

'However,' he continued, as if she'd never spoken, knowing it would rile her, determined to gain the upper hand, 'if

I had the opportunity to get to know you I might change my mind. Spend a few days with me, *bonita*. I'd love the chance to put things right between us. To prove I'm not so bad after all.'

She crossed her arms over her ample chest and arched one flaxen eyebrow. 'You think me a fool, Mr Carvalho. The way to my father is not via my bed.'

Brainy and beautiful.

'Maybe not, but I guarantee you would enjoy the ride. You're tempted—admit it.'

'As much as I am tempted to skydive from thirty-thousand feet without a parachute.'

He grinned—he couldn't help it. Despite her unfortunate parentage and the bauble now nestled back in her deep cleavage he kind of liked her. Such a shame she wore a harbinger of tragedy around her delicate throat. He wondered then if she truly knew of its origins, because surely no woman in their right mind would wear it if they were well-versed in the omen it carried. The wrath of his ancestors. Strange, he'd never really believed in any of it. Until now. Because clearly Nicandro had been led to it—to her—to wreak his revenge.

He wanted it back. And he would have it. *After* he'd taken her. *After* he'd slid the diamonds from her throat in a slow, erotic seduction she would never forget.

Nic ignored the remnants of his Catholic morality—the stuff that still percolated inside whatever passed for his soul these days—which were suggesting he wasn't being strictly fair, involving her. Odds were she was as crooked as her father.

'I could have you in a heartbeat,' he declared. Exaggeration on his part—she would be hard work. She was feisty and wilful and brimming with self-determination—which would make her final moments of surrender all the more delicious, precious.

'You will never have *me*, Nicandro.'

By the time he'd figured out those were her parting words he was wrestling with a bout of what was surely affront—because the little vixen was halfway to the door.

Nic lurched from the chair and reached the door before she did, slamming his palm flat on the dense block of wood. If she was shocked he'd torn from his hold she covered her surprise quickly enough—simply froze to the spot like an ice sculpture and peered at him the way someone would a cockroach.

'Want to bet?' he said, making his voice smooth, richer than cognac and twice as heady.

A cold front swept over him, pricking his skin through the superfine material of his shirt.

'Anyone ever tell you that you're supremely arrogant?'

'Often. I'm not averse to hearing compliments, Olympia. And nor do I imagine are you. You really are stunning, *querida*.'

Up close she was even more exquisite. He couldn't take his eyes off her.

'Save it, Romeo. You may be infamous for your limitless wants and desires, but I'm afraid you've reached your limit with me.'

He might have believed her if he hadn't trailed the back of his index finger down her bare arm excruciatingly slowly and relished the shimmy rustling over her body. Impossible as it was, her infinitesimal gasp and the ghostly pinch of her brow gave him the notion that she hadn't known a simple touch could affect her in such a tremendous way.

'You're scared. Maybe even petrified. Afraid I will prove you wrong? Or fearful you'll enjoy every minute of it?' He was baiting her, but there was one advantage to toying with an intelligent woman: he knew exactly what buttons to push.

'I fear no one. Least of all you.'

That haughty retort hung in the air, coaxing another smile from him. She was sewn up tighter than a drum.

'Prove it. Spend two weeks in my company. If you win and evade my bed I will desist in my attempts to meet with your father and resign my membership from Q Virtus with no fanfare. You have my word.'

Because her evasion would never, *ever* happen.

Those big violet eyes narrowed on his. 'Together with a full explanation? Because I know there's more to you than meets the eye and far more to this meeting you desire with Zeus. I want to know why.'

It occurred to him then that she must work for her father in some way. Must have come in his place this weekend. She might have already put two and two together and suspect he was at the root of the dissent at the club. Not that she could prove it.

'Of course I'll tell you everything you want to know. However, if you lose, and I take your body as mine, have you at my mercy, you'll arrange a meeting with Zeus and take me to him.'

Two days and she'd succumb. Three at the most.

For long moments she simply stared at him, and it was shocking to admit but he'd have given half of Manhattan to know what she was thinking. He'd never given much credence to the term 'closed book', but this intriguing package was still wrapped in Cellophane.

Finally she gave a heavy sigh, as if she really didn't have much of an alternative. As if he'd pushed her into a corner with his refusal to tell her anything and she had nowhere else to go but to follow him.

What had he said? Child's play.

'All right. Here's the deal. Zeus will be in Paris in eight days. *If* you win, I guarantee you'll meet at a specified time and place. You have my word.'

A smile—so small yet inordinately confident—curved her luscious lips. He wished she'd do it more often—it made his heart trampoline into his throat.

So bold she was, so sanguine, so sure he would fail and she would be the victor. He almost felt sorry for her.

'But when you lose I will have you on your knees, *Nicandro*.'

'*If* I lose I'll go down with pleasure, *Olympia*.'

Eyes locked, they stared at one another. Neither giving an inch. And he'd swear the air sparked with electricity, tiny arrows of fire that bounced from one point of contact to another. One strike of a match and they'd blow sky-high.

'Then you have a deal…*Nic*…'

Welcome to three days of torture.

Even the way she purred his name like that, drawing out the N, made him hard.

'Splendid. And every deal should be sealed, don't you agree?'

Without giving her time to bat an eyelash he slowly lowered his mouth to hers. There was no better place to start the war, and his body begged for just one kiss, one taste.

Gossamer-light, Nic brushed his lips across hers and lavished the corner of her mouth with a lush velvet kiss. Electricity hissed over his skin, his blood seared through his veins on a scream of satisfaction, and before he knew it he stepped closer. Her breasts crushed against his chest and he fingered her sweet waist while he swept his tongue across the seam of her lips, demanding entry, commanding more.

Dizzy, as if she'd put him under some kind of spell, his mind stripped itself clean and he nipped at the plump flesh and sucked gently, desperate to be inside her warm heaven. She tasted of sweet, hot coffee liqueur, and if she'd just let him in…

After a few more seconds he drew back. Frowned.

Passive, emotionless—she hadn't moved one muscle and her skin was like ice, her blood-red lips equally devoid of warmth. Even her violet-blue stare was cold and vacant.

The shock of it made his tone incongruous. 'Olympia,

you are frozen, *querida*.' A coil of serpents in the pit of his stomach couldn't have unsettled him more.

Lifting her chin she gifted him a small smile. Except it wasn't cold—it was sad.

'I *am* frozen…*querido*. Inside and out. Ah, Nicandro, you really have no idea who you are playing with, do you?'

Her hand to the handle now, she hauled the door wide and he floundered for a beat, stepping backwards, his foot crushing the small black sensor pad she'd tossed at him earlier.

The inevitable crack snapped him back to his wits. 'Hold up there, ice queen. The Petit Q. She was innocent in all this. Promise me the girl will—'

'Be removed from the premises. Good evening, Nicandro.'

Next thing he knew she was gone—the razor-sharp tap-tap of her towering heels vibrating in the void around him.

'You really have no idea who you are playing with, do you?'

Wasn't that the truth?

CHAPTER THREE

PIA PULLED THE double doors to her suite closed behind her
and fought the urge to slump against the carved wood. Bad
enough that she raised her fingertips to the corner of her
mouth to chase the faint echoes of his kiss, shimmering
over her lips like an iridescent butterfly.

Old habits truly did die hard, because for the first time
in years she was second-guessing herself—and that really
didn't bode well. Suddenly spending time with Nicandro
Carvalho seemed like a bad, bad idea. But what alternative did she have? Wait it out until he struck again? God
only knew what havoc he'd wreak next, and she could not
let that happen. Not in *her* world.

'Pia?'

She jumped clean off the floor, then flushed guiltily
like an idiotic schoolgirl who'd just had her first kiss from
a long-time crush and her big brother had been spying on
her. She didn't want to think how close to the truth that was.

'Where did you come from? I thought you were escorting our nefarious burglar to his suite?'

Jovan watched her warily from where he sat looking
incongruous—his large frame stiff and upright—perched
on the edge of her delicate gold silk daybed.

'Mission accomplished.'

Oh.

Pia's eyes shuttered at the concern marring his face. He
wanted to ask if she was okay but he wouldn't. He didn't

like making her feel weak. Emotional. Not when she was supposed to be a machine. But therein lay the problem. Machines didn't tremble with the touch of man's hand, at his finger breezing down her arm. Machines didn't suffer a glitch after a soft evocative kiss from his warm lips. And machines certainly didn't stare into his eyes and feel something close to longing, wishing for the impossible.

For one heart-stopping moment she would have done anything to kiss him back. Anything to feel his scorching heat melt some of the ice inside of her—ice that was so terribly, terribly cold. But Pia knew that surrendering to meaningless brief moments could shower you in a lifetime of regret, and he'd chosen the one route to her bed with a guaranteed outcome of failure and causing her maximum levels of pain.

He was using her. To get to Zeus. To Q Virtus. Ignorant of the fact he'd already been in Zeus's company for most of the evening. If it wasn't so humiliating and didn't exhume such loathsome feelings of worthlessness she would laugh. *Sorry, Nic, I've already learned my lessons in love.* Pia could spot a seduction routine a mile off and erect her barricades with ease.

Being used for the Merisi fame and fortune years ago had thrown her hard-earned self-respect to the wolves—with a little help from her father's constant stream of berating anger during the miserable aftershocks of her affair.

'Women are weak fools with vulnerable hearts, Olympia. You think he wanted your body? Your mind?' he'd hollered, as if the idea that any man could desire her for simply being Pia was unfathomable. *'True lust is greed for money and power. Surrender to a man and he will strip you of your fortune and glory and leave you as nothing more than a whore in his bed. Trust no man. Not even me.'*

That her hollow, cold flesh should now answer to the practised tongue of a Don Juan with criminal tendencies who was quite possibly trying to take her down could only be the cruel joke of a universe that despised her.

Now she had to drag him across Europe for the next few days, on a schedule that was impossible to change, trying to delve into the intricacies of his mind while he tried to delve into her knickers.

Not in a million years.

She'd just have to keep her head on straight and her eyes on him. The man could hardly kick up a storm if she was watching over his shoulder, and it would give her plenty of time to unearth what game he was playing and why.

The anxiety of it all—the possibility that she was in danger of having everything she'd worked so hard for taken away—made her feel sick to the stomach. *And that's not the only thing that has you rattled*, a little voice said. She told that voice to hush up.

'You look tired, Pia,' Jovan said.

She was. Bone-deep tired. But machines weren't supposed to get tired. So instead of crawling into bed she tried to pretend that she didn't ache all over, lifted her chin, strode towards her office and got back to business.

'I'm fine. You worry too much.'

That wasn't fair. He cared about her and she would be for ever grateful for that small mercy in her life. It would have all been so easy if there'd been flames of attraction between them, but there wasn't so much as a flicker—never mind the high-voltage current that was still racing through her body from—

No, no, *no*. She was *not* going there.

'Get Laurent from Paris on the phone and tell him I've found him a new concierge. Then ask Clarissa Knight to pack her bags and come to my office. She's wanted to be based near her mother for months and this is the perfect opportunity. With a bit of luck she'll find some fresh eye-candy in days, and Mr Carvalho will be reduced to a distant memory. Just make sure Mr I'm-Sex-Incarnate-and-I-Know-It doesn't see her leave.'

It was far too dangerous to keep her here, bewitched under Carvalho's spell. No doubt he'd promise her the world for more secrets, and if the girl thought Pia was casting her out of a job *and* had convinced herself in love with the Brazilian bad-boy anything was possible.

Even Pia—who'd been vaccinated against the Nicandros of the world—had sensed him drizzling charm all over her as if she were a hot waffle. Clarissa wouldn't have stood a chance. Had he slept with her? Devoured her over and over again? And why *that* imagery made her feel queasy was anyone's guess.

'You are going soft in your old age, Pia,' Jovan said.

The only thing going soft was her breasts.

'I'm not so vain that I can't admit to fault. The girl is far too sheltered to be surrounded by Q Virtus players, some of who are no better than vultures preying on female flesh, but she needed the extra money to send home and I caved.'

While those were the facts it wasn't the entire truth, and she knew it. The truth was Nicandro had used the girl, and it left a bitterly sour taste in Pia's mouth. She was utterly disappointed in him—and that was highly idiotic, because it meant she'd placed him on a pedestal just from what she'd read of him, meant her emotions had been engaged. *Fool.*

'Of course you caved. The girl genuinely needed you. I know you hate to admit it, but you *like* being needed.'

'No, I don't.' Did she?

'Okay, you don't. So, do I have the pleasure of escorting *him* to the airport?' Jovan asked, with no small amount of enthusiastic glee, as he walked towards her desk, where she was standing shuffling papers from one towering pile to another.

The fact she was making a mess to avoid this subject didn't go unnoticed.

Oh, hell, this was not going to go down well.

'No.' And since she didn't have the energy to tell Jovan he'd be escorting them both—together—and then deal with the inevitable fall-out—which was so unlike her it was frightening—she said, 'I'll explain later. Get going or you'll miss Laurent.'

Jovan did a quick U-turn and headed towards the door— and the action popped a memory like some maniacal jack-in-the-box. Nicandro's swift *volte-face*. One minute the consummate charmer, the next a predator. The *lobisomem* she'd seen from the start.

Strange, that all it had taken was one scan of his membership request, one perlustration of his past, one glance at the nebulous depths of his eyes and his moniker had bitten into her brain. *Lobisomem*: werewolf. A survivor despite or perhaps in spite of his origins. A lord of the night. His darkness a phantom entreaty to her soul.

But for several heartbeats in that room there'd been such violent anger in his eyes. A change so swift, so absolute, she'd felt the sharp edges of panic for the first time in years.

Where had it come from, that vitriol mutating his gorgeous whisky-coloured eyes to black pools of hate? Indifference she might have understood—but hate? Such a strong emotion. Made him appear dangerous. Deadly.

At first she'd thought his abrupt one-eighty had something to do with her diamonds—the only gift her father had ever given her, the only time he'd ever shown her he cared. It was the only possession she'd ever truly adored. Yet Nicandro had stared at them with a look of abject horror. It was the *why* that was bugging her. Yes, large black diamonds were extraordinarily rare—hers was one of a kind—but the way he'd gone on you would think it was an evil eye, some kind of black art mumbo-jumbo.

Rubbing at the aching spot between her eyes, she decided it was nigh on impossible to figure him out.

'Jovan, before you go, what's the name of that private investigator we occasionally use?'

He stilled beneath the archway leading back to the main suite and looked over his shoulder at her keenly. 'We have several. Though it's usually Mason, who tows the legal line—or McKay, who has no compulsion about being morally corrupt if given the right incentive.'

Another crook. Wonderful. Bad enough she was hearing rumours of Q Virtus being associated with the Greek mafia. Did she have Mr Carvalho to thank for that one too? She'd thank him, all right. With a swift knee-jerk in his crown jewels.

When she had the proof. *If* it was him.

So foolish, Pia. You're still hoping there's a perfectly reasonable explanation for all this—an explanation that has nothing to do with Nicandro Carvalho, aren't you? She couldn't answer that question and not hate herself.

'That's him—he'll do. McKay. Ask him to look into the history of Santos Diamonds. I don't suppose you remember how and when my father took control of the company, do you?'

Jovan paused. Stared at her with an indecipherable look. He *never* paused.

'Jovan? Did you hear me?' Pia hadn't seen him like this in ages. Almost haunted.

He gave his head a quick shake. 'Yes—sorry…distracted. No, haven't a clue.'

He also never lied to her.

'It's probably nothing, but let's have the information anyway.'

'Not a problem,' he murmured, in a low, hesitant tone that said trouble was coming. The kind of trouble that could rock the very foundations of her life.

She just hoped he was wrong.

As soon as the door closed behind him she dumped the papers on her desk and without thinking of posture, or performing for an audience, she collapsed into the chair and sprawled all over it.

She couldn't remember the last time she'd done this, she realised, head tipped back, staring at the ceiling. It reminded her of being no one—a forgotten girl in a basement room that shook with the heavy metal pounding from above, the acrid scent of drugged hopelessness drifting through the floorboards. The girl with a tainted past and only prospects of a no-good future.

In the next second, as if a ghostly fist had thumped the table, she bolted upright, pin-straight, and opened her laptop, pushing that girl—the girl who no longer existed—from her mind once more.

Nic woke to a warm, richly scented African morning, with a foul disposition from the unfathomable unrequited desire he'd suffered throughout the night and a note pushed beneath his door.

I am leaving at twelve noon and flying to Northern Europe on business. If you still wish to join me be ready at eleven.
Olympia Merisi

Join her? 'I do not think so, *querida*.' Did he look like a lapdog? Next she'd want him to bark.

Dios, he felt vile.

He dismissed the flash of self-honesty that his lack of sleep—when he should have slept like a babe after his major victory at the end of an eight-day quest—was making him too grumpy to think straight, and lurched out of bed with a hot head, ready to yank her into line.

His disgusting mood ruined a perfectly good morning as he showered and said goodbye to Narciso and Ryzard—taking one hell of a ribbing about the slight swelling around his lip, which they presumed was thanks to a ravenous Petit Q—and was led to Pia's private suite.

One of the brutish security guards from the night before

reluctantly let him in, and the fact that he looked a damn sight worse than Nic did, sporting a huge black eye, made him feel remarkably better.

'You're early,' was her greeting when he strode through the door, ready to play hell and inform her that *she* would be travelling with *him*.

He didn't notice her sleek, sophisticated up-do, or her flawless skin, or her kohl-rimmed eyes, or that pouty, pro-vocative red mouth. Nor did he take any interest in the sharp-as-a-blade black business suit hugging her sinuous figure and nipping her waist. Absolutely not.

Her beefcake security guard plonked a case near his feet, no doubt wishing it were his head.

'When did you arrive in Zanzibar?' Nic asked, eyeing the cluttered floor.

'Friday—same as you.'

'You have a lot of luggage for a three-day stay, *bonita*. Did you bring the kitchen sink?' Clearly her father paid her well for being…what? A glorified PA on a power trip? She could, of course, be his only heir. He'd have to kiss that out of her too.

'Not this time. That one is Jovan's,' she said, pointing to the smallest of the designer six-piece set.

'And Jovan is…?' For a terrible moment he suspected he was experiencing a flicker of jealousy.

Dios, he was all over the place. What had she done to him?

'My bodyguard.'

Yeah, right.

'And a friend.'

Sure.

His mother had had lots of so-called 'friends'. He'd actually liked a couple of them. Especially the one who took him to a Brazil game, where he'd met the players, but for the life of him he couldn't remember the guy's name. Which was odd, because he always remembered names—

was good with them. It had used to come in handy when his father would innocently name-drop to catch him out. Anything to avoid the screaming matches that had inevitably followed.

Then he realised it was because he was still staring at Jovan—her *friend*.

It took him a while—what with Othello's green-eyed monster riding his back—but he got there eventually.

'*Que?* No. No way. He is not coming with us. That was *not* the deal.'

'Oh, I'm sorry,' she said, all innocent and light, in cunning contradiction of the devilry in her eyes. 'Zeus insists. You don't want to get on his bad side, do you?'

Nic's temper gauge ratcheted up.

'Fine. But not him. I don't think he likes me.' *And he likes you far too much.*

'How observant you are, Nicandro.'

She lowered her voice to a conspiratorial whisper and leaned forward until he tasted her sweet breath.

'In truth, he'd kick you as soon as look at you. So I suggest you stay on your best behaviour.'

From nowhere he had the impulse to grin, and he let it fly in the most wicked, debauched way imaginable. Naturally he earned himself a nice, slow stunned blink from her gorgeous violet-blues.

Unrequited, my foot.

'Now I get it. He's the modern-day equivalent of a chastity belt.'

She must be worried. Downright petrified of being alone with him.

As if a third wheel would dissuade him. He'd once outrun several of New York's finest after he'd stolen a bagel for breakfast to appease his crippling hunger pangs, so he was damn sure he could lose *this* guy.

The edginess he'd felt the previous night evaporated

at the warmth in her million-dollar satisfied smile as she shrugged one cashmere shoulder. So beautiful. So *his*.

Olympia Merisi wasn't frozen. She only needed the higher heat from a slow burn to melt her resistance. He'd moved too fast, his impatience calling the shots, when he should have known better. He had to stop thinking of her as any other woman and use his brains instead of what was between his legs. Not that he'd ever had the need to switch or polish his technique, but people didn't call him a dynamic powerhouse for nothing.

The reason he'd stormed up here now seemed unimportant. Like a tug of war that wasn't worth landing on his ass for. And he was coming to realise he'd have to pick and choose his battles where this woman was concerned or they'd be at loggerheads for ever and he'd alienate her before he'd even begun. So he'd play along, for now, and slowly but surely gain her trust. When the time was right and he held her in the palm of his hand—*then* he'd take control. She wouldn't know what had hit her.

'Did you want something? You're much too early.'

'No, I simply wanted to see you sooner.' And the hell of it was that was the God's honest truth. Not that he intended to panic about it. His desire was to reach his end game and Miss Merisi was going to take him the scenic route. 'Let's do breakfast. I'm starving.' *For more than food.*

'Pia?' the guy *Jovan* said, in an overly familiar way that said he would move Nic bodily if she gave the word.

Go on, buddy, try it. See how far you get.

'Pia…' Nic repeated, staring into those huge seductive eyes and watching them flare as he rolled the shortened name around his mouth as if he liked the taste of it on his tongue. 'Very pretty.'

He watched her delicate throat convulse. 'You may call me Olympia.'

She sounded so haughty and uptight he wanted to ruffle her feathers.

'I think not. If he can call you Pia why can't I? Unless, of course, Olympia is reserved especially for me. For those fortunate enough to have shared body fluids with you.' He licked his lips to emphasise his point—to remind her that despite her deep freeze he *had* kissed her, and he would kiss her again, and next time she would melt.

Her gasp was so faint only he could hear, but any spectator would have to be blind not to see the pink flush enhancing the perfect sweep of her cheeks.

Oh, yeah, she wanted him, all right.

One look at the way her hands fisted by her sides and he also knew she wanted to thump him.

Score one, Carvalho. Ball in the back of the net.

Though it didn't take long before his smile faltered and a dart of panic sped like an arrow into his gut. Had he seriously just stamped his possessive mark on her? No, impossible. He'd merely been staking his claim for the next eight days. After that she could do whatever she liked and he'd feel neither care nor concern because he'd have exactly what he wanted: Zeus.

She was still glaring at him, her glorious eyes flashing with unconcealed irritation. At second glance he revised that to absolute fury.

'I'm going to have to say no to breakfast, Nicandro,' she hissed hotly. 'With that *none too subtle* reminder I seem to have lost my appetite.'

All this frisky repartee was a serious turn-on. Between her posture and his arousal both of them were as stiff as a board. She seriously needed to loosen up.

Right then it struck him. The key to Pia Merisi. He had to coax the woman to liberation. Unpin that hair, unstrap that dress, unhook that bra, unchain all that control. Unleash all that fire.

Undo her one button at a time.

Reaching up, he stroked the side of his finger down her smooth cheek and felt her vibrate like a tuning fork.

'Ah, *querida*. I think I've just given you a different kind of hunger—that is all.' Then he brushed his thumb over her bottom lip and pressed against it in the guise of a kiss. 'Until later, *tchau*.'

Then—in a satisfying juxtaposition to the night before—he sauntered from the room and left *her* standing there, likely foaming at the mouth, watching his retreating back.

CHAPTER FOUR

PIA KEPT HER head high as she slid gracefully into the leather interior of the luxurious Mercedes waiting outside the private back entrance of the Barattza, still holding on to her temper by the skin of her teeth, frankly amazed that she hadn't followed Nic to his suite and ripped him to shreds.

As she'd watched his retreating back, with an oppressive silence thickening the air around her, she hadn't been able to chance a look at their little audience. She only had to think of how that pow-wow must have looked to her people. Hoping beyond hope that she hadn't just plummeted in their estimation.

Sharing body fluids?

Had he deliberately been trying to belittle her? Undermine her?

Didn't he know how hard she'd had to work to be taken seriously just because she was a woman? Of course he didn't. In his eyes she was probably some stylish Jezebel, playing secretary just to feed out of the troughs of her father's cash, sullied with her own craven self-importance!

She could just imagine what her father would have said if he'd witnessed that overtly sensual display of Nicandro stroking her cheek and thumb-kissing her. Her stomach churned at the mere thought.

'You're a woman—you have to work twice as hard to gain respect. Whoring yourself out will do you no favours, Olympia.'

So at the risk of making the situation look even worse, or blowing her true identity and a plethora of secrets sky-high, she hadn't blown a fuse in front of her staff. No, she'd kept her cool. And it had almost strangled the life out of her. Still was.

When she'd made this deal with him she hadn't expected to face these kinds of problems. How it would look to other people. How she would feel about his opinion of her that her value was only high enough to grace his bed.

It stung.

It was a poisonous battle between her hard-won pride and the need to protect Q Virtus.

Dammit, she wanted him to take her seriously. To know she was a successful woman in her own right. Then maybe he wouldn't treat her like some two-bit tramp.

Tough. She was just going to have to swallow it and suffer.

It would have been so much easier if she could have cancelled this business trip to Northern Europe but the time of year was imperative. Winter was setting in and the window for her hotel rebuild was so small she had no wriggle room.

Fact was he was bound to discover some of her interests over the next few days. It was inevitable.

Well, she'd just have to play the pretty little heiress, helping Daddy to uphold the ranks as she judiciously scrutinised her every discerning word.

Or, better yet, not talk to him at all. *If* he ever got his gorgeous taut backside inside this car. Clearly his time-keeping was as abysmal as his integrity.

Briefcase to the floor, table down in front of her, she flipped up the lid on her laptop and scanned the trading page to check the stockmarkets. Her every action pre-programmed into her psyche. Her body on autopilot, going through the motions like the machine she was.

Until from the corner of her eye she saw the man himself stroll from the hotel as if they had all the time in the world.

It was that insolent swagger that revved her temper—the very temper that had been idling for hours—into first gear.

As if there were a glitch in her system Pia's fingers mashed the keys, and no matter how hard she tried to re-boot, despite every firewall in her arsenal, she felt as if she was being infected with a virus. The Carvalho Virus. It even sounded deadly.

Case in point: she was now staring out of the window, watching that hateful, sublime, ripped body saunter to-wards the car beneath the bright flood of the African sun, dressed in suit trousers and a fine tailored black shirt that clung to his wide sculpted chest as the breeze licked over him, his jacket hanging from the finger curled like a hook over his shoulder.

Her stomach did a languorous, wanton roll that utterly appalled her.

There he was—a study in contrasts. With that impos-ing regal bearing and yet the dissipated air of a roguish bad-boy, with unkempt hair, huge designer sunglasses and voguish shoes. The heady mix collided to make some kind of prince of darkness.

Pia could count her past lovers with very few digits and little enthusiasm, but she instinctively knew what sex with Nicandro would be like—carnal, dark, and completely he-donistic—not her kind of thing at all. Which likely made her dead or a liar.

The door swung open and he slipped onto the leather bench, all smooth elegance as he made himself comfortable beside her. He smelled fresh from the shower and splashed with a hint of expensive cologne that prodded her hormones to sit up and take notice. She ignored them—and him—while her temper shifted into third gear. Lord, she had to calm down before she exploded.

Thinking about it, she always strove to remain on an even keel—her temper having been verbally beaten out of her years ago, when her father's patience had fizzled out and Pia had recognised her snippy tongue for what it was: fear that he wouldn't keep her. But even before that she'd never felt like this. So mad she was flushed with red-hot heat as if she were burning up. Even her clothes felt too tight, compressing her chest like a steel band that suffocated her from the inside.

So by the time the car rolled out of the hotel grounds she was raring to go, her body slamming her temper into fifth gear.

Breathe—for pity's sake, breathe.

'*Boa tarde, Pia*. Where are we headed on this beautiful afternoon?'

One roll of her name around his mouth, one perfectly innocuous question in that deep luscious voice that seemed to brush dark velvet across her nerve-endings, and just like that she lost it.

Pia whipped around to face him. 'How…how *dare* you?'

His dark brows came together in a deep frown but he said nothing, just glanced around the leather interior as if the answer to her fury lay in the cup-holders or the magazine pouch.

'Have I missed something?'

'Only your integrity, your decency and your brain—and that's just the beginning!'

After a pensive scratch of his jaw, he settled his sharp gaze on her laptop and she could just imagine what he was thinking. That she'd found some proof of his villainy to stick on him. Oh, she wished she had!

'I think this conversation would go much better if you told me the precise problem, *querida*.'

'The problem, *Nicandro*, is you belittling me in front of my staff! The problem is you making me feel three inches tall. How dare you bring up last night—a kiss that I didn't want or reciprocate in any way—in front of the very people I have worked hard to gain respect from? You know fine well that *sharing body fluids* could imply far more than a kiss and, considering you'd just broken into my private suite, how did that look? It made me look like a worthless whore with no self-respect, that's what!'

His eyebrows shot skyward. Then the mouth that had invaded her dreams curved in devilish amusement and he flicked those whisky-coloured eyes sparkling with striations of gold her way.

'You are not serious?'

He thought she was *joking*?

After she'd glared at him for a few seconds he finally got the message. 'You are perfectly serious. A *whore*?'

That was what her father would have said, wouldn't he? 'Yes, a whore. Why? Why would you do that to me?'

Glancing away, he flushed hotly, distinctly uncomfortable, and she wished to God she knew why.

'Did I dent your ego so badly it was payback?' she jeered.

'No. Absolutely not,' he said with the force of a gale.

His sincerity almost blew her away.

'I didn't think it would affect you in that way. I was…'

'What?'

He wouldn't say, but his embarrassment was acute and… well, those carved, tanned cheekbones slashed with red made her insides go a bit gooey. Whatever it was, it obviously bothered him.

In the awkward silence that followed she shifted around in her seat, not sure of her next move. Because from his point of view he didn't know who she really was.

This was why her temper was the enemy.

So in the end she let it go. The reason being, she assured herself, to get back on her even keel and wrestle back some control. Because honestly she was starting to act a little crazy. Unravelling like a tatty jumper wasn't like her at all.

'Just don't do that to me again. All right? The deal between you and I is private. I've worked too hard for my respect and it's important to me, okay?'

Shrewd—that was surely the only word to describe his expression.

'So you *do* work for your father, then?'

No, I damn well don't!

'Yes. Women *are* capable of such things, Nic. What are you? Primordial? Anti-feminist? Or just plain chauvinist? I dress well, I live well, and so you assume I freeload off my father by shuffling his papers?'

He had the good grace to look abashed. 'I think I've found one of your hot buttons.'

'How astute you are.'

'And not the one I was looking for.'

Pia threw up her arms with exasperated flair. 'And there you go again! *Must* you look at me and think sex?'

'I think I must. But come on! Give me a break. *Look* at you!' He gestured at her with his hands, as if that helped his argument. 'And, to be fair, I seem to remember thinking you radiated power. It was clear you held some. So there—see? You really must stop thinking the worst of me.'

She coughed out an incredulous laugh. 'Like *that* is ever going to happen.'

Now he threw *his* arms in the air, but his were longer, and far stronger, and the loud smack of his hand bashing off the window reverberated through the car.

'I can't win!' he growled, and followed it up with a blue streak of unintelligible curses as he flung himself back against the seat.

'As soon as you realise that, the better!' she sneered.

As for Pia—she actually felt much better. Sort of cleansed. Who knew that having an argument and not keeping everything bottled up inside her could feel so good? It was a revelation.

When Romeo seemed to find his calming centre again—which didn't take long, so she figured he shared her quick hot temper—he twisted to face her, and ended up doing a double-take at her small smile.

'I suppose you could say I've known many "pampered princesses" very well, but you are right, I'm sorry. I was stereotyping and didn't think it through and that was very bad of me. Forgiven?'

He sounded like a little boy right then. Pia would bet he'd been loved beyond reason, despite his family's lack of fortune, and the remnants of her ugly mood dissolved, morphing into a puddle of envy.

'Forgiven.'

'Good,' he said, looking back out of the window at the tropical white sandy beach as opposed to the lush plantations on her side of the car.

He seemed miles away, pensive, so when he reached over and lightly brushed Pia's knee with the very tips of his fingers she wondered if he realised he was doing it. Back and forth he went, the tickling sensation on her sheer stocking making her tremble.

'Please move your hand. Are you always so liberal with your touch?'

Just as she'd thought, he glanced at his hand quizzically as he slipped it from her leg. Heaven help her—she wanted it back.

He shrugged, flexing his wide shoulders. 'Brazilians are very affectionate people, *querida*. We think nothing of gushing about what is beautiful, or *lindo maravilhoso*, or expressing fondness with a hug or a kiss. Aren't you Greeks used to lavish displays of affection? Or did you grow up in France with your mother?'

Pia kept quiet. There were always exceptions to the rule, and the very idea of thinking about her mother made horror swarm through her veins.

Seconds later she found herself tapping away at her laptop.

'What is so fascinating that you'd rather do that than talk to me?'

She shook her head at him. 'My, my—you have an exceedingly high opinion of yourself.'

He gave her an insolent shrug that said his ego was well founded and she was telling him nothing he hadn't heard before.

'I'm working. Don't *you* have work to do? A real estate empire to run?'

'Not right now. I'm one of those people who can't read as a passenger—the headaches and sickness linger for hours.'

Her fingers paused on the keypad at that statement— the first honest words to pass his mouth and a tiny insight into the real Nicandro Carvalho that gave her a ridiculous little thrill. How pathetic was that? Then again, she'd always been intrigued by him. Much to her dismay.

'You can get pills for things like that. Anti-sickness. I'm exactly the same.'

He murmured in agreement, sounding distracted, and Pia glanced up, hopelessly drawn to the tanned column of his throat, the pulse she could see flickering as he undid the top buttons of his shirt. He must be hot, she thought, because she could feel the heat rolling off him. Hot and ripped enough to make her stomach flip-flop and her lower abdomen clench.

He was just so horridly handsome. So many angles made up his beautiful face, from the prominent bones of his cheeks to the slash of his jaw. Even his mouth was chiselled, almost carved, with that exaggerated cupid's bow punctuating his frown as he read.

'Is that Merpia?' he asked, tilting his head farther to one side for a better look at her screen.

Pia snapped out of her drooling stasis, thoroughly disgusted in herself, and threw him a baleful look. 'You have a filthy habit of snooping, Nicandro.'

He cocked one dark brow. 'Right now, I promise you I'm not being nosy—I am genuinely interested. You have an obsessive compulsion to get back to that…whatever you are doing and I'm itching to know why.'

'God, you're insufferable.'

Truly, she didn't like talking about work, and it had nothing to do with secrecy or her need for privacy. It was the turmoil she felt. Like living on a knife-edge. Sometimes she woke in a cold sweat, thinking that her father had been wrong and she really couldn't do it all—would somehow fail to juggle the million balls that were thrown at her what seemed like every minute of every day. That one of these days she'd be exposed as the illiterate nobody she was—not the mathematical prodigy and business whiz her father had excitably claimed her to be not eight months after she'd landed at his door.

I devote my entire life to a thousand jobs I never really wanted...would never have chosen if I'd been free.

The sudden vehemence of her thoughts shocked her to the core and made her feel ashamed. Every time she thought that way she felt hideously selfish. She'd been given a new life—a second chance—something many people would sell their soul for. She should be more grateful. She *was* insanely grateful. Yet sometimes she just wished the merry-go-round would stop, so she could breathe if only for a little while.

Nicandro was watching her with a quiet intensity that made her uneasy—as well as grateful that he couldn't read minds. Still, thinking about it, he'd already seen the Merpia files on her desk. It was unrealistic to think he wouldn't see things, hear things and discover things about the Merisi business during their time together. She should draft some kind of non-disclosure agreement asap.

With a drawn-out sigh she spun the laptop around so he could see the full screen.

'Merpia. *Pia. Dios, com certeza!* Of course. He named it after you. You run it for him?'

She gritted her teeth together and prayed for poise and some semblance of self-control. Merpia was her baby. Her pride and joy. Her first true personal accomplishment,

started when she'd been twenty-six years old. The one
thing she was truly proud of.

'You could say that,' she bit out.

Those gorgeous eyes grew wide as he whistled in awe.
And, though it wasn't directed at her *per se*, pleasure
flooded through her in a warm rush. It had been four years
since Antonio Merisi had been lowered into the ground,
and she still hadn't managed to outgrow her need for ap-
proval. That she was basking in it now from the wolf sniff-
ing around her life was disturbing to say the least.

'Rumour has it—'

She snatched at the opening like a life-preserver. 'You
shouldn't believe or partake in rumours, Nicandro,' she
said irritably. 'Very dangerous business. Are you a propaganda man?'

The look he gave her held a hefty amount of lethal softness and it was a timely reminder of what he was capable of.

'There is an element of truth behind every rumour,
querida. Of that I am certain.'

There they were once again, dancing around the subject of Zeus and Q Virtus and rumours and lies. Neither
of them giving anything away; they just stared at one another, locked in some kind of battle of wills, the stifling
air between them as high-octane as always.

What was he saying? That every rumour that had been
spread was partly true? That Merisi was Greek mafia?
That Zeus was a dirty dealer? A crook not to be trusted?
If Nicandro was the source he couldn't possibly have proof
of any of that.

'Case in point,' he continued, his voice still sharp as a
blade. 'Merpia. Rumour has it the *man* currently behind
the commodity mask is a genius, with the work ethic of
a machine.'

'Really?' she said, as if that particular flash was news
to her. 'I would argue it was more a combination of hard

work, a dash of good luck and superb instincts. My instincts rarely let me down, Nic. May I call you Nic?'

For some reason the familiarity of him calling her Pia had left her feeling strangely unbalanced in the power stakes, and it wouldn't do any harm to unleash *her* charm and knock *him* off his stilts a time or two.

His ruthless dominance instantly mellowed. 'Of course, *bonita*,' he said as he reached up and brushed a lock of hair from her brow. The gesture was so tender it made her ache.

Careful, Pia, he's playing you.

'So what do your instincts tell you about me, Pia?'

'That you're an extremely dangerous man and I would do well to barricade my bedroom door at night.'

While he leaned closer she edged farther back, until she found herself plastered to the leather seat, his weight crushing against her side, making it hard to take a breath.

'One day you'll leave it open and unlocked, just for me. One day you'll beg for my mouth on yours. One day you'll melt…only for me.'

Considering the heat pouring off him, she wouldn't be surprised. *Please don't kiss me again. I have nowhere to run this time and I'm not sure I'll be able to resist.*

He sank one hand into her hair and the graze of his fingertips against her scalp made her tremble.

Pia scrambled around her fuzzy brain for something curt to say. 'You're going to mess up my hair, Nic.' *What?* That was the best she could do?

A little closer and he nuzzled up to her jawline until her eyes felt heavy and fluttery and her heart leapt to her throat.

With one tiny kiss at the sensitive skin beneath her ear, he whispered, 'One day. Very soon.'

Then he was gone. Taking away his heat and that delicious scent she could practically taste. Lounging back in his seat with all the debauched lethargy of a satisfied wolf.

'So where are we headed? You mentioned Northern Europe? England?'

Considering she was in the same spot he'd left her in, mentally and physically, the abrupt change in topic threw her sideways.

'Headed?'

He grinned evilly, flashing his teeth as if he knew *exactly* what he was doing to her. '*Sim, querida*. Where are we going, this fine and beautiful day? Where are you taking me? Where will I have the pleasure of spending time with you?'

Oh, he was good. She'd thought Ethan was supremely adroit, with the most artful tongue on the planet, but he had nothing on this guy.

Worse still, for a minuscule moment some secret place inside her longed for every seductive murmur to be the truth. Hopelessly wished he wanted to spend time with her for no other reason than that she was a woman he genuinely admired and liked—wanted to get to know. *Foolish, foolish Pia.*

She'd do well to remember that every word he spoke, every move he made, had a dubious agenda. That she was protecting not only Q Virtus but her entire life.

'Not England, no,' she said, pulling herself together, mentally re-erecting her shields. 'Finnmark. Norway. The northernmost part of continental Europe.'

'*What?*' His head jerked upright, eyes wide, horrified. 'Why the devil would anyone choose to go that far north this time of year?'

She didn't tell him it was the most beautiful place on earth, where the air was so crisp and clean it cleansed the filth of a multitude of cities and a dirty past. Nor did she tell him that she hoped it would numb the sensations he wrought in her, turn down the heat that continually flared between them.

All she said was, 'You'll see.'

CHAPTER FIVE

'WELCOME TO THE Ice Castle.'

Nic opened his bleary eyes at the first words Pia had spoken since they'd left Zanzibar and focused on a staggering feat of architecture, auroral beneath the bluish twilight. A hotel made of ice.

He shivered just looking at it.

'Why would anyone in their right mind wish to vacation in extreme Norway?' he said, his tone one of utter disbelief.

Truth be told, there was a part of him still amazed that he'd followed her here and not whisked her away to some tropical desert island where privacy was gratis and he had a cornucopia of heat at his disposal.

Now look where they were. Ice, snow, ice and more ice. As far as the eye could see. Then again, didn't they have sensual thick furs and warm cabins with blazing, crackling fires in these places? Perfect for seduction.

'Why *not* vacation here?'

'Isn't the persecution of minus fifteen degrees enough?'

Dios, he loathed the cold. It reminded him of being close to dead. Those long, endless minutes when he'd watched the life drain out of his parents. Waiting, praying for the pain to stop.

'It's Finnmark, not Antarctica. It's slightly warmer—even more so inside.'

Nic noticed she said this while pulling a thick cream wool hat over her head and shoving her fingers into mitts.

By rights she should look like a twenty-year-old snow bunny, off to the Alps for a jaunt—but, oh, no, with a deft grip she kept a tight hold on the leash of her stylish sophistication.

The doors of the rough-terrain four-by-four opened and she swung her legs around gracefully and flowed from the car. Nic followed seconds later, the chill pervading his bones and numbing his blood. A violent shudder made his breath puff in front of his face in a voluminous white cloud.

'Warmer, you say? For polar bears maybe.'

'I think you'll find polar bears prefer the Arctic Circle.'

The way she said it reminded him of his buttoned-up high school teacher. The one who'd finally lost her patience with him in the art cupboard.

'I was being facetious,' he said.

'Ah, yes. Another one of your less admirable traits.'

He grinned at her over the car bonnet. 'I really shouldn't like you so much. It's asking for trouble.'

Wasn't that the truth? In the end he'd been grateful for the cold shoulder since Africa. It had given him a chance to regroup and remind himself what he was doing in the company of Zeus's daughter and why. When he took her to his bed he had to stay detached, and by God he would. So that meant no drowning in those big violet-blue eyes and no inhaling the scent of her neck as if it was nectar of the gods.

'Trouble seems to be something you are exceptionally good at.'

Nic swaggered round the front of the car, leaned in and murmured. 'Oh I'm good at lots of things. Especially heat, ice queen. Speaking of which—is this your natural habitat? Is a lion going to prowl from my wardrobe tonight?'

She nudged him away from her. 'Only if you get high enough. There's a bar on the north side that only sells vodka. Your kind of place.'

Obviously she knew more about him than he did about her. Or at least she thought she did.

'Do you watch me, Pia? When you help with Q Virtus?' Clearly she'd been sent to Zanzibar in her father's stead, and he wondered how many other meetings she'd attended. Exactly how hands-on she was.

Pia flushed a little and turned to stare determinedly at the forest of towering pine and Siberian spruce that he'd only just noticed. The silvery twilight enhanced the sweep of her cheek, the flawless pearl shimmer of her skin. He couldn't take his eyes from her—was conscious of every breath she drew, the way her full breasts rose and fell, the tiny sigh of exhalation.

'At times I have to watch everyone; don't take it personally.'

'*Have* to?' he asked, and the question made her flinch—as if she'd said something she shouldn't have. 'So you help to run Q Virtus as well as Merpia?'

Not forgetting this hotel and whatever other companies besides. He wasn't sure why he was coming over so incredulous. It wasn't as if a man couldn't manage—why not her? *Because deep down, despite the signs of power, you thought she was salad dressing. The pampered daughter of a powerful man, with a healthy ego to boot, who helps out around the office looking pretty.*

That he was comparing her to his mother bothered him. An heiress who did the bare minimum in the boardroom to reach the country club by noon. But Pia seemed to take it far more seriously than that. She hadn't stopped working for five seconds since they'd left Zanzibar; her phone continually bonged with mail, or texts, or calls from some nameless face she spoke proficiently to with that icy cool composure that simultaneously made him shiver and want to divulge her of her clothing to warm her up.

He'd underestimated her, and for a second he wondered what else he was missing. Wondered if his certainty that she would quickly tumble into his bed wasn't a product of arrogant folly.

Pia smiled wryly, as if she knew exactly what he was thinking. He didn't like being transparent. It boded ill. The only way he'd get through the next few days was to be as mysterious as her father and say nothing that would jeopardise their meeting in Paris.

'Q Virtus takes up some of my time, yes,' she said, as if choosing her words carefully.

And with the past swimming round his head like sharks intent on their prey it was on the tip of his tongue to say, *It won't when I'm finished, so I hope you have a career-change*, but she'd switched gear so quickly he reckoned he'd have whiplash by morning. Which was just as well. Because it occurred to him that the voice of his conscience was getting louder, demanding to be heard. Soon he'd be forced to listen to the repercussions of crushing Pia's world, along with her father. And he didn't want to hear it—didn't want to know.

'You have two choices of sleeping arrangements.'

'I thought you'd never ask, *querida*. Show me the way.'

She shook her head, as if despairing of an incorrigible boy. 'Either one of the cabins, or inside the hotel on an ice bed. Whichever you choose it will be hiking distance from my room, I assure you.'

Ice bed? Like hell. 'But who will keep me warm?' he asked, lending his voice a seductive lilt that promised sinful debauchery.

Nic told himself the tremor that rustled over her was thanks to him and not to the abysmal temperatures in this godforsaken place. He had to snatch encouragement where he could.

'I'll send a member of staff with extra blankets—and before the thought even enters your head, Carvalho, the staff are strictly off-limits here. Please spare me the headache of getting rid of another girl.'

That was another thing. He didn't like the reminder that he was responsible for getting a Petit Q fired. He'd been on the phone all morning, trying to find her, all to no avail. It was as if she'd disappeared like a spectre into the night. It made him distinctly uneasy.

'What's the matter, Nic?' she asked sweetly—a striking contradiction to the inscrutable fire in her kohl-rimmed eyes. 'Worried about your little friend?'

Dios, he was becoming as transparent as glass. But he lavished himself with the theory that she was jealous and used the opening for what it was. *Perfect*.

'Maybe all the rumours of you Merisis being Greek mafia make people suspicious?'

She let loose a humourless laugh. 'What colourful imaginations people have. I promise you, the Merisis have never had any association with the mafia, and when I find out who started that uproar he'll have to answer to me.'

'Not to Zeus?'

'Oh, absolutely. Zeus too. And if you think *I'm* scary you've seen nothing yet.'

'Scary? You are a pussycat, *bonita*.'

'Keep pushing and you'll feel my claws,' she grated out. Nic grinned. 'Promises, promises…'

The main doors opened before them and Pia's countenance shifted, lighting up like a child on Christmas morning. Such elation, such a beautiful sight. It made something unfurl in the space behind his ribs and flap like the wings of a bird. *Weird*.

Arched tunnels were held aloft by ice columns currently being sculpted by artists with chisels and picks. In the next room ice chairs were being carved into throne-like works of art. In fact the actual artwork was so stunningly intricate the time it must have taken to create the place had to be astounding.

Pia was talking away with a luminous light in her eyes that was just as breath-stealing. 'The walls, fixtures, fittings, even the drinking glasses are made entirely of ice or

compacted snow and held together with snice. Which I
suppose would be your equivalent of mortar.'

'You love this place, don't you?' he asked.

Splaying her fingers, she glossed over a smooth ice table.
'I like art, and this place is a year-round art project. I like
to see it planned and built, the ice chiselled and shaped.
I love the fresh crisp air. I can finally breathe in purity
rather than the fumes of a car or a jet. This place is magical to me. When it melts in spring I always feel sad, but
when it's rebuilt, given another chance to come to life and
give joy, I feel…' Her smooth, delicate throat convulsed.
'*It* feels reborn.'

Nic almost lost his footing on the discarded shards of
ice block scattered over the ground.

Mesmerising was the only word he could think of when
she talked that way. Candidly, yet almost dazed. As if she
was miles away. He'd hazard a guess she'd forgotten who
she was talking to. But Nic hadn't missed the way she'd
hitched on her words and spoken as if she'd seen so much
darkness and ugliness in her life that the idea of being reborn appealed to her.

When she caught him staring she frowned. 'Do I have
icicles running off my nose?'

Nic had no idea what possessed him, but he curled his
arm about her waist, pulled her up against him and pressed
his warm lips against her frozen little nose.

Just as before, she remained motionless. Not resisting,
not exactly passive, but it was as if he held a vat of explo-
sive energy that was too compressed and thought better of
daring to move.

After a while he became concerned that she would pass
out from lack of oxygen so he eased back. 'Better?'

A gorgeous flush pinkened her cheeks, but the pensive pleat in her brow said she didn't trust him as far as
she could throw him. Which even he could admit wasn't
very far.

Gingerly, she stepped backwards. 'Yes, thank you.'

'You're very welcome,' he said huskily, wanting her back in his arms, crushed tighter against him. 'So, are we the only guests here?'

'Afraid so. Other guests won't arrive for another week or two.'

She backed up another step, creating a gulf as vast and bleak as the Grand Canyon. If she wasn't the main player in his game of revenge he would be worried that the distance made him feel…empty.

'I think we should turn in for the night.'

'Let's not. The night is still young. I say we ditch our bags and hit the bar. Join me?' When she gave her head a little shake he unleashed the big guns and smiled with every ounce of sinful charm in his arsenal. 'Please, *bonita*?'

Hot loganberry juice warming her hands, Pia tipped her head back to gaze at a sky full of darkness and began to count the stars within a mind grid. When they didn't make an even number her clavicle started to itch so she started again. Anything to distract her from the man lounging obscenely close beside her—those dark bedroom eyes lingering on her throat as he threw out pheromones in great hulking waves.

There really shouldn't be anything sexy about a man padded out in warm gear, knocking back vodka as if it was mineral water.

Pia had coaxed him outdoors before he either drove her insane or destroyed the bar. His mere presence had cranked the temperature in the room so high she'd imagined the ice melting, pouring down the walls in silvery droplets until there was nothing left but the midnight stars.

Right then she felt the shift in the air. 'Wait for it… watch.'

'I am watching.'

'No, you're not, you're watching me.' And it was starting to annoy her. The contrived deceit of it. Why would Nic truly be interested in bedding a cold, uptight, neurotic mess like her? He wouldn't. This was a bet, a deal, and she'd do well not to go all jelly-legged next time he kissed her frozen nose. '*Now.* Look up.'

A whirlwind of pale green light appeared and swirled above, the streaks tossed about with abandon. Then dark red clouds of fire pulsated in waves and arcs, undulating against the midnight sky and darting towards the heavens.

It was a collision of energetic charged particles that never failed to make her heart float in her chest and her blood sing a chorus of joy that she was still alive.

'*Dios.* I take back everything I said. This is amazing, Pia. I've heard of the Northern Lights but this…'

'Aurora Borealis—named after Aurora, the Roman goddess of dawn, and Boreas, the Greek name for the north wind.'

Nic tutted good-naturedly. 'Should've known the Greeks would have something to do with it.'

Pia pursed her lips to contain a smile. Okay, so she had this fluttery feeling going on in her chest. It was bizarre. Not at all like the soft and gentle flapping of butterflies' wings people spoke of—no, no, no. More like pterodactyls swooping and clipping her heart with every pass. Actually, maybe bizarre was the wrong word. Terrifying was more like it.

She snuck a peek at him from the corner of her eye, then cursed herself for the urge.

Languid and sprawled out on the bench seat beside her, head tipped back, thick glossy hair curling in waves over his collar, he was simply too gorgeous for words. He was gazing upward, his whisky eyes full of awe and Pia shuddered with the need to taste the liquor glistening on his full mouth.

Why did looking at him make her want so much? Long for him to pull her into his arms.

The ache in her chest bloomed into self-disgust when he caught her staring and conjured up one of those glorious smiles that did odd things to her internal organs. Like jiggle them around a bit.

'What's the plan for tomorrow?' he asked.

'I'm touring some land where we're considering building more warm lodges. I'll be gone all morning.'

'*We* will be gone all morning,' he shot back, in that honed Carvalho dominating tone.

The very one she ignored.

'I can't see the huskies liking you, *Lobisomem*. They know a threat when they see it. Astute creatures.'

'I've never understood that moniker,' he said.

She didn't miss the way he'd brought the topic right back round to Zeus. She chalked up the ability to his incredibly shrewd mind. The *why* of it was what escaped her.

'Maybe Zeus saw a predator in you.'

'What's with the Greek mythological connotations anyway?'

'My great-grandfather started the club and he was obsessed with the stories. He was also a successful businessman in his own right, and if you ask me I'd say the control went to his head. In the years before he died he apparently believed himself a god. Sounds like a whacko to me.'

'Does your father believe himself a god, Pia?'

His voice was hard enough to shatter the bench they sat upon.

Had her father believed himself a god? 'I have no idea.' Sometimes she'd had no clue what had gone through his head.

'None? Are you saying you aren't close?'

She resisted the compulsion to shuffle in her seat. 'If you're speaking in terms of general proximity then no, we're rarely close.' She knew fine well he wasn't, but this was the last thing she wanted to discuss. Just prayed he'd drop it.

'I'm talking about emotions, *querida*, and you know it. A trip to the zoo when you were in pigtails. A loving face in the crowd at your school recitals. A celebratory meal when you passed your exams. Now sharing a bottle of wine and laughing over dinner, reminiscing over the good times. *Close*. As a father and daughter should be.'

A mass of stark yearning hit her shockingly hard in the solar plexus and she bowed forward, pretending to adjust the ties on her boots to ease the pain. She was unsure why she should feel that strongly, since her father had given her the important things in life—a roof over her head, food on the table and some measure of calm.

She sat upright and drank the last mouthful of loganberry, the sweet tartness exploding on her tongue. 'Not in the least,' she said. Only to wish the words back a second later. How pitiful they sounded. The empathy in his eyes didn't help. Whisky eyes, warm enough to melt her heart. *Impossible*.

'Any brothers or sisters?' he asked.

Translation: *Are you his only heir?*

Pia held an exasperated sigh in check. She wasn't sure how much longer she could take this. Every word, every touch had an ulterior motive. Most likely even his warmth and sincerity. And *still* there she was, cradling that soft, secret place inside her, hopelessly wishing he spoke the truth and wanted nothing more than to genuinely know her. Such a fool. She knew better.

'No brothers or sisters. You?'

'Only child too. One of those impossible dreams, but my mother… Well, let's say she wasn't particularly maternal.'

Join the club.

It wasn't until he said, 'Not close to her, then?' that she realised she'd said it out loud. Good God, she *had* to get away from him!

Digging her feet into the ground for a firm hold, she stood tall. 'I need some sleep. There's no need for you to come along tomorrow, so do yourself a favour and stay warm in your chalet bed.' *Give me some peace—leave me be, please.*

'You couldn't *pay* me to sleep on ice. I suppose to you it's like coffins for vampires.'

He said it with a wicked smile, as if he was trying to lighten the mood, but it went down like a lead balloon.

She gave him a withering glare. 'Aren't you hilarious? You should've been a comedian.' Though in a way he was right. She wanted the cold to numb the sensation of him, banish the heat he injected into her veins.

'I still don't understand what would possess you to sleep in the main hotel on packed ice. Believe me, if you knew what it was like to sleep on the streets—'

'It's an experience,' she said quietly, glancing at the doors to the Ice Castle with a painful kind of desperation.

'Ah,' he said derisively, and the change in him drew her eyes back to his. 'Like those celebrities who go to developing nations and starve just to know what it feels like. Except they can't *possibly* know what real, true, gripping hunger feels like. So if you're trying to prove something…'

On and on he went, and his tone got harder and more cynical. Right then he reminded her so much of her father that she started to shake and she…she… *Don't say it, Pia. Don't do it.*

Throat raw and swollen, every word hurt as they tore from her mouth. 'Maybe I do it not only for the experience but because I've been there, and I need to remember where I've come from so I can see what I've achieved. Maybe I like to feel the cold biting into my back in order to feel grateful that I'm one of the lucky ones and I now have a warm bed every night. And *that*, Mr Carvalho, is something I'll never take for granted. *Ever. Again.*'

Pia squeezed her eyes shut, hating both of them in that moment. She couldn't believe she'd just told him that.

Oh, come on, Pia, deep down you wanted him to know

you've shared some of his darker days, that you have some-thing in common. That you're more than the sum total of your parts.

Nic blinked up at her, jaw slack. 'When? I don't under-stand…'

'For the first seventeen years of my life. So don't you *dare* judge me!'

'Where was your father?'

'I wouldn't know, okay? I didn't meet him until I was seventeen. Now, if you'll excuse me, I need some sleep.' Her voice sounded quivery and she hated it—*hated* it. And—*oh, my God!*—the backs of her eyes were stinging.

'Hey, hey…' he said, launching from the bench and reaching for her, strong arms wide open.

Pia backed away. 'Don't.' *Or I'll beg you to hold me and I refuse to crumble, especially in front of you.*

He clenched his hands into fists and then raked his fin-gers through his hair. 'Okay, but let me come along in the morning. I'd love to see the land. I promise no more talk of your father—the past is out of bounds. I just want to spend some time with you. Okay?'

She said nothing.

'Okay?' he repeated, this time adding a touch of con-cern and a dash of despair to his act. And that was the final nail in *his* coffin.

CHAPTER SIX

SHE'D GONE WITHOUT him. The beautiful, obstinate, control freak that she was.

Nic let go of a sigh, heavy with annoyance and frustration.

One step forward, two steps back. For every tiny piece of information he squeezed from her she retreated farther away from him and he only had himself to blame. Pushing, pushing, *pushing* her to talk about her father, her past. Clearly that cool, calm composure had cracked under the strain.

The virtue of patience had been a blessing to him in the past few years. He'd had little choice but to bide his time. Until now. Now he wanted her surrender. *Needed* it to get to Zeus and destroy Q Virtus, he told himself for the millionth time. And yet…he *did* want to spend time with her.

The hell of it was, she intrigued him. He wanted to know how her mind ticked. How she juggled so many balls. What drove her. Why she hadn't known her father for the first seventeen years of her life.

So many questions that had nothing to do with taking Zeus to Hades and everything to do with the invisible rope that pulled him towards her when she was near. Like the *femme fatale* she was. Spell-binding him, luring him in, toying with him like a cat would a mouse.

His mouth twisted at the ridiculous notion. Nic knew

what he was doing, had a firm grip on the reins of his control, and no woman had the power to beguile him in deceit.

The log burner crackled, popped and hissed as he peered out of the window at the heavy grey skies, wondering how long she'd been gone and if she'd make it back in time before those laden clouds wept snow over the packed ice. An idyllic picture that struck him as nature's trick to disguise peril.

Nic smiled wryly and shook his head. Granted, he didn't feel like himself this morning, but now even the weather was duplicitous? What was more, the slosh and churn of worry inside him was a surprise he hadn't foreseen. Nor was the thought of her cosying up to her *friend* Jovan on a wooden slatted bench, covered in heavy fur rugs, being hauled by huskies across the snowy plains. A scene from some dreary romantic chick flick that likely flicked her switch. And why did that idea drive him to drink like a crazy *pessoa*?

Ah, careful, Nic. Jealousy will take you into the realms of obsession and beyond.

Like hell it would.

The irony of the situation knocked him sideways with the heft of a midfield striker. To anyone looking in there he was, waiting for the little wife to come home, and just like that he was staring at his father pacing the floors, fists clenched, waiting for Nic's mother to return from some shopping trip with friends, or lunch with her clique, or—worse—a night dancing about town. Always obsessing. Possessive. Angry when she wasn't home. Furious when she ignored him. Unstable. Erratic. Unnatural in Nic's eyes.

Narciso had asked him why he was considering marrying Eloisa Goldsmith. Truth was, while he'd loved his parents, after years of witnessing their volatile marriage he refused to sign up for the same fate.

Such love. Such passion. Such a hideous disaster.

His mood now a mire of filth, sucking him into the dangerous quicksand of the past, he slammed his feet into his boots and shoved his arms into the puffy warmth of his ski jacket. The thought of standing here waiting around for Olympia Merisi to grace him with her presence was taking him from vile to hostile.

Nic pulled the cabin door closed behind him and negotiated the packed ice, his feet crushing the thin dusting of new-fallen snow as he tramped down the path towards the main lodge. Huge white puffs of his breath formed in front of his face as he cursed the lack of Wi-Fi in his room. 'Going back to nature' translated to revisiting the Dark Ages as far as he was concerned.

The lodge greeted him with a warm blast of air and the sharp tang of espresso, but that, amazingly, wasn't the source of his overwhelming surge of relief. In the far corner of the main room sat Pia's sidekick, talking animatedly with another man, and he *hated* how the sight mollified him beyond measure. For pity's sake! He was not jealous. Or obsessed. He wasn't anything of the sort.

By the time he'd settled in front of his laptop and fired off a few e-mails to encourage the ruckus and fan the flames at Q Virtus he craved a long drink and his sanity. So he did what any sensible person would do in this situation. Rang his grandfather. To remind himself exactly why he'd chased a woman across Europe.

'Nicandro!' Instantly that gruff voice eased the tension that threatened to spiral out of control.

'Avô, how are you, old man?'

'Fine, fine, my boy. Just whooping Oscar here at Gin Rummy. Man doesn't know how to lose gracefully. Spat his teeth out twice in the last five minutes.'

Nic laughed out loud. 'You're a shark, Avô.'

'How was Zanzibar?'

'Hot.' In every way imaginable. Shocking. Satisfying. Frustrating. Nic condensed twenty-four hours of breaking and entering, gun-wielding, being tied to a chair and meeting the most stunning woman in the world to, 'Nothing to write home about.' Else the man would have heart failure and it was Nic's turn to look after *him*.

'Are you on your way back? I have a date with Lily tonight but I can put her on the back burner.'

Nic pictured that old Cary Grant style movie star face and silver hair. 'No, old man. No need. Go see Lily—enjoy yourself. I've stopped off in Finnmark, Norway. Minus fifteen if we're lucky.'

'*What?* Who the devil wants to go to Norway?'

Nic grinned, thinking they'd been almost his exact words.

'Forgot your origins, boy? Brazil—land of soccer and samba. A Santos needs heat. What's in Norway? A woman?'

Nic could hear the usual cacophony of chortles and chatter in the background and his heart ached. *Dios*, he missed this man. '*Sim*, Avô. A woman.'

'A special woman if Nicandro Carvalho traipses after her.'

Special? Yeah, she probably was. Not that it mattered.

'A necessary woman.' *If I'm to restore your glory. Place Santos Diamonds back in your hands before I lose you.*

The mere thought made Nic press his lips together and fight the sting at the back of his eyes. The fact that his grandfather had only a few good years left had kicked him into high gear, and he wouldn't downshift or stamp on the brakes until he'd reached the end of the road. A gift for the man who'd cradled him as a baby when his mother could not. Or maybe would not. What did it matter? Nic had still loved her like crazy. Her stunning face and her million-dollar sassy smile. She'd been zest and spirit and fiery heart and, yes, a big ol' handful of trouble—but there'd been something endearing about that. At least to him.

The one time she'd attended a football match she'd stood in seven-inch stilettos, a long cigarette in her hand, huge sunglasses covering half her face, yelling at the referee to 'Get that dirty brute off my son's back!' After that Nic had appealed to her well-deserved vanity, told her she distracted the players—no lie: her figure had stopped traffic—and asked her to stay away, else his reputation would have gone to the dogs.

His reflection in the window gazed back at him, wistful and nostalgic, and like a freight train another image rolled over him, just as vivid.

Himself at fourteen, when she'd picked him up from school—two hours late—raised a perfectly plucked brow and asked if he'd lost his virginity yet. He'd blushed and stammered and told her to shut up.

Hopeless in the maternal stakes, truly the farthest thing from a tree-hugging, celery-crunching supermom, but what she *had* been was a glorious, fun-loving woman who hadn't deserved to die. Certainly not with a cry lodged in her throat and a bullet in her head. Triggered by the man who—

Pain so acute it set his heart on fire made him gasp sharply, and he tried to cover the choking noise with a cough.

'Nic, my boy? What's wrong? Is there something you're not telling me?'

The concern in his grandfather's voice yanked him back to the here and now, just as it had done thirteen years ago and then continued for endless harrowing months as he'd harangued him to stand, then to walk—one small step, then two, then four. While Nic had bathed in a vile pit of despair and rage, wishing he'd just died in the same red river as his parents and the dreams of his youth.

There he'd been, dubbed the next Brazilian football sensation, destined to play with the best team in the world, lying with a bullet in his back. *Game over.*

Nic squeezed his eyes shut and cleared his throat. '*Non*, Avô. Everything is well. Everything is going to be just fine. As it should have always been.'

The sound of aged breathing, heavy from Cuban cigars and cognac told Nic he hadn't quite managed to disguise his turmoil.

'What have I always told you, Nicandro? Stand up, walk forward. Do not turn and look back or you will fall.'

Impossible. He was so at rock-bottom there was no void beneath him in which to plunge. *You also told me there were answers to be found, people to repay, legends to restore. So I stood and I walked forward to do just that.*

'Worry not, Avô. We'll talk again soon.'

'No, Nicandro, my boy, *wait*. Promise me you will return safe.'

'Always. *Tchau*, Avô.'

Nic's thumb pressed the 'end call' button and he gripped the handset as he stared beyond the glass. Beyond the cobwebs of frost glistening on the panes. Beyond the thick pelts of snow driving from the east. To the dark clouds laden with the promise of a continuous storm. Nature at its most dangerous.

By the time he'd sobered up he was frowning at the darkness. *Where are you, querida? Don't disappear on me now. I need you.* To quench this lust. To incinerate this incongruous need. To get him to Paris for the next step in his end game.

Sensing Jovan shift at his side, Nic shoved his fists inside his jacket pockets. 'She should've been back hours ago.'

Black eyes glared at him. 'Like you care. Or maybe you just care for the wrong reasons. I am on to you, Carvalho. You are not what you seem and I am watching you.'

The poor attempt to intimidate Nicandro Carvalho made him smile coldly. 'How does it feel to want a woman who doesn't want you back?'

'You tell me,' Jovan sneered, before walking away.

Nic's fists clenched with murderous intent as fire raged behind his ribs. Had she told her *friend* their chemistry was one-sided? Told him not to fret because she felt nothing but ice inside? Yet what really bothered him, he realised, was that the man might be right, and Nic felt his heart sink with the thought that she didn't desire him at all. That those seductively coy glances and the burning heat in her violet-blue eyes was all an act.

But what was seriously disturbing was that right now he couldn't care less. Either way, he wanted her back here. With him.

The striking solitary landscape was tinged with blue from the cold and deep orange from the sun's struggle towards the horizon and Pia breathed deeply, trying to ease the anxiety knotting her insides. Or was it guilt that she'd left without Nic?

'I'd love to see the land…spend time with you…'

He'd seemed so sincere, but every time she wanted to think the best of him she napalmed the idea.

'The storm is coming in, Miss Merisi. I vote we take a shortcut back to the Castle early. Either through the forest or across the lake.'

'One moment,' Pia told her guide, Danel, as she snapped another shot of the clearing. 'This land is perfect—especially with the salmon river close by for cold sea fishing.'

She'd taken enough photos. He knew it. She knew it. Problem was, she didn't want to go back. Not yet. She only wanted to ignore Nic's magnetic pull a while longer, to enjoy the beauty and tranquillity before he dragged her into another whirlwind of unwanted memories, unfathomable need and sleep deprivation.

'Miss Merisi, please. We must head back.'

Pia closed her eyes, inhaled a lungful of cleansing air and trudged back towards the sled. 'I don't mind which way—your call.'

'We'll cut across the lake. Much quicker.'

Once she'd settled in her seat the silence was broken by

the panting of the huskies and the soft whoosh of the sled gliding over crisp white snow. As they skirted the dense woodland of towering spruce the scent of pine infused her mind and the rhythmic rocking lulled her tired, sore eyes to close. As long as she didn't dream of her mother again—anything but that…

She must have dozed, because the next thing she knew the sled had jolted sharply to the left and the sound of spooked huskies filled her ears with piercing whimpers.

Pia bolted upright. 'What's wrong?' Then she shivered violently as streaks of icy water ran down her face, soaked her hair. God, she must have been out of it.

Danel struggled with the reins as snow thrashed against his face. 'Storm came out of nowhere. Hold on—we'll take cover in the forest.'

Fear lodged in her chest and she gripped the edge of the bench until her knuckles screamed. *Don't panic. You've been through worse, far worse than this.*

The sled veered right, the movement holding her on a knife-edge. Visibility was virtually non-existent, and then it all happened so fast her head spun.

The sled tipped. The sound of grinding wood tore through her ears. As did the distinct crack of ice.

Danel yelled over the furious howl of the wind, his words muffled. Obscured. Then she was tossed up into the air like a ragdoll, only to plunge to the hard-packed surface, the agonising crash sending pain shooting through her body.

A cry ripped from her throat, then her head smacked off the unforgiving lake and her last thought—that she'd done the right thing, was glad she'd left without Nic and he was safe back in his cabin—was obliterated as the lights went out.

He'd had enough. Nic couldn't take it any more.

The thundering, purposeful stride that had brought him

to this place, this woman, took him to the manager's suite on the other side of the lodge via the snow that swirled in eddies and whorls, whipping at his skin and biting through his clothes.

Nic burst through the door, sending papers flying off the desk. 'I want a search party out there for the last hour of light. She's been gone too long.'

'We don't have anyone to send—'

'I'll go myself. Give me a map of their route and get me a four-by-four. I can ice-drive with the best of them.'

'I am sure all is well, sir. I—'

'Do it. *Now*.' His lethal voice caromed around the room and he watched the ruddy complexion of the man pale and bead with sweat. And all the while Nic's guts roiled with worry and dread and an outcome that didn't bear thinking about.

Nor did the reasons why.

CHAPTER SEVEN

PIA'S TEMPLES THROBBED, pain swirled around her head, but worst of all she was cold. So cold. And she was so tired of being cold.

This couldn't be real, but it felt so much like reality it was frightening. She kept having brief flickers of *déjà-vu* as hands grabbed her arm, manacling her at the shoulder and wrist, bruising as they pinned it to the bed.

'No, no, *please*—get off me!'

White light flickered in front of her closed eyelids, the black beats in between like snapshots of time replaying in her mind...

Voices. Her mother's shrill. And Pia knew Mama was on the ledge again, fighting with an opium haze of madness, because her panic slithered through the cracks in Pia's basement door like curling wisps of smoke, threatening to choke her.

Karl yelled, 'We've gotta run—they're coming after us.'

Pia's legs buckled as drawers opened and slammed shut. Drug money. The dealers. Coming after them. *Oh, God.*

'It's her damn fault, that useless kid of yours. No good for nothing. She didn't take the money.'

No, no! When she'd gone to deliver the money they'd wanted far more than cash from her and she'd run. *It wasn't her fault—it wasn't. It really wasn't.*

'So we'll take her to Merisi and he can pay seventeen years of child support so we can disappear.'

Pia froze, ear pressed against the hollow door as the bottom fell out of her world. Child support? She had a daddy?

'To Zeus? No, Karl, he'll kill me.'

Her mother's voice shook. She was terrified.

'He doesn't know.'

Kill her? He sounded worse than *this* nightmare. She'd be trading one hell for another.

Nails black, deeply encrusted with dirt, Pia clawed at the door. Heart thumping frantically. *Don't leave me here, Mama. Take me with you. Please. I'll be better. I'll be good—do whatever you want. Just please take me with you.*

Then they were in Pia's room and holding her down, and she was thrashing and twisting and trying to sink her teeth into the arm that was pinning her hard.

'No, no, *no*—get off me!'

A big hand slapped across her cheek, setting her skin on fire, but she just got back up and clawed and hissed and screamed for her life.

Until that cold metal pricked her arm and freezing liquid seeped into her veins and peace finally stole her pain.

Memories, always ready with daggers—as Nic knew—were stabbing her subconscious, making her voice a wavering chord of desperation as she lay half-naked and ghastly pale beneath a blanket on his bed.

He couldn't keep still—just paced back and forth alongside while her slow, shallow breathing and mumbles and cries gripped him by the throat. He should have searched for her sooner. Another hour lying on the cracked ice of the lake, soaked through to the skin, and she would have been dead. Another hour from now and she *would* die if they couldn't warm her up. Hypothermia had set in, and unless she calmed down and allowed the drips...

Dios, she looked so vulnerable. *Was* so vulnerable. It was a fist in his heart as he remembered what it felt like to feel paralysed.

Another shriek ricocheted off his taut nerves.

'Do something, for heaven's sake!'

The man who *claimed* to be the senior of the two medics hovering tried to hold her arm still once more, but her every contorted muscle and frozen vein screamed genuine fear.

Pia brushed down her arms, her movements frantic yet uncoordinated as she shivered and slurred. 'Please...*please*, no! Don't do this.'

On and on she went, crying out for her mama, then talking of Merisi, Zeus—private, personal nightmares—and he *hated* it. Hated that she was baring her soul in such an anguished, agonising way in front of complete strangers. He wanted them gone. Would have banished them from the room if he could.

Instead he said, in a voice that brooked no argument and warned of dire consequences, 'She's delirious—has no idea what she's saying or doing.'

Nic watched silvery tears trickle down her temples as her energy depleted and she turned to look him right in the eye. '*Please*...don't...do this to me.'

That was it. That heart-wrenching plea coming from a woman like Pia was the final straw.

'Stop. Just *stop*! Her heart must already be at risk from the strain, and if she gets any more worked up—'

'She needs to get warm quickly. Intravenous fluids are the way to go. Unless we bypass her blood, warm it through, but that's still going through a vein.'

'That's it? Those are our options? *Dios!*' His voice sounded as if he'd swallowed a razorblade. He couldn't stand seeing her like this. It made him want to crawl out of his own skin.

'My only other suggestion would be for you to get in there. Skin to skin. It'll probably take longer, but it should still work.'

Right—*right*. Why hadn't he thought of that? *Because she obliterates your brain cells, that's why.*

'This would have been useful ten minutes ago,' he gritted out. With a deft roll of his shoulders his heavy coat slipped down his back and he tossed it over the nearest chair.

'We didn't think there would be a problem, and…' This from the second medic. A tall redhead who was staring at his hands as he uncuffed his shirt.

'You may leave.' He punctuated the words by grabbing his shirt at the tails and tearing it open.

The redhead's lips parted and colour flushed her white skin as buttons bounced off walls and pinged off the floors. He toed off his shoes and went to work on his trousers and her eyes trailed down his flexing biceps, across his wide chest, then paused as he hooked his thumbs into the waistband of his briefs.

Fighting the shivers that could only have come from being outside half the night in minus fifteen freaking degrees, Nic stared down at Pia, lying on the bed, eyes closed, trembling.

Commando or not?

She was out of it, but he didn't want her waking up in his bare arms being frightened. Didn't want her to think he'd taken advantage of her for a second. *Innocent* wasn't a word he would associate with her, but where sex was concerned, or being comfortable naked, in your own skin…? He wasn't so sure about that.

'I can leave her bra and panties on, yes?'

'They look insubstantial enough, so I doubt they'd make much difference.'

'From this moment it is not your place to look,' he growled, throwing in a lethal glare for good measure. Ridiculous as it was, his protective instincts had kicked in with a ferociousness that astounded him. 'I repeat. You may leave.'

He ushered them out through the door, agitated by the way the redhead was devouring him with her eyes. Why couldn't Pia look at him like that? Then maybe she wouldn't have swanned off without him this morning and he would have been there all along to keep her safe.

Once he'd locked his door behind them he was back to the bed, fingers flexing on the corner of the blanket. Nervous? Eager? He didn't know. His concern was so overwhelming it drowned every other emotion out.

Gingerly, he pulled the covers back, just enough to allow him to slip beneath. Nic tried to shut off every thought in his head, loath to admit to the arousing anticipation of feeling those lush curves against him. Then he sent up a prayer of thanks that he'd kept her in her underwear as— *Fala serio*, could someone cut him some slack, *please*?— frivolously skimpy as it was.

Under the covers, he didn't pause to take a breath, not wasting a second of time when his heat could be seeping into her body, protecting her life.

It hit him then. What he was doing. Saving the daughter of the man who'd destroyed his parents and almost taken Nic's life. He could hurt Zeus in the same way—make him feel the same pain Nic had felt for so long. An eye for an eye. But the fact was it wasn't in him. Not even if Pia had pulled the trigger herself. He simply wasn't made that way. Life was too precious to take.

No pause, no hesitation, he tucked one arm under her shoulders and eased her against him, front to front, skin to skin, cheek to cheek. All her softness against his hard strength. Cold flesh against heat. He'd expected a struggle, at least a murmur of protest. What he got was a contented purr when, like a kitten, she burrowed and nuzzled closer, as if trying to climb into his body, where it was warm, so she could go to sleep, protected and safe.

Nic cupped her head, tucked her into the warm space where his neck met his shoulder and gently wrapped his leg around hers until they were one, until the only thing that could be missing was his hardness sliding inside her.

Oddly enough, this felt closer—an affection he'd never experienced before. Far more intimate than sex could ever be.

Nic lay there, holding her, gently stroking her hair, burying his nose in the damp waves, inhaling the cold scent that lingered on her body and there…right *there*…was the faintest hint of that velvety black scent she wore like a sultry signature: jasmine and gardenia and something elusive that sang to his body in a siren's song. And, *Dios*, it turned him to stone. He shifted and cursed under his breath, trying his damnedest to ignore the lush satiny dips and curves that fitted perfectly against him.

Tried, too, to quieten every alarm bell shrilling in his head, not to think about what might have been for the first seventeen years of her life. *Too late.*

At the age when Nic was kicking a football around a field and fishing in the river with his Avô, with not a concern or care in the world for anyone or anything, Pia had been living in her own kind of hell. The fact that she'd been subjected to drugs and abuse from her own mother made him want to lash and snarl and bite like the werewolf she claimed him to be. He realised, too, that her father must have taken her in, taken care of her…

It was a conflicting choking agony to want to feel gratitude to the man who'd caused his parents' deaths, if only for a second. It tore at his heart even to think it. Yet he was glad Pia had found a better life and a reason for living.

'Is that why you work so hard for him?' he whispered as he kissed her flaxen hair.

Nic finally allowed himself to think of the high likelihood that he'd take Pia down with her father. It made his ribcage contract but he'd come too far for too long to be swayed by emotions now. *She'll hate you. Yes, she will.*

He flinched as she startled him with a soft reply.

'Keep me,' she breathed.

What was she saying? That she worked so hard so her father would keep her?

Nic squeezed his eyes shut and used every weapon at his disposal, every memory he could find, to banish the tumultuous thoughts storming through his mind.

She whimpered and Nic hushed her. 'Sleep *querida*, I have you.' For now.

CHAPTER EIGHT

PIA TRIED TO rouse herself time and again from the murky waters of sleep but it kept tugging her back into the nebulous depths. First there'd been darkness and moonlight, then the glare of the midday sun, but her bones had ached so badly she'd snuggled back into the hard-packed mattress and let it happen.

Not this time. Now the warm scent of expensive cologne tempted and teased her senses awake. Skin and a light dusting of soft hair against her cheek—warm, so warm, and achingly wonderful. She sighed in contentment.

She felt as if she'd slept for days, and as she coaxed her eyes open to the golden fingers of dusk stroking the windowpane she wondered if that were true.

Had she ever been so lazy and sweet inside? Never—

Pia jerked upright so fast the room spun like a whirly top. What the—?

Her gaze snapped to Nic, lying beside her, and her belly clenched with hot longing at the sight of him—so strong, so masculine, and yet so vulnerable. Face relaxed, as if sleep was his only peace, those long sooty black lashes rested against the tender skin beneath his eyes in decadent arcs.

She was dying to run her hand over his defined chest, that rigid six-pack and his flat, ripped stomach, the hipbones jutting just shy of his boxers…

Then it hit her. He was practically naked. And so was she!

'*Nic…?*' Grabbing the sheet, she covered her breasts and

bottom-shuffled sideways to the edge of the bed. What had he done to her? What had *they* done? 'You…you…snake!'

Stretching with all the lethargic might of a big sleepy lion basking in the sun, he blinked up at her over and over, as if clearing the fog from his eyes. It took a while, and Pia just sat there watching him, her mind all over the place, trying to figure out how on earth she'd got into his bed. Then suddenly he snapped wide awake, and looked so ridiculously happy to see her that her heart leapt.

'You're awake?'

Pia pinched the back of her hand in self-test mode. 'I'd like to say that's a stupid question, but actually I have no idea.' Maybe she was still asleep and this was a dream. *A dream, Pia? Don't you mean a nightmare?*

He grinned wildly. 'Yep, there's that sharp tongue I like so much. You are definitely awake, *bonita*. You had me worried for a while there.'

When his hot gaze dropped to her lace bra he stared at her so hard she craved a shower. Whether hot or cold she couldn't say. Why did every day with him feel like Russian Roulette?

'Don't think for one minute this constitutes the terms of our bet!' At least she hoped to God it didn't. It rather depended on what had happened. Why couldn't she remember? This was awful. *Awful!*

Mischief sparkled in his whisky eyes, lighting them up with flecks of gold as he rolled onto his side playfully and propped his head on one hand. 'I didn't take you for a shirker, *querida*. You *did* beg.'

'I…I…I did?' She had? *Noooo.*

Nic raised one devilish brow and ran his tongue over that gorgeous mouth suggestively. 'Oh, yeah. I told you no over and over again, but would you listen?' He shook his head and tutted. 'No.'

There he was, the perfect picture of dissolute debauchery, tiptoeing his fingers over the rumpled linen and giving her thigh a sultry little stroke.

Pia shuddered and grappled with the blanket to cover her legs, but he was sprawled over them and he couldn't give a stuff—just smiled that bone-melting, tummy-flipping smile and kept on talking.

"'I'm cold, Nicandro.'"

The way he imitated her voice in a brazen purr and batted his eyelashes made her recoil in horror.

"'Please come to bed with me. I neeeeed you. Please.'"

She gasped in outrage at her own behaviour. Mentally scanned her body parts for sensations of wear and tear. Wear and tear? What was she? *A car?*

Okay, so she couldn't remember what *après sex* felt like, but she was darn sure she would feel something—right?

During her moments of castigation, as her mind flitted like a bird from one branch to another, he'd tugged the blanket away and inched closer, prowling like a feral wolf with hunger in his eyes. Pia looked down and watched his long fingers splay over the slight curve of her stomach, then curl around her waist.

Heat sizzled over her skin and her breath grew so shallow she began to hyperventilate.

'Come here, my beautiful Olympia. Kiss me. Just as you did last night.'

A tight, choking disbelief caught her by the throat. But there was no calculation in his eyes, none of the shrewdness she'd noticed in him before, and this joyful, impish innocence was a sharp deviation when she knew he had the tail of a scorpion.

Worse still, when had she got so lonely that she didn't care? Just wanted him near her.

'What did you do to me?' she asked, voice trembling as her pulse careened out of control.

Oh, God, she felt angry, and helpless, and frustrated that

she couldn't remember. But most of all—most alarmingly of all—she felt cheated!

With that thought, she tumbled backwards off the bed and landed in a sprawled heap. No grace to it whatsoever. Then she scrambled to her feet and edged away.

Predator. That was surely the word to describe him in that moment as he crawled across the mattress on all fours—big and agile and poetry in motion—the wickedness in his eyes making her lick her dry lips.

'Ah, you want me to *chase* you?' He drew the word out and added a naughty lilt to it.

'No!'

He sighed theatrically, as if they'd been through all this before. 'Which means yes.'

'No, it really doesn't! What is *wrong* with you?' He was being so frisky and light-hearted. Worlds apart from the practised charmer she'd come to expect.

And his body... *Wow.* All sex and power. The man might be Brazilian but he was like a Greek god. Broad shoulders and carved pecs, rounded thighs and long, athletic sculpted legs sprinkled with dark hair. Quite simply, he was delicious.

Slam. Her back hit the wall and he pressed up against her and thrust his hands into her hair. 'Shall I remind you, Pia? Remind you of the taste of my mouth?'

Yes. *Yes!* Nooooo—bad idea. Really.

She remained frozen, her blood pumping too fast in some places and too slowly in others. Her brain, for instance—no blood at all in there.

Nic cupped the back of her head, his fingers the perfect amount of tingly pressure on her scalp, and leaned in. He kissed the rim of her ear, nibbled on her lobe and whispered, 'Try to remember this one, would you, *bonita*?'

'I don't think...we've done this before.' Because it felt as if she was on the edge of discovery, at the gates of a bold new world. And it was exhilarating and scary all at once.

Electricity arced between them, the shock so violent that Nic jerked back an inch or two and locked onto her eyes. As they stared at one another, her breasts brushed against the hard wall of his chest with every stuttering breath she took. Heaven help her, she wanted it. *Him*. His kiss. Right now.

'You make me crazy, Pia,' he murmured, his gaze intense and considered. His breath a hot rush over her face. 'You turn me inside out and that is the honest truth.'

Leaning in, he touched his lips to hers and she felt as if she'd been plugged into the national power grid. Closing her eyes, she started to panic. Unsure if she could remember how to respond.

Then he laved his tongue along her lips and she opened up, unfurling to him, giving him her all. And in that moment she didn't think or plan or have an agenda. She simply moved and gave him permission to go deep and wet and erotic. Which was exactly what he did, with a feral growl that made her skin tighten.

One hand on her lower back, another between her shoulderblades; he pressed her sweetly but firmly against him. She'd never felt anything like it. Unbearably wonderful.

Pia squirmed closer. He pulled her tighter. *More*. More of the languorous touch of his tongue against her own. And she moaned at the sharp, masculine taste of him—potent and alluring.

It was the hottest, raunchiest, most sensual kiss she'd ever received in her life. He was practically licking her soul.

Nic tightened his hold and she went pliant, revelling in this place where neither of them was alone, letting her body bend to his will as the terror of yearning and the thrill of feeling overwhelmed her.

He started talking out a scene—what he craved doing to her—the words rolling lyrically from his talented mouth. 'I want to taste you everywhere, learn every dip and curve of your beautiful body, feel every inch of you in my hands.' He punctuated the words with the movement of those clever fingers, trailing down her arms—leaving goosebumps in his wake—then sliding them up her rib-cage to cup her lace-covered breasts. Just that slight ease of pressure off her shoulders, the heat emanating from his touch, was the most delicious sensation on earth.

He kissed words along her jaw and ground his hips, pushing his groin against her. Pia moaned long and loud as the hot flesh between her legs beat a wanton tattoo and clenched, desperate for him to be inside her.

'I want to feel your surrender, Pia. Will you give it to me?'

Another kiss. Another hard press. More heat curling through her veins, swirling through her abdomen.

'I want to slide down your body and take your orgasm in my mouth. I would do anything...*anything* to taste you. Just once. Before I thrust into your glorious body and take you to heaven and back.'

She squirmed, gyrating back against him.

'You'd love that, wouldn't you, Pia? Me inside you. Taking you long and hard and deep.'

Yes. *Yes.*

Next thing Pia knew, she had *his* back plastered against the wall and she was kissing *him* ferociously—her hands in his thick glossy hair, up on her toes so his huge thick erection nudged her lace panties—unleashing a torrent of carnal need she'd had no idea she was capable of. The scent of him, the feel of his hard body under her seeking hands, was so heady she couldn't get enough. It sent her hormones, her adrenaline, her desire for him into orbit. And when he fisted her hair with one hand and squeezed her left breast with the other stars burst behind her eyelids.

Nic groaned. She almost climaxed. And the shock of it, of being so out of control, burning from the inside out, was like an arrow of ice spearing into her psyche.

Ice.

Mortification prickled over her skin and she wrenched away from him.

'You are ice and fire, Pia,' he breathed, that wide chest heaving.

Ice. *Ice.* Huskies whimpering. Ice cracking. Freezing water seeping into her skin.

'You…you…' It was worrying that that was all the eloquence she had. But, honestly, she was turning into a vacuous bimbo without a lick of sense. He was playing with her!

'Are a good kisser?' he suggested, still breathless, still too suave and sinful for his own good. '*Sim*, I know. You aren't too bad yourself. Come back here and we'll practise some more.'

The way he was looking at her was scary. As if he had voodoo powers—whether for evil or for good she *still* didn't know. But it was the kind that made her think he would keep her drugged on sex for weeks if she let him.

Never in a month of Sundays!

'You, *Lobisomem,* are the lowest of the low.'

Face flushed, he cocked an arrogant brow. 'You weren't saying that when you had your tongue down my throat, *querida.*'

'That was before I remembered the snowstorm. When was that? Yesterday? What happened? How did I get back here?'

He raked a palm across the high ridges of his abdomen as if his chest ached. 'I found you.'

Nic had come looking for her? 'Did you find Danel, too?'

'Yes. He fared a little better than you and came to visit earlier. And, before you ask, the huskies are also fine. They ran for cover in the forest.'

'Good. That's…good.' It hurt even to think, and when she tentatively rubbed the sore mound on the side of her head she winced at the deep throb of pain.

Okay. So he'd rescued them. But—

'How did I end up in your bed?' And on the verge on surrendering! 'Clearly you would've slept with me, taken advantage, just to win a bet,' she said scathingly. 'You would've let me believe it was too late!'

A dimple popped in his cheek as he clenched his jaw and those eyes grew dark with shadows. 'No. Instead I would've stopped before we'd gone too far. Told you you'd been sick with hypothermia and frightened of the needles, and that if I hadn't climbed into bed with you to warm you up death would've been mere hours away.'

Pia swayed where she stood, clinging to hostile suspicion as if it were a life raft. A raft that bobbed and tipped precariously as she recalled waking time and again, wrapped in a cashmere mist: Nic holding her tight, as if she were something precious.

He'd saved her life. First by searching for her and then holding her throughout the night and well into the day. Never moving from her side. And his touch hadn't been grudging or just necessary, because he wanted something in return. It had felt cherishing, gentle, almost covetous. A touch she'd never felt before but wanted to again. Desperately.

Tears stung the backs of her eyes. Not because she was hurting or upset or distressed but because the torrent of strange contrary sensations was close to overload. She was fighting this thing between them with everything she had, and right now it was breaking her.

It had to be the close call with death making her so emotional. *Had* to be.

Nic's sudden launch off the wall made her flinch, and she panicked in case she'd been staring with no filter on.

'I did what I had to do,' he said, brisk and decisive.

Pia could literally see him gathering up the tattered remnants of his control.

'Had to?' she repeated stupidly, commanding her body to stand tall, chin up, projecting nonchalance.

Bending at the waist, he swiped a T-shirt from the floor. One that looked as if it had been tossed away haphazardly in haste.

Smoothing the crumpled material down his chest, he finally met her eyes—and the sardonic smile he tipped her way wasn't quite right. It was sort of forced into hardness, and it made her stomach dive to the rug.

'Oh, I get it,' she said, imposing upon her tone its usual sass. 'How can you win our bet if I'm six feet under, right?'

He didn't bother denying it, just shoved his limbs into clothes as if he wanted nothing more than to run from the room.

All the happiness and wonder and joy from that life-shattering kiss drained out of her and in the void—as if clearing the toxic mess of emotions had given her the space to think clearly again—she picked over his words.

'Frightened? I was frightened of the needles?' Good God, what had she said?

'Petrified, Pia.'

He was looking at her so oddly she couldn't catch her breath. A humourless laugh was trapped in her throat, fluttering, as if she'd swallowed a moth. A choking, frantic tickle.

'Did I talk much? Say anything…interesting?'

A surge of shame hit her with the stunning force of a tidal wave as her filthy past crashed over her, coating her in anguish and dread. The possibility that Nicandro Carvalho might know where she'd come from, who she'd been. The damage he could cause her with that kind of information at his disposal. *But he doesn't know that you're Zeus. Just keep it together.*

'You made little sense, Pia, and said nothing of interest to anyone, I assure you.' All this talking was while he avoided her gaze, and she was positive he wasn't telling her the entire story.

Was he saying her secrets were safe with him? Could she

trust that? Maybe she could, because otherwise he would have pushed for more, just as he always did. Poked and prodded until he uncovered a rotting bed of grime.

'Pia!'

It wasn't until Nic shouted her name from across the room that she realised she was about to keel over.

'*Dios!* I'm such an idiot. You shouldn't even be out of bed. You'll be weak for days.'

'Your concern is so touching,' she jeered, covering her embarrassment with sweet sarcasm.

He swept her up into his arms as if she weighed no more than a child and walked across the floor, his bare soles slapping on the hardwood, before gently lowering her to the bed.

Pulling the blankets over her, he tucked her in. She shouldn't adore the extraordinary contentment of being fussed over, and nor should she consider going to the bathroom so he'd do it all over again.

'You are still sick, Pia. No more cold. No more ice. Tonight you sleep in my bed and tomorrow morning, when the sun rises, I'm taking you somewhere warm.'

Not a chance. 'If I'm sleeping in this bed, *you* are on the couch—and what's more I'm not going anywhere *warm*. I have a stay-over in Munich and then—'

'I don't care if you have a meeting with the Queen of England at Buckingham Palace. We made a deal. I came here—now it's your turn to go where I wish. I have business in Barcelona, so to Barcelona we shall go.'

She didn't like that look. That arrogance and audacity and command. It was a powerful combination of traits that had made him a dominant force in real estate and one of the most sought-after men in the world.

'And if I say no?'

'You'll be breaking the terms of our deal and I'll take that as forfeit,' he said, with lethal softness.

'What terms?' She pulled the sheets higher over her

body, practically up to her nose. A bit late, of course, but her pride was on the floor in tatters and she needed all the help she could get.

'To spend time with me.'

Pia filled in what he wasn't saying. *To prove I am not so bad. To let me gain your trust.*

Yeah, right.

Collapsing back onto the pillows, she closed her eyes. He had a point. Fact was, she had little choice but to follow him. She still needed answers, needed to know if Nic was behind the propaganda, and she'd given her word. So she'd just have to play nice with the other children and compromise.

'Fair's fair, I suppose. I'll have to cancel my meeting in Munich.' She'd swear she could feel hives pop from her skin. Skin that begged for the scrape of her nails.

'You say that as if it's the end of the world. You've never cancelled a meeting before? Ever?'

'No.'

He paused with his arm halfway into the sleeve of his jacket and looked up. His hair was a tousled mess from her fingers. So gorgeous. 'Do you ever stop? Even for a moment?'

No. 'Why would I?'

'To live. Have fun. See friends. Be happy.'

'I do live.' She had no idea what fun was. As for friends—she didn't have the time. 'I am happy.' *Liar.* Pia and happiness were barely on speaking terms. And since when was she bothered?

She wished she could hit him right now.

'You keep telling yourself that while I head over to the lodge. I need to make the travel arrangements to Spain.'

Barcelona.

It was a horrible mistake. It had all the hallmarks of a

tragic ending. In fact she was starting to feel like the lead in a Shakespearean comedy.

So why was she sitting here, handing over control, waiting for him to turn the next page?

CHAPTER NINE

NIC SLAMMED THE Bugatti into fifth gear, pushed his foot to the floor and spun down the B-10 coast road heading into the heart of Barcelona town. On his right, the long sun-drenched waterfront skimmed the blue crystalline waters of the Balearic and on his left reclining in her seat, was the woman who was turning him inside out.

With a need for speed that echoed the years that had passed he drove himself harder, farther, faster. Running from his mournful memories or towards his predestined future, he wasn't sure.

This was all getting a bit close to home, he thought wryly, his accusation to Pia still fresh in his mind. *'Do you ever stop? Live. See friends. Be happy.'*

The hypocrisy of his words didn't escape him. Avô was rather fond of telling him he needed to slow down, play harder, be happier.

Happy? He couldn't remember the last time he'd felt the sweet tendrils of joy curl around his heart and lift the cumbersome weight of rage. Before yesterday, that was. His relief at seeing Pia up and about had floored him and he didn't want to over-analyse that. It certainly didn't mean he was developing any sort of...*feelings* for her. That would take the crowning glory for stupid moves on his part.

But, if he was being totally honest with himself, for the first time in years his purposeful stride had faltered. Nic would never forget the look on Pia's face—the fear that he knew of her past, the shame that had eviscerated the beautiful pink flush after his kisses.

Yes, okay, he'd wanted to push—to ask why, to dig, to find something he could use to demolish her father. Instead he'd stood there and looked into those exquisite violet-blue eyes, with the sultry taste of her lingering in his mouth and hadn't been able to do it. Couldn't make her relive it. Only wanted to soothe her, help her forget, make it all disappear. Not cause more pain while he was rocking her world, shaking the foundations she'd built her pride upon.

She'd never forgive him, but there was little likelihood they'd meet again after his meeting with her father. Nic would go back to New York and likely marry Goldsmith's daughter, place Santos Diamonds back in Avô's hand. As for Pia, she was strong. The strongest woman he'd ever met. She would close this chapter in her life, stand up and move on, doubtless ruing the day they'd met.

Hands white on the steering wheel, he breathed through the tightness in his chest.

It wasn't as if Pia would be left with nothing, he assured himself. Merisi seemed like an octopus, with tentacles that reached far and wide, so Nic doubted he'd ever know the full extent of his business interests. But one thing he would never falter on—Q Virtus must fall. The coliseum that had held the gladiatorial battle of Santos versus Merisi and witnessed his family's demise. And Zeus must be exposed for the crook he was.

Then he could crawl beneath a rock, as far as Nic cared. Maybe he'd leave Pia to manage what Nic had left alone. He hoped so, because he didn't want Pia starting again from nothing. Not after what she'd been through.

Nic was more anxious than ever to meet the man. Q Virtus was finally cracking under his strain, and by the time they reached Paris the vast majority of members would have disowned it, never to return. Nic had given them enough doubt to disease their minds and ensure they jumped ship while their reputations and businesses were still intact. He couldn't wait to see the look in the other man's eyes when faced with his nemesis. Couldn't wait to tell him his club and the Merisi legacy were dying.

Dammit, he *needed* that meeting. He just had to bed Pia to get there.

The thought was a mighty hand at his throat that gripped without remorse. Why was he suddenly uncomfortable with the idea? It wasn't as if he was seducing her under duress—she wanted him just as much as he wanted her. Mutual pleasure was theirs for the taking, and if the attraction between them had been strong before, now it was off the charts. As if they'd tasted nirvana and craved another shot.

Barcelona town came into view—all grandiose architecture and Gothic flair—and he sneaked a sideways glance at his temptress.

With the top down in his ferocious little supercar, the wind had whipped at that perfect film noir up-do as if taunting her to cut loose and gave her cheeks a healthy lustrous glow of pink. The hypothermia had taken its toll, and she'd slept for most of the flight, but out in the warm air, with huge sunglasses covering half her face, a small smile teasing her mouth, head tipped back as she looked up at the children waving from the bridge, he thought she'd never looked more beautiful. Or so young.

'You know...take away the laptop and the phones and the bodyguards and you look twenty years old, *querida*.'

Pia rolled her head on the cushioned pad to face him and her eyebrows shot skyward. 'How old do I look *with* them?'

'All serious and scowling? Forty at least.' Hideous exaggeration, but he was all for inflation to make his point and get a rise.

'Oh, charming! I thought you were aiming for my bed— not to get pushed off the roof!'

Nic threw his head back and laughed. He couldn't remember the last time a woman had made him laugh, made him lie in wait for the next outrageous thing to come out of her mouth, made him want to find the nearest bed and touch that sinuous, sultry body again. Ice and fire personified.

'So, unless you want me to think the worst you'll have to tell me how old you are.'

'Didn't anyone ever tell you never to ask a woman her age?'

Blame it on the sunshine. Blame it on the town he'd always loved and the opportunity to show it to Pia since she'd confessed she was a virgin to these parts and he suspected her travels were devised for oppressive boardroom play. Hell, blame it on the laughter in his heart, but the words just tumbled out.

'*Sim*, my mother. She used to pay me to tell my friends she was ten years younger. Said she would rather carry the stigma of teenage pregnancy than be seen as old. Mamãe was a great lamenter that you're only as young as you feel.'

Sabrina Santos would have liked Pia, he decided—very much. Talk about irony.

'You speak of her in the past tense. Did you lose her?'

Nic could feel her scrutiny burning into his cheek and found swallowing past the emotional grenade in his throat was harder than he'd expected. 'Yes. A long time ago. Both of my parents are dead.'

Gripping the gearstick, he downshifted as pedestrian traffic became dense and he could see children lining the streets. Distracted as he was, when he felt the startling yet unbearably sweet stroke of the back of Pia's finger down his ear and jaw he flinched.

'I'm sorry, Nic. Your mother sounds like she was a hoot. You must miss her. Miss them both.'

More than you could ever know—and I have your father to thank for it.

The violent need for vengeance flared back to life and it took everything he had to keep his emotions in check. The air grew taut with an uncomfortable silence and from nowhere he wished she would touch him again, so he could feed off a comfort he really didn't deserve.

Instead she filled the quiet. 'Well, if she was right, some days I feel one hundred.'

'But not today.'

'No,' she said softly. 'Not today. This place is just…so stunning. Amazing.'

She raised her arms in the air and he imagined she could feel the cool breeze kiss her palms, whistle through her fingers.

'If I tell you how old I am, will you answer me a question honestly?'

'I'll try my very best,' he hedged.

'I'm twenty-eight.'

Dios, very young. He hadn't expected that. It wasn't that she looked older; it was the way she carried the weight of the world on her shoulders almost effortlessly at times. Then again, with her past, he imagined she'd had to grow up quickly—much as he had.

'So…' she began, threading her fingers into a prayer-hold, knuckles white.

Her pregnant pause made his stomach pitch.

'Have you ever had any business dealings with Antonio Merisi, my father?'

Personally? 'No.'

'I'll never have sex with you, Nic.'

He didn't miss the hard core of determination or the frayed edges of remorse. She desired him, but with this damn bet between them… He was beginning to see the error of his arrogant ways there. One look and all he'd been able to think of was taking her, having her body beneath him, cocksure she'd tumble into his arms within hours. The woman screamed *sex* and he hadn't seen past that *femme fatale* persona. But beneath the façade was a vulnerability that made him ache.

'Why don't you just tell me why you want to meet him,

tell me what the problem is, and I'll try and fix it. I'll find a way. It's the least I can do after you...'

'Saved your life, Pia? Held you in my arms for hours on end?'

Nic waited until he'd pulled to a stop at a crossing before glancing over at her—she was staring at the Barcelonians cluttering the pavement, the back of her hand pressed against her mouth. He'd give his eye teeth to know what she was thinking.

'You can't help or fix it,' he said, wishing she could with all his heart. 'I don't want to discuss him, Pia. Not today or tomorrow. Not until Paris. This time is for you and I. You almost died two days ago and it makes me want to remind you how to live. Forget the bet, *querida*. For the next two days, here in this town, we'll be the best of friends. *Without* benefits. You want to see this city—I can see it in your eyes. So we'll go out. Eat delicious Catalan food that will make your mouth water. Enjoy the sun. See the sights and have some well-deserved fun.'

He truly wanted that, he realised. Just to feel like a man again—a man out with a beautiful woman and no cares in the world.

'What do you say?'

Violet-blue eyes—narrow with cynicism—peeked over the top of her sunglasses. 'I sense a subplot.'

With a chuckle he shook his head. 'Must you be so suspicious?'

She glared at him with a pensive pout. 'I'm not having sex with you, Nicandro.'

He peeked over *his* sunglasses and gave her a sinful wink. 'You keep telling yourself that, *bonita*.'

Pia *did* tell herself that, until it became a mantra in her mind and a torrid persecution in her body.

Nic was like a child with a new toy, and her suitcases had barely hit the floor of his palatial penthouse before he was dragging her down the frenetic La Rambla, strolling through the medieval alleyways and secluded squares of the old city, lyricising about every madcap Gaudi façade. Copious café's dotted the avenues, and she drank oodles of vanilla latte—espresso was Nic's poison—and paused to listen to the buskers, watch the pavement artists and be amazed at the living statues.

Pia adored every single minute of it. In fact she fell head over heels in love with the utter chaos and complete charm of it all.

Which just about described her new *friend* too.

Nic—or should she say tour guide *extraordinaire*—was amazing, with light-hearted mischief gleaming in his eyes as he spun her off in yet another direction. He was wonderful. Until the sight of her business suit sent him into an agitated state of incredulity.

'Don't you own any casual clothes, Pia? Anything that is not black?'

To which she haughtily responded, 'Black makes me look thinner.' Which, apparently, had been the wrong thing to say.

'That is the most ridiculous thing I've ever heard, Pia! I don't want you to look thinner, I want to see those glorious curves illustrated in colour!'

Pia considered the truth of that while she leaned against a drinking fountain in one of the squares, wincing at the pulsing sting of blisters on her heels and toes.

Meanwhile, Nic seemed to be having another fit—arms slashing in the air, frustration leaching out of him.

'Take them off, *querida*. I mean it. Look at your poor little feet! All squished.'

Down he went onto his knees in front of her with suave elegance and eased both shoes off her feet.

Pia frowned. 'What are you doing?' There was some fairytale about a shoe, she was sure.

'Playing Prince Charming.'

'Didn't he put the shoe *on*?'

He waved his hand in the air. 'Semantics.'

Then he grinned up at her—so utterly gorgeous—and shoved his sunglasses upwards to sit on his head, visor-like. She'd swear in any confession that her world tipped on its axis.

Wavy dark hair ruffled by the fingers of the breeze tumbled over his brow and curled around the upturned collar of his bright pink polo shirt. His white linen trousers were pulled tight over his spread thighs and she could see the thick ridged outline of his masculinity and remember the feel of it against her—

'Ohhh. That is *bliss*.' She drew the word out as if it had ten syllables as he pressed into the arch of her foot, banishing all thought. 'Keep going. More. *Harder*.'

He growled from his position between her legs. 'If you don't stop moaning in that smoky, sultry voice of yours I'll have you up against that wall over there and *harder* will take on a whole new meaning.'

Right now she'd probably let him. Spectacular—that was what he'd be. The thought should have shocked her, because sex didn't rate above 'okay' in her book.

Pia closed her eyes, tipped her head back and lost herself in his ministrations. No one had ever given her a foot-rub before—in fact it was the most selfless thing anyone had ever done for her. Those big hands were gentle yet firm, and the slow rub had her arching like a cat.

'*Dios*, look at you. This is torture. We have to move.'

No! Don't stop. 'Walk in my bare feet?'

'Hop on my back and we'll go to the boutique on the corner. I'm buying you new shoes and some decent casual clothes if it's the last thing I do.'

She wasn't sure which idea appalled her most. 'I can buy my own clothes, thank you very much, and there's no way I'm getting a piggyback into a exclusive designer store. How will *that* look?' The idea was preposterous.

He looked at her as if *she* was preposterous. 'Who cares? You might cut your feet otherwise, and you'll never get *those* back on.' He pointed to the offenders with a disgusted sneer, then spun around and lowered into an elegant crouch. 'Hop on.'

Pia swallowed hard as she eyed his wide shoulders. 'I can't believe I'm doing this,' she muttered, inching her skirt up her thighs and sneaking a peek to see who was watching. 'I weigh a ton. I could break your back.'

'You weigh one forty at the most, Pia. *Do it.*'

That commanding tone made her shiver. 'Fine. You asked for it.'

Hands hooked on his shoulders, she executed a graceless little jump and—thank God!—he caught her effortlessly, curling those big hands around her upper thighs as he stood tall.

'I like this,' he said, his thick, rich tone telling exactly how much.

Embarrassed beyond belief, she buried her face in his neck as he sauntered down the street, easy as you please, as if he did it every day of the week. It was all completely surreal. But the astonishing thing was her acute discomfort soon gave way to an odd bubbly feeling…maybe giddiness?…as people passed by and said things like, *Hola!* or *Bon dia!*, smiling at them as though they were sweet sixteen, madly in love and a delightful sight to behold.

And pretty soon she found herself smiling back and hanging on to Nic, her arms wrapped around his shoulders, wrists crossed on his chest, revelling in the feel of all his hard ridges and hot flesh. He felt glorious. Safe. Nuzzling his neck, she breathed in his earthy masculinity and felt his groan rumble up through his back and vibrate over her breasts.

'Good?' he asked.

Pia wasn't certain if he meant the feel of him, the smell,

or her lack of shoes, and decided the answer would be the same for all three. 'Divine.'

Another growl. Another deep rumble vibrating over her chest. And her heart thumped against the wall of her ribcage. She was loving the effect she had on him. No matter what, that wasn't a lie or a secret, and she clung to that as tightly as she clung to him.

For so long he'd played the starring role in her tawdriest fantasies—was it any wonder her resistance was slowly crumbling, leaving her to consider what would happen if she surrendered? Caved. Gave him his meeting. With Zeus. With *her*. Surrendered not only her body but also her true identity, her life. Not for a relationship—she wasn't *that* naïve, and in truth she wasn't interested in putting her heart on the line again for anyone, not after the humiliation of Ethan—but for one night in his bed.

One night of Nicandro Carvalho in exchange for risking it all. Would it be worth it? Probably not. Not to her. Not for sex. A fleeting pleasure versus losing Q Virtus. The old dinosaurs at the club would have her neck in a noose in no time if they knew a woman ruled their world. Heck, she'd only just managed to induct a number of serious-minded businesswomen into the fold, and that had taken her years. Dragging the place into the twenty-first century would turn her grey, she knew.

Rotten, stinking, filthy old laws.

But maybe he'll keep your secret, Pia. He knows about your past, virtually promised he'd tell no one. Maybe she could reveal herself. Trust him.

The infernal internal argument raged on, fuelling her anxiety and frustration. Too many maybes. Too many risks. Especially considering the rumours and the trouble at Eros.

But maybe she'd jumped to the wrong conclusions and he *had* just been looking for Zeus. She had no proof he was responsible apart from the fact that he'd broken into her office and had been snooping, but the more she knew of him the more she thought it was exactly the kind of risky, troublesome thing he'd do to find someone who, to be fair, was impossible to see. It didn't mean he was to blame for all her problems, did it?

Convincing yourself now, Pia? Maybe so, but if he wanted to cause trouble why save her life by holding her in his arms through the night? Why order her to sleep on the flight with fervent concern in his gaze? Why show her around the city and enjoy every minute? Massage her feet. Give her a piggyback so she didn't cut herself.

No. Just...*no*. It didn't fit. Any of it.

Lost in the tangled web of her thoughts, she didn't notice the glass plate frontage of the boutique until Nic came to a stop.

Pia wriggled to be let down. 'You can let go now.'

'I don't want to,' he said, with no small amount of petulance. 'I love feeling you against me, Pia.'

Whether it was his sincerity, the heat between them, or the gruff repressed need in his voice, she wasn't sure but she dipped her head and kissed him open-mouthed on the soft skin beneath his ear.

'Thank you for the ride, big guy.'

It had been considerate and caring and he needn't have done it. Who could blame her for being confused? This wasn't the man she'd met in Zanzibar—the calculating wolf who doubtless had an agenda. This man felt real. And, God help her, she wanted him. Wanted to trust him with everything she was.

Nic loosened his hold and she dropped to the warm stone pavement. Then he spun around, cupped her face and kissed her back tenderly, affectionately, on the mouth.

'Any time, *bonita*.'

As soon as they stepped over the threshold the store assistants were all over him like chocolate syrup—even the browsers couldn't take their eyes off him. Not that she blamed them. *And I've kissed him!* A startled thrill washed over her—the kind she hadn't had in for ever. *I've kissed him and I want to do it again. And again.*

Within half an hour Nic had packed her off to the changing rooms with a pile of clothes and Pia tore off her fitted jacket and skirt. The only way she could describe how she felt in that moment was free. As if her suit had been made of steel and she'd never known it. Eyeing the pile, overwhelmed and not sure where to even start, she heard a child-like whoop, knew it had something to do with Nic, and pulled the curtain aside to spy.

Standing on one leg, he balanced a dark red and blue Barcelona football on top of his elevated sneakered foot and held it there for long moments for the rapt attention of a young boy. After a while he gave a little kick, and Pia's jaw dropped as he started bouncing that ball over and over again. Never dropping it once. A back-kick and it was balanced on his nape with an expertise that had the entire store mesmerised. A second later he was nudging it a few inches into the air with his head repeatedly—she thought they were called headers but, hey, she'd never been into football…she could be wrong—and the young boy was grinning and clapping and cheering with utter delight.

Pia felt a silly smile on her face and her heart began to float in her chest. Before she knew it, snapshots of impossible dreams flashed in her mind.

He would be a wonderful father.

After a childhood of no authority, no order, no harmony, Antonio Merisi's controlled world had appealed to her so much she would have done anything to stay with him. And she had. But, looking back, it had been much like going from anarchy and chaos to despotism. A kind of tyranny.

Nic, on the other hand, was a glorious fusion of chaos and control. He could be commanding and dominant one minute, mischievous and wickedly sexy the next. As a daddy he'd be firm when he had to be, but probably the first to climb the nearest tree or jump in a nearby lake. And in that moment she envied the woman who would share that life with him.

An almighty shattering—like the sound of a hideously expensive vase being knocked off a shelf by a wayward football—splintered throughout the store.

Nic cringed so deeply his eyes squeezed shut. The little boy snorted, earning a glare from his mama. And Pia? She slapped a hand over her mouth to stop her giggle ripping free. And since when did she giggle? *Ugh.*

Contrite, Nic shrugged those big shoulders and smiled crookedly, almost blushing as he apologised to the staff. Pia honestly didn't know why he bothered, because they were all in love with him and he could have trashed the shop for all they cared. He could buy the place fifty times over and they knew he'd pay his dues.

After discarding a few outfits that she wouldn't be seen dead in, she settled on a sheer white T, a pair of jeans, a glamorous loose-fitting blazer and the softest pair of suede boots that made her feet sing. Then, before she could second-guess herself, she started to pull out the pins in her hair. Would Nic like her hair down? Even when she'd been sick it had stayed pinned back, so he'd never seen it—probably didn't know it was so long. Heck, maybe he wouldn't even care.

What's happening to you, Pia? What is he doing to you?

By the time she'd squashed her self-doubt, pulled the curtain back and stepped out, Nic and his partner in crime were sitting on the floor, leaning against the wall, chattering about the greatest football players of all time.

Pia cleared her throat. 'Are you boys behaving yourselves?'

Two faces jerked up. Two mouths—one big, one small—dropped.

'Wow. She's pretty. Is she your girl?'

Now it was Pia's turn to blush scarlet. Heat spread up her cheeks as Nic just sat there. Blinking. Staring.

Eventually he launched to his feet. 'I would like her to be. Do you think she should?' he asked the boy.

'Totally. You're cool.'

'This is my thinking exactly,' he said, with an arrogant nod that made her roll her eyes.

Pia watched him prowl towards her and covered up her unease by cocking her hip. 'Ta-da! Whadaya think?'

'I think that mouth of yours was made for better things than to speak slang, *querida*.' He walked around her, eyeing every curve, every nip, every inch. 'And I think you look ridiculously young, amazingly cute, a whole world lighter and the most beautiful woman I've ever seen.'

'Oh.'

'Speechless? *Dios*, has the world ended?'

'Sometimes I crave kicking you in the shin.'

From behind, he whispered huskily in her ear. 'Let's not get into cravings. Mine would make your toes curl and they are becoming more and more impossible to ignore.'

At the touch of his palm cupping her behind, she melted into a puddle.

'Your lush derrière was made for jeans—you know that?'

Oh, God. Then she felt him toying with a thick lock of her hair, the tug on her scalp sending her dizzy.

'You've finally unpinned your glorious hair. *Dios*, Pia, what are you trying to do to me?'

I'm not sure. Make you want me for me—not for who I am or what I can give you. Show you I'm more than the siren you want in your bed. Make you see me.

When he'd come full circle she stared at his mouth and he grinned wickedly.

'Want a taste, Pia?' he said, in that luscious, growly voice that made her tummy flip and her heart do a triple-somersault in her chest.

So of course she changed the subject. 'Where did you

learn to play football like that? You could've been a professional.'

It was as if she'd caused a power cut. The lights flickered. Blanked out. Then the stark flare of anguish in his eyes was so strong Pia had to root her feet to the floor to stay upright. What did they say about hidden depths? She'd never seen that kind of pain in him before. That depth of emotion.

'Nic? What did I say?'

Pain morphed into something hard and cold that made her shiver. But as quickly as it had come, it was gone.

'I was a pro. A long time ago.'

Oh, God, no wonder. 'So what happened?' she asked softly.

Turning his back on her, he stalked towards the cashier's desk. 'Injury. Let's go.'

She wanted to ask him how and why and when, but something told her he'd clam up even further because it would be opening a Pandora's box.

How awful that must have been for him. Having his dreams ripped away. And they *had* been dreams—no one could have missed the joyful, almost wistful smile on his face as he'd performed for the little boy.

Nic paid the bill after he'd given her a warning glare not to argue—in truth she'd never had anyone buy her a gift, and today had been so special she didn't want to bicker—and then asked for all the boxes to be delivered to his penthouse at the hotel. There seemed to be far too many, but she was so distracted with thoughts of his shattered aspirations she didn't question it.

When they'd left the store Nic reached for her hand, and this time Pia took it. She'd avoided his hold all day, but she had the distinct impression he was asking for comfort.

His strong, warm grip tightened, as if he were pleased, but once they were sauntering down the tree-lined avenue he flipped back to his jovial rakish self.

'Now we can hit the town,' he said. 'Dinner and a club—our first date.'

Pia stumbled on an invisible crack in the stone. 'Date? Do friends go on dates?' She couldn't even bear to think of her last date. It made her feel physically sick.

He placed his hands on her waist to steady her and cocked an eyebrow knowingly. 'Friends who want nothing more than to rip each other's clothes off? All the time.'

'There'll be no clothes-ripping tonight.'

Absolutely not. Here she'd been, unravelling at the seams, and he'd just reminded her of a time when giving her trust to a man had royally stitched her up.

His whisky eyes sparkled down at her and her stomach did a hot, sultry roll.

'You keep telling yourself that, *querida*.'

She *was*, dammit, and it didn't seem to be working a jot!

CHAPTER TEN

DUSK HAD PUNCHED through the day in a bruised swirl of rouge and the same violet-blue as her eyes, and the air was sharp-edged with salt from the Balearic Sea.

She'd gone quiet, Nic mused, drawn inwards with a small pensive frown, and the only reason he could think of was the way he'd given dinner the innocuous title of a 'date.'

Still, he held her hand in his warm grip, unwilling to let go, knowing full well they were coming off as two inseparable lovers, and ushered her into the best tapas bar in town: a tiny undiscovered hole-in-the-wall discerning locals flocked to.

He leaned in and gave her arm a nudge. 'You have been on a date before, haven't you?'

Dios, she must have. Look at her. Those jeans made the blood rush to his head and his groin, making him simultaneously dizzy and hard.

'Casual' suited her to perfection. While he lusted after the sexy siren in power clothes, this was a softer look that gave her a girl-next-door vibe and made her so approachable that strangers thought nothing of striking up a conversation whenever they paused. A world away from Finnmark, where she'd been the high-class businesswoman in total control, verging on anally retentive, who'd had everyone on tenterhooks trying to anticipate her next move.

'Of course I have,' she scoffed—a tad defensively, in his opinion. Not many dates for Pia, then. Interesting.

While she snapped her spine pin-straight and hiked up her chin Nic laughed inwardly. If she thought those dense ice walls would perturb him she had another think coming.

'Nicandro! It has been too long, *amigo*!'

He grinned at the sight of Tulio Barros, the best chef on the planet, dark, short and sharp, with a wicked taste in art. 'It certainly has, my friend. Glad to see the place hasn't changed.'

The bar's main wall was a pastel canvas of tasteful yet evocative nudes from a bygone era, while the other three remained exposed brick. The rich scents of tapas baking, the dark wood slab tables and heavy chairs, the cream tiled floor—all lent the intimate space the warmth this part of the world was famous for. Nic loved it; somehow it reminded him of home, of Brazil, a place he hadn't visited in twelve long years.

The conversation exploded into a bout of, 'How have you been? How is business? Who is this beautiful lady?' and Nic curled his arm around Pia's waist and made introductions.

He could literally feel the tension ease from her body as Tulio soaked her in his Spanish charm and pointed to a small private table in the corner. 'Go sit at my table and I will bring some Sangria and my best dishes of the day, yes?'

Pia weaved through scattered handbags and chairs and eyed the seating.

Nic gave her another nudge. 'Trying to work out how to sit the farthest away from me?'

She pursed her lips. 'Yes.'

He chuckled darkly, getting a kick out of her blatant honesty. 'Something I will never allow. *Sit.*'

With a gorgeous little glare she slid along the bench and Nic followed, until they sat in the corner at right angles, knees bumping, flesh touching and Nic in his element, with a perfect view of the room and her beautiful face aglow from the intimate lighting.

Tulio poured tall glasses of Sangria—which she sucked through a straw, her full lips working rhythmically—and the man went all-out to tease her out of her shell with creamy squid rings, known as *chocos*, *patatas bravas* with creamy *alioli*, *llonganissa* sausage and *tigres*—stuffed mussels to die for.

Nic wanted to let loose a string of Brazilian curses as his trousers became too tight for comfort. He knew he was staring but, *hell*, she ate as if she was making love to her food. As if she savoured and gloried in every delicious morsel. And it was the most provocative sight he'd ever seen.

Those little licks, the slow, erotic roll of her tongue, watching her cheeks concave as she drank deeply—it all had him in a state of agony, with a hard-on that just wouldn't quit and a craving for her to take him inside the hot cavern of her mouth. It was killing him.

He tried to think of the last time he'd had no-holds-barred sex for hours on end, but all he could remember were some awkward dates and some passable yet mediocre sex. After that he'd told himself it just wasn't worth the hassle.

He'd meant to ask how many dates she'd been on—continuing their earlier conversation—but the nibbles and tentative bites and succulent licks were messing with his brain.

'How many lovers have you had?'

As for that steel band around his chest, tightening as he waited for her answer…? That was *not* jealousy or insecurity or obsessive behaviour. He simply needed to eat. When he ceased being riveted by her.

But this, apparently, had been the wrong thing to ask when her mouth was otherwise engaged.

Choking on a mussel, she lurched forward, and Nic rapped on her back until she could breathe without turning blue.

'Are you trying to kill me? That is none of your business!'

He gave her back a sympathetic rub and leaned closer to murmur in her ear, 'Which means none. Are you a virgin, *bonita*?'

'No!' Half the restaurant's patrons whipped their heads their way and she thumped his thigh under the table with her fist. Then she whispered furiously, 'For pity's sake, have you ever heard of a twenty-eight-year-old virgin?' Snapping upright, back pin-straight, she sniffed—a tad haughtily, if you asked him. 'I've had lovers.' Yeah, definitely defensive.

'Good lovers or mediocre orgasms at best?'

Jaw slack, eyes enormous, she shook her head at him. 'Do you have *any* filter between your brain and your mouth?'

'Mediocre, then. Hmm.' He brushed his fingers over his lips and smiled inwardly when he caught her staring and she licked her own pout. 'Why do you think that is?'

Had to be control. Pure and simple. He didn't believe in any of that garbage about there being 'The One' with whom sex was not just great, or even fantastic, but *life-changing*. How could sex be life-changing? What ludicrous hogwash. As for Pia… Come to think of it, he remembered how she'd frozen on the verge of her climax back in Finnmark. He knew the signs. He'd never left a woman unsatisfied in his life.

'You'll never experience earth-shattering, cosmic, star-realigning pleasure until you give up control. *Always* you have to be in control, Pia. If you let go the power of ecstasy you feel will be fifty-fold. You stopped yourself back in my cabin, didn't you?'

A hot flush slashed across her cheeks. *Busted.*

'I know a woman close to the edge, *querida*. If I had touched you where you were wet and wanting me you would have exploded.'

Darts of pique shot from her eyes, the violet deepening to the colour purple. '*Wow*, Nic, it's a wonder you can get that head of yours through the door. I just don't think I'm made for it. It's nothing to get excited about for me.'

Dios, no wonder she'd resisted him this long. '"*It*" being sex? You *can* say it, Pia. It's not illegal or immoral in this country.'

'Good job, since you'd have been convicted ten times over. Worldwide.'

She stuffed a meatball in her mouth and—call him a masochist—he followed every move.

'Strange that *innocent* would never be a word I'd think of with you but often that is exactly what you seem. You need educating, Pia.'

'And I suppose you'd be the man for the job, right? You'd make it your civic duty to ensure Olympia Merisi experienced a good orgasm?'

His face was a veritable invitation to debauchery in that moment, he knew. 'Ah, *querida*, I promise you there'd be *way* more than one—and "good" wouldn't even come close.' Nic leaned forward, dipped his head and drizzled whisper-soft kisses up the curve of her jaw before murmuring in her ear, 'By the time I was finished with you, you wouldn't know which way was up.'

Those gorgeous breasts began to heave as she struggled to suck in air.

'I think you've been hanging around ego-inflators too much, Nicandro. You really shouldn't believe everything women tell you. Money is the greatest aphrodisiac, and it makes the most expert liars.'

Her voice was more ice than fire, and the cold front washing over him prickled his skin.

Slowly Nic straightened as a lightbulb switched on and flooded his mind, illuminating every aspect of Pia with new meaning. Moreover, he'd have to be blind not to notice the pain that pinched her brow. Hell, he could virtually see her praying that he wouldn't jump on her *faux pas*.

'Let me guess. Some cad broke your heart, Pia?' It was pure conjecture but she was ripe pickings for anyone who knew her father. Heiress that she was. 'I imagine men are either intimidated by you or they're after your father's money. Is that about right?'

A heart-wrenching combination of reluctance, hurt and rage darkened her eyes and punched him in the gut.

'You could say that,' she said, in that hard, icy tone he hadn't heard for days and frankly had never wanted to hear again.

Now he understood the frozen façade a little better. Once bitten twice shy. Cliché, but true.

'What happened, Pia?' he asked gently, knowing it was a bad idea to push but incapable of stopping himself. He didn't like the idea that some man had damaged her, and that didn't bode well in light of his grand plan.

She stroked the smooth skin between her eyebrows in that way she did when she was deliberating. Unsure. Then she seemed to come to a decision, because she jerked up her chin and nailed him on the spot.

'I dropped my guard for no more than a minute. I believed every lie that came out of his mouth. I came to trust him. Then one night we went out on a date and I heard him telling his friends he was bedding Zeus's daughter to get into Q Virtus, and she was so easy he could marry her tomorrow and have the world at his feet.'

Nic's stomach took a nose-dive. No wonder she was holding back, defiant, rebelling against the insane biological chemistry between them. She'd been used, and the fact was in her eyes Nic was using her too—for a meeting. Wasn't he? Of course he was.

He tuned back in to her brittle voice. 'And do you know what my father said to me? He said, "Trust no man, Olympia. They all have an agenda. You want people to take a *woman* seriously? You stop acting like a whore.'"

The way she said *woman*—as if it was something to be ashamed of—rang alarm bells in his head. Hell, no, he wasn't having this—and it had nothing to do with any deal.

'Enjoying making love and being close to a man doesn't make you a whore, Pia. You have so much beauty stored inside you, and if you don't stir it up and let it flow out it will wither and die. Sex—making love—makes you feel alive. There's nothing to be ashamed of about that.'

The delicate curve of her throat convulsed. 'Are you saying this as a man who needs me in his bed to gain an audience with Zeus, or as a *friend*,' she taunted, reminding him of his words. 'A friend without benefits.'

'A friend. I promise you.' Oddly enough, it was the truth. 'Forget who I am or why we're here, sharing one another's company and great food. Do *not* let your past ordeal with a man dictate a future of a cold, solitary life. Was he your last lover?'

'Yes,' she said quietly, distractedly, as she glanced around the room, her gaze bouncing from one loved-up couple to another almost wistfully.

Nic swallowed hard, reached for her hand on the table and wrapped his fingers tight around hers, squeezing until he had her full attention. 'Keeping your distance, holding people away from you, denying yourself affection and a loving touch doesn't make you stronger, Pia. If anything it makes you weaker, because you're doing it out of fear.'

Her blonde brows drew down into intent little Vs, as if what he was telling her was far beyond mentally taxing. That over-active, constantly analysing brain of hers would be her downfall, he was sure.

'You're a beautiful, sensual woman, Pia, not meant to be alone. There's so much fire inside you. No matter what happens between us, promise me you'll remember that.

Be open to trying again. Not all men are dishonest, lying philistines and...' Nic trailed off.

I'm not either, he wanted to say, but that would be a barefaced lie. At least to her. Ironic that the one woman he wasn't being honest with was the one he wanted most.

Suddenly he felt as if someone had just picked him up and torn him clean down the middle. He wanted to crush the fool who'd bruised her heart, but he was about to do the exact same thing. Take advantage of her name, of who she was, exploit her for his own ends, use her just as badly as her last lover had.

Settling back in his seat, Nic closed his eyes, unsure if he could do it. Maybe he could find some other way to get to Zeus. *And what if you can't?* He was so close. After so many years he was now days away from facing the man who'd taken his parents from him, stolen his legacy, ruined his life.

Torn—so damn torn. Why was this tearing him apart? Why did he want her so badly? Why was he even considering her happiness before his own? His father's obsessive compulsions sprang to mind, but he squashed them just as swiftly. He was *not* his father!

Dammit, why was everything going so disastrously wrong?

Pia sat at the glass-topped table in Nic's penthouse, laptop open in front of her, gazing at the stunning sight of nightfall—a swollen waxy moon and a sky bursting with diamond-studded brilliance, its glow shimmering over a town that bustled with cosmopolitan chic glamour and frenetic energy.

Nic was backing off. Had been since the restaurant last night. The big seduction routine had crashed to a halt with the subtlety of a ten-car pile-up.

Often she caught him staring at her intently, with a voracious hunger that made her want to crawl out of her skin, but otherwise he was the perfect gentleman. Nic—*the perfect gentleman?* It was surreal. Maybe he'd been taken over by an alien life force or something. It was worrying to think he had such depth.

She'd half expected him to cancel their trip to the Picasso Museum that morning but, Nic being Nic, the idea hadn't seemed to cross his mind. Nor had cancelling tonight—their last night in Barcelona—and escorting her to his samba club in the old town. If someone had told her a month ago that she'd be sitting like some idiotic schoolgirl with a crush, counting down the hours, she'd have told them they were mentally insane. Yet here she was. Verging on lunacy.

Except no other man had ever looked at her the way Nic did. Predatory. Hungry. Just the heat in his whisky-coloured gaze, running hotly over her skin, their flames dancing in the dark depths like a physical manifestation of the blazing inferno that continued to rise up between them had Pia willing to do anything and everything he desired.

The bing-bong of an incoming e-mail diverted her attention to her mailbox.

No news. Nothing to link Carvalho to the hype at QV. He looks clean. Know more when I've spoken to PI in the morning.
Be careful, Pia.
J.

Careful? Wasn't she always careful? Always playing by the rules, using her head, emotionally barren. But with Nic she felt every sensation as if her senses were torn open and raw. As if she'd been held under the power of sensory deprivation her entire life—and maybe she had.

Her thoughts were severed by the ping of the elevator and the sight of Nic—all sweat and ripped muscle—coming back from his run.

Heaven help her, one look and her body simultaneously sighed in relief and flamed with heat, like some primal animal seeing her mate.

His hair was damp, the thick waves plastered to his brow. Beads of sweat dripped from his temples and clung to his chiselled jaw. And she could just imagine those corded, flexing muscular arms and his thick, powerful thighs moving with athletic grace as he pounded the pavement.

He scratched the hard ridges of his belly absently as he sauntered over, his dark gaze searing, as if he'd missed her face. 'Working again, *querida*?'

'Some problems at the club.' Pia looked at him closely but he didn't flinch at the mention of Q Virtus.

'Let your father deal with it, Pia,' he said, brisk and decisive.

She almost told him she didn't have that option.

'We'll leave in twenty minutes. I'm taking a quick shower.'

Can I be a fly on the wall?

Honest to God, he was sex incarnate, and the thought of another night lying alone in his huge bed in the guest room, thinking of how he'd made love to her mouth, how his thick hardness had nuzzled against the apex of her thighs, was a new form of persecution.

One hand on his hip, he didn't move an inch towards the shower, just stared at something beyond her left shoulder, and as she looked closer she could see stress bracketing his eyes. 'Is everything okay, Nic?'

Finally he met her gaze and his mouth shaped for speech, as if he wanted to tell her something. Something important, if his deep frown and tight jaw were anything to go by, and Pia felt as if she teetered on the edge of a cliff, waiting for a fall. His eyes lingered on her for long moments but he didn't answer her, didn't say a word, and after a frustrated clench of his fists he stalked off to the massive en suite bathroom.

Pia blew out a breath she hadn't known she was holding and slumped against the chair.

'By the way,' he said, loud enough to be heard through the penthouse. 'There's a box on your bed; you'll need it for the club tonight.'

There was?

Pia launched from the seat and tried not to dash through to her room like a child on Christmas morning. There on the pristine white sheets of the enormous four-poster bed was one of the boxes from the designer boutique; signature black, with a huge gold velvet sash tied into a sumptuous bow.

Her breathing grew a little fast and she rubbed her hands down her jeans.

A gift. Nic had bought her a gift. The man she'd watched from afar, the man who'd saved her life, the man who desired her like no other ever had. Surely this shouldn't feel so huge, so momentous, and yet that was exactly how it felt.

Arms wide, she curled her fingers under the lid and lifted, heart pounding with anticipation and excitement and the thrill of him doing something especially for her. Again.

Pia tossed the lid aside, looked down and sucked in air so fast her throat burned and tears stung the back of her eyes.

A red sheath lay on black tissue and with trembling fingers she stroked the embellished silk bodice and low-scooped neck, adoring the hand-stitched beads that tickled her palm. Lifting it from the wide straps, she noticed the fitted waist and the chiffon skirt that would kick out from her hips—a little flirty, a whole lot of fun—and flare out when she spun. It wasn't something she'd have chosen in a million years, but as she dressed in a daze, slipping the fabric over her head, letting the silk whisper over her skin and kiss her cleavage, for the first time in her life she felt like a billion dollars.

Odd how she could have bought hundreds of dresses just like this but had never wanted to—never had the need to dress up for anyone. But this… This dress was worth more than her fortune—at least to Pia—because it was a gift from the heart of a man who had to care. He *had* to.

And it was about time she admitted to herself that she cared right back. Had wanted him before they'd ever met face to face. Question was, did she have the strength to go for it? Surrender to him? Give him her body and reveal who she was? Take the ultimate risk?

Lost in thought, she lifted her left leg like a flamingo, reached down and nudged her foot into one glittering red stiletto. Then the other.

A quick glance in the mirror and she knew exactly what was missing.

Grabbing her jewellery case from the dark wood vanity, she slid the catch and opened the box, her heart doing a little pitter-patter as she spied the large black teardrop diamond and remembered the day her father had given it to her. No affectionate kiss on the cheek or words of love, but she'd known he'd cared for her in his own way and that had been enough. More than she'd ever expected or hoped for.

Lifting the chain from its bed of velvet, she watched the prisms from the chandelier above glint off the smooth black surface and the flash of a memory dimmed her buoyant mood. *Zanzibar.* The pure loathing in Nic's eyes had been strong enough to make her feel genuine fear.

Shivering, she gave a cursory glance towards the door to see if he was out of the shower, wondering if anything had been unearthed about Santos Diamonds. Then, to preserve her fragile optimism, she snapped the case shut. Maybe Nic truly *did* have voodoo suspicions about black jewels, and he was in a strange enough mood as it was.

When she stepped out into the hallway the sound of rushing water lured her towards the open doorway of his wholly masculine en suite bathroom.

Steam poured over the top lip of the towering glass enclosure, pluming in the air with moist heat, and when she took a tentative step closer her heart gave a pang at the sight of him. Ached so badly she could hardly stand it.

Arms braced on the black granite tile, head down as the water poured over him in a hot wet rush, he looked utterly torn. Frustrated. Demoralised.

As if sensing her presence, Nic lifted his head and twisted at the neck until she could see his profile. Water dripped down his nose and he wiped his face over his hard bicep to clear his eyes.

'Pia?'

He was so beautiful. From the hard sculpted lines of his back to the tapering of his waist, the dimples at the base of his spine and the perfect firm curves of his sexy butt.

Moisture dotted in between her breasts as her blood heated.

'Did you buy the dress before or after you smashed the place up?' she asked, her voice thready as she unravelled before him.

'Before I broke a two-thousand-euro vase? Yes. Do you like it? The dress?'

'I love it, Nic. Thank you.'

He gave a small nod. 'You're very welcome.'

She couldn't look away—could only imagine what it would be like to strip off his gift, walk in there and act out any of the various tawdry fantasies she'd conjured up over the past week. And all the while he didn't move a muscle, kept his body averted, and she started to ponder if he was thinking of her in the same way. If he was as turned on as she was.

'You need to leave…*now*.'

Her stomach twisted with pure and painful longing. 'What if I don't want to?'

Tipping forward, he banged his forehead off the wall and ground out, 'I'm not making love to you, Pia.'

The penny dropped. In fact it was as if she'd hit the

jackpot and all the nice shiny coins were pouring out in a gold rush.

He didn't want her to feel used. The way Ethan had made her feel. *Now* she understood. *Now* she wanted him more than ever. He would *never* purposely hurt her.

Pia smiled, but all she said was, 'You keep telling yourself that...*querido.*'

CHAPTER ELEVEN

'I'VE CHANGED MY MIND.'

At Nic's voice, Pia tore her eyes away from the limousine window and the sight of La Catedral, with its richly decorated Gothic façade graced with gargoyles and stone intricacies. Then she cursed inwardly.

One look was all it took tonight. Her lower abdomen clenched with want—empty, so needy she bowed slightly to ease the ache.

Nic put her in mind of a roguish prince in his wicked midnight-blue suit, with his unruly hair black in the dim light and curling seductively at his forehead and nape. He'd eschewed a tie in favour of an open collar and the sight of his smooth tanned throat was making her weak at the knees.

'About what?' she asked, cringing at the quiver in her voice.

'This is the most beautiful I've ever seen you.'

'You say that every time I change clothes.'

One side of his lush mouth kicked up. 'A man's prerogative, *querida*. Are you going to dance with me tonight?'

His voice, she noticed, was still thick and rich, but there was a hesitant tone there too and it matched his manner. As if he was so deep in thought, so conflicted, he was tearing himself apart. Clearly he didn't want to talk about it—she'd asked him often enough—but that didn't mean Pia wasn't listening.

'Yes, I want to dance. But I'll warn you now I have no idea how.'

'I can teach you the samba in five minutes. Or the rumba. Have a little faith—your body was made for dancing.'

The dark interior charged with an electric current that gave a sharp ping when Nic glossed his warm palm over her knee and drew tiny circles with his thumb over and over. A covetous touch that made her pulse spike. She wanted to feel him inside her so badly she could barely sit still. It was getting worse, she realised, this inescapable want. It was as if she just couldn't breathe without him touching her.

Squirming in her seat, she scrambled for something to say. 'This is *your* club we're going to?'

'Yes. Barcelona is one of my favourite cities in the world and a friend of mine—an actor, believe it or not—was bemoaning the lack of good dance clubs when he came into port. Next thing I knew I'd opened one. Una Pasion Hermosa—A Beautiful Passion.'

The car rocked to a stop outside a trendy upmarket nightclub with an endless queue and a dizzying red carpet.

Just like that her sangfroid flew out of the window. 'Good name. Is it a celebrity haunt?'

'Generally. Depends who's in town.'

The car door opened to the excitable cacophony of the crowd and Nic flowed from his seat—all sleek masculine elegance—and held out his hand.

She stared at it like an idiot, trying to ignore the nauseating curl in her stomach.

'Pia?'

Oh, God. Deep breath, hand in his and up she went, swirling into the foyer in a blur of blinking camera lights, ducking her head self-consciously, coming unglued with the idea that people would try and figure out who she was. Nic might be used to the limelight but she wasn't. She chose instead to stay behind the scenes. Very few knew her true identity and she wanted to keep it that way.

'Nic,' she whispered furiously. 'Maybe this isn't such a good idea. Won't people know you? Wonder who I am?'

He shrugged with so much insolence she could have whacked him. 'Only my staff really knows who I am, and they are paid very well not to make a fuss. They're used to high-end clientele and I doubt anyone will look twice at us.'

Nic wrapped his hand around hers tightly, as if sensing she was about to go nuclear with the power of angst-laced adrenaline rushing through her veins, and she felt the flow of tension drift from her body on a slow sweeping wave.

Come on, Pia. You don't want to ruin your last night fretting about things that might never be, do you? No. She wanted to enjoy every second. Live in the moment. Out in the real world. For once not hiding.

Nic led her to one of the private booths set on an elevated dais and Pia slid into the overstuffed velvet bench seat, feeling the seductive bass line of the Brazilian samba pound through her blood.

'What's your poison, Pia?' he said, leaning over, his whisky eyes aflame with heat and desire.

'You choose. I don't want to make any decisions tonight. I want to just…*feel*.' Her voice sounded unreal. Loose. Licentious. As if her body was slowly taking over the power of her analytical mind.

Nic ordered French 75s and they were delivered minutes later, served in champagne tulips. Pia blamed the heat for what she did next: knocked back the first gulp with so much abandon she almost blew her head off.

'Wow. Potent stuff. Someone just shot a flame-thrower down my throat.'

'For a potent lady,' he murmured, lips carved with a devilish smirk. 'A gutsy, lusty blend of gin, champagne, lemon juice and sugar.'

The way he puckered his lips and said *'sugar'*, with a

naughty, intoxicating lilt, sent the delicious tart-sweet cock-tail straight to her head. And all she could see was the swarthy sexy mess of his dark hair, the lights flickering over his aristocratic face, the smooth bronzed skin of his throat.

Good God, this sensation of recklessness was like being on a brutally intense rollercoaster and she wanted the ride to go harder and faster, way beyond control.

When Nic caught her staring and raised an arrogant brow she tore her eyes away, more than a little perturbed at her complete lack of morals. Was she coming off as some kind of…? *Of what, Pia? Whore?*

No. No, she wasn't going there. What had Nic said? Being close. Affectionate. Yearning for a lover's touch. She'd never had that before. That was probably why it had made her feel so dirty to be used. She'd allowed Ethan to make her feel worthless. But this give and take, connection and tenderness, had its own kind of beauty and there was nothing dirty about that—he was right.

Proof of that was in the crush of dancers moving sinuously across the floor to the unique samba beat. Under the brilliant strobes they were all beautiful arches and lines, weaving in light and shadow.

She focused on the couples who appeared to be lovers and picked up the nuances of their behaviour. The man tucking his lover's hair behind her ear, kissing her jawline, the tip of her nose, nuzzling her collarbone—all fiery heat, promising dizzying pleasure. More than anything she wanted to be close and affectionate like that with Nic.

'You're looking at them with such heart-shattering longing, Pia. What is going through that pretty head of yours?'

She didn't answer—couldn't…not with such a great lump in her throat.

'Maybe you are ready to dance, yes?'

'Now or never.' And she meant that literally. Something told her tonight was her last chance, her only chance with him, and if all she ever had was the heady sensation of his body moving against hers—even fully clothed—then so be it. She'd take it. It would be enough.

Pia stepped onto the pulsing dance floor and before she could think about where to stand or how to move Nic was there, taking control, taking the lead.

Aggressive, dominating, he curled his left arm around the base of her spine and pulled her to him, crushing her breasts against his chest. Then he clasped her right hand tightly in his—a silent declaration that he wouldn't let her fall, wouldn't let go. The moment was achingly wonderful, and as she looked up into his eyes and saw the longing reflected back at her she knew she was done for. Knew she'd never feel this way again.

'That's it, *querida*. Relax. Give all that control over to me.'

She had the notion they were talking about more than dancing, and she was already halfway to coming undone and unravelling quickly.

'Feel the contagious beat in your blood. Let the music move you; let it flow through your body and follow my lead.'

His voice was a giddy narcotic all on its own as he confidently steered her around the whirl of tight bodies and swaying hips.

Pia clutched his strong upper arms, loving the sensation of honed muscle beneath her fingers, and yet he bent them and moved with such masculine grace he was a stunning sight to see. His hands splayed across her lower back, where he gripped her tight and then moved their hips in a figure eight—all sensuality and sin—and then she was twirling like a top as he executed a perfect spin.

Just like that she was dancing, and she'd never felt so connected to another person in her entire life.

A second later she slammed back into his chest, palms flat, panting softly, breasts swollen and heavy, nipples peaking against the lace of her bra, begging to be touched.

Nic gazed down at her, all broody and dark.

It was like dancing with the devil, she realised. His every movement was a wicked invitation to vice, his covetous touch was possessed with danger, his scorching hot body created to spawn lust.

That was when she noticed. Nic wasn't the only one looking at her. Them.

'People are watching us,' she breathed.

'And most are obscenely envious of me, *querida*. Not to mention turned on.'

Well, they weren't the only ones.

His grip was firm but tender, holding her in the way a musician might prise the best from a rare instrument, and with every undulation, every sinuous return of her hips, her body hummed like a piano wire and she felt a hiccup of orgasmic pleasure. Not a full-on climax but a short, sharp, sweet jolt that was gone in an instant. Then another would hit, and suddenly she was shaking with uncontrollable need.

'Nic?' *Oh, God.* This was a whole new level of sexual tension.

Their bodies were so close from the waist up they barely moved. Her cheek now rested against his and the smell of his skin made her head spin, as if he was twirling her round and round the floor. When she inhaled through her mouth she could taste him, and her mind began to wander imagining a scene playing out...

Nic holding her down—wickedly naked—as they danced to an earthly wanton tune in his bed.

Dizziness hit her like a truck and the next thing she knew she was on her tiptoes, pressing her lips to his. *Kiss me, please.*

He hesitated and dread thrashed its monstrous tail, whipping her insides until—*oh, yes*—he thrust his hands into the fall of her hair and coaxed her mouth open with his tongue. Until she was seduced into an erotic play that had her nerves singing as he kissed her with such unrestrained passion she thought she might faint.

Beneath the mastery of his plundering lips the ache between her thighs grew to painful proportions full of emptiness and need. And impatience gathered inside her, right *there*, at the base of her abdomen, its frustrating heat spreading outward.

Pia undulated against him, stroking the thick erection that pushed against his seam over and over.

'*Dios*, Pia. You're killing me,' he groaned into her mouth, his hands unsteady as they moulded to her body.

His touch was electric and it seemed to be everywhere and nowhere all at once. She needed him to do something. To take control. Take *her*.

That was another thing he'd been right about. It was all about control for her, and she didn't like giving hers up. It made her afraid of being hurt. But in giving up her power and control to Nic, in return he'd give her something she needed far more right now. The assurance that what she had to offer of herself was worth giving to someone. That *Pia* was worth it. That her past hadn't tainted her beyond value.

'I want you, Nic. So much…' she whispered as she nuzzled across his jaw, and the last vestiges of doubt dissolved beneath the power of his searing heat. 'Take me back,' she implored. '*Take me*.'

So foolhardy. So reckless. So inevitable.

Emotion roamed across his features, shifting from conflicted to cautious to aroused and everything in between.

Pia watched the war raging inside him…

Then her heart smiled.

The limousine was dark. Streetlamps flashed at regular intervals, flaring through the shadowy black leather interior. And he tried to say no, to hold on, but within seconds of them tumbling into the car she was straddling his lap and gyrating against him. It was biological fireworks and he was only human, right? He'd been desperate for her since the day they'd met.

His agonising erection nudged the mound of her lacy briefs, pressing into her hot wet folds, and his mouth was on hers, ravenous, devouring, stunningly erotic.

For the first time in his life he was incapable of restraining his impulses—his body's carnal urges were stronger than his cast-iron will.

It was all hands and mouths and thrusting hips, murmured begging and endearments that made no sense, but they were both past the need to care about anything but pleasure and release.

The desire, already voluminous, became so acute he thought he was going to have a heart attack. How he was going to last the eight-minute drive was beyond him.

The sound of cloth tearing reached his ears, and when he felt her hungry hands on his chest he let out a low groan.

'Pia, slow down—or I swear you'll be on the floor in ten seconds flat.'

It seemed her version of 'slow' varied widely from his, because her open mouth glossed down his chest and licked over the flat copper disc of his nipple.

Nic hissed, but the sound was cut off when he felt her fingers at his waist, unbuttoning his trousers.

He should stop her, really. But, dammit, he didn't want to. Just wanted to feel her hot hands on him, her fingers wrapped around his pulsing thick length. Just. Like. *That.*

Nic's brain blew a circuit or two, but that didn't stop him from looking down. *Big* mistake. Her tongue snaked out and licked into his belly button before travelling down, down...

'Pia...' he growled with warning.

'I've wanted to do this since I saw you tied to my chair,' she said, in that smoky, sultry voice that drove him wild. Dropping soft, moist kisses down his length, she breathed hotly, 'Did you want me then? Think about me doing this?'

'*Dios*, yes—*yes!*'

Her hot wet tongue flicked and licked around the swollen head of him, the soft sensual pressure spiking his pulse and firing his blood. His every thought fragmented. Then her mouth opened wide and his vision blanked.

'*Pia...*'

He gritted his teeth as her lips slid down his erection on a soft suck, her tongue circling every sensitive nerve-ending.

Nic cried out, then bit his lip to stifle the sound. 'Pia... you need to slow...stop.'

Somehow his hand had taken on a life of its own and he weaved his fingers into her flaxen hair and gently thrust into the slick heat of her mouth, begging her to make love to him harder, faster, and he lost it—let his head fall back onto the cushioned leather and undulated, gasping at the wicked pleasure of it all.

What she was doing to him in the back of a limo...what people could see if the windows weren't tinted—Pia was driving him out of his tiny mind. And without warning it was all suddenly too much. Electricity charged his skin and his hair stood on end as his body tensed, the power rising like an unstoppable wave.

'Pia...too much... I'm going to... You need to move. *Now.*'

But she didn't move, only gave a tiny whimper and a groan of unadulterated pleasure that vibrated down his groin. And that was it. His entire body seized as his orgasm hit him like a crack of thunder, the sensation both unexpected and anticipated, and mind-numbing pleasure reverberated outwards, stealing his breath.

Heart pounding in his ears, his harsh rasping breath filled the stifling air as he scrambled for his brain to kick in.

When he figured he could talk again, or at least try, he swallowed. Hard.

'That was incredible. *You* are incredible.' Nic reached down and hauled her back into his lap, then buried his nose in her hair and clutched her to him. 'I want you naked and in my arms and in my bed. I want to hear your cries echo through the room, and it has nothing to do with any deal or bet or power-play. Screw the meeting, Pia, let us have this night.'

He'd find some other way to get to Zeus—without using her. He couldn't do it. He wanted something honest and real with her, and taking away their deal was the only way.

She eased back and the streetlights flickered over her exquisite face as he watched her confusion morph into a sweet kind of happiness.

'You mean it?' she whispered. Hopeful. Beautiful.

'Every word.'

With a glorious little smile she kissed him, soft and slow. It was almost shy, distinctly vulnerable, the way she needed to keep touching him.

Nic kept a tight hold of her, tasting himself on her tongue, luxuriating in a tender intimacy he'd never known. Especially after an act so sensually erotic. But then he'd known from the first that she would turn any idea in his head upside down and shake it up. She was unpredictable, and that was the one thing he loved and feared most about her.

His revived need was a living, breathing ball of fire, burning his patience to cinders, and he worshipped her, lavishing patient moist affection over every millimetre of soft, scented pearly skin he could reach.

Pia gripped his upper arms—each nail a brilliant half-moon of perfect agony—and just as he tilted sideways and rolled her onto her back across the wide seat the car shuddered to a stop.

'*Gracas a Deus.* Perfect timing.'

Hovering above her, Nic revelled in the way she arched her back and tipped her head in a non-choreographed compulsion of pure obedience. He knew exactly what she wanted—Nic to take control, to show her the kind of earth-shattering pleasure he'd promised.

Reaching up, she cupped his face and confirmed it. 'I want you so much, Nic. I want you to need me, take me, make me feel like you said I would.'

'No pressure, then.'

She laughed, the sound so glorious he knew there was no place he'd rather be—and that wasn't only astounding, it was terrifying.

'Just take it all away. Melt the ice inside me. Make me feel alive, just once.'

I want him. Need him so much. It was laughable, because as if any need this elemental was really a choice.

It was a beautiful, terrible desire—one she'd sworn she'd never let herself feel again. In truth, she could hardly compare what she had with Nic to her past—it was like water to wine—but it was a door that led to heartache. Not the loving kind but the using kind—the kind that made her feel cheap and worthless. So she'd sealed herself off, determined never to reopen herself. Yet here she was, opening up once more.

But he'd said no deal. That this was no game. To forget about tomorrow and live for tonight. If he wanted her that much it must mean something. *Had* to.

Tomorrow she'd give him Zeus and he would trust her. They would talk and together they'd find a way to figure it all out.

Pia was strung so tight the slightest pluck on her strings resonated, and when the elevator doors pinged shut she flinched. But Nic was right there, cinching her waist, lifting her up until she was level with his mouth and kissing her with thrust after languorous thrust of his tongue, licking into her mouth, taking her higher and higher, until she was a floating cloud of sensation.

'Wrap your legs around me, *bonita*, let me feel you.'

She did just that and ground her pelvis against him—the aftershocks sending rippling shivers down her spine—while she kneaded the hard ridges of his upper back.

Nic nuzzled down her throat, across the bare skin of her chest, dropping moist, luscious kisses across the curve of her breast where it swelled above her bodice, breathless in his need.

'I need to see you.'

That was the only warning she got before he lowered her to the ground and pushed the red satin straps off her shoulders.

'I'm so hungry for you I could eat you alive.'

A dizzying pulse of excitement made it difficult to think, but if any doubts lingered his answering passion razed them to the ground.

In a red blur, fabric swished down her body and pooled on the floor. And when Nic took a step back to gaze down at her, displayed under the harsh light, she shook inside, wanting to cover herself up. She wasn't as lithe as his usual conquests, not so toned, not so sculpted, more soft and generous.

'*Dios*, Pia, look at you. You take my breath away.'

Tentatively she lifted her chin, and what she saw in his eyes melted the final shards of ice in her heart. Reverence. Ferocious desire.

With one finger he reached out and drew a line from her collarbone down the deep cleavage of her breasts—*thank you, push-up lacy bra*—and farther still over the slight rise of her stomach to the dip of her panties.

He let out a low rumbling groan. 'You're killing me, here. Those sexy stockings and seams. I am keeping them on, *querida*, and licking up every line. Turn around.'

The command in his voice was unmistakable—wrapped in silk and satin and awe and tenderness, but there nonetheless.

Her panties sliced across her cheeks and she gave another little thank-you for bum squats as she gave him what she hoped was a seductive look from beneath her eyelashes and turned, arms spread wide, palms flat to the mirrored wall.

Never had she felt so confident, so provocative, so sexual, so insanely turned on.

'Heaven help me,' he growled. 'I think I've just come again.'

She laughed—she couldn't help it—and watched his reflection, the heat in his eyes, the desire that made her blood thicken in her veins. But there were other emotions there too. Affection, and a pride that made her giddy heart leap to her throat. For a moment she considered that this might mean far more to her than was wise.

Then he was on his knees and fulfilling his promise—kissing up her stocking seams, his lips as soft and teasing as the touch of a feather—and she trembled where she stood.

Her hot panting breaths steamed the mirror and she watched her own eyes grow heavy and slumberous as he went higher, higher…reaching the bare pinch of skin where her thigh met her bottom.

'Nic?' Tremors ran up her legs and gathered at the soft folds of her femininity. Her inner walls clenched with an unbearable need for something inside. *Nic* inside her. Filling her up. Making her whole. *'Please.'*

He nudged her legs wide and she cursed the stilettos making her teeter as his dextrous fingers slipped forward to stroke her where she was hot and wet and— 'Oh, my God, Nic!'

'So close,' he murmured, kissing the nape of her neck. 'But I won't let you come yet, Pia. I forbid it. You have to wait until I'm deep inside you.'

'I hate you,' she whispered adoringly.

His dark chuckle was interrupted by the *ping* of the elevator doors and the sharp noise was the final pluck on her nerves. Her legs buckled beneath her.

'Whoa, *bonita*. Oh, no, you don't.' Nic swept her into his arms, held her against his chest and strode into the penthouse, down the hall to his bedroom—where he laid her in the centre of his huge satin-drenched bed.

She writhed in pleasure as his gaze soaked up her sumptuous black bra, skimpy chiffon panties and stockings.

'Now, *that* is a picture I will never forget,' he said, his voice thick with passion as he stripped in front of her, shameless in his skin.

Those hot eyes were burning, threatening to incinerate her where she lay breathless, waiting for his muscled physique to come into view.

He was so fabulously tall that from her position on the bed she felt as if she was staring up at the cathedral in the square.

Lascivious and wolfish, the smile on his mouth was as heady and thrilling as the need etched tightly across his gorgeous face. And the last vestige of her sanity went the way of his snug hipsters when he took himself in his hand, circled his fingers and brushed his thumb across the head of his erection in a way that made the air whoosh out of her lungs.

He was winding her up like a musical toy, and the coiling tension became so acute she almost feared the inevitable striking chorus of release.

Softness came up to swallow her back as hardness descended from above and she found herself sandwiched between heaven and hell.

'What am I going to do to you first, *querida*?' He unlaced the ribbon bows of her panties, tied at her hips, and tugged the lace free.

Just the pull of the fabric against her folds tore a whimper from her throat. She didn't care what he did as long as he did *something*.

'I think you are too close for more play, Pia,' he growled as he lavished her with more kisses across her collarbone, up her throat.

Pia twisted, nuzzling his face to find his mouth, and at the first thrust of his tongue between her lips her heart pitched.

She strained towards him, canting her hips, bowing her whole body, while her emotions whiplashed from wanton desire to wholehearted devotion. 'Make love to me like you promised,' she begged. 'Please, Nic. *Please.*'

'*Dios,* Pia, you are on fire. Burning up.'

He pushed her down into the mattress, pinned her beneath his body, his hands forming sweet warm shackles about her upper arms, and pushed inside her in one long, hard, powerful thrust. And—*oh, yes!* She revelled in the wicked slide into oblivion.

Their eyes locked—his stunned whisky depths meeting awestruck violet-blue—as they shared one breath, the moment so profound she wasn't surprised to feel a tear escape the corner of her eye.

Right then it occurred to her that she'd just made a fairly spectacular misjudgement. One night would never be enough and she'd dream of this man always.

Gazing down at her, Nic brushed damp hair back from her forehead and the tenderness of the gesture wrenched her already wide open heart. So she turned her face to hide in the crook of his neck and breathed deeply.

'No, Pia, don't do that. Don't hide from me. Not tonight.'

'I…' *I need you.*

As soon as she obeyed him and glanced back up he began to move—slow and shallow at first, teasing her to a cataclysmic high—until she was writhing beneath him and his thrusts became deeper, harder, more powerful than anything she'd ever known. Until where Nic ended and she began was the ebb and flow of an erotic wave of pleasure.

She wanted to touch his skin, feel the flexing muscle of

his ripped body beneath her palms, but those sweet warm shackles only moved upward to hold her wrists above her head with one of his large hands. The other skimmed down her cheek, farther down her throat and over her chest, to cup her breast and squeeze the aching flesh.

A desperate moan blistered the air—his or hers, she wasn't sure, didn't care—as he rubbed over her nipple, then sucked the tight peak into his hot mouth.

'Nic… Nic…' She chanted his name over and over and it seemed to fuel his inner fire. Not to move faster but to slow, as if he knew she was close and wanted to prolong the agonising pleasure.

'One more minute—then I will let you fly.' His voice shook, his hands were unsteady from holding himself back, and she realised he was in as much pain as she was.

'Nic…*please*.'

'So beautiful,' he murmured, still moving at that maddening pace, keeping her on the edge of a shattering fall.

Pia dipped her chin, silently begging for his mouth, and he gave her what she wanted—*needed*—and simultaneously thrust his tongue into her mouth and slammed his hips forward with a tiny undulation that rubbed her sweet knot of nerves once…twice…

'Nic!'

'Now you may come. *Now*.'

Lightning bolts of sensation gathered in her core like a bright white pinpoint of light—a star about to go supernova—and the cry that tore from her throat felt wrenched from her soul.

Bursts of pleasure shot outward and those streaks of lightning tore down her spine and crackled along her nerves with an almost spiteful ferocity—the sheer intensity stealing her breath and holding her on an erotic plateau that made her vision blank, her mind faze out and life cease to exist for long, endless moments.

She came to as Nic released the shackles from her body

and soul and rose above her, chasing his own nirvana. He captured her lips in a deep kiss that was tinged with desperation. Held her with a reverence she'd only ever dreamed of, making her feel accepted and worthy and wanted beyond reason. So perfectly *herself* that falling was inevitable.

His cries were wrecked and ravaging as his orgasm tore him apart and Pia licked at his lips to taste his pleasure—pleasure *she* had given him—ecstasy he'd found only in her.

His glorious weight descended and she felt safe and cared for, and cherished in the crush. And she knew it was coming—was powerless to stop it.

The overwhelming cacophony of emotions—joy and fear and adoration and amazement—refused to be ignored, and they rose up within her and escaped in a breath suspiciously close to a sob. Nic gathered her in his arms and held her with fierce strength—stronger than a mighty god. Almost devout. It was the culmination of such an amazing night that she wished she could freeze the moment in time for ever.

CHAPTER TWELVE

Who'd have thought Nicandro Carvalho was a cuddler?

Pia smiled, reminiscing about the way he'd followed her around the bed like a heat-seeking missile. When he hadn't been making love to her, that was. One minute he could be deeply intense and dominating, his lovemaking so powerful it wrought tears, and the next he was light-hearted and fun, making her laugh out loud with teasing touches and that wicked, incorrigible grin. He thought nothing of saying something outrageous mid-thrust as he took her against the wall or pleasured her on his knees. She'd never imagined couples could make love in so many different ways. But, then again, maybe that was just Nic. Maybe only he could be like that.

The high of the night still rushed through her veins but there was a dark cloud closing around her, obscuring her euphoria, obliterating her joy. It was over. Time to get back to the real world, check on work, unveil the truth and tell Nic exactly who she was.

Pia eased from his hold and slipped from the bed with a slight wince, deliciously sore and tender. She told herself not to look back, only forward. Yet still she couldn't resist one glance at the sheets that held the impression of their lovemaking and the beautiful tall, dark man who'd taken her to heaven.

Heart heavy, she snuggled into a soft fluffy robe and wandered into the kitchen for her early dose of caffeine.

Ten minutes later she sat at the glass-topped table, coffee in hand, her laptop open at the financial section of a Saturday newspaper.

Eros had taken another kicking, she noticed, feeling the punch of it in her stomach and an after-ache of dread.

Pia flipped through the pages to check Merpia. Looked okay. Back to the stock exchange…flick, flick, flicking the pages—

Her fingers stilled on the keys. She backed up—heart thumping—sure she'd seen his name… *Nic's name…there.*

Goldsmith stock climbs as a merger in matrimony with real estate magnate Nicandro Carvalho is revealed.

What?

Fingers now flying, Pia jumped from one site to another through various links, with a sickening fear that instead of being poised for flight into a brave new world, she'd propelled herself well past the edge, no wings in sight, and was about to plunge into a black void that would swallow her whole.

Somehow she ended up in the New York society pages, her throat so tight she couldn't breathe, her heart beating so hard and fast she could barely see, let alone read the words.

Carvalho out and about in Barcelona with a mystery blonde.
Goldsmith heiress leaving the Fortuna mansion under cover. Hiding tears?
Billionaire Nicandro Carvalho at his nightclub in Barcelona with a new playmate. Who could she be?

'Oh, my God,' she breathed, her fingers fluttering over her mouth, the tears scorching the backs of her eyes making the hideous photograph of her and Nic distorted and blurred. She looked like a tramp. She looked like the whore her father had told her she was—and, goddammit, she felt like it!

And that girl—the girl Nic was apparently marrying—looked genuinely devastated as ravenous newshounds circled her, ready to catch her fall on candid camera. Suddenly Pia was grateful for them, because she'd ignored the truth, convinced herself there was more between them. Instead she'd fallen under his spell, surrendered herself to him body and soul during his magnificent last act.

Hadn't she learned *anything*? Had the past taught her *nothing*? She was only good enough to use. Worthless for anything more.

Pia slammed the laptop down, bolted upright, sending the chair screeching across the floor, and stormed through the living room, headed for his bedroom, furiously brushing at her tears because she would *not* cry in front of him—she would not.

The shrill of her phone cast her to stone. The phone she'd been ignoring most of the night. Something she'd never, *ever* done before.

She didn't have to look at the caller. She didn't have to greet Jovan or say a word. Because in that moment she might not know the *why* but she certainly knew the *who*.

'Pia? Tell me you got my message—tell me you are *not* still with him.'

Self-loathing so thick she almost choked on it. Humiliation so sharp she almost cut herself on it. Pain so powerful it almost crushed her bones. Heartbreak so shattering she could hear her soul weep.

She could barely breathe for hating. Herself or Nicandro Carvalho, she wasn't sure.

'Pia, are you there? I still cannot believe he is alive. I was *there*, Pia. At the Santos mansion. I was *there*! Where are you, dammit?'

'In bed with the enemy. Am I not?'

CHAPTER THIRTEEN

Eiffel Tower—Monday six p.m.
Zeus will be there.

THAT HAD BEEN her goodbye. The only lingering tangible evidence to prove she'd been in Barcelona at all and that Nic hadn't lived a dream was the red samba dress, every shoe and scrap of clothing he'd ever gifted her and her black velvet scent on his skin.

Nic stepped out of the glass elevator on the top floor of the Eiffel Tower and walked to the railing, to stare unseeingly at the breathtaking architecture: the Arc de Triomphe, the Champ de Mars—on it went, along with the slow drift of the River Seine, everything that embodied Paris…the city of love.

Knuckles white, he gripped the iron bar as the scathing wind whipped through his hair and pierced his skin with needles of ice. His thick black overcoat with the collar up failed dismally to keep him warm as the shadows of the past had him in a stranglehold.

She'd seen the pictures splashed all over the news. She must have. All the damning articles about his upcoming marriage. A marriage he hadn't even fully committed to. *Yet.* And the way he was feeling right now, Goldsmith could go to hell.

Yeah, right, Nic. You want Santos Diamonds so badly you'd deal with the devil himself.

He squeezed his eyes shut and raked his palm over the hard ridges of his aching stomach, trying to ease the pain of an all-encompassing sadness. One night with Pia and nothing looked the same. Pushing inside her had somehow been the most perfect, most important, most heartbreaking thing he'd ever done.

He'd never pictured a world where his need for revenge would collide with his heart to mingle and smear together, distorting his views, until the future looked vague and devastating.

'Hello, Nicandro.'

His heart stopped.

His first thought: she'd broken her written word. Zeus wasn't coming.

His second thought came hard on the heels of that, because deep down he knew Pia would never break her word. It was sacred to her. So when realisation hit his eyes sprang open to land on her statuesque frame—flaxen hair pinned back, designer powerhouse black suit, long cream cashmere coat, lips coated in armour, eyes glacially cold.

The ice queen was back, and that was more devastating than the implications of what he faced.

Had he been played all along? A first-class double-cross?

Snippets of conversation, visions of business papers and the ultimate feminine power flashed through his mind and, like pieces of a complex conundrum, all slotted into place, fitted together to create a perfect picture of truth.

Dios, he'd been so blind.

The realisation grabbed him by the throat and he found he could barely speak past the iron fist. 'Good evening, Olympia. Or should I say *Zeus*?'

'You may call me anything you desire, Mr Carvalho, while I hear the truth.'

He smiled ruefully as his entire world shifted beneath his feet. 'Is Antonio Merisi dead?'

'Yes, he is.'

Thirteen years. Thirteen years of waiting for his chance to ensure Antonio Merisi felt even a tenth of the pain Nic or his *avô* or indeed his parents had felt gone with three little words and a contingency he'd never have considered in a million years. But why would he have when Zeus's name still lingered on people's lips?

Olympia Merisi. Zeus.

Nic was sure he should feel something. Anger. Rage. Hatred. The need to lash out and scream at the injustice of it all. Except his whole body was devoid of sensation. He was numb. Nic supposed the only saving grace was that the toxic wrangle of emotions Pia had left inside him had been numbed too.

'He died of a heart attack four years ago. I now own and control his companies, as well as my own—and let's not forget Q Virtus.'

Knowing what was coming, he lifted his eyes to hers and locked on to those chips of ice.

'Do I have *you* to thank for the revolt that has brought my club to its knees, Nicandro?'

'Yes.'

'Did *you* manipulate the stocks and shares at Eros International?'

'Yes.'

'Are you trying to annihilate my world, Nicandro?'

'Yes.' No point denying it. Every word was true. 'Except it wasn't *your* world, Pia. Not in my eyes.'

'Oh, but I think it was. You knew I was inextricably linked, regardless. Let's not open the doors to the past just yet. Let us pretend my father is here to answer for his sins. What have *I* ever done to you? What heinous crime could *I* have committed for you to take revenge on my body and on my world?'

'Not you *per se*, Pia. This was not person—'

'Do *not* tell me this was not personal, Nic.' Fire had

obliterated the ice in her eyes until they were a deep violet-blue. 'You made it personal when your mouth touched mine. You made it personal when you held me down and took my body.'

Closing his eyes, he swallowed. Hard. He wanted to deny it, but what good would that do? At the heart of the matter she was right. She was simply laying out the facts in all their stone-cold merciless glory. He could tell her he hadn't known her at the start. He could tell her he'd fought with his conscience. But at the heart of the matter she was still right.

'You're right, of course. The moment I saw you, found out you were his daughter, my mind was set. Destroy him and take from you as he took from me.'

'And what did my father take, Mr Santos?'

'My entire world.'

'Yet here you stand, a new man.'

Right then he realised what she'd said. *Santos*. 'How…?'

'While I was falling into your deceitful practised arms Jovan was digging into your real world. I asked him to check out Santos Diamonds back in Zanzibar. The way you looked at me when I was wearing that necklace…with such vitriol…it wouldn't leave me. Would you believe he actually lied to me too, that day? Something that will take me a long time to get over.'

She'd trusted Jovan implicitly. Had started to trust Nic. Then the bottom had fallen out of her world. So now here she stood, unable to trust a living soul.

The implications of what had happened to her were hitting him as hard as the bullet that had pierced his back all those years ago.

'He said he had no idea what had happened to Santos Diamonds. Turns out he was right there all along.'

Nic frowned deeply. 'At the house? No.' He shook his head vehemently. 'I would have recognised him.'

But would he have? Thirteen years was a long time

to pass without any physical changes. Nic hadn't had the greatest viewpoint of the room back in the Santos mansion, and what was more when they'd met in Zanzibar he'd been too busy fighting Othello's green-eyed monster to see past Jovan's relationship with Pia.

'He was there. He thought you'd died that day.'

Nic thought he'd heard a chink in her icy armour, but when he glanced over she wasn't even looking his way and her cold façade remained unreadable, unreachable. *Dios*, it was heartbreaking. All her laughter, all her smiles, all that fire in her eyes and in her soul gone. Destroyed by him.

Self-loathing sucked his throat dry. When had he become a man he barely recognised? The kind of man who would wreak his revenge on an innocent woman. Had the years of rage and resentment, the obsessive fixation on vengeance, left him so callous, so cold?

'I know my father played dirty with yours. I know your parents died that day, and I am—' Her voice *did* crack then, and he watched her throat convulse. 'Truly sorry for your loss. For all of it. But that's all I know—and considering Jovan was outside until almost the end that's all I ever will know. You have my oath that I will not breathe a word. I only ask that you speak to Jovan for a moment or two. He was under orders to be there and retrieve the debt and I believe what happened has haunted him ever since. He would like to apologise, to explain…'

Her voice didn't just crack—it disintegrated.

And why shouldn't it?

She'd just found out her father had been no more than a greedy, ruthless common crook. A man who'd sent his scapegoats to collect on a bet that he himself had rigged. All because he'd wanted Santos Diamonds. Nic would hazard a guess she didn't even know he'd hailed from the Greek mafia. She was likely standing there wondering if she'd known her father at all. In the space of twenty-four hours Nic had betrayed her, her trust for Jovan had faltered and her father—the man she'd thought she'd known—had died another death in her heart. Was it any wonder she was frozen to the core?

His body flooded with sensation, the agony returning fifty-fold and he reached for her, cupped her beautiful face. 'Pia. *Bonita*, I am so sor—'

She wrenched away, taking a large step back, and he watched her blink furiously. 'Please don't touch me. I don't even know who you are.' She bit down on her lips and closed those stunning violet-blue eyes for a beat or three. 'I have no idea who I shared a bed with. What was deceit and what, if anything, was truth.'

He could taste her misery in his heart and he wanted to choke on it. Could hardly speak past the lump in his throat. 'Pia…*please*, let me explain.'

'No, I… Jovan is waiting in a black limousine at the base of the Tower, if you'd like to speak to him, and I sincerely hope that you find happiness in your…'

Her chest quaked, as if she was holding back a sob, and it tore at his heart.

Then she whispered, 'Goodbye, Nic.'

Head high, she turned her back on him and walked away.

CHAPTER FOURTEEN

DARKNESS HAD FALLEN over Paris.

Glittering with dazzling promise, lit with elegant flair, the Eiffel Tower stood tall and magnificent, the perfect image from a romantic storybook, ignorant of the fact that Pia's heart had shattered on its top floor.

Suitcases stood by the door of her suite and Pia shoved the last of her business papers into her briefcase and pulled the zipper shut.

If she'd thought the aftershocks of her last affair were bad, they were sugar-coated candy compared to this. This bone-deep sorrow. This heart-wrenching pain. This anger and self-hatred that simply wouldn't cease.

She'd been woefully unprepared for the chaos Nic was capable of unleashing, but as she'd torn down the walls and released all the terrifying implications it had become clear that Q Virtus was no more. Her one promise to her father and she'd failed to keep it.

Pia collapsed on the sofa, surrounded by the caliginous gloom.

Ah, yes, her father. The brilliant and unpredictable scion of a long line of Greek *Godfather*-wannabes. That is, phenomenally wealthy, untouchable criminals.

And she hadn't known a damn thing.

How could that be? Yes, he'd been cold, hard, but she'd honestly thought he'd been honourable at his core. He'd taken her in, saved her life, and she'd spent years desperately trying to repay him and earn his pride. Such an arduous pursuit—because nothing she'd achieved, no amount of money she'd amassed, had been good enough. She'd still felt dirty, tainted. And right now that made her furious. How dared he call her trash when he'd lived such a life? At least she had honour, integrity. Wasn't that worth more than dollar signs?

A hard rap at the door yanked her from her ugly pity-fest and she shoved her arms into her coat, picked up her briefcase and went to catch her flight.

In swung the door and Pia swayed on her feet. Had to do a double-take in case her traitorous imagination had conjured him up from her basest fantasies.

No. He was here. At her door. In all his dark, brooding glory, wearing the same black overcoat and the same depth of pain in his eyes.

He seemed so tired. A profound exhaustion of the soul.

It shattered her heart all over again.

She'd never given a thought to the possibility that Nicandro Carvalho could be so damaged. His polish was usually so brilliant and bright; he shone like a guiding star. But now the gloss was rubbed away it had left something so marred and cold she could plainly see the evidence of his mortality in the rigid lines of his body, and it all made a bittersweet kind of sense.

Pia wanted to take him in her arms, stroke his hair and soothe his pain. A glutton for punishment, clearly. All along she'd been a means to an end. She'd let a man use her, play her, for the second and final time in her life.

Lifting her chin in the face of adversity, she found her voice. 'What are you doing here, Nic? I couldn't possibly have anything else you desire.'

Had he even wanted her in the first place? She had no idea. It had all seemed so real. She still couldn't believe how hard and fast she'd fallen under his spell.

'Can I come in for a few minutes, Pia?'

When she hesitated he begged her with his eyes.

'Please let me speak to you, *querida*. I need to explain. About Goldsmith too—you deserve at least that from me.'

Yes. Yes she did.

Leaving the door open, she walked through to the living area, leaned against the vast plate glass windows and crossed her arms to stop herself from reaching out, begging to be held, for him to take the pain and emptiness away. And what did *that* say about her? Not anything she remotely liked.

Through the shadows she watched him enter the room, his footsteps hesitant, vague, as if he was no longer sure of his place in the world. She guessed that might happen to a man who'd been so driven for thirteen years, only to have the rug pulled from beneath his feet at the final hour.

Pia hated her father right then. For ruining Nic's life. Stealing his parents, his dreams. All she had to do was remember the utter joy on his face at that boutique, playing ball with that gorgeous little boy, and she wanted to cry all over again.

Nic mirrored her position a few feet in front of her and leaned against the table.

'Q Virtus,' he said decisively, and it was the very last thing she'd expected.

'Ah, yes. The rumours leading to its downfall. Mostly true I would say—wouldn't you?'

'Yes, but unless we do something the club will fall. You must know that.'

'Of course I do, Nic. You've made it so that the members no longer trust me—and they have no idea who I even am.'

'Exactly. That's the answer, Pia. You have to show yourself. We need to fix it.'

'We?' She laughed bitterly. 'There is no "we", Nicandro, and I can't reveal my identity. I'll lose it all. Then again, what does it matter now? You've already made certain of that.'

The acerbity in her tone made her cringe, because if she was being honest she couldn't blame him. To lose so much all in one night. All because of her father's greed.

'The old rules of the club state that only a Merisi male can lead, and my past is such…' She swallowed past the rise of despair. 'It's dirty—you know that well enough. Listen, I don't blame you for this… Or maybe I do, but I don't hate you for it, or fail to understand your motivation. Nor do I want to see you ever again. So if that's all you came for—'

'Pia, *listen* to me.'

There it was. That commanding Carvalho tone that made her shiver.

'The old rules of the club are archaic—who better to change them than the woman who's made it more successful than ever before. *You* are the law, Pia. Change it! Stand in front of them and show yourself. Quash the rumours dead. I guarantee no one in his or her right mind will leave. Worst case scenario: a couple of the troglodytes pack up and go—who cares? I bet you good money that, for some, a woman at the helm they can trust is of far more import than the ghost of a man who is mired in filth.'

'My past isn't much better.'

'*Don't*, Pia.'

His voice turned hard, so dominant her blood fired through her veins.

'Do not lower your worth to his level. I will *not* allow it. Know what I think?'

'I never know what goes on in that head of yours, Nic. You're a closed book.'

'Not any more. Turn any page and I will read you a line.'

'I'm not interested.' *Liar.*

'I think you know you could've approached the members before now. No doubt you've convinced yourself you aren't good enough. You're ashamed of your past. I think your father made you that way instead of telling you to be proud of the woman you've become and to stand tall before them.'

He was truly intimidating when he was this way—brooding and torrid. Even his body was pulsating, telling her he wasn't in total control and that moreover he couldn't give a stuff.

Frowning deeply, she sifted through his words. Or she would have if he'd given her half a chance.

'Don't you see? That damn hypocrite is still controlling you from the grave. Not only do you work to the extreme, as if you're still trying to prove your worth to him, but you're *hiding*, Pia—behind a curtain of shame. When you're probably one of the richest, most successful women in the world.'

Stunned, she blinked over and over. He was right. She never stopped, was always working, and no matter her success it was never enough. Not for her. Why couldn't she just be proud of herself? Forget the past and move on?

'You brought the female members in, didn't you?' he asked, yanking her from her musings.

'Yes. I was trying to drag the place into the twenty-first century. But to say it hasn't been easy is an understatement.'

'It would be if you were a visible power to contend with. You have more strength and honour than most of the men I know. How you run the companies, the club…I have no idea, Pia.' He moved a little closer, out of the shadows and no one could miss the awe written over his face. 'I am so proud of you.'

Oh, God. 'Don't say that,' she said brokenly. *Don't make me think you care. Not again. I can't take it.*

Nic took another step towards her, reached up and cupped her face in his hands. Hands that weren't quite steady as he stroked over her cheeks with the pads of his thumbs.

'Nothing of what I felt about you, how I wanted you,

was a lie. I've never wanted any woman the way I crave you, Pia, and that is the truth. I never want you to believe you were nothing to me. *Ever.*'

Pia caught herself nuzzling into his hand, so skin-hungry, so desperate for his touch, so dangerously wanting to believe him. To trust in the sincerity darkening his eyes. And it was more than she could bear, because distrust lingered as if hope had been violated beyond repair.

'I think you should go.' She tried to steel her voice but heard the deep shift of higher emotion and knew he'd heard it too.

Leave. Please. Just walk away. Her heart was breaking. Why did she have to fall for a man who'd used her every step of the way? Who was apparently marrying another woman in ten days?

'Pia…' He softly kissed her temple, her cheek, and when he pulled back and looked down at her she felt the agony and torment in his expression in her own soul.

Suddenly words were spilling, tumbling, pouring from her mouth. 'I'm sorry you lost your parents that way. I'm sorry your dreams were stolen in the night. I'm sorry he destroyed that life. But I'm glad—*so* glad—you found the strength to stand tall and make another.'

Tears filled his eyes, pooling precariously. 'Pia…'

'Go. Marry your sweet bride. Be happy. As I will be.'

He jerked back as if she'd struck him and thrust his hands into his hair, ravaging the sexy mess. 'I haven't agreed to marry her! *Dios*, Pia. I wouldn't have slept with you if I had! I made Goldsmith retract the statement and say we were in talks, which is the truth.'

She had seen that, but reading it and hearing it from his lips were two entirely different things.

'Talks? A merger? Do you really want something so cold?' It didn't suit him at all. Didn't make sense. Unless… 'Do you love her?' It came out as a whisper, because even asking him hurt so badly.

Then. *Then* she knew. And emerging into the reality that she'd fallen madly in love with him was as stark and cold as being born, leaving her naked and shivering and utterly defenceless. How could she have been so stupid?

'No, I don't love her, Pia. Which is the entire point. I want Santos Diamonds for my grandfather—before I lose him too. I promised him.'

Pia frowned, trying to piece together what he was saying, but before she even had a chance to open her mouth and ask what the hell he was talking about he flung his arms in the air with all that Brazilian flair and passion she loved so much.

'And dammit, I don't want to feel like this!'

'This?' God, the look in his eyes. Torment. Utter torment.

'This…this *agony* when I look at you! This obsession to hold you in my arms. This craving to have you *now*. Like you are air and I can't breathe without you. This unnatural possessiveness that grabs me by the throat and makes my heart want to explode every time I touch you, kiss you, see your smile, hear your laugh and know it will be over any minute now.'

Her heart was beating so fast she was sure she'd pass out at any moment. Unsure what all that really meant.

He vibrated with a torrid combination of possessiveness, violence, sorrow and an almost desperate hunger. It all worked to pull her into a near fatal frenzy as the end of their game came into sight.

'Pia…'

Like a blistering storm he closed the gap between them, thrust his hands into her hair and crashed his mouth over hers, crushing, devouring.

She tried to pull back, she really did, but it was the first time she'd felt anything close to alive since she'd left him.

The salt of his tears exploded on her tongue and in the back of her mind, though she knew he was using her once more in order to feel something other than pain, she let him take and take and take. Bury his sorrow, his anger, deep inside her.

Somehow they made it to the bed, just skin against skin, frantic, desperately trying to soothe. And then he was moving inside her—one minute slow and somehow devout, the next angry and ferocious as he ran through a tumult of emotions and unleashed them all on her body one by one.

Murmurs filled the air—some she could neither hear nor understand, others so heartbreaking she was on the verge of tears.

'It wasn't meant to be this way,' he whispered against her throat, before inhaling her scent deeply.

This wasn't making love or sex; this was Nic ripping her soul out of her body with his goodbye.

'Please tell me I haven't hurt you.'

Then her own tears came, and she clutched him to her so he wouldn't see her own heartache drawing lines down her temples, down her cheeks.

'You haven't hurt me. You could never hurt me,' she breathed, the lies spilling from her as easily as the tears.

'I would die first,' he vowed as his climax raged through his body.

Pia followed him into the light, that supernova burning bright, only for it to flicker and die as if it had never been.

And when she woke he was gone, leaving the cold seeping into her heart once more. Frozen to the core.

CHAPTER FIFTEEN

Avô tapped him on the shoulder and Nic jolted back to the present. Though he'd swear he could still feel her petal-soft skin, taste her rich, evocative scent on his lips.

He'd hoped the craving would have paled by now, ten days on. Lust could burn—Nic knew that. But he'd never felt it threaten to incinerate every rational part of him. Obliterate all the careful shields he'd built to make him a functioning member of society, leaving this savage, beastly Neanderthal filled with need and want.

He spun round and thrust a glass of cognac to Matteo Santos, all the while drinking his own in one powerful mind-numbing shot.

'There is a parcel here for you—just arrived. Open it.'

Nic didn't even glance towards the antique monstrosity of a table in Goldsmith's study. 'No. Let Eloisa open the gifts.' Women liked that kind of thing, and she'd made no bones about the fact that wealth and security were her reasons for marrying him. Nic wasn't interested.

He watched the marquee rise up beyond the leaded windows and for the first time wondered what kind of husband he would be.

Fair? Definitely. Supportive? He'd try his very best. Loving? Honourable? Was it faithful to marry one woman and dream of another? The woman who'd left him suffocating in the smouldering ashes of an incomprehensible wanting. It struck him as a kind of cheating all on its own.

'It is not a wedding gift.'

'Have you suddenly developed psychic abilities, Avô?' He was being as facetious as hell today, but he knew what was coming. Knew he couldn't avoid it any longer. Not when Avô had finally cornered him in the same room.

One grey eyebrow arched. Dark brown eyes glittered with annoyance. 'You are not too old for me to whip your hide, boy.'

As if. Matteo Santos had never done so much as flick his ear.

'I want to know what the blazes we are doing here, because from where I'm standing you look like you have another gun to your head—and I am getting too damn old and cantankerous to pick you up again.'

'I did not ask you to pick me up last time.' Even as he said it he cringed with self-disgust at the disrespect and ingratitude of those words. But, *Dios*, he was dying here. Dying as conflict and turmoil roiled in the darkness of his mind. Spectres of anger and regret were circling like vultures, ready to feed off his soul.

'No, I damned well *made* you. Told you to get up and walk again and not let the bastards win. Told you to find something to live for—'

'And I did.'

'Yes.'

He gave a bitter laugh that raked over Nic's skin like the claws of a feral cat.

'Revenge. I know fine well what drives you, my boy. Always have. And I let you, probably even encouraged it, just so you'd take one step, then two. Then four, then ten.'

Avô's voice cracked and Nic felt it in his bones.

'Just so you'd eat and sleep and wake. So I would not lose you too.'

The old man's eyes started filling up and Nic's heart lurched—the first movement it had made, its first sign of life since he'd left Pia, beautiful and warm and safe in her bed.

'And I am grateful, Avô,' he said brokenly.

'Are you really?' he demanded. 'Because from where I'm standing you're just choosing a different kind of death. A longer torture and a slower suffering. You may as well have died on that floor with my glorious girl and her useless husband.'

One fat tear trickled down Avô's cheek and it broke the dam inside him.

His voice was so thick with pent-up emotion it shook, barely audible even to his own ears. 'I only wanted to give you back what you lost. Santos Diamonds. The lost Santos Empire.'

'Excuses.'

White-hot anger filled him. 'No!'

'Yes! You are *not* your father!'

Nic braced his weight off the stained glass windows and blasted the weather pundits who had lyricised for days about this perfect sun-drenched day, clear and calm and hot enough to fry *huevos* on the pavements. Instead the sky was a bruised swirl of black and grey, the atmosphere sharp with chaos as storm clouds thundered across the New York skyline like the wrath of the gods, ready to beat him with their displeasure.

'I don't want to discuss my father,' he said, loath even to think of that day.

'Maybe I do.'

'Please don't,' Nic begged. *Not now. Not today.*

'I lost my daughter, Nicandro, and you can't get her back. And if you do this I will have lost you too. You really think money and diamonds can redeem souls, mend hearts, replace love?'

Nic's mind gingerly touched the words.

Love? Was love like being in the rapture of heaven and

the torture of hell? No. Love was surely sweet and kind. Not possessive and obsessive madness. Unnatural.

The scepticism in his mind masqueraded as logic and argued vehemently with him.

Being with Pia in Barcelona hadn't felt unnatural. It had felt right. Heart-stoppingly perfect. It was when he was without her that it all went to hell.

Pia…

Her name spun inside him like a key tumbling a lock. Even his skin remembered her touch—like a kiss from a ghost.

Was it possible that he'd just walked away from the only woman he could ever truly love? And was Santos Diamonds worth giving her up for?

'No, I tell you!' Avô hollered across the oppressive stately room. 'It's impossible. So I ask you again—what are we doing here?'

'Goldsmith owns Santos Diamonds and his daughter is a suitable wife.' He sounded like an automated message.

'For many, I am sure. For you? Poppycock! As for Santos Diamonds—who cares? Let it go. You either continue to live in the shadows of the past or you break into a new dawn.'

Nic squeezed his eyes shut and bowed his head.

It suddenly became glaringly obvious that he was clinging to Santos Diamonds like a life raft, still desperately trying to reach the end game he'd worked so hard for. Because otherwise it would have all been for nothing and what did he have left?

Pia…you could have a lifetime of Pia, a little voice whispered. Taunting. Teasing. Coercing his heart to beat again. *If* she'd even consider having him after what he'd done to her. He still couldn't believe he'd taken her like an animal in Paris. He wouldn't be surprised if she never wanted to speak to him again.

'I'm scared,' Nic said, unable to let go of the possibility

he would some day turn into the man his father had become in the end. A monster.

'The other side of fear is freedom, my boy. Only when we are no longer afraid do we begin to live. This is your chance for true happiness. Let me see you happy before I go. Knowing there is someone in the world you cannot bear to lose and that you are not spending every single moment holding her to your heart is an unthinkable tragedy.'

Pia stood in front of the double doors leading to the boardroom, thinking how apt it was that she'd been living—*hiding*—in this darkness for so long.

Q Virtus members were gathered around the seventy-foot conference table. One chair was vacant and for that she was grateful. She was unsure if she would have had the strength to do this if Nic had been here. This morning the front-page headlines had been dominated by photographs of the happy couple at a gala dinner last weekend. They'd looked sweet together, she thought begrudgingly.

She should hate him for dredging up all of her loneliness and rage and feelings of worthlessness. For giving her hope of an unconditional love from someone who accepted her for who she was and where she'd come from. But the fact was, how could he ever love her? She had no breeding, like his wife. Her own father had ruined his family. Nic would never look at her with adoration—only resentment for the power of his desire for her. He'd made that clear in Paris.

And he must care for this woman he was marrying, Pia thought, to go ahead even after she'd sent him the package. It had taken her days, fighting with her conscience and her heart, to make a decision. Her head had told her to let him rot in a miserable marriage that was nothing more than a con. While her heart had loathed the fact that her father's actions had placed him at the altar to start with. In the end her heart had won out and she'd gone to visit his grandfather.

Pia couldn't help but smile at the memory.

Striking even in his seventies, the silver-tongued devil had trounced her at Gin Rummy, told her she had 'spunk' and kissed her goodbye. It would be very easy to love a man like that. More so because of his absolute devotion to Nic. He'd hugged her long and hard with tears in his eyes when she'd lifted her necklace—the Santos Diamonds—from the velvet cushion and given them to him.

The only gift her father had ever given her. Going in there, she'd thought it would wrench her apart to give them up. But it had felt so right—like fate. As if somehow she'd been led—by Nic—to this man to return his legacy and make good on the sins of the past.

Then he'd winked at her when she'd given him a note for Nic. One she'd rewritten over and over to make sure that no emotion lay between the lines. That her love didn't pour from the page. Telling him to ask Goldsmith exactly how much stock he owned in Santos Diamonds.

So as far as she was concerned the past had been put to rights. Now it was time to make good on the future. If Nic had given her anything it was the strength to do this. To be proud of the woman she'd become and stand tall before them.

Chin up, she took a deep breath, then another, trying to fight past the anxiety flurrying inside her as she walked down the hallway, concealed by the shadows. Then the double doors slowly opened before her, luring her forward, guiding her into the light.

Stunned gasps were a susurrus around her head and Pia could hear their surprise, feel their shock. This was tantamount to a revolution. This was their new beginning. And hers too. No more hiding. She'd blasted Nic for his dishonesty, his betrayal, but hadn't she too used subterfuge and chicanery to run this club? Yes, she had.

And now she wanted to draw off this last veil—to bring her whole self to the stage. She didn't want to be Olympia

Merisi, the tainted girl who had been groomed into the son her father had never had. She didn't want to sit in her ivory tower behind a curtain of shame and hide any longer. *And if the club falls?* whispered the little devil on her shoulder. Then she'd have done her utmost to be honest and true to them and to herself, and that was more important than upholding a vow to a man who'd thought nothing of destroying a family to fuel his greed.

Yes, despite everything she'd loved her father. He'd saved her, given her a future, but surely after twelve years her debt had been repaid.

This was for Pia.

She stood in front of a high-backed leather chair—a ludicrous throne she'd toss out at the first opportunity. She wouldn't lord it over anyone. In this room they were equals.

'Good evening, ladies and gentlemen,' she said, her voice strong enough to carry through the room as she looked every single man and woman in the eye, her heart steadying as her inner strength bolstered her will. 'I am Zeus. And I believe we have business to discuss.'

She hadn't seen him. Wouldn't even glance at his empty chair—a chair he'd asked Narciso and Ryzard to leave empty so as not to distract her. And Pia certainly didn't need to borrow his courage, even though he'd gladly give it for eternity, because she had the strength of a lioness all on her own.

What she needed was to be loved. Adored. Cared for and cosseted in the way only a lover could. She needed to laugh and smile, have piggybacks and wear jeans, go dancing and give Nic the power to make her feel alive. She needed *him*. Nic just had to convince her of that.

When he'd walked away from his shambles of a wedding all at once he'd wanted an entire future with her—afraid of nothing, side by side, walking into a new dawn to live their dreams. He wanted them fused and naked and damp between his sheets. And in the morning he wanted to kiss that face, cherish all that heart-stopping endearing beauty so tenderly she wouldn't wake, only turn to seek his lips, trusting him, loving him.

That was what he wanted. That was what he was here to beg for.

Nic watched her work the room, brewing and stirring the crowd like a cauldron until magic bubbled in the air. She declared the old laws null and void in this age of a new day, when women were becoming more powerful in their own right and could bring much to Q Virtus. She mentioned Ryzard's wife, Tiffany, who sat straight and tall beside her husband, a look of shock and awe on her face.

And she wasn't the only one. Every man in the room couldn't take his eyes off her, mesmerised by the power, the determination emanating from her. He only hoped to God *he* was the only one seriously turned on, because he had more important things to do than warn off suitors tonight. *Jealous, Nic?* Yeah, what if he was? Nic was his own man, comfortable in his own skin, and that would never change.

In a move that was simply genius, instead of leaving the way she'd come, exerting her influence and power, Pia made her way around to shake hands. One man. One woman. Equals in every aspect. A show of trust that no matter what had gone before her reign she would run the club with honour and integrity.

From the ashes of despair and the flames of fiasco she rose like a phoenix, and his chest felt crushed by the weight of his pride and love for her.

When the doors finally closed behind her she didn't look up to where he now leaned against the conference table, wood cutting into the base of his spine, aiming for a sexy, insouciant pose and royally messing it up by having a seriously bad case of the shakes.

Nic crossed his arms. To stop himself trembling or pulling her into his arms and demanding a second chance he wasn't sure. But if he had any sense—debatable, considering he'd just come from his own abandoned wedding—he would use a gentle hand to coax and lure.

His resolve was shattered when she slumped against the door, clearly fighting the urge to crash to the floor. But she wouldn't. He knew it.

'You were magnificent, *querida*.'

Up came her head, so quickly it smacked off the door—*ouch*. Then down she went, landing on her lush bottom with a soft thump.

Nic had to grit his teeth against the overpowering compulsion to grin at the effect he had on her, thanking his lucky stars it wasn't one-sided.

'What…what are you doing *here*?' she said, the snippy emphasis on 'here' accompanied by a messy arms-and-legs scramble to her feet.

Nic pushed off the table, let his arms fall to his sides and compared his nervous terror to the day he'd clambered from his bed, glaring at the rails that would teach him to walk again as if they were the devil's pitchforks and taking his very first step. He actually thought this was worse.

'Shouldn't you be…?' She wafted her hand around as if searching for the right words as she clung to the wall and walked around the boardroom, getting as far away from him as she could. 'On your honeymoon? In bed with your wife?'

Barely, he stifled the impulse to run over there and grab her. *Dios*, she was so beautiful she made him ache. 'Where are you going?'

'As far away from *you* as I can get. Are you going to answer my question?'

'People only tend to go on honeymoons when they're married, Pia.'

That stopped her. Barnacle-like, she clutched the hardwood panelling at her back.

And he'd had enough.

Nic strode forward purposefully.

'Stay right where you are, *Lobisomem*.'

'No.' He growled in frustration when she stepped forward and started to skirt around the table—on the opposite side to him. 'I'm going to spank you for that.'

'I'd love to see you try.'

He laughed wickedly and darted to the left.

Pia darted to the right and he growled again.

'Now, now, Nic—be serious.'

'Worried, *querida*?'

'Yes. I mean no. Stay back!'

'Lesson number one,' he said, lowering his voice to a commanding tone that he knew would make her shudder from top to toe. 'You are not the boss of me, Olympia Merisi, and when I tell you to stop, you stop.'

She sneered but it was a dire effort. 'Not in this lifetime. Now, run along to your bride and leave me be!'

'*Dios*, I have no bride!' Not yet, anyway.

'Oh? Realised she was marrying a wolf in sheep's clothing, did she?'

'No, she found out I was in love with someone else.'

'What? Who told her that?'

'I did.'

She blinked the confusion from her violet-blue gaze. 'Oh, I see. When you got my note and realised it was all a con you had to get out of it, right? Poor woman—you probably broke her heart.'

'I did not break her heart! Love was never in the equation. I— Wait a minute. Note? What note? And what do you mean *con*?'

She pursed those lush lips. 'You didn't receive my note this morning?'

'No. You wrote to me, Pia? What did it say? Tell me,' he ordered, his agitation at her avoidance ratcheting into the red zone.

Slowly she shook her blonde head. 'I don't think I will. Not until you tell me why you're here.'

His patience snapped and he launched himself atop the table, skidding over the highly polished surface on his backside and landing in front of her wide-eyed and stupefyingly beautiful face.

Then he backed her up until she slammed into the wall.

'Ah, this is much better. You know I prefer the personal touch.' Palms flat to the wall either side of her head, he buried his face in her neck and inhaled deeply.

Gracie de Deus. Finally.

Pia wriggled and pushed at his chest—quite hard, actually. Not that it moved him. They both knew it was a half-hearted effort. 'Why…why didn't you get married?'

Nic straightened up and cupped her jaw, dropping a tender kiss on her temple. 'Because one day I met an amazing woman I intended to wreak the ultimate revenge upon and she was unlike anything I'd ever known or seen before in my life. She scared me, and I'm a man who doesn't handle fear well, Pia. I told myself she was a means to an end and that I'd seduce her into my bed to reach my end game. What I wouldn't admit, even to myself, was that she was slowly stealing my heart.'

'She was?' Pia breathed.

He dropped another kiss on the tip of her nose. '*Sim.* Minute by minute. Hour by hour. Day by day. Until I didn't know what was up or down. Until every breath I took was for her.'

She gazed up at him with a little pleat in her brow. 'Then why…?'

'Why did I leave you lying in your bed while my heart was breaking?'

'Yes.'

'Because I didn't want the same kind of marriage as my parents. My father was obsessed with my mother. Possessive beyond control. My father fired the first shot in that room, Pia. He killed my mother.'

Shock flared in her eyes. 'Oh, my God.'

'My father lost Santos in a rigged deal at Q Virtus—you know that bit. But what you probably don't know is that it was my mother's money—my mother was the Santos heir. My father even had to change his surname to take control. Which he did without question, because he was obsessed with her. But it was an unhealthy kind of love. He often stalked her when she went out. Flew into jealous rages when they got home if she'd even spoken to another man while they were out together. Screaming matches would last for hours. He even locked her in the attic once so she couldn't go out. But the more he pushed her the more she rebelled—and let me tell you she was a reckless, zesty woman to start with. So volatile, Pia. All of it…'

'Sounds like my childhood,' she said, her gaze dropping to the open collar of his black shirt. 'Volatile.'

'I know, *bonita*,' he said, curling one hand around her nape and holding her close for a long. precious moment. 'Is your mother still alive?'

'No, she died of a drug overdose a couple of years ago. I never saw her again after she left me outside my father's house. He gave her fifty thousand dollars to disappear and in a way I felt as if I owed him.'

Nic could hear the pain of being abandoned and the sorrow in her voice at what might have been if her mother had been a different kind of woman.

'I take it your father never married her?'

Pia shook her head.

'Once a Santos marries that's it. Stuck for life. Which was the problem with my mother and father. There's a myth—a legend based around the necklace. The Heart of the Storm. It says only a true intended Santos can wear the jewels or provoke the wrath of the gods. Same if a Santos union is broken. Superstitious nonsense—that was my

retort. But the moment I saw them around your neck…
Looking back, a tiny part of me—one I had no intention
of acknowledging—had always known you were meant for
me, and I think they led me to you, Pia.'

Lips curved, she beamed up at him and his heart flip-
flopped.

'I think there was more than revenge on your mind back
then, Nic.'

'Yes, I know. Our fathers have a lot to answer for.'

Cinching her waist, he lifted her up and carried her to
a high-backed leather chair, where he sat with Pia straddling his lap. Then he tucked a stray lock of hair behind
her ear and went on.

'When my father lost the empire to your father and
Merisi's men came to take ownership of the mansion—the
necklace—my parents had a huge showdown. I walked in
and didn't know what the hell was going on, but my father
was getting more and more agitated. My mother was yelling, screaming that this was it, she'd had enough, she was
leaving him…' Nic closed his eyes, reliving the memory.
'He snatched the gun out of the pocket of one of Merisi's
men, turned and just…shot her in the heart. Right there in
front of me. Next thing bullets were flying, the room was
steeped in panic, and one of the henchmen killed him. I got
caught in the middle of it all. One bullet in the back and it
took me over a year to walk again.'

'Oh, Nic, I'm so sorry.'

'I needed something to live for, Pia. Finding your father,
making him pay for rigging that deal, for sending thugs
to my home to threaten our lives and pushing my father
to the brink… As far as I was concerned Antonio Merisi
had put the gun in his hand and virtually pulled the trigger.
Revenge was all I had to live for. And after that I wanted
Santos Diamonds. That was all I had to live for. Until you.'

'I wish you'd trusted me—told me all this. Now I understand why you'd marry her.'

'I just didn't want that kind of erratic marriage. Goldsmith's daughter is nice...timid; there'd have been no jealousy, no furious outbursts of possessiveness to shake the foundations of our home. No insanity to take one of our lives. But I was missing something in all this. I'm not my father. I am nothing like him.'

'No, you're not.'

'I am my own man.'

'Yes, you are.'

'And you—you are not my mother. Don't get me wrong, I adored the woman, but to marry a woman like her...?' He shuddered.

Pia smiled and shook her head in that way she did—as if he was past help. Where she was concerned, he was.

'But you know the downsides of a safe marriage, Pia? No passion, no adoration. No heart banging with one look. None of that weird bird-flapping in my chest. No violent tug when you're near that changes into a harrowing emptiness when you're gone, as if you're the other half of my soul. *Dios,* I was so proud of you tonight.' He wrapped her hands in his larger palms and kissed her thumb, her knuckle, stroked her hands over his cheeks, craving her touch all over his body. 'I've missed you so much, Pia. Felt I was dying without you.'

'I've missed you too,' she said, the words tremulous and watery as she leaned in to kiss him. Long and slow and deep.

Nic struggled to come up for air. 'That will be enough for me. Maybe you'll grow to feel more when I've gained your trust again, and I'll be grateful for that.'

'And maybe I've loved you from the start.'

He'd swear his heart paused in that moment. 'Maybe or definitely?'

'*Definitely*, definitely.'

Nic grinned as that heart of his floated to the ceiling. There was a God after all—

Hold on a minute…

'And yet,' he growled, suddenly annoyed with her, 'you were willing to let me marry another woman?'

She arched one eyebrow and gave him a load of sass. 'I gave you a choice. Something *I've* never truly had. Until tonight. Until I chose to come out of hiding. To stop living in my father's shadow. Just like you told me to. Ever since he died I've honestly thought I was free. Controlling my own life for the first time ever. But, like you said, he was still controlling me from the grave. I was still carrying the stigma of my past when instead of being ashamed I should've been even prouder of myself for what I've achieved. For coming so far.'

'Damn right you should.'

She leaned forward until the tips of their noses rubbed in an Eskimo kiss. 'You whirled into my life like a hurricane and showed me a taste of life outside the cage I was living in. Just the thought of stepping back into the darkness was more frightening than going forward into the light. So I decided that I'd give you all the facts and the choice was yours to make.'

'What facts?'

'That Goldsmith was trying to pull the wool over your eyes. He only owns forty-two per cent of Santos, Nic.'

'*What?* That dirty louse! I *will* flatten his unfortunate beak of a nose after all. That— Hang on—who owns the remaining shares?'

Her satisfied smile made her eyes sparkle. 'You do.'

'I think I would know this, *querida*.'

'Only if your grandfather told you that I signed my shares—my fifty-eight per cent—over to you at eight this morning. Santos Diamonds is back where it belongs. I gave him the necklace too—laid it right in the palm of his hand.'

Blinking, jaw slack, he stared at her until her words stopped caroming around his head like pinballs and he let them compute. Then she blurred in front of him. 'I don't believe it. You *love* me. To do that you must love me.'

She held his face and kissed away the tear that slipped down his cheek. 'Of course I do. With all my heart. I'm so surprised you didn't realise about the diamonds. You should know the majority shareholder would always keep possession of the jewels, Nic. Didn't you see that in Zanzibar?'

He shrugged helplessly. 'All I could see was you.'

She let loose a half-laugh, half-cry and wrapped her arms around his shoulders, holding him to her, blissfully tight.

'Marry me, Pia. Please,' he begged.

She squeezed him tighter. 'I'll think about it,' she said.

And while her tone was teasing he knew she was asking for some time. Time to learn how to trust him wholly, completely, and after everything he'd done he couldn't blame her for that. It would be torture, but he'd wait.

'And if I say yes I won't want you to take my name, Nic.'

'There is little chance of that, Pia. You'll be taking mine and there will be no arguments. Our power struggles will begin and end in the bedroom, *bonita*. With me in charge!'

She shut him up with another kiss—this one deep and passionate, messy with emotion and unbearable need— until he reluctantly pulled back to dive into her violet eyes.

'This is going to sound ridiculous, but it has been plaguing me and I…'

'What, *querido*? Tell me.'

'What can I give you, Pia, that you don't already have? That you can't buy for yourself?'

Tenderly, lovingly, she ran her fingers through his hair, brushing it back from his brow. 'Your heart, your gorgeous smile and the way you make me laugh. The way you make love to me. Take control.'

Her voice dropped, sultrier than ever, and she licked across the seam of his lips and undulated over his lap with a sinuous serpentine movement that made him hard in seconds.

'I love it when you make me fly. Only you can do that. Only you can take away the loneliness inside me, and when I sway only you can help me stand tall. Don't you see?' she whispered. 'I need you and I'd give it all up to have you always.'

Nic swallowed thickly. 'You would?'

'In a heartbeat. And maybe…one day…you can give me a baby so I can take her to football matches in my stilettos and shout at the referee.'

Nic cupped her lush backside and grinned. He could see her doing exactly that. 'Don't you mean him?'

She arched one flaxen brow. 'Girls can make excellent football players, Nic. There'll be no inequality in my house.'

'God forbid.'

He cinched her small waist, then smoothed upward to cup her perfect breasts. Where he lingered, toying with her through the layers of silk and lace until she flung her head back and moaned. He wanted rid of her shirt. *Now.*

'I can do all of that, Pia,' he promised, unveiling her pearly skin one button at a time and flexing his hips so she could feel his hard desire.

'Oh, you can?' she said, a little breathless, a whole lot turned on.

'*Sim.* Starting right now. I'm going to make you go supernova.'

'In the boardroom?' she asked, aiming for horrified. The flush in her cheeks ruined it. 'I'll never be able to have a meeting in here again.'

'Well, unless you have a bed upstairs, I'm not moving an inch. Ten days I've been without you. Never again.'

'My penthouse is upstairs. Take me there.'

'Oh, I'll take you, Pia. I'll take you to heaven and back. Then do it all over again. Every day of our lives.'

EPILOGUE

One year later...

'DON'T TELL ME...' Narciso smirked as he glanced up at the towering white sails that flapped in the breeze as the super-yacht schooner sliced through the South Pacific. 'Your wife of twenty-four hours *is* Ophion shipping.'

Nic grinned. 'Yep. Nice boat huh?'

'Boat...yeah. It would be very easy to feel emasculated by her power—good job you're the most self-assured, arrogant ass on the planet.'

'Sure is.' And after the best year of his life he was just as obsessed, just as madly in love, and it was the most awesome feeling in the world.

Narciso caught sight of his huge smile. 'I couldn't be happier for you, buddy. It's about time she made an honest man out of you.'

Nic curled his thumb and stroked over his thick platinum wedding band, glorying in the fact that he finally had his ring on her finger.

At first she'd kept him dangling from a great height, but he'd managed to keep the panic at bay, knowing she needed time to believe she could trust in his love. Then they'd been busy juggling corporate balls and building Q Virtus into the phenomenon it was today. No longer simply a gentlemen's club since Pia's unveiling had lured a multitude of highly successful businesswomen into its ranks. No longer steeped in archaic rules and masks of secrecy—at least not inside closed doors. Nic had no doubt the club would go down in history as the most respected of all time. Thanks to Pia and her courageous heart.

So this was the first chance he'd had to insist she became a Santos. Who would have thought the person he'd set out to destroy would become the very reason he lived and breathed?

Which reminded him…

'I believe I owe you something.' Nic delved into the pocket of his sharp black suit, lifted his fist and slowly unfurled his fingers.

One look and Narciso burst out laughing. 'A gold pig. I forgot about that. Well, she certainly brought you to your knees.'

'Who's on their knees?' Pia asked, her arm snaking around his waist as she sneaked up from behind.

Nic nuzzled at the soft skin beneath her ear and inhaled her black velvet scent. 'I will be. Later, *bonita*.' Easing back, before he dragged her below deck to their opulent satin-drenched suite, he took hold of her hand and gave a little tug until she twirled in the air. 'Or should I say Aphrodite?' He whistled long and low, glorying in the soft blush that bloomed in her cheeks.

'If I wasn't married…' Narciso muttered, ribbing him as always.

'I would tie you up below deck,' Nic tossed back. 'And—'

'Hey, that's my job,' Ruby said, joining their little cluster and giving Narciso a soft punch in the gut. 'And you *are* married, mister.'

'Blissfully, madly, deeply, devotedly married.'

Nic didn't miss the way Narciso splayed his hand over the slight swell of Ruby's stomach with an adoring possessive touch.

'Something you want to tell us, there, buddy?'

He winked with devilish satisfaction. 'Twenty-two weeks and counting.'

'Whoa—the next Warlock of Wall Street!'

Backslapping and congratulations lured Ryzard and Tiffany into the mix and the conversation quickly veered into a guessing game of 'Who will our children become?' And since Ryzard's firstborn had already made his introduction to the world Tiffany kicked off. Election-style.

'Early signs indicate Max will be equally predisposed to world domination as his father and grandfather.'

'Ah, yes,' Nic said. 'How is your father liking the White House?'

'More so when he has his grandson in his lap, I think. I'd bet good money that right now Max is crawling over his knee in the Oval Office, or he has the First Lady and her security detail catering to his every whim.'

'That's my boy,' Ryzard quipped, laughing as he tucked Tiffany into his side.

'As for our newlyweds here,' Narciso intoned with a wicked smirk. 'Nic tells me they're planning a football team.'

'What?' Pia spluttered.

Nic did his best to keep a straight face and failed dismally. 'I said no such thing—although it would be fun making one.'

Truth was they'd decided to wait, both of them needing to spend some time just the two of them, but he wasn't blind to the longing in those seductive eyes. She had her heart set on a honeymoon baby, so tonight was the night.

Pia's blush deepened, as if she knew exactly what he was thinking, and he got a smack for his lascivious mind that was basically an excuse for her to feel him up.

'I adore you,' he whispered, kissing the flaxen fall of her hair tucked behind her ear. 'With all my heart.'

'I love you too—so much. Sometimes I'm afraid I'll wake up.'

'No fears, *querida*. I'll always be right here by your side.'

She sought his mouth with her lips and it wasn't until he heard the ladies gasp that he managed to pull away from her addictive taste.

The yacht was manoeuvred into dock and even Nic's eyes widened at the view of the tropical island at dusk, their path lit by flaming torches, wending its way through lush vegetation towards the colossal mansion rising from the earth in palatial splendour.

Ryzard was the first to find his tongue. 'I've never seen anything like it. Welcome to Atlantis.'

Their new venture was based on the lost city—a luxurious ten-star resort steeped in mythology and the latest technology exclusively for members of Q Virtus. Their wedding party was the first to stay, and the yachts lining the harbour told him their guests had already arrived for the reception. Avô and Lily were among them—as healthy and full of life as ever.

Right on time a man with a golden tray appeared and Nic coerced everyone into taking a crystal flute.

Grasping Pia's hand, he raised his glass in a toast. 'To my wife, Mrs Olympia Carvalho Santos, for making me the happiest man alive. And to each and every one of you—thank you for being here to celebrate with us. It's a new dawn, my friends. And I wouldn't want to share it with anyone else.'

A chorus of, 'Hear-hear,' filled the air, and the champagne flowed well into the night as they all danced in their brave new world.

* * * * *

If you enjoyed this book, make sure you've also read the previous two instalments of THE 21ST CENTURY GENTLEMAN'S CLUB, *both already available:*
THE ULTIMATE PLAYBOY *by Maya Blake*
THE ULTIMATE SEDUCTION *by Dani Collins*

"Make a wish."

A kiss. In that moment all Luke wanted was to turn her to face him, to lean down and touch her sweet lips with his.

"Like to know what I wished for?" he asked, voice low.

Della's eyes drifted shut. "You're not supposed to tell. It won't come true if you do."

"Maybe," he said, his mouth so close to her ear that his lips brushed her lobe as he spoke. "But if you knew what the wish was, perhaps you'd grant it."

He pressed a light kiss on her neck, just below her ear. Della held herself still but didn't pull away. "I don't have any magical powers to grant wishes."

"I'm not so sure."

Rachel Bailey developed a serious book addiction at a young age (via Peter Rabbit and Jemima Puddleduck), and has never recovered. Just how she likes it. She went on to earn degrees in psychology and social work but is now living her dream—writing romance for a living.

She lives in a piece of paradise on Australia's Sunshine Coast, with her hero and four dogs, where she loves to sit with a dog or two, overlooking the trees and reading books from her evergrowing to-be-read pile.

Rachel would love to hear from you and can be contacted through her website: www.rachelbailey.com

Recent titles by the same author:

NO STRANGER TO SCANDAL
WHAT HAPPENS IN CHARLESTON…
RETURN OF THE SECRET HEIR
MILLION-DOLLAR AMNESIA SCANDAL

COUNTERING
HIS CLAIM

BY
RACHEL BAILEY

Published in Great Britain 2014
by Mills & Boon, an imprint of Harlequin (UK) Limited,
Eton House, 18-24 Paradise Road, Richmond, Surrey, TW9 1SR

© 2013 Rachel Robinson

ISBN: 978-0-263-24996-5

Harlequin (UK) Limited's policy is to use papers that are natural,
renewable and recyclable products and made from wood grown in
sustainable forests. The logging and manufacturing processes conform
to the legal environmental regulations of the country of origin.

Printed and bound in Spain
by Blackprint CPI, Barcelona

COUNTERING
HIS CLAIM

For Amelia.
For all the fun and love you bring.

One

With a final, fond look at the Melbourne skyline, Della Walsh stepped onto the boarding bridge of the *Cora Mae,* the luxury cruise liner she called home.

Ahead on the deck, she spotted a group of people in business suits clustered around a tall man with his back to her. She hesitated, assessing the crowd. All she could see of the man in the center was broad shoulders encased in a tailored business jacket, a straight confident bearing and hair of darkest blond that tapered in against his neck. But that was enough to draw her attention and keep it there. The ship's captain stood beside him and from various vantage points, beyond the grand foyer, groups of curious staff intently watched the interaction.

Which meant, most likely, the man in the middle of the action was *him.*

Luke Marlow, the man about to inherit the *Cora Mae,* had arrived.

Curiosity nibbling, she stepped into the foyer. Many senior crew members, including herself, had been invited to the reading of Patrick Marlow's will today, and all of them had one question uppermost in their minds—what would his nephew and heir, Luke Marlow, do with the ship once he had control? Sell? Refurbish? Interfere with the day-to-day running?

Della was probably more interested in their guest than most—she'd been hearing snippets of Luke's life from Patrick for years. It was possible she knew more about this man than she knew about some of her friends.

As she drew closer to the small crowd, she could hear Captain Tynan say, "We'll get that cut seen to straight away."

Luke Marlow held up a hand wrapped in what looked like a blue handkerchief. "No need. I'll run it under the tap and throw on a bandage."

The captain spotted Della. "Dr. Walsh! Good timing. Mr. Marlow has a cut that might need a couple of stitches."

She pasted a smile on her face, and stepped forward, prepared to offer medical assistance as if he was any other patient, not the man who would soon be her boss. "Good afternoon, Mr. Marlow. If you'll follow me to the medical suite, we'll take a look at your hand."

As she spoke, Luke Marlow slowly turned to her, his steel-gray gaze scanning her face before coming to land on her eyes. The air seemed to sizzle and spark; a wave of goose bumps rushed across her skin. Was she nervous because he held her future in the palm of his hand? Or was it his fallen angel's face—sculpted cheekbones, strong straight nose and sensual lips—that unsettled her? Whatever it was, the effect was unwelcome and she squashed it.

"Now that you mention it," he said thoughtfully, his

eyes not wavering from hers, "I think it might need stitches."

The captain nodded, satisfied. "I'll take care of your staff and a purser will collect you from Dr. Walsh's office and bring you to us when you're done."

As if in slow motion, the crowd parted and Luke Marlow covered the distance between them. He stood within touching distance, looking at her expectantly, and her heart thumped hard and erratically. Tall and charismatic, he filled her vision, making her breath come too fast, as if casting a spell over her....

Her smile slipped. This couldn't be happening. She'd vowed never to let herself feel attraction to a man again. Ever. And *this* man was about to become her boss. Perhaps determine her future. Refusing to give in to her body's blind response, she pulled herself to her full height—which leveled out in the vicinity of Luke's chin—and found that professional smile again.

"This way," she said, indicating the direction with her hand.

Luke inclined his head and stepped away from the dissipating crowd. When they walked farther into the foyer with its elaborate furnishings and chandeliers, she wondered if he noticed the eyes following him from every direction.

"Tell me something, Dr. Walsh," he said, his voice pitched somewhere between sexy-low and curiosity.

Steeling herself against the shiver that threatened to run down her spine at the timbre of his voice, she led him through the foyer, to the bank of elevators. "If I can."

"Is there always a group that size waiting to greet guests?"

The elevator arrived and after they stepped in, she

pressed the button for the third deck. "No, but then you're not an average guest."

He arched an eyebrow several shades darker than his hair. "What sort of guest am I?"

The only guest who's made my knees go weak. She paused for a long moment. He wasn't merely the only guest who'd affected her this strongly, he was the only *man* who had since… She shied away from the thought and schooled her features into casual ambivalence. "We've heard you'll likely inherit the *Cora Mae* today."

"Ah," he said and sank his good hand into his pocket.

He'd thought they wouldn't know? Patrick Marlow had made no secret over the years that he considered his nephew his heir. "Rumors travel quickly around a ship."

"Rumors?" That eyebrow rose again. "There's more than one?"

Three hundred and thirty people lived and worked on the *Cora Mae*. Some were seasonal staff who wanted to see the world. They tended to work hard and party harder. But there was a solid core of people who did more than merely live on board—they'd formed a community. This ship was their home. And both groups were alive with speculation and snippets of information about Luke Marlow. Patrick had often spoken to her about his only nephew, mentioning his privileged background, his success with Marlow Hotels and the respect he garnered in the business world. But those stories from a proud uncle hadn't prepared her for the toe-curling effect Luke had in person.

The elevator doors slid open and she led the way down a narrow, carpeted corridor while the man in question waited patiently for his answer. "Several rumors," she acknowledged, "most of which probably have no basis in fact."

"Humor me."

She allowed herself a small smile at the idea of telling the man who would soon control both her career and home about the gossip doing the rounds. "I don't think so."

They arrived at the medical suite and Della stopped at the reception desk just inside the door to speak to the duty nurse. "Jody, is Dr. Bateman in?"

Something about Luke Marlow affected her. Perhaps it was his power over her future as her boss. Or the strange magnetism he had as a man. Or simply her unsettled nerves about the reading of Patrick's will in an hour and the accompanying sharp reminder of her friend's death only twelve days ago. Regardless, she knew if she didn't feel 100 percent comfortable, it would be more appropriate to hand him to a colleague for treatment.

Hearing his name, Cal Bateman stepped into the reception room and Della's shoulders loosened in relief.

"Cal, Mr. Marlow might need some sutures in his hand." She turned to their patient. "Dr. Bateman will take care of you."

But when she turned to go, Luke's smooth, deep voice stopped her. "No."

Her heart skipped a beat and she swiveled slowly back around. "Pardon?"

Luke stood facing her, dominating the room with his height and presence, his expression neither stern nor encouraging. "If I need stitches, I'd like you to handle them, Dr. Walsh."

Puzzled, she looked at him. Why should it matter to him which doctor he saw? "I assure you, Dr. Bateman's surgical skills are second to none. He did some advanced training in plastic surgery, so he'll leave less of a scar than I would."

"I don't mind a scar," Luke said, unconcerned. "I want you, Dr. Walsh."

Her chest tightened. Was he flirting with her? No man had tried since…her husband. She deliberately cultivated an unapproachable aura to prevent it. Though, Luke Marlow didn't seem the sort of man who bothered taking notice of such things. She held back a sigh. Either way, it didn't matter. She was a professional. She'd treat Patrick's nephew, a man who made her pulse jump, and she'd do a good job of it.

"Of course," she said. She led him into her consulting room and began collecting the supplies she'd need. "Take a seat over here, please, Mr. Marlow."

"Luke," he said and sank into the patient chair.

"I'd rather keep to Mr. Marlow if it's all the same to you." She took her white coat from the hook behind the door and thrust her arms through the sleeves before turning back to him. "Chances are you'll be my boss in a few hours."

"It's not all the same to me. You're about to pierce my skin with a sharp needle and I'd feel more comfortable if we moved past formalities."

Della regarded him for a moment as he stretched out in the black vinyl chair, shoulders relaxed. He wasn't nervous, sutures or no sutures. But since he'd be inheriting the *Cora Mae,* he called the shots. She nodded once. "Luke, then."

He looked at the badge attached to her white coat. "Dr. Adele Walsh," he read. "Can I call you Adele?"

She held back the flinch. Only her husband had called her Adele. An image of Shane's dear face rose up in her mind, threatening to overwhelm her. She focused on Luke. "I prefer Della."

"Della." He blinked languidly as he regarded her. "I

like it. Now that we're on more intimate footing, tell me what the other rumors are."

Before she could restrain it, a chuckle escaped at the way he'd maneuvered. "Well played, *Luke*." She leaned back on the sink and folded her arms under her breasts. "Do you really want to waste time here talking about rumors?"

He met her gaze directly, deep gravity in his silver-gray eyes. "I suppose not. But there is something I would like to ask."

For less than an instant, her breathing stalled—she could guess what his question would be about. Still, the topic was bound to be raised sometime; better to have it dealt with before the will reading.

She took a breath and found a reassuring smile. "Ask whatever you'd like."

"We've been told one of the doctors on the ship cared for my uncle through his illness. A woman."

"Yes," she said, her voice not quite steady.

"Was it you?"

A ball of emotion lodged in her throat, so she gave a nod for her reply. Part of her still couldn't believe Patrick was gone. He'd been such a vibrant man, full of personality, and suddenly he wasn't here to chat and joke with. And Patrick's death had brought her grief over losing her husband two years ago back to the surface.

Luke's gaze was steady and solemn. "Thank you for doing that for him."

She swallowed and found her voice. "You're welcome. But there's no need to thank me—I considered Patrick a friend. He deserved the chance to live out his days on the ship instead of ashore in a hospice."

"One thing confuses me. None of his family knew he was dying. He and I spoke several times on the phone over the past few months and he didn't mention it. He used to stay with my mother every three months for a couple of days, and we knew he was too unwell to come recently but no one suspected things were that bad." Elbows resting on the chair's armrests, he steepled his fingers under his chin. "Why didn't we know?"

She thought back to several conversations she'd had with Patrick where she'd suggested he tell his family how serious his cancer was—or closer to the end, that he let her call them. But he'd been adamant. He didn't want them to see him frail and wasted, and he didn't want to endure their reactions to seeing him in that state. He said he wanted them to remember him as he'd been, but she'd wondered if it was denial—if a distraught family had arrived, he would have had to face his own mortality head-on.

She tightened her crossed arms a little. "Patrick was a proud man and he thought it would be for the best this way."

"How long was he unwell?" Luke asked quietly.

"He'd had cancer for almost a year, and he'd been ashore for two rounds of chemotherapy, but it became more serious about four months ago. Even then, he was still mobile and involved with the running of the ship until about three weeks before he died."

"Was he in any—" he frowned and seemed to think better of the word "—much pain?"

"I administered morphine and other medications as required, so his discomfort was minimal." On occasions she'd even had to convince him to take the pain relief. Patrick had been of the soldier-on mold.

"Was there…" Luke hesitated and ran his good hand through his hair. "I honestly mean no disrespect, but was he seeing any other doctors, as well?"

He needn't have worried; she understood. If their situations had been reversed, she'd ask the same question, want to know that *her* uncle had been given the best possible treatment.

"He was under the care of a specialist at the Royal Sydney Hospital, and I had regular contact with her. I can give you her details if you'd like to talk to her yourself." Luke gave a single shake of his head so she continued. "For the last two months of his life, Patrick personally paid for an extra doctor to take over my regular duties so I could focus solely on him. We also brought a specialist nurse on board so there was someone with him twenty-four hours a day."

Though, even when the nurse had been on duty, Della had found it difficult to leave him, and had checked in often.

Luke nodded his acceptance of the information as he let out a long breath. "Will you be at the will reading?"

"Yes." Patrick had made her promise to attend, saying he'd left her a little something. Telling him he didn't need to had made no difference. "Quite a few of the crew have been invited."

"I hope Patrick left you something for what you did for him, but if he didn't have time to change his will, I'll make sure you receive something of meaning."

With a twinge of grief in her chest, she realized that the generosity in his expression reminded her of Patrick, and of the stories he'd told about the man before her. She'd often wondered if Patrick had exaggerated his stories about his nephew or if Luke really was a prince among men.

"That's sweet of you," she said. "But there's no need. I was doing my job and as I said, I had a lot of respect for Patrick. I counted him as a friend. I wouldn't have had things any other way."

"Either way, I'm grateful you were able to be there for him."

"I appreciate you saying that," she said and meant it. She'd often wondered if Patrick's family would blame her for their not knowing about his illness. "And if you're going to make that will reading, we need to take a look at your cut now."

He glanced down at his watch. "You're right."

She washed her hands, sat down across a table from him and set out the sterile cloth. "Lay your hand over here," she said as she slipped on a pair of gloves.

Luke looked into Dr. Della Walsh's eyes and laid his hand, palm up, on the table. She was an intriguing woman. It couldn't have been easy caring for his stubborn uncle out at sea, yet the information from the ship's captain when he'd rung the family twelve days ago was that Patrick's care had been second to none. But it was something else that had compelled him to insist she handle his stitches—something that radiated from within her. She wore no makeup yet her toffee-brown gaze captivated him more than any preening society woman. Her eyes held depth, intelligence and the promise of something more.

Breaking the eye contact, he frowned. It didn't seem right to think this way about the doctor who'd cared for Patrick until his death, especially when that had been so recent that he could still feel the permanent punch to the gut the loss had created.

Della looked down and gently unwrapped the blue handkerchief he'd tied around his hand. It wasn't much of a cut, more a good-size nick at the base of his thumb, but she was treating it seriously. That made him feel even better about Patrick's care in the past few months.

"I'll just give you some local anesthetic," she said as she

drew up a needle. The two jabs into the fleshy part of his palm stung, but Della's hand, soft and warm through the gloves, stabilized his as she administered the drug. Then she swiped the area with an antiseptic and gave it a quick wash with clear fluid from a bottle marked *sterile saline*.

She bent her head and scanned his palm closely. "How did you do it?"

"Car accident."

Her eyes flew to his, then roved down his neck, across his shoulders, assessing everywhere she could see. "Are you hurt anywhere else? And the others in the car with you?"

"We're all fine," he said with a casual shrug. "To be fair, you could hardly class it as an accident. I was pouring some sparkling water from the minibar into a glass—"

She blinked. "I thought this was in a car?"

"Stretch limo." He'd needed to meet with several of his staff, and hated wasting time traveling, so the price of a larger vehicle to accommodate the meeting was easily worth it. "The driver had to swerve hard in traffic, just hitting the bumper of another car. The glass in my hand caught the corner of the fridge as I swung forward, and it shattered."

"You were lucky," she said, returning her attention to his palm.

The cut was minor, but it had led him here, so perhaps he had been lucky. His gaze was drawn back to the doctor's silky brown hair as she bent her head forward.

"Can you move your thumb for me? And the index finger?"

Obediently, he bent his thumb and finger in turn.

"Okay, good. Tell me if you can feel this."

The featherlight touch of her gloved fingertip ran across the planes of his fingers and thumb. "Yes."

She nodded, satisfied, and picked up a pair of tweezers. "I'm just checking for glass fragments while the anesthetic takes effect. This shouldn't hurt," she murmured.

Her dark lashes swept down over creamy pale cheeks as she worked. Under normal circumstances, he'd have asked her out for a drink, maybe dinner, but that would cross a line now that she would soon be an employee.

Besides, he doubted Della would take him up on the offer. The signals she'd been sending had been limited to professional concern, both for his hand and because he was Patrick's nephew.

She skimmed a finger over a long, straight scar along the length of his thumb pad. "This looks like it would have been a nasty cut."

A faint smile pulled at his mouth. "Childhood accident." Though, it had been far from an accident—it had been with conscious, purposeful intent that, at thirteen, he'd sliced his thumb with a pocketknife and pressed the injury against similar ones on three friends' thumbs. They'd become blood brothers that night in a darkened boarding school dorm room. He looked at the scar, remembering how his youthful enthusiasm had made him slash long and deep—as though more blood would deepen the bond. Maybe it had, because he was still closer to those guys than any other person on the planet.

Della put the tweezers down, then picked up the needle. "How does it look?" he asked.

"It's only minor," she said, all polite reassurance. The needle pierced his skin and he felt a slight tugging as she sewed the stitch. Della worked quickly and efficiently after the first one was in place, knotting and cutting. Her hands as they worked were graceful and capable, like Della herself.

After she tied off the third one, she rose and removed

her gloves, saying over her shoulder, "Have you had a tetanus shot recently?"

"About a year ago."

"That will be fine. You shouldn't need antibiotics—the cut was clean, and there was no foreign material." She washed her hands then turned back to him. "You'll need the stitches out in about seven days. If you're still here, come to the clinic and either Cal or I will do it. If you've left by then, see your local doctor."

A twinge of regret surprised him. "I'm only here for a couple of nights." He'd come for the reading of Patrick's will and to spend a few days assessing the ship's operations. He'd disembark when they reached Sydney.

"You're not staying for a full run?" A fine line appeared between her eyebrows. "To experience the *Cora Mae* out in the Pacific?"

"That won't be necessary." His plans for the ship didn't include her cruising the Pacific or anywhere.

"Then you'll need to see your own doctor in a week, Mr. Marlow," she said with her courteous, professional smile. "Ring him earlier if you have any concerns or your hand shows signs of unusual pain, redness or swelling."

With a start, he realized the appointment was over. He was seconds away from walking out the door and in all probability wouldn't see her one-on-one again. Which was probably for the best—that impulse he'd had to invite her for a drink might reemerge, and he wouldn't start anything with a future employee who never spent more than one night in any given city.

He nodded, and rested a hand on the doorknob. "Thank you for the medical care, Dr. Walsh. I appreciate it."

"You're welcome, Mr. Marlow," she said, her voice even, unaffected.

Something about this woman intrigued him, and that was rare. What if, despite the obstacles—

Walk away now, the sane part of his brain said. *This is not a woman for you.* Which was true. He shook his head ruefully and stepped through the door, only just reining in the impulse to turn back for one final look over his shoulder at Dr. Della Walsh.

Two

Less than an hour later, Della rushed along a carpeted corridor to the boardroom where Patrick Marlow's will was probably already being read. She hated being late. Hated it. Being late meant drawing attention to herself and that made her uncomfortable anytime. And this was such an important occasion.

The life of a shipboard doctor wasn't frantic like a medical career based in a hospital, but occasionally there would be a run of patients. Just after Luke had left the clinic, they'd had a minor influx of passengers returning early from shore—a child with a bee sting, another with a twisted wrist after a fall, a young woman with a migraine and a man with a bad case of sunburn. She couldn't have left them all to Cal.

She flicked a glance at her watch. Only three minutes past two—hopefully people were still taking their seats.

Arriving late to Patrick's will reading seemed disrespect-
ful, and the thought made her skin prickle.

Gently pushing open the door, she let out a breath—
although people were seated, there was still murmuring
as the short, gray-haired man at the front table shuffled
papers on his desk. Most chairs were taken, but she was
relieved to see a vacant aisle seat in the back row. She
slipped in and greeted the woman beside her.

"Have I missed anything?" Della whispered.

"No," Jackie said. "He just asked everyone to take their
seats. It's a bit surreal, isn't it? I still can't believe Patrick's
gone, let alone that we're all sitting around to talk about
his money." Jackie ran the housekeeping department and
had been friends with the ship's owner, as had many of
the senior staff.

Tears stung the back of her eyes but Della blinked them
away. "Even knowing how sick he was at the end, part of
me kept believing he'd pull through."

"Well, *he* thought he'd pull through," Jackie said, shaking her head, her smile a bittersweet mix of admiration
and sadness. "He was still making plans the last time I
saw him."

Breath tight in her lungs, Della had to pause before her
voice would work. "Determination and optimism were
probably what kept him going longer than his special-
ists expected."

"You were a big part of that, too, Della." Jackie took
her hand and squeezed, and Della appreciated the warmth,
the solidarity. "We all know the long hours you put in with
him, going above and beyond. The way you devoted yourself to making sure he was as comfortable as he could be.
And Patrick knew it, too. He sang your praises whenever
he could, told us he was indebted to you."

Della managed something of a crooked smile, but this

time her constricted chest wouldn't let her reply. Thankfully, the man at the front of the room cleared his throat and introduced himself as Patrick Marlow's lawyer and executor of his will.

As he spoke, Della's gaze drifted to Luke Marlow, also in an aisle seat, but in the front row beside the captain. His back was tall and straight in the chair and, just as when she'd first seen him when she was boarding a few hours ago, she found it difficult to drag her attention away. There was something magnetic about that man.

Then he slowly turned and searched the crowd before his gaze landed on her. A shiver of tingles ran down her spine. His head dipped in acknowledgment, and she nodded back, before he turned to the front again. Della tucked a curl behind her ear and tried to put Luke Marlow from her mind as best she could. She was here for Patrick.

The executor had finished his preamble and come to the division of assets. He'd left a collection of rare and first edition books to his sister-in-law, Luke's mother, who, the executor noted, hadn't been able to attend; he left some personal effects such as cuff links and a tie clip to various members of staff.

"Regarding the ownership of the cruise ship, the *Cora Mae*..." The executor paused for a muffled cough and darted a quick glance around. "I leave a one-half share to my nephew, Luke Marlow."

The room was silent for the longest beat as though everyone was too shocked to move. Then a wave of murmuring washed over the small crowd.

Luke had inherited *one half*? As Della struggled to make sense of the phrase, her gaze flew to Luke. He sat very straight, very still.

One half meant...there was someone else. She could feel the sudden wariness of every crew member present—

if their future had seemed uncertain five minutes ago, it was now even more unpredictable. She ran through Patrick's stories of his family in her mind for possibilities, scanned the rigid bodies sitting in the front row. Although their tension was nothing compared to that emanating from Luke as he sat motionless, waiting, focused.

"The other one-half share," the executor continued, "I leave to Dr. Della Walsh."

What? Her heart skidded to a halt then leaped to life again, thumping hard in her chest, each beat a painful hammer in her ears. *Oh, God.*

Surely there was a mistake. She replayed the words in her head, looking for where she'd misunderstood, but found nothing. What had Patrick done?

People turned in their seats to face her, some with mouths open, others with confused frowns, a few whispering her name in incredulous voices.

Even through the bewilderment, the irony struck her—despite rushing and managing to arrive before the proceedings had begun, every pair of eyes in the room was on her, after all. A bubble of hysterical laughter rose up, then died again when Luke pinned her with fierce gray eyes.

She leaned back against the chair, away from the force of his unspoken accusation. Abruptly, he stood and the crowd's attention switched to him. Her skin went cold as he stalked down the aisle then stopped to loom over her.

"Dr. Walsh," he said through a tight jaw. "A word in private, if you please."

He held his hand out, plainly expecting her to rise and precede him out of the room. Her jellied joints felt unequal to the task but after a moment she managed to force herself to her feet. As she swiveled, she nearly stumbled. A firm warm grip encircled her elbow, steadying her, saving her from that ignominy.

She turned to thank him but her throat seized as she met the hard glitter in his eyes. Her stomach flipped. With all the grace she could muster, she allowed him to guide her out to the corridor.

Once the door to the boardroom had shut behind them, he looked from closed door to closed door. "An empty room where we can talk undisturbed?"

Willing her brain to work, she indicated the door on the left and he headed for it, still gripping her elbow. It was smaller than the room they'd come from, designed for meetings of no more than ten people, furnished with a rectangular table surrounded by chairs and one porthole.

As soon as the door clicked closed, Luke released her and his hands moved to his hips, suspicion and anger radiating from every inch of his six-foot-plus frame.

"Tell me something, Dr. Walsh," he said, his voice harsh and a sneer curling his top lip. "What exactly did you do for my uncle to earn yourself half a ship?"

It took a moment but then his meaning slammed into her. He thought she'd used her body, sold herself to manipulate sweet, lovely Patrick for financial gain. Rage charged through her veins, hot and wild. Before she'd even realized her intention, her hand was swinging toward him. His eyes widened. He began to turn away, but it was too late.

A crack echoed as flesh met flesh. The force of her slap jerked his head sideways. Heat and pain streaked across her palm, leaving the rest of her body icy cold, and the jolt shuddered all the way up her arm to her shoulder.

And then she froze. She'd struck another human being in anger. The violence felt ugly, alien…she felt alien. She looked down at her upturned palm. Warily her gaze crept up to Luke's face, to the red imprint of her hand on his cheek and a wave of nausea cramped her stomach.

* * *

Luke swore under his breath. He'd never been slapped before. Now that he had, it wasn't an experience he wanted to repeat in a hurry. His cheek hurt like hell.

Della's hand still hung in the air as if she didn't know what to do with it now. Her face was blanched of color. Whatever else he may think of her, he could see the slap was out of character. Not that it mattered. What mattered more was that he'd lost his temper. If he were to succeed, control would be his friend. Control over himself, leading to control of the situation. No more angry outbursts—a cool head would win the day.

He spun away and strode over to the other end of the room, trying to find his bearings. He glanced up at a framed photo on the wall of the original *Cora Mae* proudly entering Sydney Harbour over fifty years ago. Patrick's *Cora Mae* had been named after the ship in the photo, which had been Luke's grandfather's, and that ship had been named for Luke's grandmother, Cora Mae Marlow. Now he was effectively sharing his heritage with a stranger…at least until he could rectify the situation. A heaviness pressed down on his shoulders.

What had Patrick been *thinking* to put him in this position? He scraped both hands through his hair and blew out a breath.

"I have to know," he said, still facing the photo of the *Cora Mae*. "When we met earlier and you stitched my hand. Were you aware then that Patrick was leaving you half the ship?"

He turned to face Della. She'd slipped into a chair, her head was bowed, her hands in her lap—her left hand held her right wrist as though she was afraid of what it might do next. Those were the long slender fingers that had stitched his wound with such dexterity, such tenderness. Who'd have thought they'd be capable of delivering such a stinging rebuke.

"No." Her gaze didn't waver. "I had no idea."

He surveyed her, curling his fingers around the top of the chair, feeling the padding give under his fingertips. She was the doctor who'd nursed Patrick through his final illness, when he'd been at his most vulnerable. Had she used that time to sway him? To garner a financial reward? Perhaps exerted subtle—or not so subtle—influence over a susceptible, sick man?

He released the chair, dug his uninjured hand into his pocket and rocked back on his heels. "It's a pretty big gift to be a surprise."

"Patrick had said on more than one occasion that he was grateful I'd arranged for him to be cared for on the *Cora Mae*. The ship was his home and he was afraid he wouldn't be able to stay here. Which was why he tried to hide his symptoms as long as he could." Her eyes closed tight for a long moment, and when she opened them again, she focused on the ceiling. "He also said he'd leave me 'a little something' in his will."

Luke let his silence ask the questions.

She folded her arms under her breasts. "I told him it was unnecessary, that I was just doing my job."

"But you did more than your job, didn't you?" he asked softly. "You were with him almost constantly."

"Yes." Her eyes flashed but her voice was even and calm. "I loved Patrick and I would have done anything for him. I know what you're implying but I didn't care for him for any reward. He was part of my onboard family as well as a mentor and a friend."

Luke paced across to the porthole, giving himself a few moments to regroup. Patrick was *her* family and her friend?

Why hadn't his uncle asked for him? He'd have dropped everything in an instant if he'd known Patrick was so seriously ill. He'd have wanted to be at the old man's side, wouldn't have cared that he was frail or tired or any of the other things that the illness had caused. He just wished he'd been there, to talk to him, to hold his hand, to watch over him. A hot ball of emotion lodged in his throat.

Was this part of his problem with Della? She *had* been here, she had talked to Patrick, helped him, perhaps comforted him in his hours of need. Her competence had provided succor, and Luke wished he'd been a part of that care. It made his voice harsher than he'd intended.

"He was a *friend* with the capacity to make you a rich woman."

"Challenge the bloody will, then." She looked glorious in her anger, her dark eyes shining bright and color high on her cheeks. "Drag it through the courts. Make it look like Patrick wasn't of sound mind. Knock yourself out."

Her angry words brought him up short. It would go against the grain to tarnish Patrick's memory by publically claiming his uncle was incompetent. But he might not have a choice. This was his heritage—how could he just let that go?

The silence was thick and heavy, and when a knock came at the door, it startled him back to the surroundings.

Della turned and wrenched open the door. A crew member stood on the other side. "The executor would like Mr. Marlow back in the room. He's outlining personal effects, so I expect you'll be mentioned again."

Luke nodded then turned to Della. "This conversation isn't over."

"I look forward to continuing it," she said, and stalked from the room.

He watched her leave—the movement of her hips under the soft fabric of her trousers, the bounce of her dark curls at her shoulders—and shook his head. Wasn't this going to make it hell for negotiating? The last thing he needed was this simmering desire, this spark with his uncle's doctor— and the part-owner of Luke's ship. He'd already paid the price of handling her with uncontrolled emotion. A stinging slap and the knowledge that his fierce self-discipline was not as unassailable as he'd believed.

Next time they met, his control over his temper and his body would once again be ironclad.

Della sat in the back row for the remainder of the will reading, listening to various possessions being allocated to family as well as crew members who had been treasured friends. Although she tried to prevent it, her gaze kept straying to Luke Marlow, his accusations replaying in her mind. The first—that she'd been more than a doctor to Patrick—still sat in the air like a blight on Patrick's memory. And the second—that she'd somehow influenced Patrick to leave her half the ship when he was in a vulnerable state—was abhorrent. But admittedly, Luke didn't know her well enough to know she could never stoop to doing something like that. Which didn't stop the insult from eating at her gut like acid.

There was an aura of restrained tension in and around Luke's body as he sat facing the front. Others may not notice, but she'd been watching him before the executor had announced that Patrick had left them half the ship each and there was a definite difference in the set of his shoulders now. She could imagine he was probably grinding his teeth, as well. Life had probably come so easily to him—born into a wealthy family, having the advantages of looks, charm and intelligence—that being disappointed like this was likely a new experience. Luke and disappointment probably hadn't even been on speaking terms until now.

But that wasn't her problem. And if he wanted to challenge the will in court, so be it. Patrick had been lucid until the last couple of days and there was a large group of people on board who'd be able to testify to that. She might not have been expecting to be left a gift this size, but neither was she about to throw it away simply because a rich man was used to getting his own way. She needed time to think about it all, to let it settle in her mind.

As the executor wound up and said he'd be in touch again with all the beneficiaries, Della sneaked out the door. She wasn't in the frame of mind to deal with the questions and comments from the crew, or for Luke to pick up their unfinished conversation.

Temples pounding, she hurried down the corridors until she reached her cabin. After a cup of coffee and half an hour to catch her breath, she rang her parents to see if they'd known of Patrick's intentions. Despite her father becoming close friends with Patrick while he was captain of the *Cora Mae,* they were as surprised as she, but they were thrilled.

She skipped lunch, her stomach in too many knots for food, and sat staring out her porthole, playing the morning's events over in her mind. By dinnertime, she hadn't come to any conclusions, but knew one thing. She had to face the ship. There was no doubt that this would be the hot topic of gossip and the thought made her cringe, but she refused to hide out. The captain was expecting her at his table tonight. She dressed for dinner in her favorite teal satin dress, which always made her feel good—but it would have a tough job tonight.

One final deep breath before she opened the door, ready to face the questions that were surely coming. Face the stares. Face the man.

Luke sat at the captain's table, engaging in small talk with the captain to his left, but most of his attention was on scanning the crowd for Della Walsh. He'd spent the afternoon trying to track her down. First stop had been the medical suite but she hadn't been on duty and the staff had been protective, refusing to give out her details. In fact, wherever he'd tried, he'd come up against a brick wall— the crew of the *Cora Mae* were like a shield around their doctor. But the captain had told him Della was expected at dinner tonight and she'd never missed dinner at his table when she was expected. So Luke had arrived early and bided his time. He would talk to Dr. Walsh about Patrick's will tonight.

His gaze flitted from person to person, taking in the suited men, the women in richly colored evening gowns, the sparkling jewelry. Then he saw her weaving her way around the tables and his heart skidded to a halt. The fabric of her dress caught the light from the chandeliers and shimmered, her brown hair in soft waves on her shoulders. Her dark eyes met his for a sweet moment before her attention was snared by a woman at her elbow. Beautiful was such an inadequate word.

He stared at her for a full five seconds after she looked away, only vaguely aware of whatever the captain was saying beside him. Then he pulled himself up. He'd met a lot of attractive women in his life—some he'd dated, some he'd merely admired, one he'd married. But he had a golden rule: *never be distracted by a woman; never rely on anyone.*

Aside from his disastrous marriage, he'd managed to live his life pretty much according to that rule. The only exception was for his three friends—the blood brothers he'd made at boarding school, where he'd made the cut in his thumb that Della had noticed when she'd done his stitches. He still saw them regularly, particularly to play billiards, but even with them he'd always managed to keep part of himself hidden. Safe.

He wasn't in danger of breaking the second part of his golden rule—to never rely on anyone—with the ship's doctor. But it seemed he might need to watch himself in terms of being distracted by Della Walsh.

He'd admired her this morning when she'd done his stitches, but watching her now as she came another few steps closer before she was waylaid again, his reaction was stronger. Deeper. Perhaps it was seeing her in an evening dress. Perhaps he was more keenly attuned to her since the will reading. Whatever it was, he would not be distracted from the pressing issue: the unresolved questions involving ownership of the *Cora Mae*.

Della finally made it to their table, and an usher seated her in the vacant seat to Luke's right.

"Good evening, Dr. Walsh," he said.

She raised an eyebrow, obviously noting his use of her title after making a fuss about using first names in her medical suite. But he needed to remind himself that they were now locked in a business situation. He wouldn't jeopardize the future of his family's assets over a beautiful woman. He'd learned that lesson already and wasn't in a rush to repeat it.

Luckily, when his ex-wife had taken him to the cleaners, his father had still been alive and Luke had yet to inherit the family business. If he'd been blind to Jillian's machinations for another year or two, the outcome would have been much worse.

Della shook out her napkin and laid it across her lap. "Good evening, Mr. Marlow."

"I hope you had a pleasant afternoon. Unfortunately, I had no luck locating you to continue our discussion."

"I'm sorry to hear that," she said pleasantly enough, but it was clear she wasn't sorry in the least. "How fortunate that you're on a cruise ship equipped with many ways to fill your afternoon."

Before he could reply a middle-aged man in the crisp white uniform that indicated his senior crew member status stopped at Della's shoulder. "Della, I was so pleased when I heard the outcome of Patrick's will. We're all so glad for you."

"Thank you, Colin." Her chin lifted ever so slightly, as if she was meeting a challenge. "I appreciate it."

He glanced at Luke, as if remembering he was there. "And you, too, Mr. Marlow."

"Thank you," Luke said. But he'd caught the undercurrent—the crew was pleased that one of their own had inherited a share of their home and workplace. Understandable, even if the situation wouldn't stand like this for long.

Colin turned back to Della. "You'll be resigning your post as doctor, I assume."

"I haven't made any decisions yet," she said calmly. "Besides, I wouldn't want to leave Dr. Bateman in the lurch."

The man laid a hand on her shoulder and gave a friendly squeeze before moving along. Uncomfortably aware that he hadn't liked seeing another man's hands on Della's bare flesh, Luke watched her over the rim of his wineglass as she straightened the cutlery beside her plate. She'd changed when the man had said he was happy for her. And now a woman sitting two seats farther along than Della leaned over and congratulated her, and again, Della seemed uncomfortable. Almost as if her colleagues being happy for her made her nervous. Interesting.

When Della turned back, Luke laid a hand over her forearm to ensure her attention wouldn't be stolen this time. She glanced up, as if startled by the touch, but he left his hand on the warmth of her skin. "We need to talk. To finish the conversation we started earlier."

Her tongue darted out to moisten her lips. "I know."

A man hovered at Della's shoulder and she began to turn, but Luke tightened his grip on her forearm to a firm but gentle hold. Della held his gaze and the man stepped away.

"We can't talk privately here," Luke said. "As soon as dinner is over we'll go somewhere where no one can interrupt." He glanced around at the people nearby who were subtly—or not so subtly—watching them. "Or eavesdrop."

She scanned his face for long moments before nodding. "I know a place."

"Good," he said and turned to face the table again. "As soon as we've finished eating, you'll take me there."

He'd prefer to go at once, but was prepared to be civilized. And it was better for the crew to see them handling this in a calm manner. Skittish crew members would spook the passengers.

As would a challenge to Patrick's will through the courts. Which was why he'd prefer to resolve this as quickly and as privately as possible. Of course, if he couldn't obtain the outcome he wanted privately with Della, a legal challenge was still plan B.

Della smiled at an older couple taking their seats on her other side. "Welcome back, Mr. Flack, Mrs. Flack."

She turned back to Luke. "Mr. Marlow, this is Mr. and Mrs. Flack. They're regular patrons of the *Cora Mae*."

Mr. Flack leaned across to shake Luke's hand while his wife said, "Lovely to meet you, Mr. Marlow."

Luke stood and reached down in front of Della to shake the guests' hands, an action that gave him a burst of her perfume, a brush of her arm. He refused to let it affect him, and took his seat again.

The wine waiters came and delivered their drinks, and soon all ten seats at the table had filled and Captain Tynan led the conversation among the group. He was obviously an old hand at this, and it gave Luke an opportunity to observe Della some more. Preparation was the key to any confrontation, and he had a lot riding on their meeting after dinner.

After the waiter had taken their meal orders, the main conversation trailed off and Luke turned to Della. "Tell me about yourself."

She took a sip of her wine before answering. "You didn't come to dinner to talk about me. How are you finding your cabin?"

Luke toyed with the stem of his glass as he watched her. In some ways, Della reminded him of a cat—detached and ready to turn and walk away at the slightest provocation. What would make a professional, independent woman like Della feel that way? Was it the conflict with him over the *Cora Mae,* or her reaction to him personally? It was an intriguing question. But he allowed the change of subject to pass without comment.

"Surprisingly comfortable," he said and leaned back in his chair. The duplex suite they'd been able to find him at short notice was much more spacious and luxurious than the cruise ships of his childhood. Ships had come a long way in twenty-five years, or at least his uncle's had. "To be honest, I'm a little surprised at the high standard."

"The *Cora Mae* is a luxury cruise liner. Our guests expect nothing less than absolute quality." She tilted her head to indicate the expansive dining room, decorated in opulent whites and sparkling crystal, its walls draped in lilac gauzy fabric. In the soft glow of the room's light, she was breathtaking. His pulse picked up speed. She wore a simple teal evening gown and the lightest of makeup, her nut-brown hair hanging in loose, shiny curls. Yet, for all her understatement, there was a magnetic charge that surrounded her.

He cleared his throat. "Have you had a busy time in the medical rooms since I was there?"

"I was only on duty until the will reading, so there wasn't too much," she said, absently wiping a finger through the condensation on the side of her glass.

"No other stitches?"

One side of her mouth pulled into a reluctant smile. "You were the only one. After you left I saw a case of sunburn, a twisted wrist from a fall over a mat and one child with a bee sting."

"Was the mat on the ship?" he asked casually, words like liability and lawsuit flashing through his mind.

She shook her head. "A guest who'd been ashore for the day."

He nodded and sipped his wine. He'd only just inherited the ship—well, half the ship—and legal action or other complications weren't the best way to start.

He tipped his glass toward her. "So I was the most interesting patient of the day?"

"You could say that," she conceded with a smile.

"Then I'm glad my suffering was of service," he said

slowly. For a fleeting moment, the veil lifted and awareness flashed in her toffee-brown eyes. Something in that
awareness, in the yearning that lay behind it, called to
him on a primal level, made his blood pump faster, hotter.
His muscles tensed, then she blinked and the expression,
and the moment, were gone. He'd felt a similar pull when
she'd first arrived at the table. There was some chemistry
between them, no denying it. Also no denying that Della
wasn't happy about it.

He'd never had to try too hard with women before—
even Jillian, the wife who'd left him in such grand style,
had practically handed herself to him on a platter. The
fact that Della—despite her attraction to him—would be
more comfortable somewhere else fascinated him more
than he would have predicted.

Their meals arrived and Della was drawn into other
conversations. Luke talked to the captain beside him and
others around the table, but part of his attention remained
on Della, whether he wanted it to or not. He knew when
she took a bite of her roast vegetable salad. Knew when
she touched her mouth with her napkin. Listened to her
gentle laugh. Smelled a faint vanilla fragrance when she
ran her fingers through her hair. And he silently cursed
himself for it. Because in less than an hour, she'd once
again be his opponent.

Three

Della unlocked the door to the ship's library and led the way, flicking on the lights as she went. The room was usually staffed by a crew member for the few hours a day it was open, and outside those times it had become her secret space.

Luke glanced around at the shelves of books and nodded. "Will we be interrupted by people needing a book for nighttime reading?"

"Opening hours are long over. No one will come in until ten tomorrow morning."

He arched an eyebrow. "Is it normal for the ship's doctor to have a key to the library?"

"Not especially," she said and felt the corners of her mouth tug into a smile. "My father used to be captain of this ship, and he gave me the key because he knew how much I loved it in here. I let the new captain know after Dad's retirement and he was happy to leave the arrangement as is."

The librarian had also told the new captain that Della helped keep shelves in order on her frequent visits, so on that point alone he'd been keen to keep her access unfettered. When she couldn't sleep, she liked handling books. Putting them in their proper place. Creating calm and order from chaos. She'd also occasionally bought books when she went ashore and donated them to the library, loving the feeling of being part of this special place.

"Of course," Luke said. "Your father is Dennis Walsh. Patrick mentioned him occasionally."

She wasn't surprised Patrick had mentioned his friend, but she didn't want to discuss her family with Luke Marlow. So she indicated two upholstered armchairs, arranged at right angles to each other, and they sat. Then she waited.

Luke rested an ankle on his knee and steepled his fingers. "I've been thinking. For whatever reason, Patrick wanted to leave you something more than, say, a rare bottle of wine. He didn't have much cash or other assets since most of his wealth was tied up in the *Cora Mae,* so by giving you half the ship, knowing I'd buy you out, he was able to leave you a generous financial gift."

Luke seemed so sure, so confident of himself and his words. It was in the set of his shoulders, the angle of his jaw. She hadn't had that sort of confidence in years—and she certainly didn't have it about Patrick's intentions.

She tilted her head to the side as she studied him. "What makes you think he didn't *want* to leave me half a ship?"

"Patrick's father was Arthur Marlow, my grandfather," he said without hesitation. "He started a company called Marlow and Sons. It owned many ships, including the original *Cora Mae,* which was named after his wife."

She knew the ship's history from Patrick, and had a feeling where Luke was going with this. "There's a portrait of your grandmother hanging in the lobby. I'll show you later if you like."

"Thank you, I'd appreciate that." He nodded in acknowledgment of her offer. "When Arthur died he split the company equally between his two sons. My father sold his ships and bought hotels instead, which he passed to me when he died. Patrick stayed in ships—he started with several but during some lean times, consolidated down to the flagship, the *Cora Mae*. After it became apparent he wouldn't have children of his own, Patrick made it very clear that he wanted to reunite the family company through me."

She leaned back in her chair. There was logic to his story, to his sense of expectation of inheriting, but life didn't always fit into neat boxes, or sit on the shelves in the correct order like the books that surrounded them. Sometimes the unexpected and the irregular were part of life, too. She had no idea what Patrick had been thinking, but he *must* have had some reason for leaving her half a ship. She just had yet to understand his purpose.

"So," she said, choosing her words with care, "because the *Cora Mae* has been in your family, it should simply stay in your family?"

His eyes narrowed. "Cora Mae was my grandmother. We're talking about more than an asset owned by someone I'm related to. This ship is part of the fabric of my family."

"And you think Patrick didn't intend for me to keep the half he gave me?"

"It's the only thing that makes sense." He shrugged his broad shoulders. "I'll buy your half-share and you get the windfall my uncle wanted you to have."

She glanced through the porthole at the moonlight glinting on the rippled surface of the ocean. Allowing

Luke to buy her out was the easiest option, sure, but she wouldn't be railroaded.

"What happens if I don't sell my half to you?" she asked, turning back to him.

"An untenable situation is created. Both of us would have 50 percent so neither would have a controlling interest. We'd have to agree on all major decisions for any real management to happen."

She could see his point, and understood the inherent problems in the current arrangement, but one thought kept floating to the surface—what if Patrick had wanted her to have half the ship for some reason? He'd known how much Della loved the *Cora Mae*. Della had grown up on the ships her parents worked on, and her father had been captain of the *Cora Mae* until his retirement twelve months ago. When he'd offered her a job as a doctor working alongside her mother, she'd jumped at the chance, then spent a year working and cruising with her family. Her mother had retired at the same time as her husband, but Della had stayed. She felt more at home out to sea than she did on land. And the *Cora Mae* was her favorite of the ships she'd lived on, so the sense of ownership she had for the ship probably wouldn't surprise anyone.

She stood and smoothed her hands down her dress. "I'm going to have to think about this, Luke. Selling you my half isn't something I'd do lightly."

In a flash, he was standing beside her. "How about this. Sell me a 10 percent share. I'll pay double its worth, so you'll still end up with a substantial lump sum." He pulled a folded piece of paper from his pocket and handed it to her. "This is the valuation of the ship that I had done a few days ago. Take 10 percent of that bottom figure and double it."

Della felt her eyes widen as she gripped the page. It was more money than she'd dreamed of.

"There will be stability to the management," Luke continued, "and you'll still get to keep your connection to the ship, plus the cash. Everybody wins."

Her breath caught. The idea of having a hand in the future directions of her beloved *Cora Mae,* the promise of the money and the freedom that would bring...it was overwhelming.

Yet, what if Luke was wrong and Patrick had wanted her to have half the ship for some reason? The will reading had only been a few hours ago and in that short time there had already been twists and turns to the situation. It was too much to take in at once.

"I need to think it over." She refolded the page and handed it back to him. Instead of taking it, he enfolded her hand in his, crumpling the paper inside their two sets of fingers and infusing her hand with warmth.

"The longer this draws out, the worse it is for the ship and her crew. They need stability," he said, his voice and eyes both urging her to agree.

Her stomach dipped. So many people would be affected by her decision. But that only made it more imperative that it was the right one.

"I'm sorry, Mr. Marlow," she said, straightening her spine. "This is too big a decision to rush. I'll contact you when I've made up my mind."

He gazed at her for a long time, far from happy. "I won't wait forever," he said, and walked out, leaving her in the library alone.

Thirty-six hours later—thirty-six hours in which he'd neither seen nor heard from Della—Luke walked along a path in the Sydney Botanical Gardens. They'd docked in Sydney that morning, and before he could find her, Della had left the ship. He was out of time and patience, so, after finding out the direction she'd headed in, he'd followed her.

He didn't have the luxury of time to sit around and wait any longer. Even without the mess of Patrick's will to sort out, he had a full-time job running Marlow Hotels. He would not twiddle his thumbs waiting for a summons from Dr. Della.

Scanning the crowd, he finally saw her up ahead. The graceful way she moved, the cloud of soft brown hair that sat like a halo around her head. His pulse picked up speed and for a few dangerous seconds, he forgot why he needed to see her and simply appreciated her. But he wouldn't allow himself the indulgence for long. Too much was at stake.

"Nice day for a walk," he said when he drew alongside her.

As she turned, her eyes flared in surprise then narrowed. "Mr. Marlow. What a coincidence."

"Not so much," he said with a casual shrug. "The captain told me you had the day off."

"And you guessed that in a city of four and a half million I'd be in this exact spot." She arched a dark eyebrow. "Impressive."

A smile tugged at the corners of his mouth despite his best intentions. "The captain might also have mentioned that you have a fondness for the Gardens."

"Ah." She glanced across at a display of native flowers. "Considerate of him to throw that information around. Crew privacy is usually respected."

"I'm not a random passenger. And you're no longer a mere crew member of the *Cora Mae*."

"Perhaps, but I am still the ship's doctor."

Yes she was, but a young doctor with the world at her feet cloistering herself away on a ship made about as much sense as Patrick's will. He glanced over, looking for a clue, but he found nothing. He needed to understand—to work out what had happened with his uncle, it was important to figure out the woman who was at the center of it all.

"I've been wondering something," he said and dug his hands into his pockets.

Her eyes flicked to him then back to the trees they were passing. "I have a feeling I'll regret this, but tell me."

"I've seen your résumé. Why are you wasting your medical skills on a ship where you're hardly using them?"

"I see patients every day."

"For seasickness and sunburn?"

"Some of the issues are minor, but we're trained to handle outbreaks of contagious diseases and disasters out to sea. And passenger death is not unheard of. It's imperative that the ship's medical staff is highly trained and capable."

"I don't doubt it. But why would someone as young as you, with her whole promising career ahead of her, want to settle into a job where she could do ninety-nine percent of the tasks with her eyes closed?"

"I like the job," she said with a dismissive wave of her hand. "Is that what you tracked me down to ask?"

Cupping her elbow, he led her to the side of the path so he wouldn't have to share her attention with the plant life of Sydney. "We need to resolve the ownership of the *Cora Mae* sooner rather than later. I have a job to get back to—I'd only planned to sail this first leg to Sydney then fly back to Melbourne. I need an answer to my offer."

Her hand fluttered to circle her throat. "So soon?"

"Our situation has been reported on the news and if we leave it much longer, the uncertainty could affect my company's shares on the stock market."

"I don't know—" she began, but he cut her off.

"How about this? The ship is scheduled to leave Sydney at midnight. Come to my cabin for dinner tonight. We'll have privacy to thrash this out and come to an agreement. Then I'll disembark before the *Cora Mae* sets sail for New Zealand."

A tiny frown line appeared between her brows, then she blew out a breath. "You're right. How does five-thirty suit?"

"Perfect," he said and relaxed his shoulders. He'd resolve this and be on a flight to Melbourne in the morning.

They walked for a minute in silence, Luke's thoughts dwelling on Patrick and what he could have intended by leaving half the ship to Della Walsh, if he'd been thinking at all when he wrote the will. But the other thought that had been pestering at the edges of his mind was why Patrick had felt it necessary to keep his illness a secret from his own family. That's what family was for—to support each other in the hard times.

And if Patrick hadn't made the call, then his doctor should have.

He planted his hands low on his hips and found the gaze of the doctor in question. "I need to know something. Once you knew how serious Patrick's cancer was, once you knew he wouldn't survive it, why didn't you override his wishes and ring his family?"

Uncertainty flashed across her features. It had been fleeting, but he'd seen it. Then she found her calm composure again and crossed her arms under her breasts. "I have a question for you. Why didn't you ever visit Patrick?"

Regret and grief and guilt coalesced into a hard, hot lump in his gut. "That's irrelevant," he snapped. He didn't have to justify himself or his actions to a virtual stranger.

"Patrick invited you often." Her voice was soft, probing. "If you'd come aboard, especially in the last year or so, you would have found out for yourself that he was seriously ill."

"I've never been fond of sailing. Besides, I saw him when he came ashore so there was no reason." But that answer didn't satisfy the guilt that was eating at his gut, so he offered her a tight smile. "I need to get back to the ship to make some calls. I'll see you at five-thirty."

He turned on his heel and left.

At five-thirty, Luke showered and changed for dinner with Della. Walking down the stairs of his duplex suite, delicious anticipation sizzled through his bloodstream, making him pause. How long had it been since he'd looked forward to dinner with a woman this much? Della intrigued him—every word she'd said, every action, raised questions that begged him to find answers. Or challenged him the way she had this afternoon about Patrick. Either way, he was thinking about the lovely doctor far too often.

There was a danger in this.

He straightened his spine. He would not be distracted by a woman. His ownership of the *Cora Mae* was at stake.

He glanced around the suite's dining room. The concierge had offered him staff from the butler service for the night, but he'd declined. These negotiations were delicate and they'd need privacy.

He strode from the carpeted staircase to the living room bar and found it well stocked with spirits, wines and soft drinks. All contingencies covered. He knew little about Dr. Della other than that she lived on a ship and had medical training, but at least he'd be able to cater for whatever drinks she preferred.

As he was reaching for a bottle of white wine, there was a knock at the door. Bottle in hand, he crossed the room and drew the door open. His breath caught deep in his throat. She wore a simple floral summer dress and heeled sandals that accentuated her shapely calves. Her loose hair shone in the hall lights, and his hand twitched, wanting to reach out and wrap one curl around his fingers.

Della smiled, but her eyes remained wary, as if still considering the wisdom of this meeting.

He cleared his throat and opened the door farther to allow her to pass. "I'm glad you came."

"Thank you," she said softly, but didn't enter.

Placing a hand under her elbow, he gently guided her over the threshold. "Come in." When she took two small steps into the room, he closed the door and held up the bottle still in his hand. "Would you like red, white or champagne?"

She swallowed, her posture watchful and guarded. She was obviously deciding whether this meeting would be strictly business or whether she'd concede to a certain level of social nicety. He held her gaze, not pushing, not giving her the easy escape, either.

She nodded once, decision made. "White, please."

A spark of satisfaction zinged through his system—she was going to play nice. It would allow him more opportunity to resolve the situation just between themselves, without getting courts and lawyers involved.

He poured them both a glass of sauvignon blanc and showed her to an armchair. "Are you hungry?"

"I only had a light lunch, so yes, I am," she said.

He offered her the in-suite dining menu. "Since you're hungry, we should order now."

Della took the spiral-bound booklet but didn't open it. He realized she lived here—she probably knew the options by heart.

He leaned back on the couch and laid an arm along the top. "What would you suggest?"

"Depends what you like. Everything is delicious so you can't make a bad choice." She shrugged a shoulder then sat, still and watchful. He saw a way to create some trust that could move them past her guardedness and help the negotiations that would begin soon.

He closed his menu. "Why don't you order for both of us?"

Her eyes narrowed a fraction, assessing the sincerity of his suggestion. "How do you feel about Italian?"

"I could be tempted."

"Can I use your phone?"

"Please." He reached for the handset on the table behind the lounge and passed it to her.

She dialed, then lifted her gaze to him. "Hi, Angie, it's Della. Is Edoardo on tonight?" She smiled. "Can you ask him if he has enough of his eggplant parmigiana to send two servings up to Luke Marlow in the starboard owner's suite?" There was a pause. "Excellent," she said and disconnected.

He took the phone from her outstretched hand. "Am I right in assuming you've ordered us something that's not on the menu?"

"You would be right." She inclined her head, acknowledging his guess. "Edoardo used to occasionally make this dish for himself, then as people started tasting it, they'd put in a request for some the next night and it grew into a bit of a legend. Now he comes in early for his shift and makes a dish for any of the staff who want some. So he usually has a few plates' worth of it at the back of the kitchen."

There was a bigger story here—a piece of the Della Walsh puzzle. He gave her an unhurried appraisal. "You have three hundred and thirty staff members aboard the *Cora Mae*. He makes enough for them all?"

She shrugged. "Many work over the dinner shift, either in food service or entertainment, and on their break they eat at the staff canteen."

"There would still be a lot of staff off duty," he said.

As her lashes swept down then up, she reminded him of the movie stars of the sixties—beautiful, sophisticated and unattainable. One step removed from her surroundings, as if watching the world—him—from behind an impenetrable facade.

"Not all staff know about the secret parmigiana, do they?"

"We have a large amount of casual workers. They come on for a year to see the world, and then they leave to settle down somewhere."

"Not you." He took another sip of his wine and watched her over the rim.

"I live here," she said simply. "As do a core group of employees."

The people who'd formed the protective circle around Della after the will reading. The people who seemed to constantly stop to congratulate her on her windfall. "The parmigiana crowd."

"If you like."

He placed his empty glass on the coffee table and sat back. "Don't you think you'll want to leave to settle down on land at some point? Marry?"

"I won't marry," she said with certainty.

There was more to that, but he could see by the set of her chin she wouldn't share. Not that he blamed her for that attitude—his marriage to Jillian had been the worst mistake he'd ever made.

He changed tack, still trying to build some rapport so

she wouldn't be so resistant to him and would finally agree to sell her share of the ship. "Tell me about the *Cora Mae*."

Her eyes warmed. "She's a beautiful ship, a floating piece of heaven. A sanctuary." The last word was a murmur, as though it slipped out as an involuntary afterthought. She cleared her throat and continued. "The architecture of the shopping deck alone was a huge design task and won several awards."

Luke listened with half an ear as Della continued to espouse the merits of the ship, but one word replayed in his mind. *Sanctuary*. Why would Dr. Della Walsh—attractive, intelligent, well-educated—need a safe haven? She should have the world at her feet.

Perhaps it had something to do with that guarded expression he'd seen a few times, the one hiding an old hurt.

He caught himself, annoyed. What was he doing wondering about the private thoughts of this woman? That was a completely different matter to building rapport. He blew out a breath then met her gaze. Time to finish this charade.

"Dr. Walsh, what will it take for you to sell me all or part of your share of the ship?"

Four

Della cast a quick glance around Luke's suite—one small microcosm of the ship she loved, its gold-and-maroon furnishings, the rich wood and curved walls. What would it take for her to sell her share of Patrick's ship?

"It's not that simple," she said, shifting in her seat. "If I'd known Patrick was leaving me half the *Cora Mae*, naturally I would have told him not to. And in that conversation, he would have been able to explain why he was doing it. But I never had the chance to discuss it with him, so I'm not privy to his reasoning. And make no mistake, his reasoning faculties were sound till the end. How can I give it up if I don't know why I have it in the first place?"

Luke's shoulders tensed. This was obviously not the direction he wanted the conversation to be heading. "So, what—you're holding out for a secret letter, or a clue to his intentions?"

"Maybe. I don't know." Now that he'd said it aloud,

she realized she had been hoping a letter from Patrick would surface that explained his will, however unlikely that would be—if he'd written one, it would have been attached to his will, or in the papers the executor held. But there had to be *some* hint somewhere. "Surely we'll work out why he left it this way?"

"It's more likely that we'll never find out," Luke said, sounding as annoyed about that possibility as she was.

She crossed her ankles and smoothed her skirt over her knees. "I'm sorry, Luke. I can't give you an answer yet."

He rubbed his fingers across his forehead, as if he could smooth out the lines that had become embedded there. "Surely you can't *want* to be a part-owner?"

"Since coming to work and live on the *Cora Mae* two years ago when my father was captain, I've developed a certain sense of…ownership. I became good friends with Patrick, partly through his close relationship with my parents, and because of our frequent discussions about the ship, I often thought about changes I'd love to see."

"Your training is in medicine," he said slowly, "not in business management."

"That's a fair point. But I have lifelong observations of shipboard life. With my inside knowledge of how a ship works, having been part of discussions about ships with my family since I was a child, and later with Patrick, my input into the *Cora Mae*'s future could be worthwhile. And I have to admit—" she allowed a small smile to slip out "—part of me relishes the chance to try."

Luke tapped a finger on the table, his gaze not wavering from her face. "What about your medical career?"

"I always thought I wanted to follow in my mother's footsteps as a ship's doctor. But perhaps I'd like to follow closer to my father's path and have a greater say in this ship's future."

Eyes searching, he took a long sip of his wine and swallowed, as if biding his time.

"So now we've explored my intentions," she said, "how about you tell me what your plans would be for the ship. Would you keep the current Pacific route?"

He didn't move, yet something changed. Luke was suddenly a businessman again, looking at her with all the assurance of a CEO delivering a business plan. "There are still some details to be ironed out, but I'm planning to anchor her in the Great Barrier Reef as Marlow Corporation's first floating hotel."

"What? Why?" She blurted out the words before she could stop herself, her entire body recoiling from Luke's plan.

"Costs will be reduced by eliminating fuel and related expenses, and with the permanent location, guests would be able to get up close and personal with one of the seven wonders of the natural world. They'd have everyday access to excursions such as snorkeling the reef."

She sucked in her bottom lip. The idea of the *Cora Mae* no longer cruising the oceans as she was meant to was devastating. "Why not just buy or build a hotel on one of the islands? Tourism is already a booming industry up there."

"Land is limited," he said, unfazed by her dismay. "Most of the islands are already owned by tourism operators or are in private hands. Anchoring the ship will, in effect, create my own piece of real estate in one of the most desirable locations in the world."

"Wouldn't it have a dreadful environmental impact on the reef?"

He waved a hand. "Not at all. With the technology and systems we'd have in place for waste management, water and power generation, there would be virtually no impact at all."

"But, she'd be tethered to the one spot." Della frowned, not hiding her distaste. "Robbed of her freedom."

He smiled at that, then sobered. "It's a business decision. I can't let sentimentality trump financial factors."

"So, you'd chain the *Cora Mae* down to make more money. She'd have—"

She was interrupted by a knock at the door. Luke pushed out of his armchair and strode to the door, probably pleased by the distraction. A steward with an in-suite dining trolley greeted him, and Luke stood back to let him pass.

As the steward entered the room, she recognized him and smiled. "Hi, Max."

"Good evening, Dr. Walsh," the man replied with a flirtatious smile. Max had asked her out a couple of times in the past; she'd declined but he'd been cheerily optimistic about trying again in the future.

Luke looked sharply at Max, probably assessing the situation all too correctly. Then, as Luke's gaze landed on her, a warm shiver flittered across her skin. There was something in his eyes, a heat, a thought she couldn't quite read, but one she could tell involved her. The world around her faded as his silver-gray eyes held her spellbound. Then his jaw clenched and the connection vanished. He turned away and dismissed Max with the polite reply, "I'll take it from here, thanks," before wheeling the trolley to their table.

Della blinked, attempting to orient herself to the room again—the moment of connection they'd shared had been as intense as it had been brief and it had left her slightly breathless.

But it couldn't happen again. Forming an attachment to

any man—let alone the one she was in the midst of delicate negotiations with—was not in the cards. She folded
her arms tightly over her chest, reminding herself of the
scarred imperfection that lay beneath her blouse. The
mugger who'd stolen the life of her husband and left her
for dead had given her one last gift—a torso bearing the
scars of his stabs and slashes. A torso that would never
appeal to a man like Luke, who would be used to nothing
less than perfection.

She had no intention of baring those scars to anyone—
ever. Odd how her body seemed to have its own agenda,
not caring that it was so undesirable, only wanting a man's
touch, a man's caress. Luke's caress.

Involuntarily, her muscles tensed. For two years, she'd
lived a celibate life and preferred it that way. It was the
only path open to her—even in the unlikely event that a
man might see past her scars, she would never, *never* risk
loving and losing again.

"You know," she said with as much nonchalance she
could muster to cover her lapse, "that's part of Max's job.
To bring the food to the table and serve it." She stood and
moved across to the carved wood dining table, its glass
top set lavishly for a dinner for two.

Luke looked up. "I prefer that we're alone tonight,"
he said.

"So we can argue in private?" she asked, tensing.

"No, not argue, discuss." He gave her a crooked grin.
"Maybe it will be a little heated at times, but it's still a
discussion."

"Okay. A discussion."

"And while we eat, I propose a truce." He held her gaze
a moment too long.

She nodded once and took her seat, her false casualness evaporating. Something had changed between them. And she didn't have any idea how to undo it.

Luke served the two plates of eggplant parmigiana and refilled their glasses. Bending to place her glass before her emphasized the solid breadth of his shoulders, and she was struck by the disconcerting question of what it would feel like to touch the shape of the muscles that led from his neck to the tops of his arms. Shaking her head, she almost groaned—within seconds of wanting to undo the change that had happened between them, she was in danger of becoming carried away by a nice set of shoulders.

"Well, it smells good," he said, breaking into her thoughts.

She looked down at her plate. This dish had become her comfort food. She sliced a piece of the meltingly soft eggplant coated in crispy golden bread crumbs and popped it in her mouth, savoring the textures and flavor.

"How much of your childhood did you spend on ships?" Luke asked.

"From when I was three." She tucked a wayward curl behind her ear. "My father worked his way up to captain when he was quite young and with Mum being a ship's doctor, they raised me on ships across the world. I feel more at home on a ship than on land."

"What about your education?" he asked with a raised eyebrow.

"They homeschooled me, and after I finished high school, I went ashore and trained as a doctor."

He cut a piece of eggplant, but held it on his fork as he regarded her. "You said you came to the *Cora Mae* two years ago, yet your father was captain here for six years. Did you stay ashore after qualifying in medicine?"

She hesitated. Talking about that time in her life made everything inside her clench tight, but she took a deep breath and steadied herself to answer him. It was time to start moving through the stranglehold those memories had kept on her.

She looked down at her food, gathering herself, then up at Luke. "While I was training, I met someone. We married and set ourselves up on shore." How inadequate the words were to describe the love, the life that she'd shared with Shane.

"What happened?"

"He died," she said, her voice not even wavering, perhaps for the first time. "After, my father offered me a job and I took it. I might not have been aboard this particular ship before that for more than a holiday, but I…it felt like I was coming home." And that was more than enough said about her past. She took her last bite of eggplant and when she'd finished chewing, laid her cutlery on her plate.

They needed to get back on track. Back to focusing on their shared ownership of the *Cora Mae*. She fidgeted with her napkin. Perhaps it would be better if she came at it from another direction.

"How many hotels do you own?" she asked.

"Twenty-three, across Australia and New Zealand."

She might be responsible for people's health but it was one person at a time. She couldn't imagine the magnitude of making daily decisions for a company that large.

"Do you enjoy it?"

He stared at her for a moment as if he hadn't comprehended the question, then shrugged one shoulder and reached for his drink. "It's what I do."

A little window of insight opened before her and she couldn't resist peeking in. "But you must like working in the hotel industry?"

Luke toyed with the stem of his glass. "To an extent."

Della found herself leaning infinitesimally forward, intrigued. "Then why go into it?"

"It was my father's company, so I grew up working in it. From the kitchens and housekeeping when I was on school holidays, to the reception desk and the corporate headquarters when I was on university breaks." A rueful smile tugged at his mouth, as if he hadn't admitted this often. Or at all. "I don't really know any other industry."

It was sweet to hear of a father helping his son to get a leg up in the industry. "Was he teaching you at home, as well?" She could imagine his father talking about the business over the dinner table, explaining the decisions he'd made that day at work.

"I barely saw my parents," he said with a voice that was too neutral, too deliberately even. "I went to boarding school when I was thirteen. And, unless I was with Patrick, I worked in the hotels during holidays."

Della held her breath. Beneath his confident laid-back exterior, this man was covering a scar or two of his own. Patrick had never mentioned that Luke had been sent away to school, and now that seemed like a telling oversight.

"That must have been difficult. Lonely," she said gently.

He dismissed her words with a wave of his hand. "I think it's time we moved on to another topic."

He was right. It was none of her business how he was raised. She took another long sip of her wine, then brought the conversation back to where it needed to be. "Were you serious about turning the *Cora Mae* into a floating hotel?"

"One hundred percent. I've looked into it in the past, so my staff has already done some of the background work and created a plan. Right now they're hard at work hammering out the details."

A sudden thought struck—was this the real reason Patrick had left her half the ship—he'd known what Luke intended and wanted Della to prevent it?

She laced her fingers together and took a breath. "Had you talked about this plan for the *Cora Mae* with Patrick?"

He blew out a dismissive breath. "I'd broached the subject."

"And?"

Luke shrugged. "He could see the merits of a permanently anchored cruise ship as a hotel."

"But what about the *Cora Mae?* Did you discuss her specifically with him?"

"Not in any depth. There was no need to. This was several years ago now and Patrick was still fit and healthy with no hint of the cancer that was going to kill him."

"I see." She dabbed the edges of her mouth with the napkin, then laid it carefully on the table. "There's no doubt in my mind that Patrick would have wanted the ship to keep cruising. I think this is why he left me half the *Cora Mae*—so that I could stand as her advocate after he'd gone."

Luke speared his fingers through his hair. "Much as I wish Patrick was still with us, he's not," he said, his voice a little rough around the edges. "We can't run a business trying to second-guess what he wanted. We have to do the best we can at the present time."

How simple that sounded. How convenient and neat. But it wasn't the way she worked. She moistened her lips and lifted her chin a fraction. "I'll do everything in my power as a half-share owner to keep the *Cora Mae* cruising." It was her responsibility. She wouldn't let Patrick down.

"Della, you can't afford to buy me out, so your vision for the ship will be hard to implement. We'll either need to agree, which is seemingly unlikely at this point, or you need to sell me a portion of your share."

"But why does it need to change? The ship is profitable, isn't it? You can appoint a manager. You can appoint me. I'll carry on the work that Patrick did. There's no reason for the *Cora Mae* to be tied down and her engines left to rot."

"Except profit, Della. It will be much more profitable if she is tied down."

"She's special, Luke. If only you could look past the size of the black numbers on the accountant's balance sheet, you'd see."

"Profit is the bottom line," he said patiently. "That's the way the business world works."

"And the way you work."

"To me, it's second nature." Something in his expression flared to life as he spoke the words.

She lifted her wineglass and sipped as she considered him. She needed to understand him to have any chance of changing his mind. "It's more than that, isn't it?"

He nodded, conceding her point. "It's life itself. My business is the only thing in my life that's never let me down. The only constant and reliable aspect. People, on the other hand, shift their loyalties with a change in the wind. They can never be relied on in the tough times." His gaze suddenly snapped back to hers as if only now realizing how much he'd revealed. Deep frown lines appeared across his forehead.

"I'm sorry," she said. It wasn't her place to pry. "I shouldn't have—"

He shook his head, dismissing her concern. "If nothing else, I think we've established that we're coming from two completely different places, so we'll have to agree to disagree on certain aspects of our situation."

He was right, of course, but there had to be another way. There was always another way.

"Tell me, what do you think of the ship so far?"

"She seems nice enough," he said as he refilled their wineglasses.

"She is. You could live here full-time and never miss the land."

His gaze sharpened. "You never miss the land?"

"Never. But I meant the guests," she said before he could use her comment to focus back on her. "We have all the services you could possibly need, from hairdressers to a day spa to fine restaurants." She ticked off amenities on her fingers as she went. "You're already familiar with the business resources, the internet and cell phone access. And for recreation, the rock climbing wall, tennis courts and ice rink are hard to beat. There's even half an acre of lawn on Deck Twelve if you miss the feel of land beneath your feet or want an on board picnic."

Luke arched an eyebrow. "So you never yearn for a city or a town?"

"There are more facilities here per person than in a city, and every few days we stop at one of the world's most exotic locations." And that was the key. Sailing from port to port was the essence of cruising. Of the *Cora Mae*.

Luke put his knife and fork on his empty plate and pushed it to the side. "I can see the appeal, Della. But I won't base a business decision on the idea that sailing is a charming lifestyle."

Della rubbed a finger against her temple where the pressure was building from her mind whirling. Sailing was about more than charm—she had to find a way to show him. It seemed there was only one option left.

"Luke, I have a request. Give me one month aboard the *Cora Mae* to convince you of the merits of cruising, of changing ports regularly. Before you make any other decisions about its future or we make any agreement about ownership, give the ship a real chance."

He drummed his fingers on the table and she wondered if she'd asked too much. A month for a businessman in Luke's position was a long time, even with the resources the *Cora Mae* had at his disposal for keeping in touch with his office.

Then he steepled his fingers. "I'll give you three weeks, but while I'm being open about the idea of a cruising ship, you need to be sincerely considering selling me a portion of your half-share, regardless of whether the ship is permanently anchored in the future or not."

"I can do that," she said, relieved. Convincing him in three weeks wouldn't be easy, but this was a challenge she couldn't back away from.

Luke raised his glass to make a toast and when she lifted hers, he clinked them together.

"Let the persuasions begin," he said with a smile.

Della floated in the crystalline blue water off a secluded beach in New Zealand's Bay of Islands. Days ashore weren't always something she took advantage of given that each location came around every four weeks, but the Bay of Islands was one place she always sneaked out to when she could. Cal Bateman was on call today, so Della was gloriously free.

Well, except for her Luke Marlow mission.

She glanced over at her mission a few body lengths away, swimming farther out in long, easy strokes, then back again. Did that man ever relax? Even when he was still, he was like a tightly coiled ball of energy.

He surfaced near her and wiped a hand across his face. His hair was much darker when it was wet, and slicked back it accentuated his gray eyes. Made them hard to look away from. Here, insulated from the real world by the blue, blue water and the powder-white crescent of beach, she could almost believe they were just two people spending time together because they enjoyed each other's company. Where she could swim the short distance separating them and wrap her arms around his broad, bare chest.

He moved through the water with the ease of a seal, and when he surfaced again, closer this time, his bare torso was slick with water. Her fingers wanted to reach out. But that would be to fall into the delusion that they were just two people out for the day, together because they wanted to be.

Instead, she was here to sell him on the concept of South Pacific cruising.

"You really take those sun safe messages you give the passengers to heart, don't you?" Luke said, indicating the long-sleeved Lycra shirt over her swimsuit.

She shrugged. "I'm afraid it's the result of having very fair skin, combined with knowing too many medical facts about the skin cancer rates in Australia and New Zealand." With the added advantage of making absolutely sure none of her scars peeked out.

"Among the highest rates in the world," he said, drifting closer. "I saw the information in the passenger briefing notes. In fact, I paid attention and applied a generous layer of sunscreen, Dr. Walsh."

"Very good," she said, trying to sound professional. Because she'd noticed. And despite making herself look away from his hand rubbing over his chest and shoulders as he stood on the sand, she'd still managed to watch from the corner of her eye.

"This place is great," he said, taking in the scenery that

surrounded them. "I've been to New Zealand more times than I can remember but never this spot."

"I'm guessing you usually fly over for meetings?"

"And there aren't too many of them on the beach," he said, acknowledging her point. "Though, much as I'm enjoying myself, why exactly are we here?"

She arched an eyebrow. At 7:00 a.m. she'd left him a message to meet her in the lobby and bring his swim trunks, and he'd been there, ready and waiting. She'd assumed the reason for their excursion had been self-evident.

"You've forgotten our agreement already?" she said sweetly. "Too much sun, Mr. Marlow?"

"The agreement was about the *Cora Mae*. Unless you're on the payroll for New Zealand tourism on the side?"

"Cruising is about so much more than the ship. It's also about the locations you can access, like this place." She swept her arm in an arc. "You spend a day or two in the luxury of the ship, then you arrive at another exotic destination. That's something a floating hotel can't offer."

"Fair point," he said, but she couldn't tell if he was humoring her or not. "So, what's in that basket I carried here?"

"Picnic lunch courtesy of the restaurant." The lunch baskets were one of the ship's specialties and passengers were invariably impressed with the quality of food as well as the small touches.

"I was hoping you'd say that. Is eleven too early for lunch?"

She smiled widely. "The beauty of life on a cruise is it's never too early or late for anything. The day is ours to order how we want. It's a step further removed from the everyday than a vacation at a hotel."

"Well, we wouldn't want to waste the opportunity." He grabbed her hand and pulled her toward the shore. His fingers were strong and warm and they sent a spray of champagne fizz through her blood, from her fingertips, to her arms and out to every cell in her body. There was no stopping it, so she dived under the water, using the action as an excuse to break the skin contact with Luke, then slicked back her hair when she emerged.

As she walked up the white sand to the shade where they'd left their things, she kept a respectable distance from the man walking beside her. This was not the time nor the man to allow herself to indulge in flights of fancy over. Especially when she had no idea if the charm he was displaying today was genuine or if it was part of his not-so-subtle plan of convincing her to sell her 50 percent. Tricky man, Luke Marlow. One not to underestimate.

She pulled the Lycra sun-shirt off over her head, and rubbed herself down with the large beach towel. As she grabbed her T-shirt she saw Luke's gaze land on her collarbone. She glanced down and saw the shoulder straps of her conservative swimsuit had moved enough to show the edges of her scars. Hands moving quickly, panic flaring in her belly, she adjusted the straps and pulled the T-shirt over her head.

Luke watched Della and frowned. The way she tracked his eyes and shied away told him something was wrong and for some reason, he wasn't prepared to let it go. She'd pulled the T-shirt on to cover any trace of the marks that marred her skin, but he stepped closer and gently pulled the neckline to one side to expose them. To prove to himself they hadn't been his imagination.

"Della, what happened?" he whispered.

"It was nothing." She turned but he moved with her, his fingers still brushing her collarbone.

"Scars like that don't come from nothing."

She didn't move. Not a single muscle. "I meant nothing important."

"It looks important. Della, won't you tell me?"

She winced. "You could find out how I got them with a simple internet search. It was in all the papers at the time."

A sense of foreboding filled the air, surrounded him, almost choked him. He cleared his throat. "I don't want to read impersonal newspaper articles. I want you to tell me."

She looked out to sea, her face too pale, her features pinched tight. "It was two years ago. There was a woman," she said, her voice unsteady. "Walking through Melbourne late at night, my husband and I heard her screams. Shane was a doctor, too, so we went to see if we could help."

Luke picked up her hand and gently stroked the creamy skin from her knuckles to her wrist. "Of course you would."

"She was down a laneway, where it was dark and deserted." She paused. Swallowed hard. "Alone except for the four men who surrounded her."

His heart thudded hard against his ribs, as if ready to physically leap to her defense. But he was several years too late, so he stood silently instead.

"We couldn't leave her," she said urgently, finding his gaze.

Squeezing her hands, he held her eyes. "I wouldn't have been able to leave her, either."

She nodded. "Shane started down the laneway, calling out, hoping to distract them. I pulled out my mobile phone and rang the police. Before I could give my location, one of them grabbed the phone from me and smashed it on the wall. They'd left the girl and were heading for us."

"Oh, Della," he said on a long breath. His whole body was too tense, wanting to stave off what had already happened.

"When I looked past the men, the woman was gone, which was the good news." She smiled, but it was the saddest expression he'd ever seen.

His eyes flicked to the scar peeking out from under the collar of her T-shirt. "The bad news being that now there were four men focused on you and Shane."

She was silent for a long time, and Luke waited. His fingers stroked the back of her hand, his other hand rubbing up and down her back. Inside he was burning with anger, with the injustice of it. But Della didn't need his anger. She needed strength, comfort and support, so he stuffed it all down as well as he could and kept rubbing her back.

"I woke up in the hospital. Thankfully, the woman had run for help. They were too late for Shane. He'd been stabbed in the chest multiple times, and the blade had pierced his heart."

Her hand felt cold, so he reached for her other one, too, and held them between his, as if he could will heat and strength into them. "I'm sorry."

Tears slipped over her cheeks and she looked out to sea.

"What did they do to you?"

"The same. Left me for dead, but they weren't as thorough and the surgeons repaired the damage."

There was nothing he could say, so he pulled her close and held her against his chest, hoping that he could soothe the tiny tremors, and that, as she relived the memory, she at least felt safe in the present moment. What had he been thinking? He was ten kinds of stupid for making her tell him the story.

Part of him wanted to distract her so she didn't have those images in her head. Kissing her senseless was the option of choice—she wouldn't be able to think of anything else, and it would satisfy the clawing need inside him. But that would be taking advantage of her at her most vulnerable. So instead, he continued to hold her.

One thing finally made sense—her aloofness with men, whether it was the flirtatious steward who'd delivered their dinner or, not least of all, Luke himself. The reason she'd pulled away when he'd noticed her scars had been embarrassment, possibly even shame. Della Walsh was unsure of her desirability. He could tell her how ridiculous that was, how she affected *him,* but she wouldn't believe him. And it was definitely the wrong time to show her. No matter that his pulse had spiked the moment he'd felt her soft curves against him as he held her and that it had yet to settle.

Finally she stirred and pulled away.

"I'm sorry," she said as she swiped at her face.

"No, Della, I'm sorry. I shouldn't have asked. You should have told me to go to hell."

One corner of her mouth twitched and his chest expanded with satisfaction that he could relieve her darkness even a little. "In fact, you can tell me to go to hell now."

Her lashes lifted as she looked up, checking to see if he was serious. "I'm supposed to be on a mission to convince you of the merits of cruising. So I don't think I'll be saying that."

But there was a spark returning to her features, and her face wasn't as pale.

"To be honest," he said, running with the idea, "you'd be doing me a favor. If we leave it like this, I'll be weighed down with more guilt than I'll know what to do with. At first it will affect my mood, but eventually it'll affect my interactions with people and my work. I could lose my friends. My company could go bankrupt."

"Is that right?" she asked, amusement beginning to dance in her eyes again.

"It would be devastating. The only way I can see to avoid total destruction is if you retrospectively pull me into line."

She ran a hand over her damp hair. "I don't—"

"Make sure you use my name when you do it. I'd be very grateful."

She chuckled and, after her desolation minutes before, it was a sound sweeter than any he could imagine.

"Go on," he urged and nudged her shoulder with his. "You know you want to."

She broke into a proper laugh and held up a hand. "Okay. Just give me a moment." Her expression turned somber but her eyes still danced. "Go to hell, Luke."

"That was good, but I didn't believe you. Try again."

Her mouth fell open in amused outrage then she took a deep breath and narrowed her eyes. "Go to hell, Luke."

There had been more heat in her words this time, but as soon as she finished, it all fell away and she bit down on a smile, as if surprised at her own daring. "Better," he said softly.

"You should be careful," she said with an arched eyebrow, "or that might become my new favorite phrase."

He'd thought he wanted to kiss her before. Now the need to draw her close and capture those lips was as strong as any need he'd felt. To fit her along his body and feel her curves against his skin. The air was suddenly too thick to breathe; he couldn't fill his lungs. Her eyes darkened and the pulse at the base of her throat fluttered. She felt it, too. There wasn't a thing in his life he wouldn't give to be able to lean in, to touch that mouth.

He wouldn't. She was still vulnerable from retelling that story and he would never be a man who took advantage of that.

He scrubbed a hand down his face and looked out to sea.

But it wouldn't be long.

Sometime soon, he'd find the right time and place to kiss Della Walsh.

Five

The next morning, Della met Luke for a tour of the ship—one of her "persuasions" to convince him to keep the *Cora Mae* in her current state. She'd racked her brain for little bits of information, any anecdotes that Patrick had told her about Luke that she could use now. She had a lot of material to work with, from an ex-wife who Patrick had hated, to Luke's impressive grades at university. But nothing that would work for her in this situation.

Then she'd recalled the perfect detail. A cook in one of the galleys had worked on one of Patrick's ships when Luke was a child and, when Della had checked with her, the cook remembered him. It was the ideal place to start. If they could get Luke to make an emotional connection to the *Cora Mae,* he might let his heart contribute to his decision.

He was so focused on cold, dry factors such as profits and spreadsheets, that before she could convince him not to permanently anchor the *Cora Mae,* they needed to be at least talking the same language. A combination of head and heart. To do that, she had to engage his emotions in the debate. Only then would she have a chance to change his mind.

Hands low on his hips, looking more devastatingly gorgeous than any man had a right to be, Luke regarded her as she arrived. "Where's our first stop on your magical mystery tour?"

"We're starting at the beginning. Belowdecks, in Galley Two."

"And here I'd expected another day of leisurely swimming."

She remembered his bare chest glistening with water droplets yesterday, and board shorts sitting firmly over a taut abdomen. Then she remembered how her body had reacted when he'd simply taken her hand in the water, and her blood began to heat.

She swallowed and turned her gaze ahead. "Maybe some other time."

But not until she'd recovered from the memories of their first swim, at a minimum.

"So is there a dress code for these tours?" he asked, rocking back on his heels.

She cast a sweeping glance over his casual trousers and polo shirt. "What you're wearing won't be a problem for today."

"Do you say such sweet things to all the boys, or is it just me?" he asked, gray eyes twinkling.

"Fishing for a compliment, Mr. Marlow?"

"You know what?" he said and cocked his head to the side. "I'm perversely enjoying the novelty of not receiving them."

Chuckling, she shook her head. "Dear me, what a tough

life you must lead to be jaded by a steady diet of compliments."

"Praise, sincerely given, isn't a bad thing. When it's simpering or calculated, and part of an agenda, it's tiresome."

With his wealth, power and those sculpted cheekbones, she could imagine he received regular insincere compliments. She reached out and pushed open the double-hinged doors to the galley. "Then I'll make a concerted effort to keep all simpering to a minimum."

"Your generosity knows no bounds," he said dryly and walked through the open door.

She threaded her way through the counters and staff until she found her quarry. "Hi, Roxie."

A middle-aged woman with round, rosy cheeks and faded red hair held high on her head in a bun turned and smiled widely. "Dr. Walsh. So lovely to see you." She took Della's hand in both of hers then leaned to look past her. "And this must be Mr. Marlow all grown up. I'd heard you were on board, but I didn't think I'd get to see you again."

A faint line of concentration appeared between Luke's brows as he offered Roxie his hand. "Have we met?"

"I don't expect that you'd remember, but when you were a little boy, you'd sometimes come down to the galley of the old *Princess Cora* and visit me."

Della crossed her fingers behind her back. Before she could make more headway with Luke, she needed something to sneak under his defenses. Hopefully Roxie would do it.

Suddenly, the frown line disappeared and his eyes widened. "Mrs. Appleby?"

Roxie beamed. "One and the same."

"You used to sneak me sultana cookies," Luke said, his eyes alive with memories.

"They were your favorite." Her face dropped. "I'm so sorry about your uncle. He was a good man."

"Thank you. I appreciate you saying so," he said, his features carefully schooled to neutral. He glanced around, then turned back to Roxie and lowered his voice conspiratorially. "I don't suppose you still bake those cookies?"

Roxie grinned. "They haven't been on the menu lately, but I baked a batch yesterday when I heard you were on board." She lowered her lashes and a little extra color rose in her cheeks. "Just in case."

"I haven't had a good sultana cookie since I was twelve." Luke smiled the charming smile that probably got him whatever he wanted. "Don't suppose that new batch is nearby?"

"Let me get a paper bag."

As Roxie bustled away, Della bit down on a smile. She hadn't won—not by any stretch of the imagination—but they'd just taken an important step in getting Luke to think of the *Cora Mae* as more than spreadsheets and figures, and she was well satisfied with that for now. She introduced Luke to one of the chefs who was still working on late breakfasts and they chatted about the kitchen's capacity and appliances. When Roxie returned with a brown paper bag neatly folded over at the top, Luke turned the charm back on. "I appreciate this, Mrs. Appleby."

"You just let me know when you want more. I'll bake a new batch whenever you need."

Della said goodbye to Roxie and led Luke out through the swinging doors.

"I'll treat you to a cookie," he said, holding the bag aloft. "There has to be at least eight in here."

"Only if I can buy you a coffee to go with it." She had to keep moving ahead—not lose the momentum Roxie had given her.

"Deal," he said.

She took him to her favorite café, A Taste of Paris, on the shopping deck, where the French chef made pastries that melted in the mouth and coffee that tasted like heaven. She snagged a table on a paved area outside the café's glass shopfront, a spot that would allow them to watch passengers splurge in the stores along the main shopping strip.

"I'll go in and order," she said. "How do you like your coffee?"

"Black, double strength."

When she came back a few minutes later with the coffees and two empty plates, she found Luke sitting with his back to the glass wall, his long legs stretched out in front of him, watching the world go by...the world of shipboard retail, at least. He opened the paper bag and offered it to her. "You knew about Roxie Appleby sneaking me cookies when I was a kid."

"Patrick told me." In fact, Patrick had delighted in regaling her with stories of Luke's school holiday escapades.

Luke laughed, a gorgeous full-throated sound. "Here's me thinking I'd been a juvenile master of espionage and indulging in some serious rule-breaking and the old devil knew all along."

She just smiled. She wasn't going to tell him that Patrick had been pleased to see his too-serious nephew getting up to mischief.

He took a sultana cookie from the bag and dropped it on his plate. "And you took me there deliberately, to attempt to establish an emotional connection between me and the staff."

She smiled angelically. "I wouldn't be giving it my best shot if I'd let the opportunity slip by."

"It's reassuring that I'm not in the hands of an amateur," he said and bit into his cookie.

"I also wanted you to put faces to the people who are depending on us. The people our decision will affect." The same faces that haunted Della's mind when she thought about the choice that lay before her.

He sipped his coffee and watched her over the rim. "But Roxie would keep her job if the *Cora Mae* becomes a floating hotel," he said as he set the cup back in its saucer. "Nothing need change there."

"Roxie might not want that job. She spent a few years on land after you knew her and had a family, and now she has a son working here on the bridge, a daughter in Sydney and another son in New Zealand with his wife and baby. I suspect she'd look for another ship doing a similar run if you anchor this one, so she could still see her children regularly."

He frowned as he finished his cookie and brushed the crumbs from his fingers. "You're not suggesting I should direct the future of my company based on where Roxie Appleby would prefer to work."

"No, of course not. I'm just helping you get to know the ship and her crew and the issues they face." Baby steps. And this baby step was merely to raise a niggle of doubt in his mind about how perfect his plan was. Which led to the next baby step. "I'm on duty after lunch but we still have some time before that. We could go ice skating, try some golf, play a game of tennis—the whole ship is our oyster. Or, how do you feel about rock climbing?"

He shrugged one shoulder. "I prefer golf."

"Mini golf, driving range or the putting green?" She ticked off the options on her fingers.

He rubbed his jaw, considering. "Depends."

"I'll tell you up front that I draw the line at being your caddy."

The edges of his sensual lips twitched. "Nice to see

you're willing to go the extra mile for your cause. But fortunately, you don't need a caddy for any of those options."

"Then what does it depend on?" she asked warily. In the short time she'd known him, she'd learned to expect the unexpected with Luke Marlow.

"Do you play?"

"I've played mini golf. What about you?"

"Never played a round of mini golf in my life," he said, obviously holding back a wince. "But real golf—" his eyes flared with passion "—that's a game I've indulged in."

Della smiled brightly. This was good news. She wanted him relaxed, enjoying himself—in the best possible mood while considering the *Cora Mae*'s future. "How about we try the driving range?"

"Sure, why not?" he said and stood.

She looked up at him, so tall and broad as he loomed over her, and her heart skipped a beat. Suddenly she could think of several reasons why not, chief among them that watching his powerful shoulders as he took a swing would likely mess with her focus on making her case for the *Cora Mae*.

She drew in a breath, pushed back her chair and stood next to him. She'd just have to be extra vigilant. Besides, she didn't *have* to watch him. She'd take a few swings herself—the activity might help her to keep her mind somewhere else.

Luke watched Della line up another shot in the driving range's nets. The golf pro on duty had tracked their shots on the computer software and given them some statistics such as the ball's speed and trajectory, plus a few tips for improvement. Then he'd moved on to another passenger in one of the three nets and left them alone to practice.

The power in Luke's shots wasn't as good as usual, but

he tried to ignore the twinge in his palm from the stitches and play on regardless.

Della put her feet together beside the tee, then moved them shoulder-width apart as Luke had shown her when they'd arrived. Her back was straight, her knees a little bent, and her sweet rear end was angled slightly, ever-so-enticingly out. She drew the club back, then a loud thwack split the air and, with considerable effort, Luke dragged his gaze away to watch where the ball hit on the net's target.

"You sliced again," he said as if he'd been watching the whole shot, not dividing his time between that and her rear end. "But not as badly."

"Do you say such sweet things to all the gals, or is it just me?" she said, recycling his words from earlier.

"What can I say? You bring out the best in me."

"Smooth talker." She pulled a face at him before bending to put another ball on the tee. "This is harder than mini golf."

He barely managed to hold back the laugh. "Just a bit," he conceded. "Though you're a natural. If I didn't trust you, I mightn't have believed this is your first time."

As the words left his mouth, Luke stiffened. *Trust her?* When had he come to trust her? His gut clenched tight. Looking back, something had changed yesterday at the Bay of Islands. Hearing her distress while telling him her story, something inside him had shifted.

Trust gave her all sorts of power over his business future…maybe even over him. He wasn't sure he liked that. In fact, he was damned sure he didn't.

And if he trusted her, then he could no longer believe she coerced Patrick to leave her half the ship. Although Patrick meaning to leave her half the ship made no sense at all.

Della moved back to let him have a turn and he stood in front of the tee, gripped the club as well as he could with the stitches in his palm, moving his arms, feet and knees to slip into the correct posture. Then he remembered where his eyes had been while she'd taken her shot....

Where were her eyes now? Would straitlaced Dr. Della do something as naughty as watch his butt while he swung? His pulse leaped but he took a breath and focused on the ball. Banter was one thing, and he might believe her story about Patrick now, but he wouldn't let himself become entangled with someone he was in business negotiations with. No matter how her rear end looked when she swung a golf club.

He lined up the shot, drew back the club and hit the ball with a satisfying thwack. He put another ball on the tee and stood back for her turn.

"What time do you go on duty?" he asked.

"Midday," she said without looking up. "Are you attempting to distract me?"

No, he thought, *to distract myself.* "Can't blame a man for trying."

"I'm just learning this game and already you're being competitive?"

He waited till she took the shot—another slice, but again, not too bad all things considered—before replying. "Competition is hardwired into my brain. Comes with having a Y chromosome."

She wrapped her fingers around the handle of her driving iron, her eyes calculating. "How about we make a wager then?"

"On hitting into the nets?"

"Too hard to score. On mini golf." She flicked a glance at her watch. "The clinic closes at three, so plenty of time for a play-off afterward."

He'd never seen the course and he'd guess she'd played it many times. Her familiarity with the holes versus his putting skill might just produce an even contest. "What are the stakes?"

"You win, we continue with the current plan of persuading each other about the *Cora Mae*'s future. I win, you leave the *Cora Mae* as a cruising ship."

He didn't try to hold back the laugh this time. "Nice try, Dr. Walsh. Lucky for me folly wasn't wired in with my competitive spirit. Let's make the stakes more in keeping with the game being played, shall we? If you win, I'll go rock climbing."

"Not challenging enough," she said, tapping one slender finger on her club's shaft. "I win, you spend a day at the ship's day spa."

He winced. "Will that involve fluffy white towels and green slime plastered over my face?"

Her lips twitched. "So I've heard."

"You've never been?" he asked, intrigued.

She shrugged, seemingly unfazed by his question. "I've been told by trustworthy people that the services are first-rate."

"Okay," he said slowly. "You win, I'll go to the day spa. I win, you go."

Her eyes rounded. He'd surprised her. A potent coil of satisfaction twisted tight in his belly. "Deal?" he prompted.

"Deal," she said.

He lined up the shot and swung, knowing he was far too pleased with himself over merely surprising Dr. Della.

At half past three, Della took the elevator to the top deck and strolled over to the mini-golf course. She'd changed into shorts and a white sleeveless wraparound top, running shoes and a baseball cap. She was here to win. Getting Luke to agree to some time being pampered had been on her agenda, but she'd known it would be a hard sell. If she won this match, problem solved. Luke would spend time at the day spa, relaxing, building positive memories of the ship to reinforce the rest of her strategy. She wanted him head over heels in love with the *Cora Mae,* so he'd want what was best for the ship, not his bottom line.

She saw him ahead, leaning casually against the counter, silver-rimmed sunglasses covering his eyes, feet crossed at the ankles, the recipient of adoring looks from the girl running the activity desk.

Della took a moment to appreciate his long lean form before Luke lifted his sunglasses to the top of his head as she approached. She glimpsed heat flare in his eyes for a split second before he smothered it. "Della, I was just telling Christina about our wager."

Christina's blond ponytail bobbed as she nodded. "I think it sounds like heaps of fun. Good luck," she gushed, eyes never leaving Luke.

Della smiled wryly. Luke had an admirer. Though, she had to admit, if she—who'd sworn off men—was affected by Luke's magnetic aura, then a less seasoned woman like Christina didn't have much hope.

They took their clubs and a scorecard and moved off to the start line, with more of Christina's good luck wishes following them.

"Apparently, you have your own personal cheer squad," she said as she wrote their names at the top of the scorecard.

"She's a nice kid," he said, and a little part of her—one she wasn't proud of—warmed at his easy rebuff of the attentions from a pretty girl. She chanced a glance at him again to check, but his eyes were roaming the first hole. It was fairly straightforward—a green felt S, relatively flat.

"I'd normally flip a coin to see who goes first," he said, "but I think ladies should go before gentlemen."

"I suggested the match, which makes you my guest, so you go first."

He arched an eyebrow. "Looks like we'll need to flip, after all." He dug into his pocket and drew out a shiny silver twenty-five cent coin. "Heads or tails?"

"Tails."

With a flick of his thumb, the coin spun into the air, turning over and over, catching the sun on each rotation. Then he plucked it out of the air, planted it on the back of his hand and held it out for her to see. Heads.

He stuffed the coin back in his pocket and rested the club across the ledge of his shoulders, behind his neck, with a wrist holding it in place at each end. "I'm ready to be dazzled by nine holes of your mini-golf brilliance."

"Right. So no pressure, then." She dropped the ball onto the black X and lined up the shot. If she could bounce it off the first curve at the right angle, it should end up somewhere near the hole. She surveyed the angle of the S and found the spot on the little white barrier wall she'd need to hit.

"You strike me as a person who thrives on pressure," he said, but she ignored him as she aimed for the spot she'd found and swung. The ball touched close to where she'd aimed, bounced away and struck the side again farther down, then rolled along to within a couple of feet from the cup. A fairly straightforward putt.

Only then did she look up at him. "Trying to distract me again, Mr. Marlow?"

"It's a pretty high-stakes game, Dr. Walsh. Nice shot, by the way."

She walked the S then hit the ball into the hole before stepping over the ankle-high wall so Luke could take his shot. He hit the spot she'd been aiming for, but it still didn't give him a hole in one. Just left him a little closer to the cup than she'd been. He tapped it in and strolled over. "We appear to be even."

"It's only been one hole," she pointed out as she recorded his score on the card.

The next hole, the windmill, put him one stroke ahead. They were back to even after the third, a hilly U.

"You don't play like a man who's never been on a mini-golf course before."

"What can I say? It's a ball game, I'm a man."

"A match made in heaven," she teased and sneaked a glance at him. No doubt that he had an athlete's body—strong shoulders, muscled chest tapering to narrow hips, biceps and forearms that flexed as he lined up his club—but even so, mini golf was its own basket of skills.

"Yep." He grinned. "You know, I feel obliged to point out that this course would be just as accessible to guests if the *Cora Mae* were permanently anchored."

"Ah, but it's more about doing something fun on the deck of a moving vessel—the exhilaration of feeling the ship sail through the water while you're playing sports is something that can't be replicated on a floating hotel."

Luke glanced at the ocean, rubbing his chin as he considered. "I'll take your word for it." He took his shot, then looked back up at her. "Have you played the course often?"

"Occasionally, when there aren't many passengers wanting to play. It's a shame it's such a clear, calm day. My specialty is playing when the going is rough." In truth, even then the ship barely rocked at all, but it was enough to affect a shot.

"A stroke of luck for me," he said with a lazy smile.

Though she was starting to wonder if it was simple luck, or if Luke's entire life was charmed—even the weather cooperated.

With six holes down, Luke was ahead by two strokes. "When you go to the day spa," he asked with an innocent air, "will you have a manicure, as well? Or a pedicure? I like the idea of your toenails in a red gloss polish."

She waited until he was about to swing. "Got a foot fetish?"

He laughed and hit badly, the ball bouncing from a little wall of cobbled rock almost back to where it had started.

"Oh, what a shame."

"Mmm." He glanced down at her sandals. "Definitely red…or perhaps a flaming scarlet."

"You're only two strokes ahead, Mr. Marlow," she said moving to set up her ball. "Try not to get carried away."

After she won that hole, she was only behind by one. She picked up another stroke on the eighth by again using his trick and distracting him before he hit, leaving them tied going into the last hole. Della bit down on her lip as she recorded the scores. If she could just get Luke to consent to all the delights of a day spa—warm oil massage, hot rocks, sauna—he might relax enough to be in a better frame of mind for her to sway him to keep the *Cora Mae* a cruising ship. All she had to do was to get him there, and to do that she needed to win this game. With the score even, it came down to the ninth hole. She squared her shoulders and laid her ball on the black cross.

Luke watched Della place her ball and size up the path to the cup. She wanted to win, that much was obvious, but he'd planned how the game would end before either of them had taken their first swing. He might not have played mini golf before, but he knew one end of a putter from the other, and he'd played more games of billiards than he'd had homemade dinners. Same principles to both games—it was all about angles and momentum.

Making the game's outcome seem natural, that was the tricky part.

Luckily he'd won the coin toss and would play the ninth after Della. It was a complex path that led over a steep slope, under a footbridge, around a fountain and to the cup. In many ways it reminded him of his relationship with Della herself—overly complicated and too many distractions preventing him from keeping his eyes on the prize.

Della managed it in four strokes. Luke thought he could do it in three. Four if he made a mistake—an actual mistake, or a deliberate one. He glanced up at Della and murmured, "Wish me luck."

"Sure," she said sweetly. "Here's to you winning a day at the spa."

"I appreciate the support," he said, then took his first shot. It passed over the hill, under the overpass to hit the side of the fountain before rolling to a stop. He was on track to win the hole. Win the round. Which was not on the agenda.

Della wanted him to spend a day at the spa, and he was willing to do it. He'd been serious about keeping an open mind regarding the *Cora Mae,* and was willing to go along with all the plans Della had to convince him to keep her cruising. Just as he hoped she was doing the same about the ship's transformation into a floating hotel.

But if he had to be trapped in the den of sweet smelling horror that he'd heard passed for day spas, then it was only fair that she had to go, too. Plus, he was curious that she lived here and hadn't paid a visit to the place where women were pampered. His eyes skimmed her delectable form. Unless… Perhaps this was about the scar he'd seen while they were swimming? She'd been so quick to cover it up and stop him from seeing any more of it—did Della have body image issues? He frowned as he walked around the outside of the ninth hole to reach his ball.

"Awkward spot," she said.

"Not too bad." As he lined up the shot, his skin warmed and he knew Della had moved closer. She was going to try and distract him. And he was going to let her. How long had it been since this doctor had spent any time being spoiled? Indulging herself? Too long, he suspected. Time to rectify that. He restrained the smile that threatened.

He swung the putter back and, on the downswing, Della said, "How are your stitches?"

He botched the shot and the ball ended up a little farther behind where he'd started. "Your concern for my health is touching," he drawled, eyeing his ball with a mocking expression. "And useful."

"Surely, you don't think I tried to put you off, Mr. Marlow. Why, that would be despicable. No—" she assumed an angelic expression "—I'm simply honoring my commitment to a patient and to the Hippocratic Oath."

He took a step back and lined up his next shot.

"So your hand isn't bothering you with the grip on the club?" she asked, moving around into his field of vision.

"It's a little tender, but nothing to worry about. I'm doing most of the work with my other hand." It wasn't like he had to put any force into these swings, so this was easier than hitting in the nets earlier. He made the shot and thankfully it hit the place he was aiming for, making it around the fountain on the rebound.

He couldn't win. But he could tie.

His last shot got the ball in the cup. "What's the score, doc?"

"We tied," she said, frowning. Clearly this outcome wasn't a welcome turn of events.

He grinned. "So, I guess we'll both be off to the spa."

Perhaps the grin was a step too far. Hand on hip, she scrutinized him with narrowed eyes. "Why do I get the feeling you planned it this way?"

He rested the club behind his neck, along his shoulders. "You have a suspicious mind?" he said helpfully.

"You said you hadn't played mini golf before."

"I haven't, but I play a lot of billiards. The principles are the same."

Shaking her head, she flashed him a resigned smile. "I've been scammed."

"Maybe, but if the day spa is as good as you say, then we're both winners."

She laughed, and as she did, her nose crinkled up. His heart stilled in his chest and the rest of the world seemed to recede. Dark hair danced around her face in the light breeze, and there was humor in her bottomless brown eyes. Nothing short of the world ending could have stopped him from laughing with her. Until he realized what he'd done.

He'd started to relax.

For the first time in far too long, he felt like he was actually taking a holiday. Despite the grief of losing the uncle he'd loved, and the mountains of work he'd managed while Della had been on shift. Despite his deep-seated aversion to relaxing around anyone but his billiards buddies because it inherently involved letting down his guard.

Despite knowing Della was someone he was locked in a high-stakes business negotiation with, someone who tugged at him so much, he knew he needed to be extra careful around her. And possibly most seriously, despite vowing that he'd never again be blinded by a woman to the detriment of all else. He silently cursed himself.

Tension flowed into his muscles, bracing his shoulders, then pouring through the rest of his body, tightening and clenching until he felt…more like his normal self. That was a disturbing thought. He filed it away for later consideration. He took down the club from his shoulders—a stupid, cocky pose—and rested it on the ground, the grip of his good hand tightening till he felt his knuckles straining.

Right now he had other, more important matters to concentrate on. He set his jaw and met Della's eyes again, this time being sure to keep his expression more suited to a business acquaintance. "So what's on the agenda tonight?"

Her eyebrows quirked, obviously noticing the change in his demeanor. The happy twinkle vanished from her eyes and he knew it was in response to his suddenly chilly tone. It made him realize just how much she'd relaxed with him.

She took a small step back and nodded with a respectful detachment. Perversely, he already missed the secret delight of the casual air that had sprung up between them. And didn't *that* just show how important it was that he'd caught his slip in time?

"I think you deserve a night off," she said with that damned polite smile she'd used when he first met her.

A reprieve. Time to get his mind in order. Just what he needed. So why did he want to push?

"Why waste the night?" he said before he could stop himself.

She bit down on her lip, then her shoulders squared. "I have some paperwork to do this afternoon, so I'll be grabbing something quick for dinner. But I can see you after that. Meet me at the main staircase in the foyer at seven."

He nodded. Before then he would get his head thinking clearly again. Because, starting tonight, they were changing tack—he was going to convince Della Walsh to allow him to turn the *Cora Mae* into a floating hotel. No more messing around.

This was business.

Six

While Della waited at the stairs for Luke that evening, she fingered the scalloped neck of her top. It was new, more daring than anything she'd worn for the past few years. The moment she'd seen the gleaming sequined mint-green garment in one of the ship's boutiques, she'd had to have it. Given her refusal to wear anything but relatively plain clothing since her husband's death, she'd found her obsession with the top disquieting. Could it be a sign that she was changing? She glanced at the fabric with the tiny gleaming discs, habit making her check that her scars were well covered.

She looked up to see Luke strolling into the lobby and all thoughts flew out of her mind. The same magnetic charge that had struck her the moment she'd first seen him on the deck hit her again—it held her gaze steady on him, enticing her to draw closer. She ran her palms down her skirt and tried to hold on to her composure. His hair was damp and freshly combed; his sky-blue dress shirt emphasized the breadth of his shoulders and chest. A need to feel that strength under her hands was so strong it threatened to pull her under.

"Good evening, Della," he said, granting her a lazy smile. "You look amazing."

"Hello, Luke," she said brightly, hoping to cover how her pulse thrummed. "Thank you. Is there anything in particular you'd like to do tonight? See one of the live shows, perhaps? Try the wine bar?"

He sank his hands into his pockets. "I assume this ship has a dance floor?"

"There are three venues," she said, relieved to be able to fall into tour guide mode. "If you like a modern atmosphere, there's a nightclub on Deck Five. And there's a retro disco on Deck Nine. Or if you prefer a waltz, the Blue Moon is on Deck Four."

"Which one do you usually go to?" He raised a lazy eyebrow.

Butterflies leaped to life in her belly. She had a feeling she knew where this was going—the wrong direction.

"I—" she began but her throat was too tight to speak. She swallowed and began again. "I don't." Even to her the answer sounded sharp, full of meaning. Not just a statement of fact as she'd intended. When he raised his eyebrows, she found herself compelled to say more. "I'm not much of a dancer. But I'll take you to whichever venue appeals. I'm sure you won't have a problem finding partners."

"I'd rather dance with you," he said, his voice as rich and smooth as darkest chocolate. Before she could think of another excuse, he held out his hand. "Live on the edge. Dance with me, Della."

She looked at the hand outstretched in front of her.

This wasn't just a hand she'd sutured; it was a man's hand. She hadn't held—*really held*—a man's hand since her husband's. It was loaded with meaning. An invitation to dance. Her mind spun on to the next threat...dancing, which required even more body contact than hand-holding. Involuntarily, her muscles tensed.

For two years, she'd lived a celibate life and preferred it that way. It was the only path open to her—even in the unlikely event that a man might see past her scars, she would never, *never* risk loving and losing again. So why go dancing? Or even share dinner with a man?

Because Luke wanted to—and she'd locked herself into a game of "persuasions" to convince him to keep the *Cora Mae* as a cruising ship. A game she didn't intend to lose. So no backing away from a simple request.

Though, if she were honest, part of her wanted to dance with this man. Would it be so wrong to give in to that part just this once?

Ignoring the trembling deep inside, she took Luke's hand and showed him the way to the Blue Moon.

As Luke led her onto the full dance floor ten minutes later with a firm grip on her hand, Della tried to remember how to breathe. She normally loved that the walls around them were painted darkest blue and studded with fairy lights that resembled little stars, but for the first time she couldn't spare them a glance.

He's walking you to a dance floor, not off a gangplank. No big deal.

But her body wasn't listening. Because, any moment now, Luke would take her in his arms—a touch more intimate than any contact from a man she'd experienced in several years. Her stomach tightened like a fist.

While the singer crooned an old favorite and with other couples scattered around them enjoying the night, they reached the center of the polished floor. Luke turned to face her, inviting her to step in. She tried to comply—to move—but her feet wouldn't work.

You agreed to this. You said you'd dance with him.

Taking a breath, she shuffled her feet until she was encircled by Luke's patiently waiting arms. Perhaps sensing her inner tension, he held her at a respectable distance and began to move them smoothly around the floor. She was as stiff as a board, but was helpless to loosen up. Being this close seemed wrong on so many levels.

"I won't bite," he said, his mouth near her ear.

Startled from her thoughts, she caught her bottom lip between her teeth. Of course he wouldn't; she was being unreasonable. They were simply dancing, the same as the other couples. The same as she used to do. Before.

Consciously loosening her muscles, she released some tension as she exhaled in a long steady stream.

"Better," he murmured.

His encouraging tone allowed her to relax more into his arms. And as she did, she became aware of the sensation of those arms around her—supportive and…nice.

The scent of a man's clean skin filled her head, and the strength of his broad shoulders registered under hand. Her pulse picked up pace, and this time it wasn't due to apprehension. He pulled her almost imperceptibly closer, and she looked up into his warm gray eyes.

"I'm sorry," she said, not knowing exactly what to say.

"What for?" he asked, his voice soft. "You've given me an entertaining day and now you're dancing with me. There's nothing to apologize for. I should be thanking you."

Kindness with no awkward questions. Her heart melted a little. The depth of his sensitivity was unexpected. She couldn't have picked a better partner for her first foray into dating. Not that this was a date, but the things they were doing were all the sorts of things normal couples did when they went out. Maybe, after Luke left, she would make more of an effort with her social life, stop cutting herself off—not go searching for a relationship, just a little company. Maybe it was time.

She smiled up at him. Other guests floated across the floor, most dressed to the nines, several dripping in diamonds or brightly colored gemstones, but she ignored them. They couldn't compare to this man.

He shifted his hand at the small of her back and rubbed a slow pattern of small circles, sending goose bumps rushing across her arms and torso. As he led her in a turn, he pulled her a little closer again. A space still existed between their bodies, but she could feel the heat emanating from him, and his breath fanning over her cheek.

Suddenly she didn't want his kindness, didn't want his gentleness. She wanted to be dragged against him—closer still—to feel his body pressed against the length of hers, to kiss and be kissed. It had been so long…

The strength drained from her body, leaving her cold. *How could she be thinking such things?* Wanting to kiss a man who wasn't her husband? Wanting to start something that could only lead to another ending either sooner or later.

She stumbled to a stop, thoughts clashing in her mind, the rigidity returning to every part of her body. How easy it was to counsel others on the stages of grief, on the turmoil of the road to recovery. The importance of not being crippled by guilt when normal needs and desires start stirring again.

She looked up at Luke. "Would you mind—?"

"Can I get you a drink?" he smoothly interjected.

"Thank you," she said, more grateful for his understanding than the drink. "A lime and soda."

He guided her over to two vacant bar stools and ordered her drink plus a scotch. Then he turned and casually surveyed the room. Perhaps to give her more time to recover.

"Looking for anyone in particular?" she asked.

"Not really." He turned back to her, all relaxed charm. "I've run into a few acquaintances in the corridors and around the ship, but you're the only person on board that I actually know."

His words unsettled her. "You don't know me, Luke," she said softly. There were so many things about her that he didn't understand.

"I think I do." His gaze rested on her mouth. "Or at least I'm coming to."

She moistened her suddenly dry lips. "Are you also coming to know the *Cora Mae?*"

He looked from the pianist sitting at the baby grand to the twenty-foot-high wine rack behind the bar and nodded. "I believe I am."

Their drinks arrived and she flashed a smile of thanks to Tommy, the bartender. She took a sip, then put her glass down on the polished wood bar. "Dare I hope she's growing on you?"

"I've become very fond of her," he said, but she couldn't tell if he really meant it, or whether he was humoring her.

Swirling the ice around her glass, she asked, "Can you see that she deserves to stay cruising the South Pacific?"

"I see your point, Della, I do," he said, spearing his fingers through his hair. "But this has to be a business decision, not a sentimental one."

She laid a hand on his forearm. "Surely it wouldn't be charity if it makes a profit."

"I don't know anything about running a cruise ship."

He placed a hand over hers as it lay on his forearm. "If I take the time to learn, it will divert my time and energy away from my own business, so I need to be very sure."

Her chest tightened and she withdrew her hand. She'd thought it was a simple matter of convincing him about the merits of cruising, but she now saw the mountain she'd need to overcome before he'd agree to leave the *Cora Mae* alone.

He took a sip from his drink and swallowed. "Tell me more about yourself, Della."

"There are so many more interesting topics." She resisted the impulse to squirm in her seat.

"You said I didn't know you. I'd like to."

"But it's not necessary, is it? Not part of the business we're involved in here. Time is precious and I need you to know about the *Cora Mae* and her crew." She ran her finger around the rim of her glass. "Did you know we have a three-story auditorium with live shows?"

Slowly, deliberately, he sat back on his stool and regarded her. Della held her breath. He was deciding whether to pursue the topic or let her off the hook—it was in the look he leveled at her. And she had a feeling that if this man pushed hard enough, she might just tell him anything he wanted to know.

"All right," he said finally, lifting his glass. "Tell me about the crew."

She breathed a sigh of relief. For whatever reason, he was allowing her to change the subject. "Well, there's the medical team, of course. Then there's our social activities team," she continued. "They organize the program of events such as the games and yoga in the mornings."

"Do you join in the organized activities?"

She practiced yoga on her own during quiet times at the gym, not in the group sessions. Having her scars peek out of her leotard during a pose and catching people's attention was not her idea of relaxation or recreation. "I'm not much of a joiner."

His slow blink told her she hadn't fooled him. "You never miss the land, yet even out here you're not much of a joiner. Interesting."

Her chest tightened. "Stop trying to decode me, Luke," she said and picked up her drink.

Luke could see he was losing her again. She'd begun to relax when they were dancing, then something had made her pull away. Despite knowing it was a bad idea, part of him wanted her back there, wanted her in his arms again. Having her there had felt damn good. Better than anything had in too long to remember. He held back an oath. Time to leave the dance club.

"I've only caught glimpses of the top decks so far," he said. "Will you show me?"

She nodded, relief sliding over her features. "Of course."

He settled his hand at the small of her back as they wove their way through the throng, and had to restrain a sigh at how good even that small touch felt. The thin fabric slid smoothly over her skin and he had the illusion that at any moment he could pull her close and wrap her in his arms—closer than she'd been when they'd danced. Close enough to feel her pressed against him. He curled the fingers of his free hand into a fist then stretched them. How would he keep his reaction to her under control for three weeks?

The clear glass doors of the elevator opened and they stepped in. As they began the ascent, he glanced at the passing levels...until he realized Della was watching his reflection. His breath caught. When his gaze met hers in the glass, she didn't look away. The effect of the stolen glance was electric, and his shirt collar was suddenly restrictive around his throat.

After an eternity encapsulated in mere moments, the elevator slowed and the doors whooshed apart, taking the reflected image of the two of them with it, and the tension that had been building in his chest dissipated.

"This is the second highest deck," Della said as they stepped out. The oddly intimate connection was gone and she was all business as she pointed up, to their left. "That's Deck Thirteen, the highest, but it only has a bar and a cluster of heated spas."

He looked up and saw people spilling out the doors of the bar, the beat of rock music floating down to where he stood. Their deck—Twelve—had only two other people, a couple strolling much farther along, absorbed in each other. "It seems fairly empty."

"It usually is at this time of night. Most people are at dinner, or the night entertainments like the theatre, or they're at a bar."

"Or dancing," he murmured, remembering the feel of her in his arms.

"Or dancing," she agreed neutrally, seeming not to be as affected as he was by the memory. "During the day, this is a popular area, though. This pool is always full of guests, and the deck chairs are used by people reading or relaxing."

They walked past a long, curved pool, with underwater lights that made the water sparkle. Before their picnic at the Bay of Islands, he couldn't remember the last time he'd been for a swim. It must have been years—leisure activities weren't high on his priority list. He worked out at the gym in his office building, sure, but that wasn't for fun, that was to keep himself healthy. He paused and looked down into the glittering depths; depths that were unexpectedly enticing. "With these facilities, you must have a dip in the water every day."

"I don't swim here," she said smoothly.

He turned to her and sank his hands deep into his pockets. "You swam with me in New Zealand."

"Usually I prefer privacy." She moved away and pointed to their left. "Have you seen the life-size chessboard?"

And it clicked into place. Her scars. She was self-conscious about her body. He wanted to take her by the shoulders and tell her she shouldn't worry—a few scars couldn't ruin her beauty. But he knew that would fall on deaf ears. He stared at her a moment longer before turning to the chessboard and her question. "I can't say that I have."

She ran a hand over the smooth top of a white pawn that came up to her shoulder. "Can you play?"

"Sure. Can you?"

"I haven't in years—" she hesitated and her eyes flicked to him and back to the board "—but I'll give it a go if you'd like a game."

Luke arched an eyebrow. This was a diversionary tactic. Della obviously wanted them occupied in an activity that didn't involve touching. Sensible woman. Logically, he should be striving for the same thing. No, not should. Would. He *would* be aiming for such activities.

"I'll take black," he said, moving to the opposite side of the board.

Della stepped across the squares and pushed one of her pawns two squares forward.

"Predictable start," he said as he picked up his knight and placed it on a square in front of his line of pawns.

She moved another pawn out. "Just because something is predictable doesn't make it wrong."

"Perhaps." Lifting the pawn diagonally to the right of his bishop, he moved it out one square. While she thought about her move he watched her, but he saw her sneak a self-conscious look at him from under her lashes. His scrutiny made her uncomfortable. She was a mass of contradictions—she surveyed the world with calm composure, rarely missing a thing he was sure, yet didn't want to be observed herself.

And whenever he asked her a question about herself, she gave brief replies, but talking about the ship or her crew, you couldn't switch her off. It wasn't modesty holding her back in discussions about herself—sharing personal information made her uncomfortable. Why would that be? Was it connected to the personal history she'd shared that day on the beach?

He looked up to the stars and a flash of movement caught his attention. Within an instant he was beside Della, one arm around her waist, pointing skyward. "Shooting star."

"Oh," she said on a long breath, her gaze following his finger.

The feel of her against him was mesmerizing. Absorbed in the moment, she'd forgotten to be on her guard and allowed her soft curves to meld into his side, her head resting back on his shoulder as she tracked the star's path.

"Make a wish," he murmured beside her ear.

A kiss. In this moment, all he wanted was to turn her to face him, to lean down and touch her sweet lips with his. It was wrong, he knew it was wrong, but the blood in his veins thundered and a delicious heat began to rise.

The star faded and the night sky again grew still, the only movement the ship's steady forward progress and the gentle breeze that danced in Della's hair. But she didn't move away. Part of him dared not move and break the spell, but the larger, rebellious part of him—surrounded by the scent of vanilla and woman—risked inclining his head down to hers, and was rewarded when she shivered.

"Like to know what I wished for?" he said, voice low.

Her eyes drifted shut. "You're not supposed to tell. It won't come true if you do."

"Maybe," he said, his mouth so close to her ear that his lips brushed her lobe as he spoke. "But if you knew what the wish was, perhaps you'd grant it."

He pressed a light kiss on her neck, just below her ear. Della held herself still but didn't pull away. "I don't have any magical powers to grant wishes."

"I'm not so sure." He pressed another kiss to her soft skin, this one at the edge of her jaw.

As he cupped the side of her throat with one hand, he felt her racing pulse and turned her to face him. A small sound of protest passed her lips even as she leaned in and placed the lightest of kisses on his mouth. It took everything inside him, but he locked his muscles tight and didn't move an inch. Della had held herself back so much, he wouldn't ruin this by pushing too far, too fast. Instead, he waited for excruciating seconds for her to come back to him. Her warm breath caressed his face as she looked from his mouth to his eyes, fighting some inner struggle. Then she tilted her head forward and stole another butterfly kiss, and again, he gently moved his lips but nothing else, despite the protests of his straining body.

Her scent curled around his thoughts, leaving little reason in its wake, but he held firm until she tipped her chin up for a third time. Now, her lips were more confident and she wound her arms up around his neck. That was all the permission he needed, all the permission he could wait for. With a groan, he pulled her in.

He deepened the kiss, tasting her, needing to be close,

connected to her. Holding her flush against him with the hand she'd stitched, he traced a path over the curve of her spine with the other, down over her hip, back up to feel the swell of the side of her breast. He'd wanted her from the moment she'd first appeared like an angel from the crowd on the deck the day he'd boarded, but now, he craved her with an urgency that rocked him. His body was ablaze; the kiss was nowhere near enough. Her fingers wound up into his hair and dug into his scalp, her mouth demanding against his.

"Della," he rasped as he wrenched his mouth away to drag some oxygen into his lungs.

She stilled and looked up at him with eyes that were suddenly alert…and stunned.

"It's okay," he whispered as he rubbed a thumb over her damp bottom lip.

She unwound her arms from his neck and let them fall to her sides. "No, it's not." She said the words quietly, almost to herself, her eyes averted. Then she drew in a deep breath and met his gaze. "Luke, you don't want to do this."

He almost laughed at how far that was from the truth. "I can tell you that my body disagrees in the most strenuous of terms."

"That's because it's under a misapprehension."

"What would that be?" he murmured as he skimmed his fingers down her spine to the dip in her lower back, trying to bring the two of them back to the place they'd been only moments earlier.

For a full second, her eyes darkened in response to his caress, before she blinked the effect away. "Your body thinks there's a chance this will go further."

"Hate to be the one to break it to you," he said lazily, "but your body agrees with mine."

She pressed lips still rosy from his kiss tightly together. "Luke, you have to know something."

"I'm listening," he said, watching the way her mouth moved, wanting to lean in again and—

"No, you really need to hear this."

His gaze flicked up to her eyes. She was right. He was paying more attention to her mouth than the words coming out of it. Summoning all his self-discipline, he took a small step back and rested his hands on his hips. "Okay, shoot."

"I'm celibate." There was a pause as he thought he'd misheard or she'd been joking, all while she watched him warily.

"Celibate?" he finally said, frowning. "Are you serious?"

She nodded as she folded her arms under her breasts. "I don't want to lead you on, to waste your time."

His mind grappled with the concept, which seemed so alien to his hormone-drenched body. "You took some kind of vow after your husband died?"

Della drew in a breath and moved the short distance to the guardrail. He followed and rested his forearms on the top rail, facing slightly away from her to give her some space.

But she apparently didn't need it—she turned to him. "No vow, but this is not a flippant lifestyle choice. I'm serious." A soft pink flush touched her cheekbones—this was difficult for her to share. Which just made it harder to understand.

"You don't kiss like a celibate person," he murmured.

"I'm sorry about the kiss. That was a mistake," she said, her gaze not wavering.

Something deep in his chest protested. "Not from where I'm standing."

"It was the first time I've kissed anyone in two years.

It won't happen again." Her voice was filled with quiet certainty. When he opened his mouth to reply, she held up a hand, palm out. "There's nothing you can say or do to change my mind. Please don't make this awkward by trying."

He let out a long breath then gently tucked a wayward curl behind her ear. "Even though I'd love you to change your mind, I do respect that you've made your decision." He rubbed an index finger across his forehead. "I'm asking questions because I'm intrigued." Everything new he learned about this woman intrigued him.

"Is this about your scars? Do you doubt I desire you?"

She shook her head slowly. "It's more complicated than that, but please don't ask me more. You're the first person I've told, and I'm only doing it now to stop you wasting any more time pursuing an impossibility." A smile pulled at the corners of her mouth, but it was unconvincing. "I've tried to head this off a few times but you're persistent."

He returned the smile, acknowledging the truth in that. "I appreciate your honesty. I'm more disappointed than you know, but it's your decision to make," he said, still not understanding, but willing to leave it for now.

"Thank you," she whispered.

After he'd walked her back to her room and left her without so much as a kiss on the cheek, Luke went back to the deck and leaned on the same railing they'd shared minutes before. Dragging in a deep breath of ocean-fresh air, he looked up at the stars again. He sure hadn't seen that coming. How could a woman who kissed as passionately as Della be celibate?

And, though he was serious that he would never push her to breaking a decision like that, he was more keen than ever to understand what made her tick.

Seven

Della froze at her desk as the nurse's voice floated from the front room through her partially open door.

"Good morning, Mr. Marlow," Jody said. "How can I help you?"

Hidden in her office, Della bit down on her lip and wondered if she could shut the door without drawing attention. She'd successfully avoided Luke Marlow since their bone-melting kiss. For a full day yesterday. Despite knowing she only had a short time to convince him about the *Cora Mae*.

She sighed. Her procrastination had to end now.

"I'd like to see Dr. Walsh about the stitches in my hand," he said, voice deep and charming.

Even from this distance, the timbre of his voice seemed to reverberate through her body, and her eyes drifted closed. Memories of their kiss surfaced in her mind— the way his hand had curled around the nape of her neck, the champagne fizz that had rushed through her veins the moment his lips had touched hers.

"I'll just see if she's available," Jody said out in reception.

Della's hands fluttered to the desktop and clasped together. Two years ago, she'd lain in a hospital bed critically ill with the injuries she'd received in the attack that had killed her husband. Shane had been her everything. Having his life ripped from her in that dirty street had been unbearable, overwhelming. In her grief, she'd made a promise to herself—never, never again would she love someone enough to leave her vulnerable to that much pain.

Intellectually, she knew she couldn't, *shouldn't,* hold herself to that long-ago promise. But emotionally, she knew it still held sway over her. Exposing herself meant stripping bare in so much more than just a physical sense. And Luke would be horrified if he ever caught a glimpse of the puckered scars across her torso. He might think he knew about a couple of dainty marks, but the reality was uglier. Anything physical between them would end before it had begun.

Not that it would ever get that far. All she was doing now was stopping things prior to reaching that point. Saving him the trouble. Saving herself the pain.

Jody slipped in through the doorway and closed it behind her. "Do you want me to pass him to Cal?" she asked quietly.

As strong as the temptation was, she knew she couldn't. She'd asked Jody and the other staff in the medical suite to cover for her if Luke rang. She hadn't explained why, and they'd been considerate enough to not ask questions. She simply needed time to get her bearings—to purge that kiss from her memory so she could focus on the reason for seeing him.

So she could face him merely as a business associate, the other half-owner of Patrick's ship. Calm, professional, unperturbed.

That meant no passing him to Cal now.

"That's fine, Jody." She drew in a fortifying breath. "Show him in."

All too soon, Luke sauntered into her office, one hand deep in a pocket, the bandaged hand held at chest height, his dark blond hair rumpled, as if he'd been on the top deck in the breeze. She remained behind her small desk, grateful for the illusion of protection it afforded her.

"Jody tells me your hand needs attention?" she said, starting the conversation as she meant it to continue—on a professional basis.

The arch of his eyebrow showed he'd noted her tone, but he didn't comment on it. Instead, he glanced down at his bandaged hand. "I think you might need to check this."

"Certainly," she said, smiling. "Jody? Can you come in here a moment?"

The nurse appeared at the door. "Yes, Dr. Walsh?"

"Mr. Marlow has some concerns about his sutured hand. Can you take down the dressing and check for signs of infection while I bring up his report, please?"

Jody nodded, holding back a smile as she washed her hands in the sink. Surprise flared in Luke's eyes, then an almost imperceptible frown as he no doubt calculated strategies to circumvent the proceedings, followed by amusement as his gaze flicked to hers and he realized he'd been outmaneuvered.

She sat back down behind the desk, feeling unreasonably smug at gaining the upper hand.

Jody moved to the table where Della had first sewn the sutures. "Mr. Marlow, if you'll take a seat and lay your hand here, I'll take a look."

In her peripheral vision, Della saw Luke set his hand out on the flat surface. After pulling up his info on the computer screen, she swiveled in her chair to find his eyes on her as Jody peeled back the bandage. As the wound was exposed, it looked exactly as Della had expected— a healthy pink with the skin healing around the sutures.

Jody wiped the area with an alcohol-infused cloth. "There's no sign of redness or swelling. Have you had any pain?"

Still looking at Della, he said, "It doesn't hurt, but I couldn't say things have felt right."

Della's stomach lurched as she took his double meaning, and she threw a quick glance at Jody, but thankfully the nurse didn't seem to notice anything amiss.

Jody pressed Luke's hand gently with her gloved fingers. "Any pain when I do this?"

"No."

Della glanced at the screen to check the date. "The stitches have been in for long enough, anyway. Jody, you can take them out."

While the nurse efficiently removed the sutures, Della made a few notes in Luke's file. With Luke watching her, the skin at the back of her neck tingled the whole time. A shiver ran up her spine, but she refused to look around.

When Jody finished, she stood, stripped off her gloves and looked to Della. "Do you need me for anything else?"

"No. Thank you, Jody," Della said, and watched the nurse leave. Then her eyes strayed to the man who remained.

"If that's all—" Della said at the same time Luke said, "You didn't return my call."

She took one breath, then another. "I haven't had a chance yet."

"You were avoiding me," he said softly, taking a small

step forward. "You told me where you stand and I said I respected that. Why would that stop us from spending time together?"

Something inside her trembled, knowing this was a make-or-break point. And she had to be completely honest. She moistened her lips.

"You don't expect more?"

"I wouldn't be averse to something more. But I think you already know that."

"There's no future with me, Luke."

"I can accept that. I'm not after a future but I do want to explore what we do have here and now," he said.

She wrapped a hand around the taut muscles at the back of her neck. He wouldn't be interested in something short-term either if he knew what she looked like under these clothes. A shipboard fling was all about fantasy, about glorious experiences. Her body allowed for neither.

"Besides," he said, moving to the side of her desk, "you were convincing me of the merits of keeping the ship sailing the high seas. Surely you haven't given up on that?"

"No," she said slowly.

"It's much harder to convince me from the other side of the ship."

"I—" she paused and swallowed "—I just thought we both needed a bit of a time-out."

"But we're past that now?" He stroked his fingers across his chin and her skin tingled as if he'd touched her own chin.

She drew in an uneven breath. "Perhaps."

He nodded once, short and assured, as if she'd agreed with him. "I've been thinking about what you said last night."

"I thought you might. But we—"

"It's about your scars, isn't it? Your celibacy is because you don't think you're desirable."

She flinched. It was one thing to think about it, another to have her insecurities presented so boldly to her face. But she couldn't lie. "Partly."

She didn't elaborate—she wasn't ready to talk about the pain of loving and losing with Luke Marlow, or anyone for that matter.

He stepped closer. "It must be hard to contemplate baring yourself for the first time after what you suffered. Hard to trust that you won't be rejected."

"Yes." Her throat felt thick and tight. His understanding was her undoing.

"You can trust me, Della," he said, his voice low as he took another step closer.

"You think that but you don't know...you don't know." She swallowed.

"Della—"

"Anyway, it's a moot point."

He looked at her with such genuine concern, she felt a tiny chink in her resolve.

"What if I guaranteed my cabin would be in total darkness?" He reached out and cupped the side of her face in his palm. "Would your answer change if you had that privacy?"

Her eyes drifted closed as she instinctively nestled her face into the warmth of his hand. He really did understand. There was a thrill in knowing he wanted her enough to create a way she could feel safe while being intimate. Intimate. Making love with Luke Marlow...

She was sorely tempted.

Her heart skipped a beat. Shane had been her only lover and she'd made vows before God that he'd be the only one. But her husband was gone forever. The scars on her body had insulated her from facing this decision…but now there was Luke. Could she take what he was offering?

She swallowed. "I honestly don't know."

"I'm having dinner in my cabin tonight." His gray eyes sparked with invitation. "Join me."

"And if I say no to your offer to turn the lights off?"

"Whatever your decision, you're welcome to share dinner. I'd prefer your answer was yes," he said with a smile in his voice, "but I'll respect a no. We still have much to discuss with the *Cora Mae,* regardless."

Join him. Such a simple request.

And maybe things between them *should* be that simple….

Maybe she was making this into something bigger than it needed to be. They'd kissed. She'd told him they had no future. He'd accepted it. Time to move on. Back to the plan.

"I'll let you know."

"While you're deciding, think on this." He moved in close, crowding her, and then his mouth came slowly down until it softly, firmly moved over hers. A molten heat flared at her core, filling her body cell by cell and she moaned. The push of his tongue, the brush of his arms at her waist, his scent surrounding her…she was lost.

Just when she was trembling with need, he slowed the kiss and eased away.

"All right, then," she whispered.

She watched a slow, satisfied smile spread across his face as he turned and walked through the door. And her stomach fluttered as she realized she may have miscalculated her ability to handle Luke Marlow.

Della knocked on Luke's cabin door that night, no closer to a decision about taking their attraction to the next level than she had been in the medical suite.

Once taken, that step would be impossible to undo. And if he reacted badly to her body—if he was horrified, or pitied her—would she be able to continue to negotiate with him about the *Cora Mae*...or would she burn with an unhealthy mix of embarrassment, hurt and resentment making business discussions impossible?

There was no way of knowing how any of the variables would play out.

At her first knock, the door swung open and he stood before her in a black polo shirt and tan pants, stealing her breath. His gray eyes were dark, his chin freshly shaved and he filled the doorway as if it were a frame made just for him.

For a charged moment, neither of them moved or spoke. The air was heavy with the possibilities of the night, sending a shiver through her blood.

Then he reached out and drew her in, placing a chaste kiss on her cheek. "I'm glad you came."

"Did you think I wouldn't?" she asked, her voice only a little unsteady. The merest contact of his lips with the side of her face sent magic shimmering across her skin, and she wanted to turn to him. Ask for more. But she wouldn't let herself get carried away—she'd need a cool head to make a decision tonight that was right for her.

As she passed him, he cupped her elbow. "I hoped you would, but I've learned not to assume anything with you."

She glanced around the room, taking in the soft lighting, the flickering candles, the two glasses sitting on the table. The stage was set for seduction. She swallowed. As for what may happen tonight, she was trying hard not to think about it just yet.

Luke indicated the bottle of white wine in the ice bucket. "How about you pour while I organize dinner?

Roxie Appleby sent me up a basket with instructions that are apparently foolproof."

"Sure," she said, grateful for something to do with her hands. She normally wasn't prone to restlessness, but standing close to Luke Marlow, close enough to smell his cologne, while they were surrounded by candles and low lighting, created an...unsettled feeling deep inside.

An unsettled feeling? Is that the best you can do to describe it after all those years of medical training? Della laughed softly at herself as she poured the wine. Her amusement dissipated her tension just a little until she took the glasses to the kitchenette, where Luke was tossing a salad. The action drew her gaze to the solid breadth of his shoulders, and she wanted nothing more in that moment than to smooth her hands across them. She'd bet they were solid. And warm. And smooth. Her pulse raced erratically. If she said yes to his proposition, she could run her hands over those shoulders tonight. Impossibly, her heart beat faster.

"Would you like yours in here?" she asked through a dry throat.

"Here's great." He laid the utensils down and took the glass she held out, brushing her fingers lightly as he did.

The temptation to let her fingers linger against his was crushing, so she quickly lifted her own glass to her lips. But before she could take a sip, he stopped her with his hand on her wrist.

"Here's to possibilities," he said, his voice smooth and low.

Everything inside her quivered. "To possibilities," she echoed.

They clinked glasses and, as he sampled the wine, Luke watched her over the rim. His gray eyes were dark, drawing her in. There was no use denying it to herself—she wanted him. Badly. Without losing eye contact, she sipped her drink, the cool liquid doing nothing to ease the flames that were coming to life inside her.

Luke took her wine and placed the glass next to his on the counter, then tugged her closer. And kissed her. Gently at first, the taste of wine was on his tongue, but within moments, it wasn't enough. She threaded her fingers through his hair, holding him in place, just as his hand crept up to cradle her nape. Heat shimmered between them, around them. Through her.

"Della," he murmured against her mouth. "I want you so badly I can't see straight."

With reluctance, she began to ease away, her breathing uneven. She didn't want to lead him on. He'd been nothing but patient with her—she owed it to him to play fair.

He ironed a palm down her back. "Let me turn the lights off, Della." His voice was ragged. "Let me make love to you."

A ball of panic began to rise at the base of her throat, but she swallowed it away. She wanted this. Wanted him. And for the first time in a long time, the want was more powerful than the fear.

"Yes," she whispered. Then, stronger, "Yes."

"You won't regret it, I promise." His eyes blazed as he smiled. "Even if dinner will be later than planned."

He took her hand and led her up the stairs to the bedroom. The curtains in front of the sliding door to the balcony were already drawn. He clicked a remote and the lights downstairs went out, leaving just one lamp casting a soft glow in the bedroom. In the gentle light, he resembled a fallen angel—dark blond hair framing his face, eyes brimming with temptation, strong nose and that mouth... Her breath snared high in her throat. She already knew the magic that mouth could create.

As if reading her thoughts, he kissed her lightly, then pulled away, his endless gray eyes looking deeply into hers. "Tell me if you want to stop." Another kiss, feather-light, lingering at the corner of her mouth. "But I'm telling you now, I intend to make sure you don't need to."

He clicked another button and darkness softly shrouded them. Her heart beat loudly in her ears—it was a pivotal moment in her life, that much was obvious. If she went through with this, nothing would ever be the same. But she couldn't walk away....

Standing on tippy toes, she tentatively placed her lips on his. She had to show him this was her choice—she knew what she wanted, and what she wanted was Luke. At the contact, she felt a groan reverberate in his chest but he didn't move, didn't take control of the kiss. Emboldened, she tugged on his bottom lip with her teeth and skimmed a hand up to his shoulders, tracing the muscles she'd been admiring in the kitchen earlier. Even though she couldn't see him, he filled her senses—the sound of his rough breaths, the feel of him under her fingertips, the scent of clean skin mingling with aftershave.

With an arm around her waist, he drew her closer, flush against him, and she sighed. Her body felt heavy, sweetly drugged by his kiss.

He turned her until her back was to him, leaving a trail of kisses as he went. Gently, he urged her arms up into the air, then slowly lifted her blouse. The double protection of the darkness and having him behind her allowed her to give in to the sensations and release the lurking fears. To just feel. His fingers lingered on her skin as they slid along her arms, teasing. Promising.

Her blouse swished to the floor at her feet, the delicate sound filling her awareness...until Luke's hands began their return journey from her fingertips high in the air, down her inner arms, to her sides and finally coming to rest at her waist. She almost melted in a puddle at his feet.

Hot breath warmed her ear. "I've been crazy with wanting you."

Pure sexual awareness skittered down her spine. Nothing existed but the two of them and this moment in time. Lowering her arms, she leaned back into him, reveling in the warmth, the strength of his chest supporting her. His heart thumped hard enough for her to feel and it resonated through her entire body, as if it beat just for her.

He undid the clasp on her bra, sliding the straps down her arms, and she felt the warm evening air brush across her sensitized breasts.

His hands drifted down her sides, and she tensed as his fingertips found the first bump of a scar. Saying he was fine with her marked body and discovering the reality were two different things, and she couldn't breathe as his fingers explored her ribs to her collarbone.

"Della, you're beautiful," he said, his voice rich and low.

"But the—"

He placed a finger over her lips, silencing her protest. "The scars are proof of your amazing inner strength. Enough to withstand something so awful. And that inner strength is something I find alluring. Irresistible."

With his acceptance, a shudder ran through her body and, finally, she was able to unleash the passion that had been securely locked away for far too long.

She kissed him. Hungrily. With all the wanting and needing she had for this man. And he kissed her right back, with as much passion. More.

The liquid heat of desire spread through her body. He held her waist firmly, keeping her upright, and the imprint of his hand on her bare skin burned with delicious heat.

His fingers found the zipper on her skirt and released it. The whisper of the fabric as it fell to pool at her feet was almost as erotic as Luke's touch. Almost.

His fingers slipped inside the waistband of her panties, urging them down to join her skirt on the floor. She stepped to the side, away from her clothes, and slipped out of her shoes. Never had she been as meticulously, as erotically undressed.

"And what about you," she murmured as she felt for his belt and unbuckled.

He laid his hands over hers, holding them. "I know this is selfish, but give me a few minutes to learn your body. I can't see it, so I need to explore. To discover."

Biting down hard on her bottom lip, she let go of the belt with its dangling ends and allowed Luke the time he asked for.

His head dipped, and surprisingly soft hair brushed against her throat, then her collarbone. As his hands and mouth moved across her skin, tingling awareness spread through her.

Each time his fingers found a scar, he placed a tender kiss on the flesh, and a little piece of her heart melted.

The heat of his tongue on the underside of her breast surprised her and she gasped. A hand cupped her other breast, while another snaked down her abdomen, to where she needed him the most.

Too restless with aching need to wait any longer, she reached for him. "My turn."

His body moved against hers as he straightened, then his voice was at her ear. "Our turn," he said, and dragged her lobe into his mouth.

Her knees swayed, and Luke guided her backward a step until the bed bumped into her calves. He leaned down and she heard the covers being dragged back. Then Luke's hands were at her waist again. Where they belonged. She eased down until she found the edge of the bed, then lay back, not letting go of his shoulders, bringing him with her. How had she held out against him before tonight? In this moment, he was everything she'd ever needed.

"Luke," she said, but didn't have the words to complete the sentence. To tell him everything she was experiencing.

He placed a lingering kiss on her lips, then pulled away. "Hold that thought. I'll be back in a second," he said. His body heat disappeared and there was a rustling of clothes a few feet away, followed by the sound of fabric landing on the carpet, then a drawer rolling open and a foil packet being opened.

Then he'd returned to her, his hands making the mattress dip on either side of her head. His breath, so close, sounded rough. "I've thought of little else than this moment for days."

"Me, too," she admitted.

He stilled. "I thought you didn't want this to happen."

"I didn't think it was the right thing to happen." Her hands searched for and found his face. Even though she couldn't see him, she wanted him to know this wasn't a throwaway remark, that each word was heartfelt. "I thought about it, though. Dreamed about it. About you."

"Della," he groaned.

He kissed a trail down her neck, over her collarbone and across to a breast, sending her spiraling back into his thrall. She knew his lips had passed over the puckered scars once more but she didn't care, and the moment his mouth closed over the peak of her breast, she forgot the scars altogether and lost herself in the exquisite sensations his tongue and teeth were evoking.

Greedy for it all, she touched wherever she could reach—fingertips across the crisp hair of his chest, nails lightly scraping along his abdomen, hand encircling the heaviness of his groin, eliciting a gasp from his lips.

She ached for him, needed him with a desperation that seemed only matched by his need for her. Whispering his name, she arched her hips, then whispered his name again.

When he entered her, nestling himself deep inside, her entire body quivered, overwhelmed with sensation, too much, needing more, urging him on. He moved in a steady rhythm, but she was past needing steady, so she wrapped her legs around his hips and murmured, "More."

A groan tore from his throat, and his movements became more urgent, frenzied. He hooked an elbow under her knee and lifted, changing the angle of her hips. The wave built higher, taking her up, up, until it broke, and for one perfect instant she was suspended in time and space, outside the world, and all that existed was pleasure and Luke. Then the pleasure came crashing down, filling every single fiber of her being.

And she wondered what she could ever need again.

With a final powerful thrust, he followed her over the edge, and she wrapped her arms around his shoulders tightly, wanting the moment never to end.

Minutes later, she still lay in his arms, he in hers, trembling with the intensity of what they'd shared. He'd been right—she didn't regret it. Not a single moment.

She'd taken a giant step in moving on with her life—allowing herself to become intimate with a man again. The question now was, how would she ever go back once Luke walked out of her life?

Eight

After he'd ordered two coffees, Luke looked back at Della. A small smile played around her mouth as she surveyed the view of the sweeping white beach with gentle wavelets lapping at the sand. He knew the vista from the alfresco dining area of the exclusive French restaurant in Nouméa was spectacular. But he was more interested in watching Della. She glowed, radiating serenity and happiness, and he liked to think he might be part of the reason. She was certainly responsible for how he felt—he couldn't remember ever feeling such a bone-deep contentment.

She'd come to him for the past few nights and, despite the darkness she needed to relax, their lovemaking had only grown more and more amazing.

She turned her head and her eyes met his. An easy smile curved her mouth and a jolt of awareness shook him.

"Penny?" she said.

"Nothing. Wondering…" He stopped, almost afraid of

what might come out of his mouth. He looked for a safe subject. "Tell me about growing up on ship."

"It was great." Her eyes softened. "There were advantages and disadvantages, of course, but I loved it." She looked into the distance, obviously remembering moments of her shipboard life, and he wanted to her to look back at him.

"What sort of disadvantages?"

She shrugged. "Always having to be on my very best behavior when I was outside our cabin. The lack of other children to play with."

"Did you play with the children of passengers?"

The waitress came with their coffees and after she'd left, Della turned back to him. "Sometimes, but they were few and far between. My parents mainly worked on cruise liners that were on the luxury end of the scale, catering more to couples and retired people than families. They were limited in the ships they could work on—not only did they need a ship with a vacancy for a captain and a doctor at the same time, but an owner who would allow them to bring a child. Most wouldn't."

He threaded his fingers through hers on the white linen tablecloth, loving the slide of skin that even simple hand-holding could bring. Three nights of Della Walsh weren't nearly enough to satisfy his craving for her.

Soon he'd convince her she could trust him enough to leave the lights on. She was beautiful, and seeing the same scars he'd felt under his hands wouldn't change his opinion. He wanted to watch her toffee-brown eyes when he entered her, see her face when she lost control.

Soon. He repressed a shudder of anticipation.

"Tell me about the advantages," he said.

Della took a sip of her coffee. "Seeing the world. Spending massive amounts of time with my parents. Meeting interesting people."

When he was young, he'd fantasized about an upbringing very similar to the one she described. "Did you go ashore much?"

She nodded, her eyes faraway. "My mother and I lived ashore until I was three, when my dad became a captain and could bring her back on board. After that, on school holidays, I'd often visit my cousins or grandparents. Sometimes a cousin would come to stay with us on the ship."

"You know," he said, leaning back in his chair, "I envy your childhood."

She raised her eyebrows. "You do?"

"I had a sister once. Sarah." Saying her name again was like a punch to the gut, even after all these years. Which was why he very rarely talked about her.

Della's face immediately transformed with concern. "She died?"

"When I was thirteen," he said, his tone matter of fact, as if that could counter the old pain. "Drowned at the beach."

She tightened her fingers that were still threaded with his. "Oh, Luke, I'm so sorry."

"Ironic, really," he said, one finger of his free hand rubbing the condensation on the side of his wineglass. "That the family who made their money in ships lost a daughter to the sea."

She was silent for a moment, leaving him to his own dark thoughts, until she said, "Was that when your father moved away from ships?"

"No, he'd been scared of the water since he was a kid, so as soon as he inherited, he changed his company to hotels. He didn't even want us at the beach that day, but my mother took us, anyway. When Sarah died, it just reinforced his fears."

"Were you close to Sarah?"

He nodded. "She was only a year younger, so we spent a lot of time together."

"Oh, Luke. Her death must have hit you hard."

"Worse than hard." He cleared his throat. "And a month later, I was sent to boarding school."

A barely audible gasp slipped from her lips. "They sent you away?"

"It was a planned enrollment. They'd always meant to send me, despite my protests." At her raised eyebrow, he explained. "Before Sarah died, I'd thought they were coming around and would let me live at home through high school."

She cocked her head to the side. "After losing one child, I wouldn't have been surprised if they wanted to keep you close."

One *might* assume that. But one would be wrong.

"I wasn't the type of child they wanted to keep close." He looked out over the azure Pacific Ocean, unwilling to let the memory have a hold on him anymore.

"What do you mean?"

"Sarah was the perfect one, always instinctively knowing how to please them." He rubbed a hand over the back of his neck. "I was…more challenging to parent."

"Let me guess," she said with an understanding smile. "You became even more challenging after losing your sister?"

He grinned. "You could say that."

Her eyes flashed in anger, but he knew it wasn't aimed at him. There was something nice about having Della on his side.

"So," she said, drawing the word out, "even though

your parents might have been softening about sending you away before Sarah died, after it happened, while you were grieving and your behavior was worse, they made you go."

The memory sat like a rock in the pit of his belly, but he wouldn't let his face betray his reaction. "That's about the crux of it, yes."

"You were just a boy." Her outrage on his behalf brought a pink flush to her alabaster cheeks. "Of *course* you were acting out."

"My parents were never particularly good at seeing things from a child's point of view," he said, his tone dry. That had to be the understatement of the year. They'd been too wrapped up in themselves and each other and barely noticed he existed.

Her eyes narrowed. "Within the space of a month, you effectively lost your entire family."

"Except Patrick," he clarified. Besides Sarah, Patrick had been his favorite family member.

She sipped her coffee, but didn't take her eyes off him. "Did you see much of him?"

"Whenever he docked in Sydney, he'd come and take me out of school for the day." Those days were some of the happiest memories of his childhood. They hadn't done anything particularly exciting, but Patrick had just had a way of making everything fun and making Luke laugh.

"Now I see why you envy my childhood—you wanted Patrick to take you out of school to live on the ship with him." She gazed at him with warm brown eyes that saw too much. He shifted in his seat, but answered truthfully.

"He told me it was impossible for a child to live on board." He'd started to wonder if Patrick had believed that, or he'd been protecting his brother who would never have consented, anyway.

"I had the childhood you wanted—growing up aboard

a ship with parents who wanted me with them. And I also lived close to Patrick for the past couple of years."

He attempted a smile. "Seems so."

"I'm sorry, Luke." She leaned closer, her gaze sincere. "That must have been hard."

With a flick of his wrist, he waved away her concern. He didn't need it. "It taught me a good lesson when I was young. Never to rely on anyone." People might promise him the world, but they never stood by him in the tough times. He had friends, sure, including his buddies from boarding school, but he would never depend on another person again, or let them close to his heart.

"What about relationships?" she asked, tucking a wayward curl behind her ear. "A good partnership needs trust. Partners need to be able to rely on each other. Surely you'd have that when you meet your soul mate?"

Soul mate? He had to cover the instinctive flinch. That was the *last* thing he wanted.

He cleared his throat. "I'm not good in relationships. I'm not interested in baring myself to another person, which they tell me is important." Though, admittedly, he couldn't remember telling anyone else the story about Sarah, or that he'd wanted to live with Patrick. Not even his ex-wife, Jillian, which probably said a whole lot about his marriage right there.

There was something about Della that made him let his guard down a bit too much. Which only meant he'd have to work extra hard to ensure neither of them got in too deep.

He tapped his fingers on the tablecloth, carefully organizing the words in his mind.

"Della," he said, capturing her gaze, "I need you to understand that anything with me can only ever be temporary." He hoped to hell she already knew it from previous conversations, but it couldn't hurt to be extra sure. And to remind himself.

Her eyelashes hid her eyes as she looked down at her hands in her lap. "So you'll always be alone?"

"It worked for Patrick, it will work just fine for me." He'd have occasional female company, and he had a strong group of friends. Alone didn't necessarily mean lonely. It meant being in control of his own life.

"Luke, have you considered that you resent the *Cora Mae?*" she asked gently. "That the person you wanted to live with as a child kept leaving you for a ship and wouldn't let you follow. And if you resent the ship, that might be behind your determination to anchor it?"

He winced. That sounded like a pile of psychobabble, but something tugged deep inside him. *Was* he trying to fulfill a boy's wish of keeping Patrick's ship chained down nearby?

He shrugged. "Who knows how the subconscious works. Either way, it also makes good business sense." He rubbed a hand across his chin. "How much do you know about floating hotels?"

"I've seen photos, heard stories."

Hearing stories and knowing specifics were poles apart. "My staff has finished working on the preliminary plans for the *Cora Mae's* conversion and I need to review them, so I'll be flying out to Melbourne for one night. Come with me."

He'd previously considered showing her the plans his vice president was overseeing and decided there wasn't much to be gained—he was confident she would sell him all or part of her share of the ship regardless, and getting into extra detail would just muddy the waters. But something had changed. He no longer wanted her to merely sell her share of the *Cora Mae,* he wanted her to understand that this really was the best thing for the ship. To agree with him. To *want* the transformation of her home.

He cared about Della. When this was all over, he didn't want her to look back on their time together with bad feelings, or to think she'd somehow lost. He'd like to think she'd remember him fondly. This situation with the ship needed to be resolved in a win-win. Della had to be convinced his plan was for the best.

She chewed on her bottom lip. "When?"

He did a few mental calculations about flight times and their next ports of call. "How much notice do you need to give the medical department to get another doctor to cover you?"

"Depends on how quickly we find one." A frown line appeared between her brows. "But I'm not sure what this would achieve—I already understand the concept."

He placed his upturned palms on the table. "I've given you the commitment of three weeks and an open mind while you tried to convince me that your plans for the *Cora Mae* are best. It's a reasonable expectation that you would do the same. I don't even need the three weeks. Just a couple of days."

She blew out a breath and nodded. "I'll make some inquiries with the doctors who cover for Cal and my holidays, and see when they're available."

"I appreciate that." His shoulders relaxed. He was surer than ever that this was the best plan for everyone. Convince her the *Cora Mae* would be better as a floating hotel, and do it quickly, before either of them formed an emotional attachment to the other.

That night, Della went back to Luke's cabin after dinner. They'd been invited to dine at the captain's table, and had agreed that their intimate relationship should stay private while so much rested on their negotiations about the *Cora Mae*. So she'd sat through the torture of not being able to touch him through an entire meal.

Well, more precisely, they hadn't touched where anyone else could see. But those long white tablecloths were excellent cover for questing hands.

"Coffee?" he asked, his eyes betraying a lack of interest in the drink.

"No, thanks." She bit down on a smile, but it escaped, anyway.

He loosened his tie. "Tea? Wine?"

"Nope." She took two steps closer, until she was within touching distance.

"So, there's nothing you want?" he asked mildly.

Her hands rested on his chest, reveling in the solidness beneath the crisp white shirt. "Oh, there's something I want. Something I've been desperate for all night."

"They'll serve anything you ask for at the captain's table," he said, one hand cupping her cheek. "What could you have possibly wanted that they couldn't provide?"

"This." And she kissed him, slowly, thoroughly, the way she'd been dreaming of since they'd sat down at dinner. Her conversations with passengers and other crew had probably been muddled, given that most of her focus had remained on the man who sat beside her, no matter who she was talking to. All she'd wanted to do was this. Just this.

Without breaking the kiss, he lifted her into his arms and carried her up the stairs to the bedroom, letting her slide down his body just inside the door.

She leaned into his neck, inhaling the scent of him as she caught her breath. "Nice move, Luke."

"Here's another one." He walked her back a step until

her shoulders bumped against the wall. "Now kiss me again."

She lifted her face and met his mouth with hers, showing him all the passion that welled up inside her when he was near.

"Della," he said, his voice ragged. "I want to see you when I make love to you."

Her blood turned to ice. Didn't he realize how impossible that was for her? Tension flowed into her limbs, the rigidness almost painful after the lovely lassitude of only moments ago.

Slowly, she withdrew her arms and wrapped them around her waist. "Isn't what we have enough?"

"What we've shared has been amazing." He leaned in, his lips so close to her ear that she could feel the warmth of his breath. "But I want to see your face when you slide over the edge. I want you to see me when I'm inside you."

Her eyes drifted closed, imagining the scene he described. She'd do almost anything to be able to see his face in those moments, too. *Almost* anything. But certainly not what he asked.

She turned her head and focused on the night sky through the window. "I'm sorry, Luke, I just can't."

With a finger, he turned her face until his eyes filled her vision again. "You don't think I can handle the way your body looks," he said softly, but with an undercurrent of accusation. Perhaps even hurt.

"If I'm…"

"Exposed," he supplied.

She nodded, accepting his word choice. It was important he understood that this was no whim, that what he asked was simply not possible. "I won't be able to relax. I'd be too self-conscious to enjoy what we were doing."

She saw understanding dawn in his eyes and began to relax.

"Okay, new plan," he said and gently touched his lips to the tip of her nose. "Leave the dress on."

He kissed her again, tenderly, and while she was distracted, he slid his hands up under her skirt, lingering over the satiny skin of her inner thighs, then hooked his thumbs in the elastic of her lacy panties, peeling them down.

"You'll leave my dress on?" she asked warily, watching his progress with removing her underwear.

"I swear." He lifted one of her feet, then the other, so she could step out of her panties. "It's not my preferred option, but at least I'll be able to see your face."

The possibility unfolded before her like a shining jewel. If she could trust him to keep his word, she'd be able to see him during those intimate moments, to connect with him on a deeper level, to watch his release. Her pulse began to race.

As Luke stood, she wrapped her arms around his neck. "If I'm consenting to the lights on, do I get a reward?"

"What do you want?" he asked with a lazy smile.

She undid the knot in his tie and slid it out from his collar, then threw it across the room. "All your clothes come off."

"That's hardly fair," he said, chuckling. "I'll keep one item, like you are. And technically you have two, since there's a bra under that dress."

"Nope, they all come off." She touched her tongue to her top lip, and watched him watch the action. "In exchange for the lights."

He blinked slowly, the corners of his mouth twitching. "You drive a hard bargain."

"And they come off now. Before we start."

A slow, lazy smile spread across his face. "I need to

watch you closer next time we discuss the *Cora Mae*. You have hidden negotiating talents." But he stepped back and quickly dispensed with his shoes, socks, trousers and shirt.

She reached out, letting her fingers dance across his skin. With the lights out the past few nights, she'd been blocked from seeing his body. Such a shame considering the shape of him. She'd seen his bare chest the day they'd swum at the Bay of Islands, but seeing it up close, being able to touch it… A hot shiver ran down her spine.

"And the rest," she said, her voice uneven. "My underwear's already gone."

"I've changed my mind." He stepped forward, pushing her back into the wall, and claimed her mouth. The kiss was hot, demanding, and she gave herself completely to its power. His hands roamed down her sides, exploring her curves beneath the fabric but leaving the dress in place as he'd promised.

He wrenched his mouth away and rested his forehead against hers, their breath mingling. "I can't wait to see more of you," he whispered.

With hands that moved an inch ahead of his mouth, he made his way along the line of her jaw, down her throat. Pausing at the sensitive place where her neck sloped into her shoulders, he gently abraded her skin with his teeth, sending sparks of desire through her system.

Unable to reach much of him as he dipped lower, she moved impatiently, stroking from the strong column of his throat down to his biceps. When his knees touched the ground, he looked up, the whole world in his eyes. Nothing could have prevented her from smiling down at him.

He gripped one of her ankles and slid a shoe off, followed by the other, then his hands slid up her legs, spreading them a little farther apart as he went. Finding the hem of her dress, he bunched it in his fingers and kept on traveling, exposing new flesh inch by inch. When he reached the juncture of her thighs, his hands trapped her hips firmly against the wall, and he placed a delicate kiss there. Then his tongue flicked out and found the core of her. A moan ripped from her throat, just as his lips joined in.

Her breathing choppy, she managed a mangled version of "please," not sure exactly what she was asking for. Luke continued his work regardless, his tongue circling and sweeping, driving her slowly crazy. She dug her nails into the muscles of his shoulders, needing something to anchor herself as her bones melted into nothingness.

His hands pushed her harder against the wall, his mouth merciless. She writhed, arms flung out to the wall behind her, hands looking for purchase as reality dissolved.

"Luke," she gasped, then pleasure pulsed sharply through her and she imploded.

He moved up her body until he stood, holding her against him, supporting her as she came back to earth. When she could breathe again, she opened her eyes to find him looking at her.

"Thank you," he murmured.

She coughed out a laugh. "I should be thanking you."

"Feel free," he said and grinned. "But I was thanking you for trusting me in the light."

She ran her hands over his bare shoulders, luxuriating in the polished smoothness. "I'm glad I did."

"Mmm, I think that should be, *I'm glad I* am *trusting you, Luke,*" he said, using a hand under her knee to lift her leg and wrap it around his hips.

A shiver raced across her skin. "Oh, yes. I *am,* Luke. And I'll be glad for as long as you want me to."

He dug his fingers under the waistband of his boxer

shorts and came out with a little foil packet that he presented to her with a flourish. "Excellent."

She looked down at the waistband of his boxers then back to his face. "How long have you had that in there?"

"About a minute and a half." He pushed the underwear down his legs and kicked it away. "I dug it out of my trousers just before I stood up."

"I like a man who thinks ahead," she said as she took it from his fingers. Pushing him back an inch to give herself some room, she ripped the packet open and rolled the protection along his length.

"You also might like this." He lifted her and wrapped her other leg around his hips so she could lock her ankles behind him. Only the thin cotton of her dress bunched around her hips lay between them.

"Like?" she said on a gasp. "This is fast becoming one of my favorite things."

His hands supported her, positioned her, and as she felt the tip of him seeking entrance, her eyes drifted closed.

Luke stilled. "Open your eyes," he said, his voice deep and rough.

She lifted her lids and found his gray eyes locked on her. "Better," he murmured. "I'm not missing out this time on seeing your eyes when we're joined."

He began to move again, small movements, merely nudging her, building anticipation until she couldn't stand it any longer. She braced her back on the wall behind her and reached down to find him, then guided him into her as she sank down.

Air hissed out from between his teeth, but he didn't lose eye contact.

The feel of him filling her while watching his face in the fully lit room made something shift in her chest. The times they'd made love in the dark she'd known it was him, of course she had, but perhaps there had been some little corner of her brain that had played dumb, thinking if she didn't see him she wasn't breaking the vows she'd once made to her husband.

But here and now there was no denying this was Luke she had her thighs wrapped around. Luke thrusting into her. Luke with his fingers biting into the flesh of her hips as he moved her to his rhythm. And she didn't want anyone else. Only him. Only ever Luke.

"Della," he groaned, his body vibrating with tension. He changed the angle of her hips and sparks shot through her entire body. Driving her fingers through his hair, she dragged his mouth down to hers.

He kissed her hungrily, then pulled his mouth back a couple of inches, and she took the chance to fill her screaming lungs. His chest heaved in and out, but his gaze didn't waver. Taking her higher, higher, to a place just out of reach, higher. Luke was whispering, eyes still on her, telling her she was beautiful, that she drove him crazy with want, saying her name. Then she burst free. Free of everything but this man. Within moments, Luke convulsed in her arms, his eyes only closing in the final moments of his pleasure.

Minutes—hours?—later, he released her legs and they stumbled to the bed. Despite her exhaustion, a joy deep down bubbled away and she snuggled against his side, completely relaxed. Supremely content.

Yet, as she lay in Luke's embrace, a dark cloud moved over her heart. Was she falling in love? Her skin grew cold. For everyone's sakes, she hoped not—despite being a good man, Luke had told her today in Nouméa that he didn't want a true relationship. He wouldn't *want* to be loved. And after experiencing the utter devastation that could come from loving someone, she would never open herself to the possibility again. If she let herself love Luke and she lost him, if he left her, it would kill her.

Glancing up at Luke's strong profile as he dozed, she mercilessly squashed down the joy that had been building. She simply wouldn't let herself love him. She'd enjoy all he had to offer, then leave with her heart intact when they parted. Simple.

The dark cloud continued to hover, making a mockery of her naïveté, but she determinedly ignored it and nuzzled in closer to her lover's side.

Nine

Three days later, Luke unlocked the front door to his Melbourne penthouse apartment and ushered Della inside. Fortunately, one of the doctors who often covered for Della's and Cal's holidays had been available to meet the ship and fill in, so Luke had quickly arranged their trip to his hometown. It was only fair that she could see what he wanted to transform the *Cora Mae* into before she made her decision.

They'd flown in from Samoa this morning and he'd spent the afternoon at his office. He'd wanted the time to sign contracts and other paperwork that had been waiting for him while he was cruising the South Pacific—to clear his plate so he could devote tomorrow to Della and the *Cora Mae*.

Della had spent the afternoon with her parents before Luke had picked her up and brought her back to his home. He'd only spoken to her parents briefly, but he'd liked them, and knowing they'd been friends of Patrick's made him like them all the more.

He pulled his front door shut behind him and carried his and Della's bags through to the main bedroom, rolling his shoulders to ease the tension. All the good effects from his time on the *Cora Mae* had dissipated the moment he'd stepped back into the Marlow Hotels office and the weight of responsibility had come crashing back down.

When he came back, Della was standing near his sofa, taking in the room. "This doesn't seem very…lived in," she said.

Loosening his tie, he glanced around his living room. "I don't spend much time here. Most of my day is at the office, and I usually spend time off with friends. Also I travel a fair bit, checking on the hotels."

Della drifted across to the floor-to-ceiling windows that showcased the city below. Twilight had descended and Melbourne was bathed in its magical glow. It was his favorite time of day, and one of the reasons he'd bought the apartment.

Yet it was the woman standing in front of the window who claimed his attention. He crossed to her, wrapped his arms around her waist from behind and glanced at the view over her shoulder. The feel of her against him brought a satisfaction to his blood that he never would have predicted.

"It's beautiful," she said, leaning her head back on to his shoulder.

"Not as beautiful as you." Gently, he turned her in his arms and captured her lips, his heart beating faster from the simple kiss. "I'm looking forward to making love to you in my bed," he murmured. A primal, possessive need deep down inside him wanted to make love to her here, in his home.

She shivered and smiled. "That's a plan I can agree to."

"But first, I'll feed you," he said on a sigh, and pulled away from her special brand of temptation. "I'm afraid my cooking skills are confined to breakfast, so we'll have to order in."

She blinked at him. "You cook breakfast?"

"Omelets, scrambled eggs with grilled tomatoes, pancakes—I have a full repertoire. Just no dinner." Partly because he was rarely home for dinner. "Have a look through the menus beside the phone and choose anything you'd like. I just need to check a couple of things."

He'd been working while aboard the ship, though not as many hours a day as he'd usually put in, and the pile of work waiting for him today was evidence that he'd relaxed a bit too much. That had to end.

As he opened his laptop and waited for it to fire up, his gaze was drawn back to Della. She was in his kitchen, ringing the local Indian takeout. Something shifted in his chest. She looked good there.

He'd never had a woman in his apartment before; he didn't like the complications it brought. The expectations it might engender. But Della was different. Mainly because he knew she didn't want a life on the land, so she wasn't thinking she could turn him into a long-term prospect.

He rubbed a hand over his jaw. No, it was more. There was something about Della herself. Her presence made him feel different inside. Perhaps it was that he could be more himself with her. She—

Heart fisted tight, he stopped himself before he could get carried away. He didn't need a woman to make him feel *anything*. He didn't need anyone.

He repeated his golden rule under his breath. *Never be distracted by a woman; never rely on anyone.*

They were lovers, and he would have her in his bed

tonight, but he wouldn't indulge in any flights of fancy about what they had together.

Della Walsh was temporary in his life.

Della ended the call and watched Luke as his fingers flew over his laptop keyboard. Despite his words being just as considerate, and the reaction he caused in her body just as strong, this wasn't the same man tonight as the man she'd known on the ship.

He didn't even look the same—there was more tension in his shoulders, his back was a fraction straighter. There was a touch more arrogance in the angle he held his head. It had begun when they'd landed in Melbourne, and had been more pronounced when he'd picked her up after her late lunch with her parents. In fact, the effect was growing stronger every minute they spent in this city.

This was Luke the businessman, the man she'd met after Patrick's will reading who'd been determined to get her half of the ship for himself. The man she'd slapped, she remembered, biting down on her lip.

Somewhere during their time together, he'd relaxed and stopped regarding her as the enemy. He'd become the man who treated her with tenderness, who had been patient about her scarred body and who laughed with her over mini golf.

Which man was the real Luke—tense businessman or relaxed lover?

He glanced up, saw her watching him and gave her a tight smile, then went back to his laptop. Embarrassed at being caught staring, she started going through his cupboards, pulling out plates and cutlery for the food that would soon be on its way. But her thoughts wouldn't be so easily diverted.

It wasn't unusual for people to act out of character on

vacation, which was what their time on the *Cora Mae* had practically become. It was why holiday flings were renowned for not lasting. An unwelcome thought that she'd been ignoring finally surfaced—it was more than two weeks since Luke had made the deal to consider keeping the *Cora Mae* as a cruising vessel, but he didn't seem to be coming around. What if he'd been stringing her along? Her stomach swooped. Perhaps he'd been pretending to be considering her wishes, charming her into trusting him, entertaining them both with a fling.

Maybe there weren't two Lukes, there was just this one, the focused businessman. And the man she'd come to know on the ship had been a role he was playing, either intentionally or because he'd been caught up in his holiday.

Had she fallen in love with a mirage?

Love...

Oh, no. Oh, God. She'd promised herself she wasn't falling in love with him. With trembling hands, she placed the crockery and cutlery carefully on his dining table.

Love...?

He shut down his laptop, stretched his arms above his head and stood. Then he cast a lazy smile across at her and her insides melted.

"How long until the food arrives?" he asked.

She swallowed, trying to keep her wits about her. "Thirty minutes."

"Enough time to show you my bed." He prowled closer, encircled her in his arms. "Come with me," he whispered beside her ear then pulled her lobe into the warmth of his mouth.

Heat shimmered across her skin. This was desire, not love. A holiday fling that would end soon. As long as she kept treating it that way, it was no threat to her heart.

She ran her hands up his solid chest. "We'd have to be quick."

"I can still make it worth your while," he said with a devilish gleam in his gray eyes.

She let him lead her down a hallway, determined to enjoy whatever time she could have with whichever Luke this was. Because it wouldn't be long before she lost him completely.

The next morning, Della stepped into the boardroom that adjoined Luke's office and glanced around. Since they were only a few blocks from his apartment building, the floor-to-ceiling windows held a similar view of the bustling city below, and the decor had the same impersonal feel. The difference was that it felt right in a business environment.

Though she'd suspected his life was dominated by his career, so perhaps it was appropriate that his home reflected his office.

"Coffee?" Luke asked, heading for a small table against the wall, lavishly laid out with coffee and tea, iced biscuits, fresh pastries and tiny cakes.

"Are we expecting a hoard?"

"Just us, though we can call in the people who worked on this project if we have questions." He glanced at the catering table. "My assistant always stocks the room if people will be working in here."

"Just coffee, then," she said and strolled over to the plans strewn across the boardroom table. There were detailed diagrams of waste management systems, power generators and water production. High piles of reports sat to the side, with an environmental impact report sitting at the top of the pile closest to her. Projected on a huge white screen was a slideshow of artists' renditions of the *Cora Mae* in her new surroundings of the Great Barrier Reef.

Luke handed her a mug of steaming coffee, then pointed to the sailors' quarters on the main plans. "As you can see, these rooms will be converted to a permanent research facility for marine biologists and other scientists. We'd also employ a full-time environmental scientist to ensure the impact on the reef is minimized."

"Interesting," she murmured as she continued to peruse the plans. They were details she hadn't expected him to consider and was pleasantly surprised to see them included.

A couple of hours and another cup of coffee later, she'd had a chance to flick through most of the presentation. Luke rested a hip on the edge of the table and crossed his arms. "Well, what do you think?"

"To be honest, it's not as bad as I was expecting," she admitted.

He cocked his head. "What were you expecting?"

"I'm not sure." She glanced up at the screen projection of the *Cora Mae* on the wall. "Maybe something akin to a caged bird."

"And now?" he asked, leaning infinitesimally forward.

"By being permanently anchored, she's part of her surroundings." She looked back to Luke, surprised at the direction of her own thoughts. "She belongs, instead of just passing through."

Luke nodded. "That permanency also means the crew would have the option of living on board as they do now, or having a home base on the coast and working a roster of several days on at a time. They wouldn't have to make the decisions that your parents did when you were first born. You would have all stayed together as a family."

"Ah, but then I would have missed out on the travel,"

she said, feeling nostalgia pull her lips into a smile. "The amazing learning experiences that most other children just aren't able to access."

He sank into a seat beside hers, curiosity in his eyes. "Like what?"

She pushed her chair out a few feet and stretched her legs as the memories crowded into her mind. "When I was twelve, we were on the *Mediterranean Queen,* and my mother planned my homeschooling projects around Ancient Greece and Rome. We studied the civilizations when we were out to sea, then walked the ruins and historical sites on the days in port."

He regarded her for a long moment, tapping a finger on his thigh as he did. "You know, you guessed when we were in Nouméa that, in some ways, you'd had the childhood I'd wanted—growing up on a ship, all the time you spent with Patrick in the last few years. And you were right. But it was also the polar opposite of the childhood I had—you experienced the freedom, the travel, while I was in boarding school day and night."

"Like a caged bird," she said softly.

His gaze drifted to the expanse of glass along one wall, but she didn't think his focus was on the view. "I think part of me probably did feel like that at the time."

"And when you talked about that in Nouméa, I asked if you resented the *Cora Mae,* and if that was affecting your decision about her future."

He nodded as he turned back to her. "I said I didn't know."

"What if it's not about resentment?" she asked tentatively. At his quizzical expression, she rolled her bottom lip between her teeth and carefully chose the words to explain. "I'm wondering how that childhood of being cooped up, of having no freedoms, no real holidays, would affect a person. Would it make them want to take a ship that traveled, that was free, and chain it down to one spot?"

He rubbed a hand over his jaw. "Perhaps. And I wonder how a person who'd grown up with a vast experience of travel, of always moving, would feel about a ship being permanently anchored? Especially if that person's one proper experience of life in one place ended in tragedy. Would they see it as an emotional issue, maybe even transfer their own fears on to the ship?"

She felt the corners of her mouth tug into a smile as she acknowledged his point. "Probably."

He chuckled. "We're a fine pair."

For a precious moment it was as if the veil of businessman had lifted and the Luke she'd known on the *Cora Mae* had reemerged. Her heart lifted, and she found the courage to ask a question that had been playing at the corners of her mind. "Do you mind if I ask something personal?"

He arched an eyebrow. "There's something more personal than analyzing my childhood and its effects on present-day business decisions?"

She smiled, then sobered. "Patrick often talked about you, so I knew a few things about you before we met. Yet some things you never mention."

He shrugged his broad shoulders. "Ask what you want to know."

"You were married," she said simply.

His expression was carefully schooled to neutral. "I was."

"You've never mentioned an ex-wife." She would have had no idea he'd been married if not for Patrick's family stories.

"It's never come up in conversation," he said smoothly and picked up the report nearest his hand.

Instinct told her to back off, but she didn't want to let it go and risk never knowing about his romantic past. "True. Yet you've mentioned that your sister died when you were thirteen, and I've talked about having been married. We've both been pretty open with each other."

"Are you saying I've deliberately avoided mentioning my ex-wife?"

She held his gaze. "Have you?"

"Perhaps," he acknowledged, and tossed the report back onto the table. "I try to avoid thinking about her if I can."

"Why?"

"Mainly because it makes me look like a fool," he said with a self-deprecating smile.

"When Patrick talked about your marriage—" she hesitated, then plunged in "—he always seemed to be angry but he never said why."

A humorless laugh puffed from his throat. "He saw through her from the start."

"What happened?"

He eased out a long breath. "She worked at Marlow Corporation, but apparently decided that it would be an easier life to marry the boss than to work for him."

Her heart clenched tight, aching for him. "She was using you?"

"From day one."

Suddenly several things made sense—his comments about insincere compliments the day they first went to meet Roxie Appleby in the galley. His suspicions about her influencing Patrick to leave her half the ship...

"Just so you know," she said slowly, "I wasn't doing that with Patrick."

He reached over and took her hand, lacing their fingers. "I realized that a while ago. Besides, I should have had more faith in Patrick's ability to size people up—he wouldn't have stood for you trying to manipulate him, even if he was sick. He was always stubborn and a particularly good judge of character."

She'd assumed Luke wouldn't be sleeping with her had he continued to believe she'd used her position to influence his uncle, but it was still a weight off her shoulders to hear him say the words. She nudged her chair over beside his and laid her head on his shoulder. He rested an arm around her shoulders.

"You know," she murmured, "you were Patrick's favorite person."

There was silence for so long she thought he wasn't going to reply. "I should have visited more," he finally said, his voice rough around the edges.

She turned, found his gaze. "He knew you'd come if he wanted you, Luke."

Tenderly, he stroked a finger down her cheek. "I'm glad you were there for him. That he had someone with your heart and your skills with him at the end."

Tears pressed at the back of her eyes. He'd given her a gift.

He leaned in and softly touched his mouth to hers, with more emotion than she thought could fit in one simple kiss. And then she knew for sure—there was no use denying any longer.

She loved this man. Loved him so much it lifted her up until she was floating.

And, though she knew it would lead to pain and grief all over again, in this moment she couldn't bring herself to care. All she needed right now was Luke. She threaded her arms behind his neck and kissed him again.

Ten

Della arrived at the medical suites for her morning shift only half an hour after leaving Luke's cabin. They'd been back on board for two days, spending every spare moment together, usually in his bed. Luke had begun to relax again once they'd boarded the *Cora Mae* in Fiji, which was great, but her own immense relief to be back on the ship had been uncomfortably surprising.

"Good morning, Dr. Walsh. Sleep well?" Jody asked. The twinkle in her eye made Della wince. Apparently the *Cora Mae*'s rumor mill was in fine working order—she'd wondered if she and Luke had been able to keep their involvement a secret, or if word was seeping out. Now she had her answer.

"Fine, thank you." Della picked up the log of calls taken since the medical suite had been open yesterday and perused it, both to keep an eye on things and to cover for any potential blushing. "How about you?"

Jody shrugged theatrically. "You know how it is. One of my roommates came in late, and another one snored, so it was hard to get some sleep." She straightened the pens on her desk then stopped and looked up at Della. "Oh, no, that's right. You wouldn't know, since you have a cabin to yourself. No one there to wake you. All on your own. All night."

Della smothered a chuckle as she put down the log book and crossed her arms. "Is there something you're trying to say, Jody?"

"No, no." Jody smiled sweetly. "Why, is there something you want to share?"

Della tapped a pen against her lips. Perhaps it would help her sort through the mess of her emotions if she talked about it with someone. She'd known Jody a couple of years and she trusted her.

Before she could decide, a call came through on the emergency line. Jody tapped a button and said, "Medical suite."

"This is the bridge. Medical team needed to Galley Two immediately. A fire has been reported. Fire teams on their way and warning about to go out to all passengers. Medical assessment and first-aid station required."

Della had already swung into action, grabbing one of the first-aid backpacks that were stored in a cupboard near the door. "On our way," Jody said, as she hung up and grabbed a second backpack.

The door to the suite opened and their other nurse, Maree, came in. Della paused just long enough to say, "Fire in Galley Two. Page Cal then meet us down there," before she and Jody slipped outside. Della's pulse was fast and erratic. Fire was a ship's worst enemy and she had no idea of the scale of what they were about to face. With any luck it would be small and already contained.

As they ran along the corridors and down the stairs, a calm message came over the P.A. system advising passengers that there was a small fire in one of the kitchens, and as a precaution Section Four of the ship would be evacuated until the fire teams declared it safe to return.

Thankfully, it was midmorning on a day in port, and most of the passengers would already be sightseeing in the New Zealand capital, Wellington. Passengers all received a solid briefing on emergencies when they first boarded, but this would be a heck of a lot simpler with most of them ashore.

They reached the closed doors that marked the edge of Section Four. Max, a steward from the premium suites, was standing guard. In the event of a fire, crew members had assigned roles—everyone was part of the emergency plans and fire drills.

"What have we got, Max?" she asked, slightly out of breath. She took in the small crowd of galley staff who had been evacuated from the exclusion zone.

Three more crew members rushed down the corridor, still adjusting their helmets, and Max stepped aside to let them through as he answered.

"The first team hasn't been in long, but the fire seems to be contained to Galley Two. There's an office on the left you can use as a first-aid station."

"Thanks." Della and Jody dropped their backpacks just as a few more of the galley staff were led out through the doors, looking a little dazed. Max pointed them to Della and she and Jody got to work checking them for burns and smoke inhalation.

Another group of galley staff emerged just as Cal came through the door and grabbed a pair of surgical gloves. "Where do you want me?"

Della looked up from dressing a minor burn on a chef's

forearm. "Check the office next door. If it's got room, take Maree and start a second station."

"Roger." Cal disappeared with Maree, then reappeared and invited some of the lined-up galley crew to the second room. Della grabbed a rubber band from the desk in the office and put her hair up. The air-conditioning would have been turned off in the next section by now and even on this side of the wall it was warming up.

More people trickled in, some coughing—most had breathed smoke before they'd made it out and many had minor burns as they'd tried to contain the fire. The smell of smoke and fire lingered in the air, but no one was panicking—they trained regularly for this.

She was confident in the fire crew's ability, but fire was unpredictable and potentially devastating, and so many people seemed to have been affected. This place was her home; the people were her second family. She sent up a little prayer that no one had been hurt badly—the only concession she could afford to make to the anxiety that crept through her—and kept working.

"What can I do?" The voice was deep and calm behind her. She turned to see Luke, so tall and solid and unflappable, and suddenly she felt centered again. "Do you have first-aid training?"

"Advanced first aid, updated every year."

"Excellent. Grab a pair of gloves from Jody. You can take her seat. Jody, there are more people coming through—can you go out and start assessing and prioritizing those waiting?"

"On it," the nurse said and vacated her seat for Luke.

Working beside him was smooth and easy—they immediately slipped into a routine where she passed him patients who only needed basic attention and he followed her instructions without question. There was a synergy to their work.

Della looked up for her next patient and saw Roxie Appleby. "Roxie, how are you?"

"Just a little burn on my wrist," she said and sat in the chair.

"Let me have a look." Della took her hand, noting that it was only a mild burn. "Did you see how the fire started?"

Roxie sighed. "It was a few stations across from me. I didn't see, but it spread fairly quickly and we all rushed to smother it with the fire blankets. A couple of cooks grabbed the fire extinguishers and the sprinklers came on, but it's still going on in there."

"I'm glad you weren't hurt more than this. Once we're done here, I want you to go up to the top deck and get some fresh air. The people we've seen will already be up there." She turned to Luke. "Luke, can you get Roxie some oxygen while I do a dressing on her burn?"

"Not a problem," Luke said, then started talking to Roxie in soothing tones as Della dressed the burn.

They worked side by side for another ten minutes before Max rushed in and squatted beside Della. "Dr. Walsh, they need you in there. They have a chef collapsed and they want your okay before they move him. He has some burns."

Della nodded and her stomach sank as she mentally ran through all the chefs she knew but hadn't seen in the first-aid station yet. "Have you got a fire suit for me?"

"Yep, over here," Max said as they walked to the door.

She felt Luke move beside her. "I'll come with you."

His reassuring presence and extra pair of hands would be valuable but she couldn't accept his offer. "It's policy not to take noncrew into a fire zone." She gave him a tight smile as she took the heavy orange suit from Max. "I'll be fine."

"Dr. Walsh," he said, sounding every inch the powerful businessman he was. "I'm a half-owner of the ship and I have an advanced first-aid certificate. You might need help and you can't spare one of the nurses from here."

She bit down on her lip as she considered. He was right—being half-owner of the ship probably meant the policy didn't apply to him. "Are you sure?"

"Absolutely." Luke's steel-gray gaze didn't waver.

Della nodded. "Jody, you'll need to take over in here, and call in a couple of the crew with first-aid training. Mr. Marlow and I are going into the galley."

She pulled the suit on over her clothes, finishing with the helmet, as Luke did the same, then they made their way into the exclusion zone, Luke carrying a stretcher. Once on the other side of the door, Luke gave her fingers a squeeze and she threw him a grateful smile.

It was dark and hot—all electricity had been turned off, but their helmets had torches and they found their way easily enough through the other rooms in Section Four till they reached the galley. Soot covered the countertops and the food that had been in the process of being prepared, and fire retardant foam was piled high in places where the fire team had worked. Even with the air filter on her helmet, she could smell the smoke in the air.

She weaved through the benches until one of the crew in an orange suit and helmet waved her over and guided her to the collapsed man he'd been sitting with. Della knelt down beside the dazed but conscious chef, who was wearing an oxygen mask and a white uniform with scorch marks. She only vaguely recognized him, and double-checked his badge to find his name was Ted before she said, "Hi, Ted. It's Dr. Walsh. You've had a fall, but you'll be fine now."

She listened to his breathing and felt for his pulse. While Luke spoke reassuringly to the man, she continued the assessment, including looking for any damage that may have occurred when he fell. He had some burns, but she was more worried about his lungs, given the smoke he must have breathed in before the fire crew had fitted the mask. Luckily, he didn't appear to have hurt himself much when he collapsed, so she gave the okay to move him. The three of them rolled the man onto a stretcher, then she and Luke carried him out.

As soon as they made it out the door and through the line of galley staff that snaked its way along the corridor, Max grabbed the handles from her end of the stretcher, and she whipped off her mask, relief sweeping through her that the worst was probably over.

"Jody, call the city hospital," she said as she stripped off her fire suit. "We need an ambulance urgently."

Jody reached for the phone and gave instructions to the ship's operator. Della hung her fire suit over a chair, then took the handles from Luke so he could get out of his. "We need to take him up to the lobby. I'll do some first aid there, so at least we're ready for the ambulance when it arrives. Are you all right to keep carrying him?"

"Yep," he said, and took his end back.

"Max, can you get someone else to carry the other end—I need to keep my hands free. Also, someone to run to the medical suite to pick up some supplies." She grabbed one of the first-aid backpacks from the doorway. "Jody, can you travel in the ambulance with him?"

"Sure," the nurse said.

Della ducked her head into Cal's makeshift first-aid room. "Maree, we're going to need you to take over in the other room—Jody's going with the ambulance. I'll be back down as soon as I can. Jody's already called in more first aiders to help you both. They should be arriving any minute."

The rest of the day passed in a blur. Della heard from Jody when she returned a couple of hours later that the chef was doing well at the hospital.

They treated more crew—the galley had been full of chefs, cooks and waitstaff serving late breakfasts and prepping for lunch, and everyone needed at least a quick check over. Luckily no one else was hurt as badly as the chef taken ashore, and everything could be handled by the *Cora Mae's* medical team. Luke worked like a Trojan on any task she set him, and handed her a bottle of water and a smile each time she turned around.

Once the last person had been seen, Della was tired and desperately needed a shower, but began the cleanup in the office where they'd had the first-aid station.

Luke laid a hand on her shoulder and looked into her eyes. "Can the others handle the cleanup without you?"

She glanced around at the rest of the team, plus the other first aiders Jody had called in. They'd all had a long day.

"They could," she said, turning back to him, "but I don't want to leave it all to them."

"You won't be slacking off. Captain Tynan wants to see us both as soon as we're free."

"Go," Cal said. "I'd rather do the cleanup with Jody and Maree than go to the logistics meeting you're about to have."

"Okay, thanks," she said on a sigh and followed Luke out the door.

As they walked along the corridors, Luke draped an

arm over her shoulders. She glanced up at him and he shrugged. "I'm pretty sure the crew all know we're seeing each other, so why shouldn't I give you a bit of support after the day you've put in?"

She thought back to Jody's comments that morning and smiled. "I think they know, too." And it felt good—right—to walk along, physically linked to the man she loved.

Yet a shiver raced across her skin. They hadn't talked about it, but they both knew their time together was coming to an end. And despite the darkened surroundings that she still insisted on when their clothes were off, there had been more intimacy, and a sense of urgency to their lovemaking since they'd come back from Melbourne. As if each time could be their last.

And once that last time inevitably happened, she wasn't sure how she'd bear it.

When they reached the meeting room, she followed Luke over to where the captain and several key senior crew members were gathered.

Captain Tynan looked up from the ship plans that were spread over the table. "Ah, Mr. Marlow, Dr. Walsh. Excellent. This will be easier with you both here. That was the advantage of Patrick living on board, too—on other ships I'd have to ring the head office to get authorization for significant repairs."

Della chewed on her lip. When she'd talked to Patrick about the running of the ship, they'd discussed big picture topics like routes and entertainments, not issues like repairs. She'd need to pay attention to this discussion to keep up.

Like a man used to being in charge, Luke strode to the captain's side and ran a hand over the detailed plans. "What do we know of the damage so far?"

The captain tapped a pen on the table in a rapid rhythm. "Obviously we haven't been able to do a thorough analysis of the affected areas yet, but from reports the fire officers gave in their debriefing, we can make some rough guesses."

"Bad?" Luke asked, glancing up at the other man.

"We don't think any of the ship's structure has been compromised, thanks in large part to the actions of the galley crew and the fire officers. The damage seems to be localized to Galley Two." The captain pointed to the area on the plans. Since she wasn't sure what to say, Della leaned over to look, despite knowing the layout of the ship like the back of her hand.

Luke straightened and crossed his arms over his chest. "Can the other galleys take on the work of Galley Two while the repairs are carried out?"

"With some changes to scheduling, yes." The captain pointed out the other galleys on the plans. "And the menu options for the premium cabins can be restricted to allow their galley to take on a larger load."

"Excellent," Luke said, obviously satisfied with the plan. "It's fortunate we're in port, so we can get access to materials and tradesmen straight away."

"And that both co-owners can give authorization to the expenses straight away, since this will likely exceed my budget."

Exceed the captain's budget? She had no idea if the *Cora Mae* had more money in reserve. Why hadn't she thought to ask that after the will reading?

Luke moved to the other side of the table to get a closer look at something on the plan. "How soon do the fire officers expect it'll be until we can get in to do a thorough assessment of the damage so we can make firm plans?"

Della kept listening to the exchange among Luke, the

captain and the senior crew, but her heart was sinking. Damages, repair costs and contingency plans. What did she know of such things? She knew about smoke inhalation, burns, fatigue and dehydration, but in this conversation she was completely superfluous.

Luckily, Luke knew what he was doing. He handled the staff and the plans like a pro. Of course, he *was* a pro—he owned a company that operated twenty-three hotels. One incident like this wouldn't be enough to fluster him.

Imagine if Patrick had left a controlling interest in the *Cora Mae* to her? These urgent discussions would be peppered by her indecision and lack of knowledge, which could only spell disaster for the ship and her crew. She wrapped her arms tightly around her waist.

And where would the money for the repairs come from? Her stomach lurched until she felt nauseous.

Heart thumping against her ribs, she edged toward Luke. "Can I see you for a moment, please?"

He nodded, though clearly distracted, then turned to the captain. "Excuse me a minute."

The room was big enough that they could stand in a corner and not be overheard if they kept their voices low, so they moved to the farthest point from the small group of crew.

"What is it?" he asked, positioning himself so he could watch the others in the room over her shoulder.

"The money." She resisted the urge to wince, and instead stood tall, prepared to meet her responsibilities. "If this will cost more than Captain Tynan's budget, then the expense will have to come from outside of operating costs, yes?"

He shrugged one shoulder, seemingly unconcerned. "Insurance will cover most of it."

"But not all."

"It's hard to say without all the information about what's been damaged," he said, his eyes tracking the movements of the people behind her.

"But from your experience…" She left the sentence hanging and his gaze snapped back to her.

He wrapped a hand around the back of his neck and let out a breath. "From my experience, there will be out-of-pocket expenses. But Marlow Hotels will cover it."

"You only own 50 percent of the *Cora Mae,*" she pointed out, "so you're only responsible for 50 percent of her losses."

The door opened and the head chef, accompanied by the purser, strode across to the table covered with plans. "We've just had a preliminary look at Galley Two."

Luke glanced over, then back to Della. "Can we finish this later? I need to hear their assessment."

He'd said "I," she realized with a resigned sigh. He needed to hear their assessment, not both of them. Which was so obviously true, and pretty much said it all about her potential role in this situation.

She took a step back and pasted on a smile. "Of course. Give my apologies to the group, will you? I have to do a few things. And don't worry about running decisions by me—you just do what you have to do."

Luke frowned, his mouth open as if about to say something, but she slipped out of the room before he could speak. They needed his management skills over at the table. And she needed to be anywhere but here.

Luke found Della on the top deck, her forearms resting on the railing, her gaze on the view of the harbor city sprawled out before them. It had been two hours since their brief discussion about the costs of repairs, and her haunted expression had been in the back of his mind ever since. It was obvious she didn't have the money to contribute to out-of-pocket expenses, but her despondency had seemed out of proportion. Perhaps it was her exhaustion coloring her reaction, perhaps there was more to it. He needed to know.

"Hey, I've been looking for you," he said softly when he reached her side. He leaned on the railing, their shoulders brushing.

"I've been here, thinking." Her voice sounded as if it came from far away. She turned and gave him a smile that didn't reach her eyes. "You were great today."

He shook his head. "I only did some basic first aid. You were the one who was great."

"I meant after the fire." She turned back to the view, her expression once again lost, and it nearly broke his heart.

"That was nothing," he said and shrugged. "Just some organizing."

"To you, maybe. To me it was more."

There was his answer—there *was* more to the situation. And everything inside him yearned to find a way to make it better for her. To see her happy again.

He wrapped one of her curls around his finger. "Della, what's going on?"

She turned her back to the railing and crossed her arms under her breasts. "During the fire, my role was clear. I was in charge of the first-aid station. You assisted me because I had the expertise. But the business decisions that followed were your area of expertise. You've lived and breathed tourism and accommodation facilities most of your life." She paused and moistened her lips. "If I had the controlling interest, the best person wouldn't have been making those decisions. I simply don't have the skill set to run a ship."

It was what he wanted to hear, exactly the realization he'd hoped she'd come to during their time together, yet the soul-deep loss in her eyes was tearing at him. "Della—"

She rested a finger gently on his lips. "It's not just the decisions, although that's enough on its own. I don't have any available funds to cover the repairs until the insurance kicks in and the extras the insurance won't cover. Or the money for when the next unexpected event occurs. Your company has the resources to run the ship the way it needs to be run. The *Cora Mae* and her crew deserve the stability that only you can provide."

He searched her toffee-brown eyes. "Are you saying you've made a decision?"

"There's really no decision to make—I'll sell some or all of my share of the *Cora Mae* to you. You can have the controlling interest, or own it outright, whichever you prefer. You're the best person for the ship, Luke."

He tightened his grip on the railing till his knuckles went white. This was no victory—he didn't want Della to give up on her dream. Yet it was the outcome he'd been working toward. The outcome the *Cora Mae* needed for stability. Why did it feel so wrong?

He released the railing and pulled her close against him, as if the contact could calm the conflicting thoughts and feelings that were thrashing through his mind and body. "We'll talk about this in the morning. You're exhausted, and that's no state to be making decisions of this magnitude."

"I won't change my mind," she said, her warning tremulous.

"Maybe not, but I refuse to negotiate with someone who's dead on her feet." If nothing else, he needed to be certain he hadn't taken advantage of her state of mind.

"Come back to my cabin, we'll get something to eat, and after a good night's sleep, we'll sort this out."

And after that? A devil on his shoulder prodded. *You'll have finished your business together. Are you ready to let her go?*

His gut fell away, leaving black emptiness. He held Della tighter and willed all the uncertainty away. It was far too soon to think about losing her. Not now that he finally had what he wanted—Della in his arms, in his bed.

Eleven

Della let Luke lead her back to his cabin. He was right—she *was* exhausted, both physically and emotionally. She wouldn't change her mind, but neither did she have the mental space to discuss the details of selling her share tonight.

When they arrived, Luke picked up the phone and ordered dinner. "But don't deliver it to my cabin for forty-five minutes," he said and disconnected.

Della's stomach growled, as if in protest. "Why not as soon as it's ready?"

He took her hand, laced their fingers and led her upstairs. "You need a chance to clean up first. You have soot smudges on your cheeks, and your hair smells of smoke. Everything will seem better after a shower."

"Good point." She'd been drenched with sweat at the first-aid station after the air-conditioning was turned off and she felt grimy. If she hadn't been so tired, getting clean would have occurred to her earlier.

Fingers still entwined, he guided her into the bathroom then turned and took her face in his hands. "Della, I know you haven't wanted me to see your scars, but let me look after you. Trust me, I promise you'll be safe."

Della let out a sigh. She was so tired, and his voice was so sure, so persuasive. And really, what did she have to lose? Their time was over—she'd sell him her share in the morning and he'd leave, probably before lunch tomorrow.

Biting the inside of her cheek to tame the butterflies in her belly, she lifted her shirt over her head and let it fall from her fingers. Then she reached behind her back and unhooked her bra before dropping it, as well. Goose bumps raced across her skin, both from the sudden contact of the cool air, and from fear of his reaction. She stood before him, exposed from the waist up. It was the first time anyone besides her doctors had seen her scarred chest.

She braced herself, heartbeat hard and erratic, and lifted her chin, waiting for his response, hoping it wasn't pity. Praying it wasn't revulsion.

Yet he simply turned her until her back was to him, unzipped her trousers and slid them, with her underpants, down her legs, pausing to let her step out of them. She frowned. Had he seen her chest? She heard the shower start, so turned and saw him pulling his own clothes off. He stepped into the shower, adjusted the water and gently tugged her in with him.

Light-headed with surprise, she looked up into his face for clues, but found only acceptance. He hadn't taken any notice of her scars. All that time worrying, and he was treating her as if she had a normal body. The relief of it brought tears to her eyes, and the weight of everything else that had happened in the previous twelve hours, from the fire to her decision to stop fighting about the ship, pushed the tears down her cheeks.

Under the warm spray, Luke encircled her in his arms and she rested her cheek against his shoulder, not bothering to hide that she was softly crying. He stroked her hair and murmured comforting words above her head.

Patrick had been right—Luke really was a prince among men.

Within a couple of minutes, the tears stopped coming. All the emotion that had bubbled inside her had been released, leaving her almost lethargic, calm.

He reached for a sponge and squirted it with soap that smelled like sandalwood and Luke, and lathered her back in slow, thorough strokes. Then he ran the sponge down her legs and along her arms. The sensation was undemanding, yet its inherent sensuality roused a heat in her bloodstream. He turned her and repeated the soaping process down the front of her arms, across her chest and belly, then along her legs, unhurried, reverentially, as if honoring her body as he cleansed her. Then he lifted her feet, one at a time, and washed beneath them, water running from his hair down his fallen angel's face in rivulets.

Straightening, he rinsed out the sponge and put it back on the end of the bath, then squirted more soap into his hands, rubbed them together until it formed a lather and gently washed her neck, up to her chin and cheeks, then nose and forehead. Della's eyes drifted closed as she allowed herself to be washed, to be nurtured. She'd never loved this man more.

With a hand supporting the nape of her neck, he rinsed her face then placed a chaste, albeit lingering, kiss on her mouth. Emotion welled up from her heart, filling her. Engulfing her. Wrapping her hands behind his neck, she captured him before he could pull away, eliciting more heat from the kiss. Her pulse jerked erratically at the slick feel of his skin against hers, the scrape of his teeth over her bottom lip, the groan that seemed to come from deep in his chest.

Before she became too carried away, she laid a hand on his chest and tore her mouth away. Then, breathing still uneven, she took the sponge, soaped it and began to wash him. She ran it over the golden skin of his back, then across his powerful shoulders. As the soap was rinsed from each area, she kissed the skin she'd cleaned. Down his arms, his chest and the ridges of his abdomen, then lower still, to the apex of his thighs. He was already aroused, and her soaping only increased his reaction, but he didn't move. Just let her continue her path down his muscular legs, washing and leaving a trail of kisses. When she stood, she soaped her hands, as he had done, and washed the planes of a face that had become so dear to her.

She ended as he had done, with a chaste kiss on his mouth, but within moments, the kiss became more. Became everything. The wet slide of his body against hers was a sensual feast, the gentle abrasion of the peaks of her breasts against his hair-roughened chest exquisite. He whispered her name against her lips and the word seemed to reverberate around the shower stall—or perhaps he was repeating it. It barely mattered as long as he kept kissing her.

She reached down, held his fullness and was rewarded with a groan. And suddenly, kissing was no longer enough. Had it ever been?

As if he could read her thoughts, Luke shunted the tap off with an elbow and grabbed a thick white towel from a shelf just outside the shower. He patted her down in the same methodical way he'd washed her, but this time he had a shade less composure as he completed the task. His eyes were darkened, his chest rising and falling rapidly. He quickly rubbed himself over with another towel, then took her hand, leading her to the bed.

When he was sheathed and balancing over her on the mattress, she cupped his face in her hands, making him pause. It was imperative that he know how much tonight had meant to her, that he'd accepted her body so unquestioningly. In one simple shower, he'd given her back her self-worth. Given her back the completeness of her sexuality. The desire in his eyes now, while her imperfect body was on display, was something she never thought she'd see again.

"No matter what happens tomorrow," she said, her voice trembling with emotion, "I'll always remember our lovemaking. I'll always be grateful for what you've done for me."

Luke looked down at Della lying beneath him, trying to think through the fog of desire that filled his head.

Had she just *thanked* him? He was crazy with lust for this woman, and she was *grateful*? As if their time together had been nothing more than pity sex....

It would have been one thing to thank him for looking after her tonight, but it was obvious that wasn't what she meant. His gut clenched tight. Had she simply been dealing with her issues while he'd been so lost in want for her he could barely see straight?

"Let's be clear about one thing," he said fiercely. "This has been about desire and need for me." Brain-melting need. He leaned down, captured her mouth in a fiery kiss, showing her what she did to him, how wild she made him. He lifted one of her legs and hooked it over his elbow, entering her in one smooth stroke. "I've wanted you from the first day," he said through a tight jaw. "I want you even more now."

He'd planned to hold himself in check, to make tonight tender, gentle. But it seemed more imperative now that he not hide his passion. Not hide how close to the edge he was, so she knew that this was *real* between them.

More real than anything else in his life.

She had nothing to feel *grateful* for.

He thrust harder, faster, telling her in plain language the effect she had on him. Her fingers bit into the flesh on his shoulders, arms, wherever she could reach, and he welcomed the tiny points of pain as proof that she was as crazy with lust as he was. Her movements beneath him became more frantic, and he reached down with one hand, found her center and felt tension fill her body then implode around him. Within moments he followed and, as he floated, he had the strange sensation that nothing would be the same ever again.

Nor would he want it to be.

Della blinked as she woke then looked around. Luke was sitting on the side of the bed, already dressed for the day in casual trousers and a polo shirt, and holding a tray with a steaming coffeepot, two glasses of orange juice and an assortment of pastries.

"Morning, sleepyhead," he said and kissed her on the forehead.

"Morning," she said over a muffled yawn. "That coffee smells like heaven."

He held the tray aloft while she sat up and tucked the sheet around herself, then set it on the mattress. "You look like heaven," he said, surveying her with a lazy smile.

A cozy warmth rose inside her, until memories of the day before came flooding back. She was giving in on the

Cora Mae. Luke would be leaving. Probably today. Everything inside her sank low and shivered.

"What time is it?" she said through a dry throat and tried to blink away the grittiness in her eyes. She'd spent much of the night staring into the darkness, contemplating her future, so she hadn't had much sleep.

He poured a coffee and handed it to her. "Six o'clock. I wasn't sure if you were working this morning."

"No, Cal has the morning shift, but I should get up, anyway." She sipped the coffee and closed her eyes as it slid down her throat, the heat calming her a little.

"I've been thinking," he said as he poured another coffee. His posture was relaxed, but there was a spark in his eyes.

Any hope of enjoying what was in all probability their last breakfast together evaporated—his tone said they were talking business. "If this is about me selling you my share, I haven't changed my mind."

"I have an alternative."

She was instantly wary. Luke the businessman wasn't someone to underestimate.

"Tell me." She took an apple pastry from the tray and sampled it.

"I'll be ringing my office this morning and instructing them to put several of my hotels up for sale. I'm going to use that money to start my own cruise line."

Della almost choked on her pastry, and Luke smoothly passed her an orange juice. "Your own line?" she asked when she could talk, trying to comprehend his meaning.

He nodded, as if this was a logical progression from his position only yesterday. "Three ships sounds like a good place to begin," he said, "then I'll grow it from there."

"Three ships," she repeated faintly. All this time she'd been trying to talk him into keeping one, and now he wanted three. His gray gaze was completely serious, perhaps even excited. She could see him making mental calculations as they were talking.

"I might not live full-time on board the way Patrick did, but I'll spend the majority of my time on the ships." He stood and paced around the room, as if the energy of his new plan wouldn't allow him to stay still. "I'll be able to work long hours, just like in the city, but afterward, I'll have all the resources and entertainments of the ship at my disposal. Not to mention days off in various ports."

It was as if their roles had been reversed and now he was selling her on the cruising lifestyle. Della sipped her coffee to give herself a moment to think.

"This is a pretty big turnaround," she finally said.

He sat back on the bed beside her. "The fire gave me a lot to chew over. Crystallized my thinking. The camaraderie of the crew during the fire and its aftermath was impressive, but I've also grown to love the lifestyle of a cruise ship." He took her hand in his. "That's thanks to you."

"I didn't think I was having an impact," she said faintly.

He gave her a crooked smile. "Being on the *Cora Mae* has helped me relax for the first time I can remember. On my deathbed, I don't want to just look back on a career. I want to look back on both a career and a life well lived. No regrets."

He'd never reminded her more of Patrick. She smiled. "I'm starting to see the family resemblance."

Luke's eyes crinkled at the edges. He was obviously pleased by the comparison. "Uncle Patrick lived his life on his own terms, and I bet he had few regrets at the end."

"You're right." She bit down on her lip, wondering how much to say about Patrick's thoughts at the end, but Luke had a right to know. "He said his regrets were mainly about you. Wishing he'd spent more time with you."

Luke blinked hard then looked away. "Patrick often invited me to stay on the *Cora Mae,* and his other ships before this one, but after I took over Marlow Corporation I was always too busy, so I only saw him when he came ashore."

"He knew you loved him. The way he spoke about you, he knew."

He swallowed hard, then cleared his throat. "Thank you for saying that. It means a lot."

"And he'd be thrilled if he knew about your plans."

"Now I understand why he lived here—now I can see what I've been missing—and I don't want to wait. If nothing else, Patrick's death has taught me that life is short."

"I'm happy for you, Luke, I really am." When they'd been in Melbourne she'd thought he was turning from the relaxed man on holidays who'd played mini golf with her into Luke the businessman. But now she could see that he'd managed to integrate all of those parts of himself, perhaps to become the man he'd always meant to be. And it made her heart sing even as it was breaking—the man he was meant to be wasn't a man she could have. He'd been clear that he'd never marry again, and she wouldn't settle for anything less than forever. Being in love and waiting for the inevitable end to their relationship would break her heart by a thousand little cuts. "Seems it's even better timing to sell you my share."

"There's a new offer on the table. I'll convert your half-share of the *Cora Mae* to 20 percent of the new company that will own and run the fleet of ships. You can be a silent partner, or you can have a more active role. It will be up to you."

She put her coffee mug down on the side table before

she spilled it, then checked Luke's face to make sure he was serious. His gray eyes were dark and steady. Seemed he was, despite his new offer not adding up. "But 20 percent is a bigger share than what I'd be bringing."

He waved the quibble away and picked up another pastry. "Without you, the new company wouldn't exist. You're the one who sold me on the concept of cruising. You deserve the extra few percent."

A vision of the life he was suggesting rolled out before her. She'd be a shareholder in a cruise ship line, as active as she wanted to be, safeguarding the *Cora Mae*. Having regular business contact with Luke after he'd moved on from their personal relationship. Having to work with him, loving him, when she knew he was seeing someone new. Bile rose in her throat, and she rubbed her arms that were suddenly cold.

She refused to subject herself to that torture.

Besides, it was time she took control of her own life. Alone. "Luke, I've been doing some thinking, too." She'd lain awake most of the night, unable to sleep with all the thoughts chasing each other in circles in her mind. "I've realized that I've been hiding on this ship. Patrick was living the life you're talking about, but I've been staying here out of fear since my husband died."

He rubbed a thumb over the frown line that had appeared in his forehead. "But you grew up on ships. You said you wanted to live at sea like your parents."

"I thought I did. But it's one matter for my parents and Patrick to make those choices. I've been scared of living on land again, which is something entirely different." Luke's acceptance of her last night had given her the insight into herself. Into the way she'd been hiding. "I realize now that I have to leave and face my fears."

"What exactly does facing your fears entail?" he asked warily.

She pulled her knees up to her chest and wrapped her arms around them tight, as if she could physically control the anxiety that was rising. "Setting up a life on land again. Getting a job in a hospital, finding a place to live. And if you still want it, I'll sell you my share of the *Cora Mae*. You have great plans for her. I know I'll be leaving her in safe hands."

Luke stilled. He'd just decided to live on board...and Della was leaving? He cleared his throat. "You're going?"

"Yes," she said and didn't meet his eyes.

He stood and stalked across the room, a rising blackness filling him. "When?"

"Soon. Now that I've made the decision, there's no point putting it off. I'll talk to Captain Tynan about Dr. Oliver, the doctor who did the locum for me while we were in Melbourne, and if he's happy with her, I'll ring her and see if she wants to apply. It could all be quite soon if things fall into place."

Soon? He was nowhere near ready for her to leave his bed. Especially not after last night. She'd shown him such trust—he'd really thought something had changed between them.

"What if I asked you to stay?" he asked, even though he had to force the words out.

"We were going to end sometime." She shrugged one bare shoulder. "You made it plain on several occasions that you're not looking for anything long-term. Maybe it's better that we end on a high note instead of letting it drag out."

How could she be so calm about this? His heart thundered against his ribs. Did the time they'd spent together mean so little to her? Then he saw her hand tremble as she tucked a curl behind her ear and his chest crushed in on itself. Della Walsh wasn't any calmer about this than he was.

And she was right—he wouldn't marry again. Wouldn't let himself get close enough to another person to rely on them, or trust them implicitly. Why not end it now instead of weeks or months down the line? In fact, if they stayed together and things deteriorated, it would only make their business dealings more awkward. Now was the best time. So why was his stomach clenched hard as a rock, as if he might lose his breakfast at any moment?

"This doesn't feel right." He ran a hand down his face, trying to clear his mind.

She gave him a tremulous smile. "That's because you're too used to getting your own way."

"Perhaps you're right." He sank down on the side of the bed again, ready to face her departure like a man.

"You should never have taught me to tell you to go to hell."

He took her hand and threaded their fingers together. "A mistake I won't repeat." He pulled her hand over and kissed her knuckles. "Della, I want you to know…"

He frowned. How did he tell her what was inside? There weren't words for what he was feeling. Yet he owed it to her to at least try. "I don't want to marry again, or even have something permanent with a woman. But if I did want that—if I was capable of it—it would be you."

A single tear slipped from her eye and curved its way down her cheek before she withdrew her hand from his to wipe it away. "I'd better get going," she said, reaching over the side of the bed for her clothes. "I need to meet with Captain Tynan, and tell Cal, Jody and the rest of the medical team."

Della slipped from his bed, quickly dressed, dropped a

kiss on his cheek then disappeared from his room. From his life. And, with his head a jumble of confusion, Luke watched it happen, powerless to do anything to stop it.

Twelve

Della eased into a chair at the nurses' station and rubbed her eyes before blinking down at the medical chart of the patient she'd just seen in the emergency room. Getting used to shift work again would take some time. Especially when she spent most of the hours when she should be sleeping lying in bed and thinking of Luke. The way he smiled. The way he said her name. The way he made love to her. Sighing, she took a long sip from her water bottle then screwed the cap back on and took a pen from the top pocket of her white coat.

Slipping back into life on land had been unexpectedly simple. The morning she'd told Luke she was leaving—had it really been just five days ago?—she'd also told Captain Tynan. He'd been happy for her to approach Dr. Oliver, who'd covered for her while she was in Melbourne. Jane Oliver had not only been keen to apply for the job but, hoping to make a good impression on the captain, had offered to fill in until the interviews were held, and had caught a flight from Australia to Wellington that afternoon.

While waiting for her replacement to arrive, Della had packed her bags—shipboard life meant she didn't own much—then rung the hospital where she'd worked in Melbourne. They were short-staffed and had been pleased to give her some locum work, starting as soon as she'd like. She'd also called her parents, who'd been thrilled by the chance to see more of her, and offered her a bed for as long as she wanted. Not wanting to give herself thinking time and risk losing her courage, she'd accepted both offers.

Once Dr. Oliver arrived aboard the *Cora Mae,* Della had done a quick hand over and left her in Jody's and Cal's capable hands. She'd already made her farewells to her friends, which she'd tried to handle quickly since she hated goodbyes. There had been a longer, more wrenching goodbye with Luke, though she'd managed not to cry, and hoped she'd at least kept her dignity intact.

Within fourteen hours of telling Luke she was going, she'd left the ship—her home—and caught a flight to Melbourne.

She'd expected the whole process might take weeks to organize, but it had fallen into place with alarming ease. And now here she was, living on terra firma, working at a hospital, just as she'd told Luke she would.

As she read over the notes she'd made in the medical chart, her mobile phone rang. Only a few people had her new number—the hospital, her parents, the crew of the *Cora Mae*...Luke. There were still a few details to sort out with the sale of her share of the ship, so she'd needed to give him a way to get in touch with her, despite knowing that prolonging their contact would only make it harder to get over him.

The new phone hadn't rung often since she'd bought it a few days ago, but each time the ringtone sounded she tensed, wondering if it was Luke. Wishing it was. Hoping it wasn't. Which was crazy—she had to get used to living her life without Luke Marlow in it.

Shaking her head at herself, she checked the number on the screen—it was one of the *Cora Mae's* phone numbers. Her heart beat double-time as she answered.

"Good morning, Della." The deep rumble of his voice flowed over her, sank down into her heart, where she ached for him, making it difficult to reply.

"Hello, Luke," she finally managed, but the words felt stilted, formal. As if, after all they'd shared, they couldn't have a normal conversation. She turned the swivel chair so she could look out at the hospital parking lot, and tried again. "It's good to hear from you."

"How have you been?"

"Busy. The hospital threw me in the deep end, with shifts in the emergency room starting the day after I came back, but busy is good."

"Have you been okay?" His voice was gentle, probing. She knew what he was asking, of course. The plan to come ashore had been about facing her fears and she loved him all the more for checking.

"You know what? I really have been," she said and bit down on a smile, proud of what she'd achieved. On the flight home from Wellington, she'd been almost sick with worry about how she'd cope back on land, in the town where Shane had been killed, where she'd almost died. It had been hard, but all in all not as bad as she'd built it up to be in her head.

After her first shift, she'd even visited the room where she'd been a patient, and found it no longer held the demons she remembered.

The hardest thing had been the comments about Shane from colleagues who remembered him, telling her how sorry they were. A couple of months ago she wouldn't have been able to bear hearing such things, but now they merely evoked a well of sadness that she guessed would always be there. She'd moved further through her grief than she'd realized. Discovered she was stronger than she'd given herself credit for, and she had Luke to thank for part of that.

"I'm glad to hear it," Luke said.

"How's the *Cora Mae* and the repairs?" she asked brightly, needing to change the subject.

"Everything is on track. We spent an extra couple of nights in Wellington to allow for local tradesmen to work on the repairs, but the captain made up a bit of time across the Tasman Sea. We docked in Melbourne a couple of hours ago."

"I didn't realize." How strange it was to not know the location of the *Cora Mae* after years of being so intimately acquainted with her schedule.

Luke cleared his throat. "Do you have any free time to drop down to the dock today? There are a couple of things I'd like to discuss with you."

Her hands trembled; she dropped the pen on the floor and leaned over to pick it up. "Sure," she said, trying to sound unaffected. As if the world hadn't just wobbled. She checked her watch. "I'm on a night shift and it ends in a couple of hours. Give me time for a shower after I finish and I'll be there."

"I'll see you then." He disconnected and Della was left staring at the phone in her hand, wondering why she'd so easily agreed to see him again so soon. Before she'd developed any distance from her feelings for him.

Given that her heart may never be free of him, perhaps

it was better to get this meeting over and done with so she could go back to building her new life. Perhaps.

Her heart thumping a crazy tattoo, Della stepped into the *Cora Mae*'s lobby and glanced around. A few crew members smiled and waved as if she just been ashore for a quick visit, and she waved back. But something was different. There was a hum of tension in the air; too many pairs of eyes were tracking her movements.

She felt Luke's presence before she saw him—a delicious shiver raced across her skin, and everyone else in the lobby seemed to slow to a standstill. The air no longer hummed, it crackled. She turned to see him walking toward her, so tall and broad and all that she wanted…

The aura of confidence that always surrounded him was there, but his gray gaze held a touch of uncertainty. From the corner of her eye she saw a crew member on the grand stairs lean over and whisper something to the person beside him. A sudden sense of déjà vu swamped her, remembering when Luke had boarded the *Cora Mae* on the day she'd first met him, but this time their roles were reversed—he belonged and she was the visitor that people were talking about.

And then Luke reached her and all thoughts of anyone but him flew from her mind. Her hands longed to reach up and stroke the planes of his face that she knew so well. Her lips tingled with the need to touch his. And her heart wanted him to take her in his arms and remove this distance between them.

"Della," he said, his voice a husky whisper. "It's good to see you." He took her hands and leaned in to kiss her cheek. The brief touch of his lips was a moment of heaven, but all too soon he was drawing away, taking a piece of her soul with him.

"Hello, Luke." She withdrew her hands, unable to endure the touch when she couldn't have more.

His gaze dropped to where she'd severed the contact and a faint frown line creased his forehead, but it quickly vanished as he dug his hands into his pockets and flashed her a wholly unconvincing smile. "How about we go somewhere a little more private?"

Given that there seemed to be hundreds of eyes trained on them, she nodded. "Good idea."

As he led her up the grand staircase, he didn't touch her. In fact, he seemed to be deliberately ensuring that not even their arms brushed. She'd been the one to let go of his hand first, yet she couldn't help but wish they still had the closeness where he could drape an arm around her waist, or he would welcome her reaching over and interlacing their fingers.

The stares followed them as they reached the next floor, and the strangeness of the atmosphere finally penetrated the claim Luke had made on her attention. She turned to him, her voice lowered. "Is there something else going on that I don't know about?"

"What do you mean?" he asked, giving nothing away.

She double-checked her surroundings as they set off down one of the promenades. "There seem to be a lot of people watching us."

He shrugged one broad shoulder. "You're more than an average guest," he said, echoing her words to him the day they met.

"So they're watching me because of rumors?" she couldn't resist asking and felt her mouth tug at the corners.

"I'm sure you understand that rumors pass quickly around a ship," he said and guided her to the door to the Blue Moon. She hesitated on the threshold. This wasn't a venue for business discussions, it was for dancing and drinking. The place she'd first felt Luke's arms around her.

He held the door open for her and she tentatively took a step inside—it was empty now, closed until evening. "I thought you might want to talk in an office or a meeting room," she said nervously.

He let the door softly close behind them and flicked a switch. Soft lighting filled the room from above and the twinkling fairy lights in the walls sprang to life. "This isn't about business, and I wanted somewhere I knew we wouldn't be interrupted."

Her heart missed a beat then raced to catch up. "You said on the phone that there were a few details we need to iron out."

"And there are," he said, his voice solemn. He took her hand and led her to the middle of the polished dance floor. "But they're details about us."

Her breath hitched high in her throat. "What do you mean, us?"

"You and me." He met her eyes steadily. "What we have together."

She flinched. Seeing him again, having a conversation like this only emphasized the aching hollow inside her. "Luke, I don't want to start up something again. I can't."

"I'm not talking about starting anything. What's between us isn't over," he said, still holding her hand.

She squeezed her eyes shut for one breath, two, then opened them again and met his gaze. "We've discussed this. If there's no future, then why would we prolong the ending?"

"Tell me something," he said, his hand sliding from her fingers up to her arm. "Is us being apart what you want?"

The imprint of his hand on her arm burned through the

fabric of her sleeve, so she took a step back, once again severing a physical connection.

"Luke, I have to be honest." It seemed there was no other way to circumvent this conversation—the last thing she wanted was to open herself up for more pain, but she couldn't see any other way to make him understand. She crossed her arms tightly under her breasts and exposed her heart. "My feelings for you were more than I expected. I *can't* see you anymore. Please don't ask me to—it would be emotional suicide."

"Because your feelings were more than you expected or wanted," he clarified, saying each word slowly, carefully.

"Please don't make this worse." Her voice wobbled, the final indignity. She turned to the door, escape the only refuge remaining. "If there's nothing to discuss about the *Cora Mae* or the sale of my share, then—"

He stepped around so he was again in her line of vision, his face pale. "Della, I asked you to come today so I could tell you how grateful I am that you spent the time showing me the *Cora Mae* and convincing me to keep her cruising. That time you invested changed my life."

She swallowed the sudden constriction in her throat. "I'm glad for you, Luke, but—"

"What I didn't realize before you left was that the change was in more than just my opinion of the ship. I know now that the lifestyle I was so impressed with was only partly about the ship and cruising. It was also about you."

"Luke—" she said, praying her tone was warning, but knowing it was probably pleading.

"The ship was different when you left—" he took an infinitesimal step closer "—as if you took something with you. It might be greedy but, Della, I want it all."

His heart was in his eyes, and that stunned her more

than anything he could say. For a charged moment, she didn't respond. "All?" she finally said, her voice an octave higher than normal.

"I want the ships *and* you." He took another step closer, till she could feel the body heat emanating from him, but he didn't try to touch her this time. "And if I had to choose just one, it would be you."

Something fluttered in the pit of her belly and she placed a hand over her stomach to calm it. "You'd give up the ships after rearranging your life to have them?"

He didn't hesitate. "No question. I love you, Della. I was in love with you before you left but didn't understand." He speared his fingers through his hair. "Or perhaps I didn't *want* to understand."

"What does that mean to you? For us?" she asked warily.

"It means I'm abandoning my stupid ideas about never marrying or letting anyone close. Once you were gone I realized that all I really need is you." He tucked a curl behind her ear. "I thought I couldn't trust anyone. I guess I was expecting people to abandon me, not stand by me in the tough times, but that's not what you're about. Your strength in moving on after such an awful past showed me up for what I was—an emotional coward. You've inspired me to want to face life fully. Hell, I want to grab life and live it to the hilt. With you."

She tried to blink away the prickling burn behind her eyes but it wouldn't ease. "Oh, Luke, I love you, too. So much."

A shudder ripped through his body, and then he was there, hauling her against him, holding her close. She wrapped her arms around him, not sure she'd ever let him go. Luke *loved* her. It felt magical, a miracle, and she laughed even as the tears she'd been holding in check began to slip down her cheeks.

"I love you with everything inside me," he murmured beside her ear, then pulled back and tenderly brushed her tears away with his thumbs. "Marry me. I know you're keen to try living on land, and I promise that if you say yes, I won't tie you down. We can live our lives ashore, or on the *Cora Mae,* or any combination you want. Nothing is more important than you."

Her heart flipped over in her chest. It was even more than she'd dreamed of. "Yes," she said and heard the tears in her voice. "To everything, yes."

She twined her arms up behind his neck and kissed him, and knew she'd come home. If they never moved from this spot again, she wouldn't mind—she could stay here in Luke's arms, losing herself in his kiss forever.

But Luke eventually pulled away, slipping a hand into his pocket and retrieving a small velvet box. Trembling, she took the box and opened it to find a solitaire diamond sparkling up at her from its white-gold band. A tear slipped down her cheek—his choice of something simple and classic showed how well he knew her.

"It's perfect," she breathed.

He smiled into her eyes. "It's you." He took the box from her hand and slipped the ring on her finger. She reached up on tiptoes and kissed him again, but before they became carried away Luke wrenched himself back, his breath coming hard and a reluctant smile on his lips. Then he strode over to the door and knocked loudly three times. The doors burst open and people flowed into the room, throwing streamers and releasing balloons. Della was stunned—all she could do was watch the commotion around her and try not to gape. A massive congratulatory banner appeared from above, and a loud chorus of cheers went up.

Jody made her way through the crowd and, grinning widely, drew Della into a hug. "I knew you and Luke belonged together. I just knew it."

Before Della could reply, Jody was edged out of the way by Max, who also hugged her and whispered, "You know where to find me if things don't work out with Marlow." With a wink, he was gone.

Della still hadn't caught her breath when Cal hugged her and then shook Luke's hand, congratulating them both. Roxie Appleby dragged Luke closer and linked his hand to Della's. "I couldn't be happier for you two," she said, her voice thick with emotion.

Della watched Roxie move away though the crowd, still marveling at the scene around her. She spotted Captain Tynan raising a glass in her direction and she waved. One of the ship's singers had started to croon a love ballad, and more people were still pouring in through the doors.

She turned to Luke and whispered in his ear, "So this is why everyone was watching me when I arrived?"

He chuckled, and drew her against him. "After you left, I was dragged aside by crew member after crew member. For two days they each had their say about what an idiot I'd been."

Della coughed out a laugh and opened her mouth to protest, but he silenced her with a finger on her lips. "They were right. And the only way to get them to stop haranguing me was to tell them I was going to get you back. Once they heard that, the story traveled around the ship like wildfire, and they all wanted to be involved. My only stipulation was they gave us absolute privacy until you'd made your decision."

"I appreciate that," she said, imagining the horror of

having a private moment like they'd shared play out in front of hundreds of people.

Luke shrugged his broad shoulders. "If you'd had an audience, you'd have felt pressured to say yes, and I wanted to be one hundred percent sure you wanted me for me."

"And what do you think now?" she asked.

He squeezed her a little tighter and rested his forehead on hers. "It's a miracle, but it appears you do love me."

"You'd better believe it," she said and smiled up at him.

When Luke dragged her away from the others and gathered her close for another kiss, she was dimly aware of the hooting from the crew, but the spectacle around her soon melted away and she became lost in the arms of the man she loved.

* * * * *

MILLS & BOON®

Want to get more from Mills & Boon?

Here's what's available to you if you join the
exclusive **Mills & Boon eBook Club** today:

✦ *Convenience – choose your books each month*
✦ *Exclusive – receive your books a month before*
  anywhere else
✦ *Flexibility – change your subscription at any time*
✦ *Variety – gain access to eBook-only series*
✦ *Value – subscriptions from just £1.99 a month*

So visit **www.millsandboon.co.uk/esubs** today
to be a part of this exclusive eBook Club!

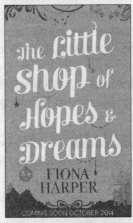